THE TALES OF EL BORAK

(A Collection of Short Stories About a Texan Gunman)

BY

ROBERT E. HOWARD

British Library Cataloguing-in-Publication Data
A catalogue record for this book is available from the
British Library

Contents

Robert E. Howard. 1

Blood of the Gods

A Shot Through the Window. 3

The Abodes of Emptiness 10

The Fight at the Well of Amir Khan. 22

The Djinn of the Caves. 32

Hawks at Bay. 46

The Devil of the Night 66

The Country of the Knife

Chapter I 85

Chapter II 92

Chapter III. 112

Chapter IV. 131

Chapter V 142

Chapter VI. 159

Chapter VII 169

Chapter VIII 181

The Daughter of Erlik Khan

Chapter I 190

Chapter II 196

Chapter III. 205

Chapter IV. 214

Chapter V 225
Chapter VI. 247
Chapter VII 253
Chapter VIII 258
Chapter IX. 266
Chapter X 278
Chapter XI. 292

Hawk of the Hills

I 294
II. 303
III. 324
IV. 337
V. 343
VI. 354

The Lost Valley of Iskander

I. The Oiled Silk Package 383
II. The Rescue of Bardylis of Attalus. 390
III. The Sons of Iskander. 398
IV. The Duel with Ptolemy the Kind 406
V. The Death of Hunyadi 418

Son of the White Wolf

Chapter I: The Battle Standard 429
Chapter II: Massacre 432
Chapter III: The Call of Blood 436
Chapter IV: Wolves of the Desert. 448

Chapter V: Treachery 459

Robert E. Howard

Robert Ervin Howard was born in Peaster, Texas in 1906. During his youth, his family moved between a variety of Texan boomtowns, and Howard – a bookish and somewhat introverted child – was steeped in the violent myths and legends of the Old South. Although he loved reading and learning, Howard developed a distinctly Texan, hardboiled outlook on the world. He became a passionate fan of boxing, taking it up at an amateur level, and from the age of nine began to write adventure tales of semi-historical bloodshed. In 1919, when Howard was thirteen, his family moved to the Central Texas hamlet of Cross Plains, where he would stay for the rest of his life.

At fifteen Howard began to read the pulp magazines of the day, and to write more seriously. The December 1922 issue of his high school newspaper featured two of his stories, 'Golden Hope Christmas' and 'West is West'. In 1924 he sold his first piece – a short caveman tale titled 'Spear and Fang' – for $16 to the not-yet-famous Weird Tales magazine. He published with the magazine regularly over the next few years. 1929 was a breakout year for Howard, in that the 23-year-old writer began to sell to other magazines, such as Ghost Stories and Argosy, both of whom had previously sent him hundreds of rejection slips. In 1930, he began a correspondence with weird fiction master H. P. Lovecraft which ran up to his death six years later, and is regarded as one of the great correspondence cycles in all of fantasy literature.

It was partly due to Lovecraft's encouragement that Howard created his most famous character, Conan the Cimmerian. Conan – a barbarian-turned-King during the Hyborian Age, a mythical period of some 12,000 years ago – featured in seventeen Weird Tales stories between 1933 and 1936, and is now regarded as having spawned the 'sword and sorcery' genre, making Howard's influence on fantasy literature comparable to that of J. R. R. Tolkien's. The Conan stories have since been adapted many times, most famously in the series of films starring Arnold Schwarzenegger.

Howard was enjoying an all-time high in sales by the beginning of 1936, but he was also deeply upset by the ill health of his mother, who had fallen into a coma. On the morning of June 11, 1936, he asked an attending nurse whether she would ever recover, and the nurse replied negatively. Howard walked to his car, parked outside the family home in Cross Plains, and shot himself. He died eight hours later, aged just thirty.

BLOOD OF THE GODS

A Shot Through the Window

IT WAS THE wolfish snarl on Hawkston's thin lips, the red glare in his eyes, which first roused terrified suspicion in the Arab's mind, there in the deserted hut on the outskirts of the little town of Azem. Suspicion became certainty as he stared at the three dark, lowering faces of the other white men, bent toward him, and all beastly with the same cruel greed that twisted their leader's features.

The brandy glass slipped from the Arab's hand and his swarthy skin went ashy.

"Lah!" he cried desperately. "No! You lied to me! You are not friends-you brought me here to murder me-"

He made a convulsive effort to rise, but Hawkston grasped the bosom of his gumbaz in an iron grip and forced him down into the camp chair again. The Arab cringed away from the dark, hawk-like visage bending close to his own.

"You won't be hurt, Dirdar," rasped the Englishman. "Not if you tell us what we want to know. You heard my question. Where is Al Wazir?"

The beady eyes of the Arab glared wildly up at his captor for an instant, then Dirdar moved with all the strength and speed of his wiry body. Bracing his feet against the floor,

3

he heaved backward suddenly, toppling the chair over and throwing himself along with it. With a rending of worn cloth the bosom of the gumbaz came away in Hawkston's hand, and Dirdar, regaining his feet like a bouncing rubber ball, dived straight at the open door, ducking beneath the pawing arm of the big Dutchman, Van Brock. But he tripped over Ortelli's extended leg and fell sprawling, rolling on his back to slash up at the Italian with the curved knife he had snatched from his girdle. Ortelli jumped back, yowling, blood spurting from his leg, but as Dirdar once more bounced to his feet, the Russian, Krakovitch, struck him heavily from behind with a pistol barrel.

As the Arab sagged to the floor, stunned, Hawkston kicked the knife out of his hand. The Englishman stooped, grabbed him by the collar of his abba, and grunted: "Help me lift him, Van Brock."

The burly Dutchman complied, and the half-senseless Arab was slammed down in the chair from which he had just escaped. They did not tie him, but Krakovitch stood behind him, one set of steely fingers digging into his shoulder, the other poising the long gun-barrel.

Hawkston poured out a glass of brandy and thrust it to his lips. Dirdar gulped mechanically, and the glassiness faded out of his eyes.

"He's coming around," grunted Hawkston. "You hit him hard, Krakovitch. Shut up, Ortelli! Tie a rag about your bally leg and quit grousing about it! Well, Dirdar, are you ready to talk?"

The Arab looked about like a trapped animal, his lean chest heaving under the torn gumbaz. He saw no mercy in the flinty faces about him.

"Let's burn his cursed feet," snarled Ortelli, busy with an improvised bandage. "Let me put the hot irons to the swine-"

Dirdar shuddered and his gaze sought the face of the Englishman, with burning intensity. He knew that Hawkston was leader of these lawless men by virtue of sharp wits and a sledge-like fist.

The Arab licked his lips.

"As Allah is my witness, I do not know where Al Wazir is!"

"You lie!" snapped the Englishman. "We know that you were one of the party that took him into the desert-and he never came back. We know you know where he was left. Now, are you going to tell?"

"El Borak will kill me!" muttered Dirdar.

"Who's El Borak?" rumbled Van Brock.

"American," snapped Hawkston. "Adventurer. Real name's Gordon. He led the caravan that took Al Wazir into the desert. Dirdar, you needn't fear El Borak. We'll protect you from him."

A new gleam entered the Arab's shifty eyes; avarice mingled with the fear already there. Those beady eyes grew cunning and cruel.

"There is only one reason why you wish to find Al Wazir," he said. "You hope to learn the secret of a treasure richer than the secret hoard of Shahrazar the Forbidden! Well, suppose I tell you? Suppose I even guide you to the spot where Al Wazir is to be found-will you protect me from El Borak-will you give me a share of the Blood of the Gods?"

Hawkston frowned, and Ortelli ripped out an oath.

"Promise the dog nothing! Burn the soles off his feet! Here! I'll heat the irons!"

"Let that alone!" said Hawkston with an oath. "One of you better go to the door and watch. I saw that old devil Salim sneaking around through the alleys just before sundown."

No one obeyed. They did not trust their leader. He did not repeat the command. He turned to Dirdar, in whose eyes greed was much stronger now than fear.

"How do I know you'd guide us right? Every man in that caravan swore an oath he'd never betray Al Wazir's hiding place."

"Oaths were made to be broken," answered Dirdar cynically. "For a share in the Blood of the Gods I would foreswear Muhammad. But even when you have found

Al Wazir, you may not be able to learn the secret of the treasure."

"We have ways of making men talk," Hawkston assured him grimly. "Will you put our skill to the test, or will you guide us to Al Wazir? We will give you a share of the treasure." Hawkston had no intention of keeping his word as he spoke.

"Mashallah!" said the Arab. "He dwells alone in an all but inaccessible place. When I name it, you, at least, Hawkston effendi, will know how to reach it. But I can guide you by a shorter way, which will save two days. And a day saved on the desert is often the difference between life and death.

"Al Wazir dwells in the Caves of El Khour-arrrgh!" His voice broke in a scream, and he threw up his hands, a sudden image of frantic terror, eyes glaring, teeth bared. Simultaneously the deafening report of a shot filled the hut, and Dirdar toppled from his chair, clutching at his breast. Hawkston whirled, caught a glimpse through the window of a smoking black pistol barrel and a grim bearded face. He fired at that face even as, with his left hand, he swept the candle from the table and plunged the hut into darkness.

His companions were cursing, yelling, falling over each other, but Hawkston acted with unerring decision. He plunged to the door of the hut, knocking aside somebody who stumbled into his path, and threw the door open. He saw a figure running across the road, into the shadows on the side. He threw up his revolver, fired, and saw the figure sway and fall headlong, to be swallowed up by the darkness under the trees. He crouched for an instant in the doorway, gun lifted, left arm barring the blundering rush of the other men.

"Keep back, curse you! That was old Salim. There may be more, under the trees across the road."

But no menacing figure appeared, no sound mingled with the rustling of the palm-leaves in the wind, except a noise that might have been a man flopping in his death-throes-or dragging himself painfully away on hands and knees. This noise quickly ceased and Hawkston stepped cautiously out into the starlight. No shot greeted his appearance, and instantly he became a dynamo of energy. He leaped back into the hut, snarling: "Van Brock, take Ortelli and look for Salim. I know I hit him. You'll probably find him lying dead over there under the trees. If he's still breathing, finish him! He was Al Wazir's steward. We don't want him taking tales to Gordon."

Followed by Krakovitch, the Englishman groped his way into the darkened hut, struck a light and held it over the prostrate figure on the floor; it etched a grey face, staring glassy eyes, and a naked breast in which showed a round blue hole from which the blood had already ceased to ooze.

"Shot through the heart!" swore Hawkston, clenching his fist. "Old Salim must have seen him with us, and trailed him, guessing what we were after. The old devil shot him to keep him from guiding us to Al Wazir-but no matter. I don't need any guide to get me to the Caves of El Khour-well?" As the Dutchman and the Italian entered.

Van Brock spoke: "We didn't find the old dog. Smears of blood all over the grass, though. He must have been hard hit."

"Let him go," snarled Hawkston. "He's crawled away to die somewhere. It's a mile to the nearest occupied house. He won't live to get that far. Come on! The camels and the men are ready. They're behind that palm grove south of this hut. Everything's ready for the jump, just as I planned it. Let's go!"

Soon thereafter there sounded the soft pad of camel's hoofs and the jingle of accoutrements, as a line of mounted figures, ghostly in the night, moved westward into the desert. Behind them the flat roofs of el-Azem slept in the starlight, shadowed by the palm-leaves which stirred in the breeze that blew from the Persian Gulf.

The Abodes of Emptiness

GORDON'S THUMB WAS hooked easily in his belt, keeping his hand near the butt of his heavy pistol, as he rode leisurely through the starlight, and his gaze swept the palms which lined each side of the road, their broad fronds rattling in the faint breeze. He did not expect an ambush or the appearance of an enemy. He had no blood-feud with any man in el-Azem. And yonder, a hundred yards ahead of him, stood the flat-roofed, wall-encircled house of his friend, Achmet ibn Mitkhal, where the American was living as an honored guest. But the habits of a life-time are tenacious. For years El Borak had carried his life in his hands, and if there were hundreds of men in Arabia proud to call him friend, there were hundreds of others who would have given the teeth out of their heads for a clean sight of him, etched against the stars, over the barrel of a rifle.

Gordon reached the gate, and was about to call to the gate-keeper, when it swung open, and the portly figure of his host emerged.

"Allah be with thee, El Borak! I was beginning to fear some enemy had laid an ambush for you. Is it wise to ride alone, by night, when within a three days' ride dwell men who bear blood-feud with you?"

Gordon swung down, and handed his reins to a groom who had followed his master out of the compound. The

American was not a large man, but he was square-shouldered and deep-chested, with corded sinews and steely nerves which had been tempered and honed by the tooth-and-nail struggle for survival in the wild outlands of the world. His black eyes gleamed in the starlight like those of some untamed son of the wilderness.

"I think my enemies have decided to let me die of old age or inertia," he replied. "There has not been-"

"What's that?" Achmet ibn Mitkhal had his own enemies. In an instant the curious dragging, choking sounds he had heard beyond the nearest angle of the wall had transformed him into a tense image of suspicion and menace.

Gordon had heard the sounds as quickly as his Arab host, and he turned with the smooth speed of a cat, the big pistol appearing in his right hand as if by magic. He took a single quick stride toward the angle of the wall-then around that angle came a strange figure, with torn, trailing garments. A man, crawling slowly and painfully along on his hands and knees. As he crawled he gasped and panted with a grisly whistling and gagging in his breathing. As they stared at him, he slumped down almost at their feet, turning a blood-streaked visage to the starlight.

"Salim!" ejaculated Gordon softly, and with one stride he was at the angle, staring around it, pistol poised. No living thing met his eye; only an expanse of bare ground, barred by the shadows of the palms. He turned back to the prostrate man, over whom Achmet was already bending.

"Effendi!" panted the old man. "El Borak!" Gordon dropped to his knee beside him, and Salim's bony fingers clenched desperately on his arm.

"A hakim, quick, Achmet!" snapped Gordon.

"Nay," gasped Salim. "I am dying-"

"Who shot you, Salim?" asked Gordon, for he had already ascertained the nature of the wound which dyed the old man's tattered abba with crimson.

"Hawkston-the Englishman." The words came with an effort. "I saw him-the three rogues who follow him-beguiling that fool Dirdar to the deserted hut near Mekmet's Pool. I followed for I knew-they meant no good. Dirdar was a dog. He drank liquor-like an Infidel. El Borak! He betrayed Al Wazir! In spite of his oath. I shot him-through the window-but not in time. He will never guide them-but he told Hawkston-of the Caves of El Khour. I saw their caravan-camels-seven Arab servants. El Borak! They have departed-for the Caves-the Caves of El Khour!"

"Don't worry about them, Salim," replied Gordon, responding to the urgent appeal in the glazing eyes. "They'll never lay hand on Al Wazir. I promise you."

"Al Hamud Lillah-" whispered the old Arab, and with a spasm that brought frothy blood to his bearded lips, his grim old face set in iron lines, and he was dead before Gordon could ease his head to the ground.

The American stood up and looked down at the silent figure. Achmet came close to him and tugged his sleeve.

"Al Wazir!" murmured Achmet. "Wallah! I thought men had forgotten all about that man. It is more than a year now since he disappeared."

"White men don't forget-not when there's loot in the offing," answered Gordon sardonically. "All up and down the coast men are still looking for the Blood of the Gods-those marvelous matched rubies which were Al Wazir's especial pride, and which disappeared when he forsook the world and went into the desert to live as a hermit, seeking the Way to Truth through meditation and self-denial."

Achmet shivered and glanced westward where, beyond the belt of palms, the shadowy desert stretched vast and mysterious to mingle its immensity with the dimness of the starlit night.

"A hard way to seek Truth," said Achmet, who was a lover of the soft things and the rich things of life.

"Al Wazir was a strange man," answered Gordon. "But his servants loved him. Old Salim there, for instance. Good God, Mekmet's Pool is more than a mile from here. Salim crawled-crawled all that way, shot through and through. He knew Hawkston would torture Al Wazir-maybe kill him. Achmet, have my racing camel saddled-"

"I'll go with you!" exclaimed Achmet. "How many men will we need? You heard Salim-Hawkston will have at least eleven men with him-"

"We couldn't catch him now," answered Gordon. "He's got too much of a start on us. His camels are hejin-racing camels-too. I'm going to the Caves of El Khour, alone."

"But-"

"They'll go by the caravan road that leads to Riyadh; I'm going by the Well of Amir Khan."

Achmet blenched.

"Amir Khan lies within the country of Shalan ibn Mansour, who hates you as an iman hates Shaitan the Damned!"

"Perhaps none of his tribe will be at the Well," answered Gordon. "I'm the only Feringhi who knows of that route. If Dirdar told Hawkston about it, the Englishman couldn't find it, without a guide. I can get to the Caves a full day ahead of Hawkston. I'm going alone, because we couldn't take enough men to whip the Ruweila if they're on the warpath. One man has a better chance of slipping through than a score. I'm not going to fight Hawkston-not now. I'm going to warn Al Wazir. We'll hide until Hawkston gives it up and comes back to el-Azem. Then, when he's gone, I'll return by the caravan road."

Achmet shouted an order to the men who were gathering just within the gate, and they scampered to do his bidding.

"You will go disguised, at least?" he urged.

"No. It wouldn't do any good. Until I get into Ruweila country I won't be in any danger, and after that a disguise would be useless. The Ruweila kill and plunder every stranger they catch, whether Christian or Muhammadan."

He strode into the compound to oversee the saddling of the white racing camel.

"I'm riding light as possible," he said. "Speed means everything. The camel won't need any water until we reach the Well. After that it's not a long jump to the Caves. Load on just enough food and water to last me to the Well, with economy."

His economy was that of a true son of the desert. Neither water-skin nor food-bag was over-heavy when the two were slung on the high rear pommel. With a brief word of farewell, Gordon swung into the saddle, and at the tap of his bamboo stick, the beast lurched to its feet. "Yahh!" Another tap and it swung into motion. Men pulled wide the compound gate and stood aside, their eyes gleaming in the torchlight.

"Bismillah el rahman el rahhim!" quoth Achmet resignedly, lifting his hands in a gesture of benediction, as the camel and its rider faded into the night.

"He rides to death," muttered a bearded Arab.

"Were it another man I should agree," said Achmet. "But it is El Borak who rides. Yet Shalan ibn Mansour would give many horses for his head."

The sun was swinging low over the desert, a tawny stretch of rocky soil and sand as far as Gordon could see in every direction. The solitary rider was the only visible sign of life, but Gordon's vigilance was keen. Days and nights of hard riding lay behind him; he was coming into the Ruweila country, now, and every step he took increased his danger by that much. The Ruweila, whom he believed to be kin to the powerful Roualla of El Hamad, were true sons of Ishmael-hawks of the desert, whose hands were against every man not of their clan. To avoid their country the regular caravan road to the west swung wide to the south. This was an easy route, with wells a day's march apart, and it passed within a day's ride of the Caves of El Khour, the catacombs which pit a low range of hills rising sheer out of the wastelands.

Few white men know of their existence, but evidently Hawkston knew of the ancient trail that turned northward from the Well of Khosru, on the caravan road. Hawkston was perforce approaching El Khour circuitously. Gordon was heading straight westward, across waterless wastes, cut by a trace so faint only an Arab or El Borak could have followed it. On that route there was but one watering place between the fringe of oases along the coast and the Caves-the half-mythical Well of Amir Khan, the existence of which was a secret jealously guarded by the Bedouins.

There was no fixed habitation at the oasis, which was but a clump of palms, watered by a small spring, but frequently bands of Ruweila camped there. That was a chance he must take. He hoped they were driving their camel herds somewhere far to the north, in the heart of their country; but like true hawks, they ranged far afield, striking at the caravans and the outlying villages.

The trail he was following was so slight that few would have recognized it as such. It stretched dimly away before him over a level expanse of stone-littered ground, broken on one hand by sand dunes, on the other by a succession of low ridges. He glanced at the sun, and tapped the water-bag that swung from the saddle. There was little left, though he had practiced the grim economy of a Bedouin or a wolf. But within a few hours he would be at the Well of Amir Khan, where he would replenish his supply-though his nerves tightened at the thought of what might be waiting there for him.

Even as the thought passed through his mind, the sun struck a glint from something on the nearer of the sand dunes. The quick duck of his head was instinctive, and simultaneously there rang out the crack of a rifle and he heard the thud of the bullet into flesh. The camel leaped convulsively and came down in a headlong sprawl, shot through the heart. Gordon leaped free as it fell, rifle in hand, and in an instant was crouching behind the carcass, watching the crest of the dune over the barrel of his rifle. A strident yell greeted the fall of the camel, and another shot set the echoes barking. The bullet ploughed into the ground beside Gordon's stiffening breastwork, and the American replied. Dust spurted into the air so near the muzzle that gleamed on the crest that it evoked a volley of lurid oaths in a choked voice.

The black glittering ring was withdrawn, and presently there rose the rapid drum of hoofs. Gordon saw a white kafieh bobbing among the dunes, and understood the Bedouin's plan. He believed there was only one man. That man intended to circle Gordon's position, cross the trail a few hundred yards west of him, and get on the rising ground behind the American, where his vantage-point would allow him to shoot over the bulk of the camel-for of course he knew Gordon would keep the dead beast between them. But Gordon shifted himself only enough to command the trail ahead of him, the open space the Arab must cross after leaving the dunes before he reached the protection of the ridges. Gordon rested his rifle across the stiff forelegs of the camel.

A quarter of a mile up the trail there was a sandstone rock jutting up in the skyline. Anyone crossing the trail between it and himself would be limned against it momentarily. He set his sights and drew a bead against that rock. He was betting that the Bedouin was alone, and that he would not withdraw to any great distance before making the dash across the trail.

Even as he meditated a white-clad figure burst from among the ridges and raced across the trail, bending low in the saddle and flogging his mount. It was a long shot, but Gordon's nerves did not quiver. At the exact instant that the white-clad figure was limned against the distant rock, the American pulled the trigger. For a fleeting moment he thought he had missed; then the rider straightened convulsively, threw up two wide-sleeved arms and reeled back drunkenly. The frightened horse reared high, throwing the man heavily. In an instant the landscape showed two separate shapes where there had been one-a bundle of white sprawling on the ground, and a horse racing off southward.

Gordon lay motionless for a few minutes, too wary to expose himself. He knew the man was dead; the fall alone would have killed him. But there was a slight chance that other riders might be lurking among the sand dunes, after all.

The sun beat down savagely; vultures appeared from nowhere-black dots in the sky, swinging in great circles, lower and lower. There was no hint of movement among the ridges or the dunes.

Gordon rose and glanced down at the dead camel. His jaws set a trifle more grimly; that was all. But he realized what the killing of his steed meant. He looked westward, where the heat waves shimmered. It would be a long walk, a long, dry walk, before it ended.

Stooping, he unslung water-skin and food-bag and threw them over his shoulders. Rifle in hand he went up the trail with a steady, swinging stride that would eat up the miles and carry him for hour after hour without faltering.

When he came to the shape sprawling in the path, he set the butt of his rifle on the ground and stood looking briefly, one hand steadying the bags on his shoulders. The man he had killed was a Ruweila, right enough: one of the tall, sinewy, hawk-faced and wolf-hearted plunderers of the southern desert. Gordon's bullet had caught him just below the arm-pit. That the man had been alone, and on a horse instead of a camel, meant that there was a larger party of his tribesmen somewhere in the vicinity. Gordon shrugged his shoulders, shifted the rifle to the crook of his arm, and moved on up the trail. The score between himself and the men of Shalan ibn Mansour was red enough, already. It might well be settled once and for all at the Well of Amir Khan.

As he swung along the trail he kept thinking of the man he was going to warn: Al Wazir, the Arabs called him, because of his former capacity with the Sultan of Oman. A Russian nobleman, in reality, wandering over the world in search of

20

some mystical goal Gordon had never understood, just as an unquenchable thirst for adventure drove El Borak around the planet in constant wanderings. But the dreamy soul of the Slav coveted something more than material things. Al Wazir had been many things. Wealth, power, position; all had slipped through his unsatisfied fingers. He had delved deep in strange religions and philosophies, seeking the answer to the riddle of Existence, as Gordon sought the stimulation of hazard. The mysticisms of the Sufia had attracted him, and finally the ascetic mysteries of the Hindus.

A year before Al Wazir had been governor of Oman, next to the Sultan the wealthiest and most powerful man on the Pearl Coast. Without warning he had given up his position and disappeared. Only a chosen few knew that he had distributed his vast wealth among the poor, renounced all ambition and power, and gone like an ancient prophet to dwell in the desert, where, in the solitary meditation and self denial of a true ascetic, he hoped to read at last the eternal riddle of Life-as the ancient prophets read it. Gordon had accompanied him on that last journey, with the handful of faithful servants who knew their master's intentions-old Salim among them, for between the dreamy philosopher and the hard-bitten man of action there existed a powerful tie of friendship.

But for the traitor and fool, Dirdar, Al Wazir's secret had been well kept. Gordon knew that ever since Al Wazir's disappearance, adventurers of every breed had been searching for him, hoping to secure possession of the treasure that the Russian had possessed in the days of his power-the wonderful collection of perfectly matched rubies, known as the Blood of the Gods, which had blazed a lurid path through Oriental history for five hundred years. These jewels had not been distributed among the poor with the rest of Al Wazir's wealth. Gordon himself did not know what the man had done with them. Nor did the American care. Greed was not one of his faults. And Al Wazir was his friend.

The blazing sun rocked slowly down the sky, its flame turned to molten copper; it touched the desert rim, and etched against it, a crawling black tiny figure, Gordon moved grimly on, striding inexorably into the somber immensities of the Ruba al Khali-the Empty Abodes.

The Fight at the Well of Amir Khan

ETCHED AGAINST A white streak of dawn, motionless as figures on a tapestry, Gordon saw the clump of palms that marked the Well of Amir Khan grow up out of the fading night.

A few moments later he swore, softly. Luck, the fickle jade, was not with him this time. A faint ribbon of blue smoke curled up against the whitening sky. There were men at the Well of Amir Khan.

Gordon licked his dry lips. The water-bag that slapped against his back at each stride was flat, empty. The distance he would have covered in a matter of hours, skimming over the desert on the back of his tireless camel, he had trudged on foot, the whole night long, even though he had held a gait that few even of the desert's sons could have maintained unbroken. Even for him, in the coolness of the night, it had been a hard trek, though his iron muscles resisted fatigue like a wolf's.

Far to the east a low blue line lay on the horizon. It was the range of hills that held the Caves of El Khour. He was still ahead of Hawkston, forging on somewhere far to the south. But the Englishman would be gaining on him at every stride. Gordon could swing wide to avoid the men at the Well, and trudge on. Trudge on, afoot, and with empty water-bag? It would be suicide. He could never reach the Caves on foot and without water. Already he was bitten by the devils of thirst.

A red flame grew up in his eyes, and his dark face set in wolfish lines. Water was life in the desert; life for him and for Al Wazir. There was water at the Well, and camels. There were men, his enemies, in possession of both. If they lived, he must die. It was the law of the wolf-pack, and of the desert. He slipped the limp bags from his shoulders, cocked his rifle and went forward to kill or be killed-not for wealth, nor the love of a woman, nor an ideal, nor a dream, but for as much water as could be carried in a sheep-skin bag.

A wadi or gully broke the plain ahead of him, meandering to a point within a few hundred feet of the Well. Gordon crept toward it, taking advantage of every bit of cover. He had almost reached it, at a point a hundred yards from the Well, when a man in white kafieh and ragged abba materialized from among the palms. Discovery in the growing light was instant. The Arab yelled and fired. The bullet knocked up dust a foot from Gordon's knee, as he crouched on the edge of the gully, and he fired back. The Arab cried out, dropped his rifle and staggered drunkenly back among the palms.

The next instant Gordon had sprung down into the gully and was moving swiftly and carefully along it, toward the point where it bent nearest the Well. He glimpsed white-clad figures flitting briefly among the trees, and then rifles began to crack viciously. Bullets sang over the gully as the men fired from behind their saddles and bales of goods, piled like a rampart among the stems of the palms. They lay in the eastern fringe of the clump; the camels, Gordon knew, were on the other side of the trees. From the volume of the firing it could not be a large party.

A rock on the edge of the gully provided cover. Gordon thrust his rifle barrel under a jutting corner of it and watched for movement among the palms. Fire spurted and a bullet whined off the rock-zingggg! Dwindling in the distance like the dry whir of a rattler. Gordon fired at the puff of smoke, and a defiant yell answered him.

His eyes were slits of black flame. A fight like this could last for days. And he could not endure a siege. He had no water; he had no time. A long march to the south the caravan of Hawkston was swinging relentlessly westward, each step carrying them nearer the Caves of El Khour and the unsuspecting man who dreamed his dreams there. A few hundred feet away from Gordon there was water, and camels that would carry him swiftly to his destination; but lead-fanged wolves of the desert lay between.

Lead came at his retreat thick and fast, and vehement voices rained maledictions on him. They let him know they knew he was alone, and on foot, and probably half-mad with thirst. They howled jeers and threats. But they did not expose themselves. They were confident but wary, with the caution taught by the desert deep ingrained in them. They held the winning hand and they intended to keep it so.

An hour of this, and the sun climbing over the eastern rim, and the heat beginning-the molten, blinding heat of the southern desert. It was fierce already; later it would be a scorching hell in that unshielded gully. Gordon licked his blackened lips and staked his life and the life of Al Wazir on one desperate cast of Fate's blind dice.

Recognizing and accepting the terrible odds against success, he raised himself high enough to expose head and one shoulder above the gully rim, firing as he did so. Three rifles cracked together and lead hummed about his ears; the bullet of one raked a white-hot line across his upper arm. Instantly Gordon cried out, the loud, agonized cry of a man hard hit, and threw his arms above the rim of the gully in the convulsive gesture of a man suddenly death-stricken. One hand held the rifle and the motion threw it out of the gully, to fall ten feet away, in plain sight of the Arabs.

An instant's silence, in which Gordon crouched below the rim, then blood-thirsty yells echoed his cry. He dared not raise himself high enough to look, but he heard the slap-slap-slap of sandalled feet, winged by hate and blood-lust. They had fallen for his ruse. Why not? A crafty man might feign a wound and fall, but who would deliberately cast away his rifle? The thought of a Feringhi, lying helpless and badly wounded in the bottom of the gully, with a defenseless throat ready for the knife, was too much for the blood-lust of the Bedouins. Gordon held himself in iron control, until the swift feet were only a matter of yards away-then he came erect like a steel spring released, the big automatic in his hand.

As he leaped up he caught one split-second glimpse of three Arabs, halting dead in their tracks, wild-eyed at the unexpected apparition-even as he straightened-his gun was roaring. One man spun on his heel and fell in a crumpled heap, shot through the head. Another fired once, with a rifle, from the hip, without aim. An instant later he was down, with a slug through his groin and another ripping through his breast as he fell. And then Fate took a hand again-Fate in the form of a grain of sand in the mechanism of Gordon's automatic. The gun jammed just as he threw it down on the remaining Arab.

This man had no gun; only a long knife. With a howl he wheeled and legged it back for the grove, his rags whipping on the wind of his haste. And Gordon was after him like a starving wolf. His strategy might go for nothing if the man got back among the trees, where he might have left a rifle.

The Bedouin ran like an antelope, but Gordon was so close behind him when they reached the trees, the Arab had no time to snatch up the rifle leaning against the improvised rampart. He wheeled at bay, yowling like a mad dog, and slashing with the long knife. The point tore Gordon's shirt as the American dodged, and brought down the heavy pistol on the Arab's head. The thick kafieh saved the man's skull from being crushed, but his knees buckled and he went down, throwing his arms about Gordon's waist and dragging down the white man as he fell. Somewhere on the other side of the grove the wounded man was calling down curses on El Borak.

The two men rolled on the ground, ripping and smiting like wild animals. Gordon struck once again with his gun barrel, a glancing blow that laid open the Arab's face from eye to jaw, and then dropped the jammed pistol and caught at the arm that wielded the knife. He got a grip with his left hand on the wrist and the guard of the knife itself, and with his other hand began to fight for a throat-hold. The Arab's ghastly, blood-smeared countenance writhed in a tortured grin of muscular strain. He knew the terrible strength that lurked in El Borak's iron fingers, knew that if they closed on his throat they would not let go until his jugular was torn out.

He threw his body frantically from side to side, wrenching and tearing. The violence of his efforts sent both men rolling over and over, to crash against palm stems and carom against saddles and bales. Once Gordon's head was driven hard against a tree, but the blow did not weaken him, nor did the vicious drive the Arab got in with a knee to his groin. The Bedouin grew frantic, maddened by the fingers that sought his throat, the dark face, inexorable as iron, that glared into his own. Somewhere on the other side of the grove a pistol was barking, but Gordon did not feel the tear of lead, nor hear the whistle of bullets.

With a shriek like a wounded panther's, the Arab whirled over again, a knot of straining muscles, and his hand, thrown out to balance himself, fell on the barrel of the pistol Gordon had dropped. Quick as a flash he lifted it, just as Gordon found the hold he had been seeking, and crashed the butt down on the American's head with every ounce of strength in his lean sinews, backed by the fear of death. A tremor ran through the American's iron frame, and his head fell forward. And in that instant the Ruweila tore free like a wolf breaking from a trap, leaving his long knife in Gordon's hand.

Even before Gordon's brain cleared, his war-trained muscles were responding instinctively. As the Ruweila sprang up, he shook his head and rose more slowly, the long knife in his hand. The Arab hurled the pistol at him, and caught up the rifle which leaned against the barrier. He gripped it by the barrel with both hands and wheeled, whirling the stock above his head; but before the blow could fall Gordon struck with all the blinding speed that had earned him his name among the tribes. In under the descending butt he lunged and his knife, driven with all his strength and the momentum of his charge, plunged into the Arab's breast and drove him back against a tree into which the blade sank a hand's breadth deep. The Bedouin cried out, a thick, choking cry that death cut short. An instant he sagged against the haft, dead on his feet and nailed upright to the palm tree. Then his knees buckled and his weight tore the knife from the wood and he pitched into the sand.

Gordon wheeled, shaking the sweat from his eyes, glaring about for the fourth man-the wounded man. The furious fight had taken only a matter of moments. The pistol was still cracking dryly on the other side of the trees, and an animal scream of pain mingled with the reports.

With a curse Gordon caught up the Arab's rifle and burst through the grove. The wounded man lay under the shade of the trees, propped on an elbow, and aiming his pistol, not at El Borak but at the one camel that still lived. The other three lay stretched in their blood. Gordon sprang at the man, swinging the rifle stock. He was a split-second too late. The shot cracked and the camel moaned and crumpled even as the butt fell on the lifted arm, snapping the bone like a twig. The smoking pistol fell into the sand and the Arab sank back, laughing like a ghoul.

"Now see if you can escape from the Well of Amir Khan, El Borak!" he gasped. "The riders of Shalan ibn Mansour are out! Tonight or tomorrow they will return to the Well! Will you await them here, or flee on foot to die in the desert, or be tracked down like a wolf? Ya kalb! Forgotten of God! They will hang thy skin on a palmtree! Laan" abuk-!"

Lifting himself with an effort that spattered his beard with bloody foam, he spat toward Gordon, laughed croakingly and fell back, dead before his head hit the ground.

Gordon stood like a statue, staring down at the dying camels. The dead man's vengeance was grimly characteristic of his race. Gordon lifted his head and looked long at the low blue range on the western horizon. Cheeringly the dying Arab had foretold the grim choice left him. He could wait at the Well until Shalan ibn Mansour's wild riders returned and wiped him out by force of numbers, or he could plunge into the desert again on foot. And whether he awaited certain doom at the Well, or sought the uncertain doom of the desert, inexorably Hawkston would be marching westward, steadily cutting down the lead Gordon had had at the beginning.

But Gordon never had any doubt concerning his next move. He drank deep at the Well, and bolted some of the food the Arabs had been preparing for their breakfast. Some dried dates and crusted cheese-balls he placed in a food-bag, and he filled a water-skin from the Well. He retrieved his rifle, got the sand out of his automatic and buckled to his belt a scimitar from the girdle of one of the men he had killed. He had come into the desert intending to run and hide, not to fight. But it looked very much as if he would do much more fighting before this venture was over, and the added weight of the sword was more than balanced by the feeling of added security in the touch of the lean curved blade.

Then he slung the water-skin and food-bag over his shoulders, took up his rifle and strode out of the shadows of the grove into the molten heat of the desert day. He had not slept at all the night before. His short rest at the Well had

31

put new life and spring into his resilient muscles, hardened and toughened by an incredibly strenuous life. But it was a long, long march to the Caves of El Khour, under a searing sun. Unless some miracle occurred, he could not hope to reach them before Hawkston now. And before another sunrise the riders of Shalan ibn Mansour might well be on his trail, in which case-but all he had ever asked of Fortune was a fighting chance.

The sun rocked its slow, torturing way up the sky and down; twilight deepened into dusk, and the desert stars winked out; and on, grimly on, plodded that solitary figure, pitting an indomitable will against the merciless immensity of thirst-haunted desolation.

The Djinn of the Caves

THE CAVES of EL KHOUR pit the sheer eastern walls of a gaunt hill-range that rises like a stony backbone out of a waste of rocky plains. There is only one spring in the hills; it rises in a cave high up in the wall and curls down the steep rocky slope, a slender thread of silver, to empty into a broad shallow pool below. The sun was hanging like a blood-red ball above the western desert when Francis Xavier Gordon halted near this pool and scanned the rows of gaping cave-mouths with blood-shot eyes. He licked heat-blackened lips with a tongue from which all moisture had been baked. Yet there was still a little water in the skin on his shoulder. He had economized on that gruelling march, with the savage economy of the wilderness-bred.

It seemed a bit hard to realize he had actually reached his goal. The hills of El Khour had shimmered before him for so many miles, unreal in the heat-waves, until at last they had seemed like a mirage, a fantasy of a thirst-maddened imagination. The desert sun plays tricks even with a brain like Gordon's. Slowly, slowly the hills had grown up before him-now he stood at the foot of the eastern-most cliff, frowning up at the tiers of caves which showed their black mouths in even rows.

Nightfall had not brought Shalan ibn Mansour's riders swooping after the solitary wanderer, nor had dawn brought them. Again and again through the long, hot day, Gordon had halted on some rise and looked back, expecting to see the dust of the hurrying camels; but the desert had stretched empty to the horizon.

And now it seemed another miracle had taken place, for there were no signs of Hawkston and his caravan. Had they come and gone? They would have at least watered their camels at the pool; and from the utter lack of signs about it, Gordon knew that no one had camped or watered animals at the pool for many moons. No, it was indisputable, even if unexplainable. Something had delayed Hawkston and Gordon had reached the Caves ahead of him after all.

The American dropped on his belly at the pool and sank his face into the cool water. He lifted his head presently, shook it like a lion shaking his mane, and leisurely washed the dust from his face and hands.

Then he rose and went toward the cliff. He had seen no sign of life, yet he knew that in one of those caves lived the man he had come to seek. He lifted his voice in a far-carrying shout.

"Al Wazir! Ho there, Al Wazir!"

"Wazirrr!" whispered the echo back from the cliff. There was no other answer. The silence was ominous. With his rifle at the ready Gordon went toward the narrow trail that wound up the rugged face of the cliff. Up this he climbed, keenly scanning the eaves. They pitted the whole wall, in even tiers-too even to be the chance work of nature. They were man-made. Thousands of years ago, in the dim dawn of pre-history they had served as dwelling-places for some race of people who were not mere savages, who nitched their caverns in the soft strata with skill and cunning. Gordon knew the caves were connected by narrow passages, and that only by this ladder-like path he was following could they be reached from below.

The path ended at a long ledge, upon which all the caves of the lower tier opened. In the largest of these Al Wazir had taken up his abode.

Gordon called again, without result. He strode into the cave, and there he halted. It was square in shape. In the back wall and in each side wall showed a narrow door-like opening. Those at the sides led into adjoining caves. That at the back let into a smaller cavern, without any other outlet. There, Gordon remembered, Al Wazir had stored the dried and tinned foods he had brought with him. He had brought no furniture, nor weapons.

In one corner of the square cave a heap of charred fragments indicated that a fire had once been built there. In one corner lay a heap of skins-Al Wazir's bed. Nearby lay the one book Al Wazir had brought with him-The Bhagavat-Gita. But of the man himself there was no evidence.

Gordon went into the storeroom, struck a match and looked about him. The tins of food were there, though the supply was considerably depleted. But they were not stacked against the wall in neat columns as Gordon had seen them stowed under Al Wazir's directions. They were tumbled and scattered about all over the floor, with open and empty tins among them. This was not like Al Wazir, who placed a high value on neatness and order, even in small things. The rope he had brought along to aid him in exploring the caves lay coiled in one corner.

Gordon, extremely puzzled, returned to the square cave. Here, he had fully expected to find Al Wazir sitting in tranquil meditation, or out on the ledge meditating over the sun-set desert. Where was the man?

He was certain that Al Wazir had not wandered away to perish in the desert. There was no reason for him to leave the caves. If he had simply tired of his lonely life and taken his departure, he would have taken the book that was lying on the floor, his inseparable companion. There was no blood-stain on the floor, or anything to indicate that the hermit had met a violent end. Nor did Gordon believe that any Arab, even the Ruweila, would molest the "holy man." Anyway, if Arabs had done away with Al Wazir, they would have taken away the rope and the tins of food. And he was certain that, until Hawkston learned of it, no white man but himself had known of Al Wazir's whereabouts.

He searched through the lower tiers of caves without avail. The sun had sunk out of sight behind the hills, whose long shadows streamed far eastward across the desert, and deepening shadows filled the caverns. The silence and the mystery began to weigh on Gordon's nerves. He began to be irked by the feeling that unseen eyes were watching him. Men who live lives of constant peril develop certain obscure faculties or instincts to a keenness unknown to those lapped about by the securities of "civilization." As he passed through the caves, Gordon repeatedly felt an impulse to turn suddenly, to try to surprise those eyes that seemed to be boring into his back. At last he did wheel suddenly, thumb pressing back the hammer of his rifle, eyes alert for any movement in the growing dusk. The shadowy chambers and passages stood empty before him.

Once, as he passed a dark passageway he could have sworn he heard a soft noise, like the stealthy tread of a bare, furtive foot. He stepped to the mouth of the tunnel and called, without conviction: "Is that you, Ivan?" He shivered at the silence which followed; he had not really believed it was Al Wazir. He groped his way into the tunnel, rifle poked ahead of him. Within a few yards he encountered a blank wall; there seemed to be no entrance or exit except the doorway through which he had come. And the tunnel was empty, save for himself.

He returned to the ledge before the caves, in disgust.

"Hell, am I getting jumpy?"

But a grisly thought kept recurring to him-recollection of the Bedouins" belief that a supernatural fiend lurked in these ancient caves and devoured any human foolish enough to be caught there by night. This thought kept recurring, together with the reflection that the Orient held many secrets, which the West would laugh at, but which often proved to be grim realities. That would explain Al Wazir's mysterious absence: if some fiendish or bestial dweller in the caves had devoured him-Gordon's speculations revolved about a hypothetical rock-python of enormous size, dwelling for generations, perhaps centuries, in the hills-that would explain the lack of any blood-stains. Abruptly he swore: "Damn! I'm going batty. There are no snakes like that in Arabia. These caves are getting on my nerves."

It was a fact. There was a brooding weirdness about these ancient and forgotten caverns that roused uncanny speculations in Gordon's predominantly Celtic mind. What race had occupied them, so long ago? What wars had they witnessed, against what fierce barbarians sweeping up from the south? What cruelties and intrigues had they known, what grim rituals of worship and human sacrifice? Gordon shrugged his shoulders, wishing he had not thought of human sacrifice. The idea fitted too well with the general atmosphere of these grim caverns.

Angry at himself, he returned to the big square cavern, which, he remembered, the Arabs called Niss'rosh, The Eagle's Nest, for some reason or other. He meant to sleep in the caves that night, partly to overcome the aversion he felt toward them, partly because he did not care to be caught down on the plain in case Hawkston or Shalan ibn Mansour arrived in the night. There was another mystery. Why had not they reached the Caves, one or both of them? The desert was a breeding-place of mysteries, a twilight realm of fantasy. Al Wazir, Hawkston and Shalan ibn Mansour-had the fabled djinn of the Empty Abodes snatched them up and flown away with them, leaving him the one man alive in all the vast desert? Such whims of imagination played through his exhausted brain, as, too weary to eat, he prepared for the night.

He put a large rock in the trail, poised precariously, which anyone climbing the path in the dark would be sure to dislodge. The noise would awaken him. He stretched himself on the pile of skins, painfully aware of the stress and strain of his long trek, which had taxed even his iron frame to the utmost. He was asleep almost the instant he touched his rude bed.

It was because of this weariness of body and mind that he did not hear the velvet-footed approach of the thing that crept upon him in the darkness. He woke only when taloned fingers clenched murderously on his throat and an inhuman voice whinnied sickening triumph in his ear.

Gordon's reflexes had been trained in a thousand battles. So now he was fighting for his life before he was awake enough to know whether it was an ape or a great serpent that had attacked him. The fierce fingers had almost crushed his throat before he had a chance to tense his neck muscles. Yet those powerful muscles, even though relaxed, had saved his life. Even so the attack was so stunning, the grasp so nearly fatal, that as they rolled over the floor Gordon wasted precious seconds trying to tear away the strangling hands by wrenching at the wrists. Then as his fighting brain asserted itself, even through the red, thickening mists that were enfolding him, he shifted his tactics, drove a savage knee into a hard-muscled belly, and getting his thumbs under the little finger of each crushing hand, bent them fiercely back. No strength can resist that leverage. The unknown attacker let go, and instantly Gordon smashed a trip-hammer blow against the side of his head and rolled clear as the hard frame went momentarily limp. It was as dark in the cave as the gullet of Hell, so dark Gordon could not even see his antagonist.

He sprang to his feet, drawing his scimitar. He stood poised, tense, wondering uncomfortably if the thing could see in the dark, and scarcely breathing as he strained his ears. At the first faint sound he sprang like a panther, and slashed murderously at the noise. The blade cut only empty air, there was an incoherent cry, a shuffle of feet, then the rapidly receding pad of hurried footsteps. Whatever it was, it was in retreat. Gordon tried to follow it, ran into a blank wall, and by the time he had located the side door through which, apparently, the creature had fled, the sounds had faded out. The American struck a match and glared around, not expecting to see anything that would give him a clue to the mystery. Nor did he. The rock floor of the cavern showed no footprint.

What manner of creature he had fought in the dark he did not know. Its body had not seemed hairy enough for an ape, though the head had been a tangled mass of hair. Yet it had not fought like a human being; he had felt its talons and teeth, and it was hard to believe that human muscles could have contained such iron strength as he had encountered. And the noises it had made had certainly not resembled the sounds a man makes, even in combat.

Gordon picked up his rifle and went out on the ledge. From the position of the stars, it was past midnight. He sat down on the ledge, with his back against the cliff wall. He did not intend to sleep, but he slept in spite of himself, and woke suddenly, to find himself on his feet, with every nerve tingling, and his skin crawling with the sensation that grim peril had crept close upon him.

Even as he wondered if a bad dream had awakened him, he glimpsed a vague shadow fading into the black mouth of a cave not far away. He threw up his rifle and the shot sent the echoes flying and ringing from cliff to cliff. He waited tensely, but neither saw nor heard anything else.

After that he sat with his rifle across his knees, every faculty alert. His position, he realized, was precarious. He was like a man marooned on a deserted island. It was a day's hard ride to the caravan road to the south. On foot it would take longer. He could reach it, unhindered-but unless Hawkston had abandoned the quest, which was not likely, the Englishman's caravan was moving along that road somewhere. If Gordon met it, alone and on foot-Gordon had no illusions about Hawkston. But there was still a greater danger: Shalan ibn Mansour. He did not know why the shaykh had not tracked him down already, but it was certain that Shalan, scouring the desert to find the man who slew his warriors at the Well of Amir Khan, would eventually run him down. When that happened, Gordon did not wish to be caught out on the desert, on foot. Here, in the Caves, with water, food and shelter, he would have at least a fighting chance. If Hawkston and Shalan should chance to arrive at the same time-that offered possibilities. Gordon was a fighting man who depended on his wits as much as his sword, and he had set his enemies tearing at each other before now. But there was a present menace to him, in the Caves themselves, a menace he felt was the solution to the riddle of Al Wazir's fate. That menace he meant to drive to bay with the coming of daylight.

He sat there until dawn turned the eastern sky rose and white. With the coming of the light he strained his eyes into the desert, expecting to see a moving line of dots that would mean men on camels. But only the tawny, empty waste levels and ridges met his gaze. Not until the sun was rising did he enter the caves; the level beams struck into them, disclosing features that had been veiled in shadows the evening before.

He went first to the passage where he had first heard the sinister footfalls, and there he found the explanation to one mystery. A series of hand and foot holds, lightly nitched in the stone of the wall, led up through a square hole in the rocky ceiling into the cave above. The djinn of the Caves had been in that passage, and had escaped by that route, for some reason choosing flight rather than battle just then.

Now that he was rested, he became aware of the bite of hunger, and headed for The Eagle's Nest, to get his breakfast out of the tins before he pursued his exploration of the caves. He entered the wide chamber, lighted by the early sun which streamed through the door-and stopped dead.

A bent figure in the door of the store-room wheeled erect, to face him. For an instant they both stood frozen. Gordon saw a man confronting him like an image of the primordial-naked, gaunt, with a great matted tangle of hair and beard, from which the eyes blazed weirdly. It might have been a caveman out of the dawn centuries who stood there, a stone gripped in each brawny hand. But the high, broad forehead, half hidden under the thatch of hair, was not the slanting brow of a savage. Nor was the face, almost covered though it was by the tangled beard.

"Ivan!" ejaculated Gordon aghast, and the explanation of the mystery rushed upon him, with all its sickening implications. Al Wazir was a madman.

As if goaded by the sound of his voice, the naked man started violently, cried out incoherently, and hurled the rock in his right hand. Gordon dodged and it shattered on the wall behind him with an impact that warned him of the unnatural power lurking in the maniac's thews. Al Wazir was taller than Gordon, with a magnificent, broad-shouldered, lean-hipped torso, ridged with muscles. Gordon half turned and set his rifle against the wall, and as he did so, Al Wazir hurled the rock in his left hand, awkwardly, and followed it across the cave with a bound, shrieking frightfully, foam flying from his lips.

Gordon met him breast to breast, bracing his muscular legs against the impact, and Al Wazir grunted explosively as he was stopped dead in his tracks. Gordon pinioned his arms at his side, and a wild shriek broke from the madman's lips as he tore and plunged like a trapped animal. His muscles were like quivering steel wires under Gordon's grasp, that writhed and knotted. His teeth snapped beast-like at Gordon's throat, and as the American jerked back his head to escape them, Al Wazir tore loose his right arm, and whipped it over Gordon's left arm and down. Before the American could prevent it, he had grasped the scimitar hilt and torn the blade from its scabbard. Up and back went the long arm, with the sheen of naked steel, and Gordon, sensing death in the lifted sword, smashed his left fist to the madman's jaw. It was a short terrific hook that traveled little more than a foot, but it was like the jolt of a mule's kick.

Al Wazir's head snapped back between his shoulders under the impact, then fell limply forward on his breast. His legs gave way simultaneously and Gordon caught him and eased him to the rocky floor.

Leaving the limp form where it lay, Gordon went hurriedly into the store-room and secured the rope. Returning to the senseless man he knotted it about his waist, then lifted him to a sitting position against a natural stone pillar at the back of the cave, passed the rope about the column and tied it with an intricate knot on the other side. The rope was too strong, even for the superhuman strength of a maniac, and Al Wazir could not reach backward around the pillar to reach and untie the knot. Then Gordon set to work reviving the man-no light task, for El Borak, with the peril of death upon him, had struck hard, with the drive and snap of steel-trap muscles. Only the heavy beard had saved the jawbone from fracture.

But presently the eyes opened and gazed wildly around, flaring redly as they fixed on Gordon's face. The clawing hands with their long black nails, came up and caught at Gordon's throat, as the American drew back out of reach. Al Wazir made a convulsive effort to rise, then sank back and crouched, with his unwinking stare, his fingers making aimless motions. Gordon looked at him somberly, sick at his soul. What a miserable, revolting end to dreams and philosophies! Al Wazir had come into the desert seeking meditation and peace and the visions of the ancient prophets; he had found horror and insanity. Gordon had come looking for a hermit-philosopher, radiant with mellow wisdom; he had found a filthy, naked madman.

The American filled an empty tin with water and set it, with an opened tin of meat, near Al Wazir's hand. An instant later he dodged, as the mad hermit hurled the tins at him with all his power. Shaking his head in despair, Gordon went into the store-room and broke his own fast. He had little heart to eat, with the ruin of that once-splendid personality before him, but the urgings of hunger would not be denied.

It was while thus employed that a sudden noise outside brought him to his feet, galvanized by the imminence of danger.

Hawks at Bay

IT WAS THE rattling fall of the stone Gordon had placed in the path that had alarmed him. Someone was climbing up the winding trail! Snatching up his rifle he glided out on the ledge. One of his enemies had come at last.

Down at the pool a weary, dusty camel was drinking. On the path, a few feet below the ledge there stood a tall, wiry man in dust-stained boots and breeches, his torn shirt revealing his brown, muscular chest.

"Gordon!" this man ejaculated, staring amazedly into the black muzzle of the American's rifle. "How the devil did you get here?" His hands were empty, resting on an outcropping of rock, just as he had halted in the act of climbing. His rifle was slung to his back, pistol and scimitar in their scabbards at his belt.

"Put up your hands, Hawkston," ordered Gordon, and the Englishman obeyed.

"What are you doing here?" he repeated. "I left you in el-Azem-"

"Salim lived long enough to tell me what he saw in the hut by Mekmet's Pool. I came by a road you know nothing about. Where are the other jackals?"

Hawkston shook the sweat-beads from his sun-burnt forehead. He was above medium height, brown, hard as sole-leather, with a dark hawk-like face and a high-bridged predatory nose arching over a thin black mustache. A lawless adventurer, his scintillant grey eyes reflected a ruthless and reckless nature, and as a fighting man he was as notorious as was Gordon-more notorious in Arabia, for Afghanistan had been the stage for most of El Borak's exploits.

"My men? Dead by now, I fancy. The Ruweila are on the war-path. Shalan ibn Mansour caught us at Sulaymen's Well, with fifty men. We made a barricade of our saddles among the palms and stood them off all day. Van Brock and three of our camel-drivers were killed during the fighting, and Krakovitch was wounded. That night I took a camel and cleared out. I knew it was no use hanging on."

"You swine," said Gordon without passion. He did not call Hawkston a coward. He knew that not cowardice, but a cynical determination to save his skin at all hazards had driven the Englishman to desert his wounded and beleaguered companions.

"There wasn't any use for us all to be killed," retorted Hawkston. "I believed one man could sneak away in the dark and I did. They rushed the camp just as I got clear. I heard them killing the others. Ortelli howled like a lost soul when they cut his throat-I knew they'd run me down long before I could reach the Coast, so I headed for the Caves-northwest across the open desert, leaving the road and Khosru's Well off to the south. It was a long, dry ride, and I made it more by luck than anything else. And now can I put my hands down?"

"You might as well," replied Gordon, the rifle at his shoulder never wavering. "In a few seconds it won't matter much to you where your hands are."

Hawkston's expression did not change. He lowered his hands, but kept them away from his belt.

"You mean to kill me?" he asked calmly.

"You murdered my friend Salim. You came here to torture and rob Al Wazir. You'd kill me if you got the chance. I'd be a fool to let you live."

"Are you going to shoot me in cold blood?"

"No. Climb up on the ledge. I'll give you any kind of an even break you want."

Hawkston complied, and a few seconds later stood facing the American. An observer would have been struck by a certain similarity between the two men. There was no facial resemblance, but both were burned dark by the sun, both were built with the hard economy of rawhide and spring steel, and both wore the keen, hawk-like aspect which is the common brand of men who live by their wits and guts out on the raw edges of the world.

Hawkston stood with his empty hands at his sides while Gordon faced him with rifle held hip-low, but covering his midriff.

"Rifles, pistols or swords?" asked the American. "They say you can handle a blade."

"Second to none in Arabia," answered Hawkston confidently. "But I'm not going to fight you, Gordon."

"You will!" A red flame began to smolder in the black eyes. "I know you, Hawkston. You've got a slick tongue, and you're treacherous as a snake. We'll settle this thing here and now. Choose your weapons-or by God, I'll shoot you down in your tracks!"

Hawkston shook his head calmly.

"You wouldn't shoot a man in cold blood, Gordon. I'm not going to fight you-yet. Listen, man, we'll have plenty of fighting on our hands before long! Where's Al Wazir?"

"That's none of your business," growled Gordon.

"Well, no matter. You know why I'm here. And I know you came here to stop me if you could. But just now you and I are in the same boat. Shalan ibn Mansour's on my trail. I slipped through his fingers, as I said, but he picked up my tracks and was after me within a matter of hours. His camels were faster and fresher than mine, and he's been slowly overhauling me. When I topped the tallest of those ridges to the south there, I saw his dust. He'll be here within the next hour! He hates you as much as he does me."

"You need my help, and I need yours. With Al Wazir to help us, we can hold these Caves indefinitely."

Gordon frowned. Hawkston's tale sounded plausible, and would explain why Shalan ibn Mansour had not come hot on the American's trail, and why the Englishman had not arrived at the Caves sooner. But Hawkston was such a snake-tongued liar it was dangerous to trust him. The merciless creed of the desert said shoot him down without any more parley, and take his camel. Rested, it would carry Gordon and Al Wazir out of the desert. But Hawkston had gauged Gordon's character correctly when he said the American could not shoot a man in cold blood.

"Don't move," Gordon warned him, and holding the cocked rifle like a pistol in one hand, he disarmed Hawkston, and ran a hand over him to see that he had no concealed weapons. If his scruples prevented him shooting his enemy, he was determined not to give that enemy a chance to get the drop on him. For he knew Hawkston had no such scruples.

"How do I know you're not lying?" he demanded.

"Would I have come here alone, on a worn-out camel, if I wasn't telling the truth?" countered Hawkston. "We'd better hide that camel, if we can. If we should beat them off, we'll need it to get to the Coast on. Damn it, Gordon, your suspicion and hesitation will get our throats cut yet! Where's Al Wazir?"

"Turn and look into that cave," replied Gordon grimly.

Hawkston, his face suddenly sharp with suspicion, obeyed. As his eyes rested on the figure crouched against the column at the back of the cavern, his breath sucked in sharply.

"Al Wazir! What in God's name's the matter with him?"

"Too much loneliness, I reckon," growled Gordon. "He's stark mad. He couldn't tell you where to find the Blood of the Gods if you tortured him all day."

"Well, it doesn't matter much just now," muttered Hawkston callously. "Can't think of treasure when life itself

51

is at stake. Gordon, you'd better believe me! We should be preparing for a siege, not standing here chinning. If Shalan ibn Mansour-look!" He started violently, his long arm stabbing toward the south.

Gordon did not turn at the exclamation. He stepped back instead, out of the Englishman's reach, and still covering the man, shifted his position so he could watch both Hawkston and the point of the compass indicated. Southeastward the country was undulating, broken by barren ridges. Over the farthest ridge a string of white dots was pouring, and a faint dust-haze billowed up in the air. Men on camels! A regular horde of them.

"The Ruweila!" exclaimed Hawkston. "They'll be here within the hour!"

"They may be men of yours," answered Gordon, too wary to accept anything not fully proven. Hawkston was as tricky as a fox, and to make a mistake on the desert meant death. "We'll hide that camel, though, just on the chance you're telling the truth. Go ahead of me down the trail."

Paying no attention to the Englishman's profanity, Gordon herded him down the path to the pool. Hawkston took the camel's rope and went ahead leading it, under Gordon's guidance. A few hundred yards north of the pool there was a narrow canyon winding deep into a break of the hills, and a short distance up this ravine Gordon showed Hawkston a narrow cleft in the wall, concealed behind a jutting boulder. Through this the camel was squeezed, into a natural pocket, open at the top, roughly round in shape, and about forty feet across.

"I don't know whether the Arabs know about this place or not," said Gordon. "But we'll have to take the chance that they won't find the beast."

Hawkston was nervous.

"For God's sake let's get back to the Caves! They're coming like the wind. If they catch us in the open they'll shoot us like rabbits!"

He started back at a run, and Gordon was close on his heels. But Hawkston's nervousness was justified. The white men had not quite reached the foot of the trail that led up to the Caves when a low thunder of hoofs rose on their ears, and over the nearest ridge came a wild white-clad figure on a camel, waving a rifle. At the sight of them he yelled stridently and flogged his beast into a more furious gallop, and threw his rifle to his shoulder. Behind him man after man topped the ridge-Bedouins on hejin-white racing camels.

"Up the cliff, man!" yelled Hawkston, pale under his bronze. Gordon was already racing up the path, and behind him Hawkston panted and cursed, urging greater haste, where more speed was impossible. Bullets began to snick against the cliff, and the foremost rider howled in blood-thirsty glee as he bore down swiftly upon them. He was many yards ahead of his companions, and he was a remarkable marksman, for an Arab. Firing from the rocking, swaying saddle, he was clipping his targets close.

Hawkston yelped as he was stung by a flying sliver of rock, flaked off by a smashing slug.

"Damn you, Gordon!" he panted. "This is your fault-your bloody stubbornness-he'll pick us off like rabbits-"

The oncoming rider was not more than three hundred yards from the foot of the cliff, and the rim of the ledge was ten feet above the climbers. Gordon wheeled suddenly, threw his rifle to his shoulder and fired all in one motion, so quickly he did not even seem to take aim. But the Arab went out of his saddle like a man hit by lightning. Without pausing to note the result of his shot, Gordon raced on up the path, and an instant later he swarmed over the ledge, with Hawkston at his heels.

"Damndest snap-shot I ever saw!" gasped the Englishman.

"There's your guns," grunted Gordon, throwing himself flat on the ledge. "Here they come!"

Hawkston snatched his weapons from the rock where Gordon had left them, and followed the American's example.

The Arabs had not paused. They greeted the fall of their reckless leader with yells of hate, but they flogged their mounts and came on in a headlong rush. They meant to spring off at the foot of the trail and charge up it on foot. There were at least fifty, of them.

The two men lying prone on the ledge above did not lose their heads. Veterans, both of them, of a thousand wild battles, they waited coolly until the first of the riders were within good range. Then they began firing, without haste and without error. And at each shot a man tumbled headlong from his saddle or slumped forward on his mount's bobbing neck.

Not even Bedouins could charge into such a blast of destruction. The rush wavered, split, turned on itself-and in an instant the white-clad riders were turning their backs on the Caves and flogging in the other direction as madly as they had come. Five of them would never charge again, and as they fled Hawkston drilled one of the rearmost men neatly between the shoulders.

They fell back beyond the first low, stone-littered ridge, and Hawkston shook his rifle at them and cursed them with virile eloquence.

"Desert scum! Try it again, you bounders!"

Gordon wasted no breath on words. Hawkston had told the truth, and Gordon knew he was in no danger from treachery from that source, for the present. Hawkston would not attack him as long as they were confronted by a common enemy-but he knew that the instant that peril was removed, the Englishman might shoot him in the back, if he could. Their position was bad, but it might well have been worse. The Bedouins were all seasoned desert-fighters, cruel as wolves. Their chief had a blood-feud with both white men, and would not fail to grasp the chance that had thrown them into his reach. But the defenders had the advantage of shelter, an inexhaustible water supply, and food enough to last for months. Their only weakness was the limited amount of ammunition.

Without consulting one another, they took their stations on the ledge, Hawkston to the north of the trailhead, Gordon about an equal distance to the south of it.

There was no need for a conference; each man knew the other knew his business. They lay prone, gathering broken rocks in heaps before them to add to the protection offered by the ledge-rim.

Spurts of flame began to crown the ridge; bullets whined and splatted against the rock. Men crept from each end of the ridge into the clusters of boulders that littered the plain. The men on the ledge held their fire, unmoved by the slugs that whistled and spanged near at hand. Their minds worked so similarly in a situation like this that they understood each other without the necessity of conversation. There was no chance of them wasting two cartridges on the same man. An imaginary line, running from the foot of the trail to the ridge, divided their territories. When a turbaned head was poked from a rock north of that line, it was Hawkston's rifle that knocked the man dead and sprawling over the boulder. And when a Bedouin darted from behind a spur of rock south of that line in a weaving, dodging run for cover nearer the cliff, Hawkston held his fire. Gordon's rifle cracked and the runner took the earth in a rolling tumble that ended in a brief thrashing of limbs.

A voice rose from the ridge, edged with fury.

"That's Shalan, damn him!" snarled Hawkston. "Can you make out what he says?"

"He's telling his men to keep out of sight," answered Gordon. "He tells them to be patient-they've got plenty of time."

"And that's the truth, too," grunted Hawkston. "They've got time, food, water-they'll be sneaking to the pool after dark to fill their water-skins. I wish one of us could get a clean shot at Shalan. But he's too foxy to give us a chance at him. I saw him when they were charging us, standing back on the ridge, too far away to risk a bullet on him."

"If we could drop him the rest of them wouldn't hang around here a minute," commented Gordon. "They're afraid of the man-eating djinn they think haunts these hills."

"Well, if they could get a good look at Al Wazir now, they'd swear it was the djinn in person," said Hawkston. "How many cartridges have you?"

"Both guns are full, about a dozen extra rifle cartridges."

57

Hawkston swore.

"I haven't many more than that, myself. We'd better toss a coin to see which one of us sneaks out tonight, while the other keeps up a fusilade to distract their attention. The one who stays gets both rifles and all the ammunition."

"We will like hell," growled Gordon. "If we can't all go, Al Wazir with us, nobody goes!"

"You're crazy to think of a lunatic at a time like this!"

"Maybe. But if you try to sneak off I'll drill you in the back as you run."

Hawkston snarled wordlessly and fell silent. Both men lay motionless as red Indians, watching the ridge and the rocks that shimmered in the heat waves. The firing had ceased, but they had glimpses of white garments from time to time among the gullies and stones, as the besiegers crept about among the boulders. Some distance to the south Gordon saw a group creeping along a shallow gully that ran to the foot of the cliff. He did not waste lead on them. When they reached the cliff at that point they would be no better off. They were too far away for effective shooting, and the cliff could be climbed only at the point where the trail wound upward. Gordon fell to studying the hill that was serving the white men as their fortress.

Some thirty caves formed the lower tier, extending across the curtain of rock that formed the face of the cliff. As he knew, each cave was connected by a narrow passage to the adjoining chamber. There were three tiers above this one, all the tiers connected by ladders of hand-holds nitched in the rock, mounting from the lower caves through holes in the stone ceiling to the ones above. The Eagle's Nest, in which Al Wazir was tied, safe from flying lead, was approximately in the middle of the lower tier, and the path hewn in the rock came upon the ledge directly before its opening. Hawkston was lying in front of the third cave to the north of it, and Gordon lay before the third cave to the south.

The Arabs lay in a wide semi-circle, extending from the rocks at one end of the low ridge, along its crest, and into the rocks at the other end. Only those lying among the rocks were close enough to do any damage, save by accident. And looking up at the ledge from below, they could see only the gleaming muzzles of the white men's rifles, or catch fleeting glimpses of their heads occasionally. They seemed to be weary of wasting lead on such difficult targets. Not a shot had been fired for some time.

Gordon found himself wondering if a man on the crest of the cliff above the caves could, looking down, see him and Hawkston lying on the ledge. He studied the wall above him; it was almost sheer, but other, narrower ledges ran along each tier of caves, obstructing the view from above, as it did from the lower ledge. Remembering the craggy sides of the hill, Gordon did not believe these plains-dwellers would be able to scale it at any point.

He was just contemplating returning to The Eagle's Nest to offer food and water again to Al Wazir, when a faint sound reached his ears that caused him to go tense with suspicion.

It seemed to come from the caves behind him. He glanced at Hawkston. The Englishman was squinting along his rifle barrel, trying to get a bead on a kafieh that kept bobbing in and out among the boulders near the end of the ridge.

Gordon wriggled back from the ledge-rim and rolled into the mouth of the nearest cave before he stood up, out of sight of the men below. He stood still, straining his ears.

There it was again-soft and furtive, like the rustle of cloth against stone, the shuffle of bare feet. It came from some point south of where he stood. Gordon moved silently in that direction, passed through the adjoining chamber, entered the next-and came face to face with a tall beared Bedouin who yelled and whirled up a scimitar. Another raider, a man with an evil, scarred face, was directly behind him, and three more were crawling out of a cleft in the floor.

Gordon fired from the hip, checking the downward stroke of the scimitar. The scar-faced Arab fired over the falling body and Gordon felt a numbing shock run up his arms, jerked the trigger and got no response. The bullet had smashed into the lock, ruining the mechanism. He heard

Hawkston yell savagely, out on the ledge, heard the pumping fusilade of the Englishman's rifle, and a storm of shots and yells rising from the valley. They were storming the cliff! And Hawkston must meet them alone, for Gordon had his hands full.

What takes long to relate, actually happened in split seconds. Before the scarred Bedouin could fire again Gordon knocked him sprawling with a kick in the groin, and reversing his rifle, crushed the skull of a man who lunged at him with a long knife. No time to draw pistol or scimitar. It was hand-to-hand slaughter with a vengeance in the narrow cave, two Bedouins tearing at him like wolves, and others jamming the shaft in their eagerness to join the fray.

No quarter given or expected-a whirlwind of furious motion, blades flashing and whickering, clanging on the rifle barrel and biting into the stock as Gordon parried-and the butt crushing home and men going down with their heads smashed. The scarred nomad had risen, but fearing to fire because of the desperate closeness of the melee, rushed in, clubbing his rifle, just as the last man dropped. Gordon, bleeding from a gash across the breast muscles, ducked the swinging stock, shifted his grip on his own rifle and drove the blood-smeared butt, like a dagger, full in the bearded face. Teeth and bones crumpled and the man toppled backward into the shaft, carrying with him the men who were just clambering out.

Snatching the instant's respite Gordon sprang to the mouth of the shaft, whipping out his automatic. Wild bearded faces crowding the shaft glared up at him, frozen with the recognition of doom-then the cave reverberated deafeningly to the thundering of the big automatic, blasting those wild faces into red ruin. It was slaughter at that range, blood and brains spattered, nerveless hands released their holds, bodies went sliding down the shaft in a red welter, jamming and choking it.

Gordon glared down it for an instant, all killer in that moment, then whirled and ran out on the ledge. Bullets sang past his head, and he saw Hawkston stuffing fresh cartridges into his rifle. No living Arab was in sight, but half a dozen new forms between the ridge and the foot of the trail told of a determined effort to storm the cliff, defeated only by the Englishman's deadly accuracy.

Hawkston shouted: "What the hell's been going on in there?"

"They've found a shaft leading up from somewhere down below," snapped Gordon. "Watch for another rush while I try to jam it."

Ignoring lead slapped at him from among the rocks, he found a sizable boulder and rolled it into the cave. He peered cautiously down the well. Hand and foot holds nitched in the rock formed precarious stair-steps in the slanting side. Some forty feet down the shaft made an angle, and it was there the bodies of the Arabs had jammed. But now only one corpse hung there, and as he looked it moved, as if imbued with life, and slid down out of sight. Men below the angle were pulling the bodies out, to clear the way for a fresh attack.

Gordon rolled the boulder into the shaft and it rumbled downward and wedged hard at the angle. He did not believe it could be dislodged from below, and his belief was confirmed by a muffled chorus of maledictions swelling up from the depths.

Gordon was sure this shaft had not been in existence when he first came to the Caves with Al Wazir, a year before. Exploring the caverns in search of the madman, the night before, it was not strange that he had failed to notice the narrow mouth in a dark corner of the cave. That it opened into some cleft at the foot of the cliff was obvious. He remembered the men he had seen stealing along the gully to the south. They had found that lower cleft, and the simultaneous attack from both sides had been well planned. But for Gordon's keen ears it might have succeeded. As it was it had left the American with an empty pistol and a broken rifle.

Gordon dragged the bodies of the four Arabs he had killed to the ledge and heaved them over, ignoring the ferocious yells and shots that emanated from the rocks. He did not bother to marvel that he had emerged the victor from that desperate melee. He knew that fighting was half speed and strength and wit, and half blind luck. His number was not up yet, that was all.

Then he set out on a thorough tour of investigation through the lower tiers, in search of other possible shafts. Passing through The Eagle's Nest, he glanced at Al Wazir, sitting against the pillar. The man seemed to be asleep; his hairy head was sunk on his breast, his hands folded limply over the rope about his waist. Gordon set food and water beside him.

His explorations revealed no more unexpected tunnels. Gordon returned to the ledge with tins of food and a skin of water, procured from the stream which had its source in one of the caves. They ate lying flat on the shelf, for keen eyes were watching with murderous hate and eager trigger-finger from ridge and rock. The sun had passed its zenith.

Their frugal meal finished, the white men lay baking in the heat like lizards on a rock, watching the ridge. The afternoon waned.

"You've got another rifle," said Hawkston.

"Mine was broken in the fight in the cave. I took this one from one of the men I killed. It has a full magazine, but no more cartridges for it. My pistol's empty."

"I've got only the cartridges in my guns," muttered Hawkston. "Looks like our number's up. They're just waiting for dark before they rush us again. One of us might get away in the dark, while the other held the fort, but since you won't agree to that, there's nothing to do but sit here and wait until they cut our throats."

"We have one chance," said Gordon. "If we can kill Shalan, the others will run. He's not afraid of man or devil, but his men fear djinn. They'll be nervous as the devil after night falls."

Hawkston laughed harshly. "Fool's talk. Shalan won't give us a chance at him. We'll all die here. All but Al Wazir. The Arabs won't harm him. But they won't help him, either. Damn him! Why did he have to go mad?"

"It wasn't very considerate," Gordon agreed with biting irony. "But then, you see he didn't know you wanted to torture him into telling where he hid the Blood of the Gods."

"It wouldn't have been the first time a man has been tortured for them," retorted Hawkston. "Man, you have no real idea of the value of those jewels. I saw them once, when Al Wazir was governor of Oman. The sight of them's enough to drive a man mad. Their story sounds like a tale out of The Arabian Nights. Only God knows how many women have given up their souls or men their lives because of them, since Ala ed-din Muhammad of Delhi plundered the Hindu temple of Somnath, and found them among the loot. That was in 1294. They've blazed a crimson path across Asia since then. Blood's spilt wherever they go. I'd poison my own brother to get them-" The wild flame that rose in the Englishman's eyes made it easy for Gordon to believe it, and he was swept by a revulsion toward the man.

"I'm going to feed Al Wazir," he said abruptly, rising.

No shots had come from the rocks for some time, though they knew their foes were there, waiting with their ancient, terrible patience. The sun had sunk behind the hills, the ravines and ridges were veiled in great blue shadows. Away to the east a silver-bright star winked out and quivered in the deepening blue.

Gordon strode into the square chamber-and was galvanized at the sight of the stone pillar standing empty. With a stride he reached it; bent over the frayed ends of the severed rope that told their own story. Al Wazir had found a way to free himself. Slowly, painfully, working with his claw-like fingernails through the long day, the madman had picked apart the tough strands of the heavy rope. And he was gone.

The Devil of the Night

GORDON STEPPED TO the door of the Nest and said curtly: "Al Wazir's gotten away. I'm going to search the Caves for him. Stay on the ledge and keep watch."

"Why waste the last minutes of your life chasing a lunatic through a rat-run?" growled Hawkston. "It'll be dark soon and the Arabs will be rushing us-"

"You wouldn't understand," snarled Gordon, turning away.

The task ahead of him was distasteful. Searching for a homicidal maniac through the darkening caves was bad enough, but the thought of having forcibly to subdue his friend again was revolting. But it must be done. Left to run at large in the Caves Al Wazir might do harm either to himself or to them. A stray bullet might strike him down.

A swift search through the lower tier proved fruitless, and Gordon mounted by the ladder into the second tier. As he climbed through the hole into the cave above he had an uncomfortable feeling that Al Wazir was crouching at the rim to break his head with a rock. But only silence and emptiness greeted him. Dusk was filling the caves so swiftly he began to despair of finding the madman. There were a hundred nooks and corners where Al Wazir could crouch unobserved, and Gordon's time was short.

The ladder that connected the second tier with the third was in the chamber into which he had come, and glancing up through it Gordon was startled to see a circle of deepening blue set with a winking star. In an instant he was climbing toward it.

He had discovered another unsuspected exit from the Caves. The ladder of hand holds led through the ceiling, up the wall of the cave above, and up through a round shaft that opened in the ceiling of the highest cave. He went up, like a man climbing up a chimney, and a few moments later thrust his head over the rim.

He had come out on the summit of the cliffs. To the east the rock rim pitched up sharply, obstructing his view, but to the west he looked out over a jagged backbone that broke in gaunt crags outlined against the twilight. He stiffened as somewhere a pebble rattled down, as if dislodged by a groping foot. Had Al Wazir come this way? Was the madman somewhere out there, climbing among those shadowy crags? If he was, he was courting death by the slip of a hand or a foot.

As he strained his eyes in the deepening shadows, a call welled up from below: "I say, Gordon! The blighters are getting ready to rush us! I see them massing among the rocks!"

With a curse Gordon started back down the shaft. It was all he could do. With darkness gathering Hawkston would not be able to hold the ledge alone.

Gordon went down swiftly, but before he reached the ledge darkness had fallen, lighted but little by the stars. The Englishman crouched on the rim, staring down into the dim gulf of shadows below.

"They're coming!" he muttered, cocking his rifle. "Listen!"

There was no shooting, this time-only the swift purposeful slap of sandalled feet over the stones. In the faint starlight a shadowy mass detached itself from the outer darkness and rolled toward the foot of the cliff. Steel clinked on the rocks. The mass divided into individual figures. Men grew up out of the darkness below. No use to waste bullets on shadows. The white men held their fire. The Arabs were on the trail, and they came up with a rush, steel gleaming dully in their hands. The path was thronged with dim figures; the defenders caught the glitter of white eyeballs, rolling upward.

They began to work their rifles. The dark was cut with incessant spurts of flame. Lead thudded home. Men cried out. Bodies rolled from the trail, to strike sickeningly on the rocks below. Somewhere back in the darkness, Shalan ibn Mansour's voice was urging on his slayers. The crafty shaykh had no intentions of risking his hide within reach of those grim fighters holding the ledge.

Hawkston cursed him as he worked his rifle.

"Thibhahum, bism er rassul!" sobbed the bloodlusting howl as the maddened Bedouins fought their way upward, frothing like rabid dogs in their hate and eagerness to tear the Infidels limb from limb.

69

Gordon's hammer fell with an empty click. He clubbed the rifle and stepped to the head of the path. A white-clad form loomed before him, fighting for a foothold on the ledge. The swinging rifle-butt crushed his head like an eggshell. A rifle fired point-blank singed Gordon's brows and his gun-stock shattered the rifleman's shoulder.

Hawkston fired his last cartridge, hurled the empty rifle and leaped to Gordon's side, scimitar in hand. He cut down a Bedouin who was scrambling over the rim with a knife in his teeth. The Arabs massed in a milling clump below the rim, snarling like wolves, flinching from the blows that rained down from rifle butt and scimitar.

Men began to slink back down the trail.

"Wallah!" wailed a man. "They are devils! Flee, brothers!"

"Dogs!" yelled Shalan ibn Mansour, an eery voice out of the darkness. He stood on a low knoll near the ridge, but he was invisible to the men on the cliff, what of the thick shadows. "Stand to it! There are but two of them!"

"They have ceased firing, so their guns must be empty! If you do not bring me their heads I will flay you alive! Theyahhh! Ya allah-!" His voice rose to an incoherent scream, and then broke in a horrible gurgle. That was followed by a tense silence, in which the Arabs clinging to the trail and massed at its foot twisted their heads over their shoulders to glare in amazement in the direction whence the cry had come. The men on the ledge, glad of the respite, shook the sweat from their eyes and stood listening with equal surprise and interest.

Someone called: "Ohai, Shalan ibn Mansour! Is all well with thee?"

There was no reply, and one of the Arabs left the foot of the cliff and ran toward the knoll, shouting the shaykh's name. The men on the ledge could trace his progress by his strident voice.

"Why did the shaykh cry out and fall silent?" shouted a man on the path. "What has happened, Haditha?"

Haditha's reply came back plainly.

"I have reached the knoll whereon he stood--I do not see him--Wallah! He is dead! He lies here slain, with his throat torn out! Allah! Help!" He screamed, fired, and then came sounds of his frantic flight. And as he howled like a lost soul, for the flash of the shot had showed him a face stooping above the dead man, a wild grinning visage rendered inhuman by a matted tangle of hair-the face of a devil to the terrified Arab. And above his shrieks, as he ran, rose burst upon burst of maniacal laughter.

"Flee! Flee! I have seen it! It is the djinn of El Khour!"

Instant panic ensued. Men fell off the trail like ripe apples off a limb screaming: "The djinn has slain Shalan ibn Mansour! Flee, brothers, flee!" The night was filled with their clamor as they stampeded for the ridge, and presently the sounds of lusty whacking and the grunting of camels came back to the men on the ledge. There was no trick about this. The Ruweila, courageous in the face of human foes, but haunted by superstitious terrors, were in full flight, leaving behind them the bodies of their chief and their slain comrades.

"What the devil?" marveled Hawkston.

"It must have been Ivan," muttered Gordon. "Somehow he must have climbed down the crags on the other side of the hill-God, what a climb it must have been!"

They stood there listening, but the only sound that reached their ears was the diminishing noise of the horde's wild flight. Presently they descended the path, past forms grotesquely huddled where they had fallen. More bodies dotted the floor at the foot of the cliff, and Gordon picked up a rifle dropped from a dead hand, and assured himself that it was loaded. With the Arabs in flight, the truce between him and Hawkston might well be at an end. Their future relations would depend entirely upon the Englishman.

A few moments later they stood upon the low knoll on which Shalan ibn Mansour had stood. The Arab chief was still there. He sprawled on his back in a dark crimson puddle, and his throat had been ripped open as if by the claws of a wild beast. He was a grisly sight in the light of the match Gordon shaded over him.

The American straightened, blew out the match and flipped it away. He strained his eyes into the surrounding shadows and called: "Ivan!" There was no answer.

"Do you suppose it was really Al Wazir who killed him?" asked Hawkston uneasily.

"Who else could it have been? He must have sneaked on Shalan from behind. The other fellow caught a glimpse of him, and thought he was the devil of the caves, just as you said they would. " What erratic whim had impelled Al Wazir to this deed, Gordon could not say. Who can guess the vagaries of the insane? The primitive instincts of murder loosed by lunacy--a madman stealing through the night, attracted by a solitary figure shouting from a knoll--it was not so strange, after all.

"Well, let's start looking for him," growled Hawkston. "I know you won't start back to the Coast until we've got him nicely tied up on that bally camel. So the sooner the better."

"All right." Gordon's voice betrayed none of the suspicion in his mind. He knew that Hawkston's nature and purposes had been altered none by what they had passed through. The man was treacherous and unpredictable as a wolf. He turned and started toward the cliff, but he took good care not to let the Englishman get behind him, and he carried his cocked rifle ready.

"I want to find the lower end of that shaft the Arabs came up," said Gordon. "Ivan may be hiding there. It must be near the western end of that gully they were sneaking along when I first saw them."

Not long later they were moving along the shallow gully, and where it ended against the foot of the cliff, they saw a narrow slit-like cleft in the stone, large enough to admit a man. Hoarding their matches carefully they entered and moved along the narrow tunnel into which it opened. This tunnel led straight back into the cliff for a short distance, then turned sharply to the right, running along until it ended in a small chamber cut out of solid rock, which Gordon believed was directly under the room in which he had fought the Arabs. His belief was confirmed when they found the opening of the shaft leading upward. A match held up in the well showed the angle still blocked by the boulder.

"Well, we know how they got into the Caves," growled Hawkston. "But we haven't found Al Wazir. He's not in here."

"We'll go up into the Caves," answered Gordon. "He'll come back there for food. We'll catch him then."

"And then what?" demanded Hawkston.

"It's obvious, isn't it? We hit out for the caravan road. Ivan rides. We walk. We can make it, all right. I don't believe the Ruweila will stop before they get back to the tents of their tribe. I'm hoping Ivan's mind can be restored when we get him back to civilization."

"And what about the Blood of the Gods?"

"Well, what about them? They're his, to do what he pleases with them."

Hawkston did not reply, nor did he seem aware of Gordon's suspicion of him. He had no rifle, but Gordon knew the pistol at his hip was loaded. The American carried his rifle in the crook of his arm, and he maneuvered so the Englishman went ahead of him as they groped their way back down the tunnel and out into the starlight. Just what Hawkston's intentions were, he did not know. Sooner or later, he believed, he would have to fight the Englishman for his life. But somehow he felt that this would not be necessary until after Al Wazir had been found and secured.

He wondered about the tunnel and the shaft to the top of the cliff. They had not been there a year ago. Obviously the Arabs had found the tunnel purely by accident.

"No use searching the Caves tonight," said Hawkston, when they had reached the ledge. "We'll take turns watching and sleeping. Take the first watch, will you? I didn't sleep last night, you know."

Gordon nodded. Hawkston dragged the sleeping-skins from the Nest and wrapping himself in them, fell asleep close to the wall. Gordon sat down a short distance away, his rifle across his knees. As he sat he dozed lightly, waking each time the sleeping Englishman stirred.

He was still sitting there when the dawn reddened the eastern sky.

Hawkston rose, stretched and yawned.

"Why didn't you wake me to watch my turn?" he asked.

"You know damned well why I didn't," grated Gordon. "I don't care to run the risk of being murdered in my sleep."

"You don't like me, do you, Gordon?" laughed Hawkston. But only his lips smiled, and a red flame smoldered in his eyes. "Well, that makes the feeling mutual, don't you know. After we've gotten Al Wazir back to el-Azem, I'm looking forward to a gentlemanly settling of our differences-just you and I-and a pair of swords."

"Why wait until then?" Gordon was on his feet, his nostrils quivering with the eagerness of hard-leashed hate.

Hawkston shook his head, smiling fiercely.

"Oh no, El Borak. No fighting until we get out of the desert."

"All right," snarled the American disgruntedly. "Let's eat, and then start combing the Caves for Ivan."

A slight sound brought them both wheeling toward the door of the Nest. Al Wazir stood there, plucking at his beard with his long black nails. His eyes lacked their former wild beast glare; they were clouded, plaintive. His attitude was one of bewilderment rather than menace.

"Ivan!" muttered Gordon, setting down his rifle and moving toward the wild man. Al Wazir did not retreat, nor did he make any hostile demonstration. He stood stolidly, uneasily tugging at his tangled beard.

"He's in a milder mood," murmured Gordon. "Easy, Hawkston. Let me handle this. I don't believe he'll have to be overpowered this time."

"In that case," said Hawkston, "I don't need you any longer."

Gordon whipped around; the Englishman's eyes were red with the killing lust, his hand rested on the butt of his pistol. For an instant the two men stood tensely facing one another. Hawkston spoke, almost in a whisper: "You fool, did you think I'd give you an even break? I don't need you to help me get Al Wazir back to el-Azem. I know a German doctor who can restore his mind if anybody can-and then I'll see that he tells me where to find the Blood of the Gods-"

Their right hands moved in a simultaneous blur of speed. Hawkston's gun cleared its holster as Gordon's scimitar flashed free. And the gun spoke just as the blade struck it, knocking it from the Englishman's hand. Gordon felt the wind of the slug and behind him the madman in the door grunted and fell heavily. The pistol rang on the stone and bounced from the ledge, and Gordon cut murderously at Hawkston's head, his eyes red with fury. A swift backward leap carried the Englishman out of range, and Hawkston tore out his scimitar as Gordon came at him in savage silence. The American had seen Al Wazir lying limp in the doorway, blood oozing from his head.

Gordon and Hawkston came together with a dazzling flame and crack of steel, in an unleashing of hard-pent passions, two wild natures a-thirst for each others" lives. Here was the urge to kill, loosed at last, and backing every blow.

For a few minutes stroke followed stroke too fast for the eye to distinguish, had any eye witnessed that onslaught. They fought with a chilled-steel fury, a reckless abandon that was yet neither wild or careless. The clang of steel was deafening; miraculously, it seemed, the shimmer of steel played about their heads, yet neither edge cut home. The skill of the two fighters was too well matched.

After the first hurricane of attack, the play changed subtly; it grew, not less savage but more crafty. The desert sun, that had lighted the blades of a thousand generations of swordsmen, in a land sworn to the sword, had never shone on a more scintillating display of swordsmanship than this, where two aliens carved out the destinies of their tangled careers on a high-flung ledge between sun and desert.

Up and down the ledge-scruff and shift of quick-moving feet-gliding, not stamping-ring and clash of steel meeting steel-flame-lighted black eyes glaring into flinty grey eyes; flying blades turned crimson by the rising sun.

Hawkston had cut his teeth on the straight blade of his native land, and he was partial to the point and used it with devilish skill. Gordon had learned sword fighting in the hard school of the Afghan mountain wars, with the curved tulwar, and he fought with no set or orthodox style. His blade was a lethal, living thing that darted like a serpent's tongue or lashed with devastating power.

Here was no ceremonious dueling with elegant rules and formalities. It was a fight for life, naked and desperate, and within the space of half a dozen minutes both men had attempted or foiled tricks that would have made a medieval Italian fencing master blink. There was no pause or breathing spell; only the constant slither and rasp of blade on blade—Hawkston failing in his attempt to maneuver Gordon about so the sun would dazzle his eyes; Gordon almost rushing Hawkston over the rim of the ledge, the Englishman saving himself by a sidewise leap.

The end came suddenly. Hawkston, with sweat pouring down his face, realized that the sheer strength in Gordon's arm was beginning to tell. Even his iron wrist was growing numb under the terrific blows the American rained on his guard. Believing himself to be superior to Gordon in pure fencing skill, he began the preliminaries of an intricate maneuver, and meeting with apparent success, feinted a cut at Gordon's head. El Borak knew it was a feint, but, pretending to be deceived by it, he lifted his sword as though to parry the cut. Instantly Hawkston's point licked at his throat. Even as the Englishman thrust he knew he had been tricked, but he could not check the motion. The blade passed over Gordon's shoulder as the American evaded the thrust with a swaying twist of his torso, and his scimitar flashed like white steel lightning in the sun. Hawkston's dark features were blotted out by a gush of blood and brains; his scimitar rang loud on the rocky ledge; he swayed, tottered, and fell suddenly, his crown split to the hinges of the jawbone.

Gordon shook the sweat from his eyes and glared down at the prostrate figure, too drunken with hate and battle to fully realize that his foe was dead. He started and whirled as a voice spoke weakly behind him: "The same swift blade as ever, El Borak!"

Al Wazir was sitting with his back against the wall. His eyes, no longer murky nor bloodshot, met Gordon's levelly. In spite of his tangled hair and beard there was something ineffably tranquil and seer-like about him. Here, indeed, was the man Gordon had known of old.

"Ivan! Alive! But Hawkston's bullet-"

"Was that what it was?" Al Wazir lifted a hand to his head; it came away smeared with blood. "Anyway, I'm very much alive, and my mind's clear-for the first time in God knows how long. What happened?"

"You stopped a slug meant for me," grunted Gordon. "Let me see that wound." After a brief investigation he announced: "Just a graze; ploughed through the scalp and knocked you out. I'll wash it and bandage it." While he worked he said tersely: "Hawkston was on your trail; after your rubies. I tried to beat him here, and Shalan ibn Mansour trapped us both. You were a bit out of your head and I had to tie you up. We had a tussle with the Arabs and finally beat them off."

"What day is it?" asked Al Wazir. At Gordon's reply he ejaculated: "Great heavens! It's more than a month since I got knocked on the head!"

"What's that?" exclaimed Gordon. "I thought the loneliness-"

Al Wazir laughed. "Not that, El Borak. I was doing some excavation work-I discovered a shaft in one of the lower caves, leading down to the tunnel. The mouths of both were sealed with slabs of rock. I opened them up, just out of curiosity. Then I found another shaft leading from an upper cave to the summit of the cliff, like a chimney. It was while I was working out the slab that sealed it, that I dislodged a shower of rocks. One of them gave me an awful rap on the head. My mind's been a blank ever since, except for brief intervals-and they weren't very clear. I remember them like bits of dreams, now. I remember squatting in the Nest, tearing tins open and gobbling food, trying to remember

81

who I was and why I was here. Then everything would fade out again.

"I have another vague recollection of being tied to a rock in the cave, and seeing you and Hawkston lying on the ledge, and firing. Of course I didn't know either of you. I remember hearing you saying that if somebody was killed the others would go away. There was a lot of shooting and shouting and that frightened me and hurt my ears. I wanted you all to go away and leave me in peace.

"I don't know how I got loose, but my next disjointed bit of memory is that of creeping up the shaft that leads to the top of the cliff, and then climbing, climbing, with the stars over me and the wind blowing in my face-heavens! I must have climbed over the summit of the hill and down the crags on the other side!

"Then I have a muddled remembrance of running and crawling through the dark-a confused impression of shooting and noise, and a man standing alone on a knoll and shouting-" he shuddered and shook his head. "When I try to remember what happened then, it's all a blind whirl of fire and blood, like a nightmare. Somehow I seemed to feel that the man on the knoll was to blame for all the noise that was maddening me, and that if he quit shouting, they'd all go away and let me alone. But from that point it's all a blind red mist."

Gordon held his peace. He realized that it was his remark, overheard by Al Wazir, that if Shalan ibn Mansour were slain, the Arabs would flee, which had taken root in the madman's clouded brain and provided the impulse-probably subconsciously-which finally translated itself into action. Al Wazir did not remember having killed the shaykh, and there was no use distressing him with the truth.

"I remember running, then," murmured Al Wazir, rubbing his head. "I was in a terrible fright, and trying to get back to the Caves. I remember climbing again-up this time. I must have climbed back over the crags and down the chimney again--I'll wager I couldn't make that climb clothed in my right mind. The next thing I remember is hearing voices, and they sounded somehow familiar. I started toward them--then something cracked and flashed in my head, and I knew nothing more until I came to myself a few moments ago, in possession of all my faculties, and saw you and Hawkston fighting with your swords."

"You were evidently regaining your senses," said Gordon. "It took the extra jolt of that slug to set your numb machinery going again. Such things have happened before.

"Ivan, I've got a camel hidden nearby, and the Arabs left some ropes of hay in their camp when they pulled out. I'm going to feed and water it, and then-well, I intended taking you back to the Coast with me, but since you've regained your wits, I suppose you'll-"

83

"I'm going back with you," said Al Wazir. "My meditations didn't give me the gift of prophecy, but they convinced me-even before I got that rap on the head-that the best life a man can live is one of service to his fellow man. Just as you do, in your own way! I can't help mankind by dreaming out here in the desert." He glanced down at the prostrate figure on the ledge. "We'll have to build a cairn, first. Poor devil, it was his destiny to be the last sacrifice to the Blood of the Gods."

"What do you mean?"

"They were stained with men's blood," answered Al Wazir. "They have caused nothing but suffering and crime since they first appeared in history. Before I left el-Azem I threw them into the sea."

THE END

THE COUNTRY OF THE KNIFE

Chapter I

A CRY FROM beyond the bolted door-a thick, desperate croaking that gaspingly repeated a name. Stuart Brent paused in the act of filling a whisky glass, and shot a startled glance toward the door from beyond which that cry had come. It was his name that had been gasped out-and why should anyone call on him with such frantic urgency at midnight in the hall outside his apartment?

He stepped to the door, without stopping to set down the square amber bottle. Even as he turned the knob, he was electrified by the unmistakable sounds of a struggle outside-the quick fierce scuff of feet, the thud of blows, then the desperate voice lifted again. He threw the door open.

The richly appointed hallway outside was dimly lighted by bulbs concealed in the jaws of gilt dragons writhing across the ceiling. The costly red rugs and velvet tapestries seemed to drink in this soft light, heightening an effect of unreality. But the struggle going on before his eyes was as real as life and death.

There were splashes of a brighter crimson on the dark-red rug. A man was down on his back before the door, a slender man whose white face shone like a wax mask in the dim light. Another man crouched upon him, one knee grinding brutally into his breast, one hand twisting at the victim's throat. The other hand lifted a red-smeared blade.

Brent acted entirely through impulse. Everything happened simultaneously. The knife was swinging up for the downward drive even as he opened the door. At the height of its arc it hovered briefly as the wielder shot a venomous, slit-eyed glance at the man in the doorway. In that instant Brent saw murder about to be done, saw that the victim was a white man, the killer a swarthy alien of some kind. Age-old implanted instincts acted through him, without his conscious volition. He dashed the heavy whisky bottle full into the dark face with all his power. The hard, stocky body toppled backward in a crash of broken glass and a shower of splattering liquor, and the knife rang on the floor several feet away. With a feline snarl the fellow bounced to his feet, red-eyed, blood and whisky streaming from his face and over his collar.

For an instant he crouched as if to leap at Brent barehanded. Then the glare in his eyes wavered, turned to something like fear, and he wheeled and was gone, lunging down the stair with reckless haste. Brent stared after him in amazement. The whole affair was fantastic, and Brent was irritated. He had broken a self-imposed rule of long standing-which was never to butt into anything which was not his business.

86

"Brent!" It was the wounded man, calling him weakly. Brent bent down to him.

"What is it, old fellow-Thunderation! Stockton!"

"Get me in, quick!" panted the other, staring fearfully at the stair. "He may come back-with others."

Brent stooped and lifted him bodily. Stockton was not a bulky man, and Brent's trim frame concealed the muscles of an athlete. There was no sound throughout the building. Evidently no one had been aroused by the muffled sounds of the brief fight. Brent carried the wounded man into the room and laid him carefully on a divan. There was blood on Brent's hands when he straightened.

"Lock the door!" gasped Stockton.

Brent obeyed, and then turned back, frowning concernedly down at the man. They offered a striking contrast-Stockton, light-haired, of medium height, frail, with plain, commonplace features now twisted in a grimace of pain, his sober garments disheveled and smeared with blood; Brent, tall, dark, immaculately tailored, handsome in a virile masculine way, and selfassured. But in Stockton's pale eyes there blazed a fire that burned away the difference between them, and gave the wounded man something that Brent did not possess-something that dominated the scene.

"You're hurt, Dick!" Brent caught up a fresh whisky bottle. "Why, man, you're stabbed to pieces! I'll call a doctor, and-"

"No!" A lean hand brushed aside the whisky glass and seized Brent's wrist. "It's no use. I'm bleeding inside. I'd be dead now, but I can't leave my job unfinished. Don't interrupt just listen!"

Brent knew Stockton spoke the truth. Blood was oozing thinly from the wounds in his breast, where a thin-bladed knife must have struck home at least half a dozen times. Brent looked on, awed and appalled, as the small, bright-eyed man fought death to a standstill, gripping the last fading fringes of life and keeping himself conscious and lucid to the end by the sheer effort of an iron will.

"I stumbled on something big tonight, down in a water-front dive. I was looking for something else uncovered this by accident. Then they got suspicious. I got away-came here because you were the only man I knew in San Francisco. But that devil was after me-caught me on the stair."

Blood oozed from the livid lips, and Stockton spat dryly. Brent looked on helplessly. He knew the man was a secret agent of the British government, who had made a business of tracing sinister secrets to their source. He was dying as he had lived, in the harness.

"Something big!" whispered the Englishman. "Something that balances the fate of India! I can't tell you all now-I'm going fast. But there's one man in the world who must know. You must find him, Brent! His name is Gordon-Francis Xavier Gordon. He's an American; the Afghans call him El Borak. I'd have gone to him-but you must go. Promise me!"

Brent did not hesitate. His soothing hand on the dying man's shoulder was even more convincing and reassuring than his quiet, level voice.

"I promise, old man. But where am I to find him?"

"Somewhere in Afghanistan. Go at once. Tell the police nothing. Spies are all around. If they know I knew you, and spoke with you before I died, they'll kill you before you can reach Gordon. Tell the police I was simply a drunken stranger, wounded by an unknown party, and staggering into your hall to die. You never saw me before. I said nothing before I died.

"Go to Kabul. The British officials will make your way easy that far. Simply say to each one: "Remember the kites of Khoral Nulla." That's your password. If Gordon isn't in Kabul, the ameer will give you an escort to hunt for him in the hills. You must find him! The peace of India depends on him, now!"

"But what shall I tell him?" Brent was bewildered.

"Say to him," gasped the dying man, fighting fiercely for a few more moments of life, "say: "The Black Tigers had a new prince; they call him Abd el Khafid, but his real name is Vladimir Jakrovitch." '

"Is that all?" This affair was growing more and more bizarre.

"Gordon will understand and act. The Black Tigers are your peril. They're a secret society of Asiatic murderers. Therefore, be on your guard at every step of the way. But El Borak will understand. He'll know where to look for Jakrovitch-in Rub el Harami-the Abode of Thieves-"

A convulsive shudder, and the slim threat that had held the life in the tortured body snapped.

Brent straightened and looked down at the dead man in wonder. He shook his head, marveling again at the inner unrest that sent men wandering in the waste places of the world, playing a game of life and death for a meager wage. Games that had gold for their stake Brent could understand-none better. His strong, sure fingers could read the cards almost as a man reads books; but he could not read the souls of men like Richard Stockton who stake their lives on the bare boards where Death is the dealer. What if the man won, how could he measure his winnings, where cash his chips? Brent asked no odds of life; he lost without a wince; but in winning, he was a usurer, demanding the last least crumb of the wager, and content with nothing less than the glittering, solid materialities of life. The grim and barren game Stockton had played held no promise for Stuart Brent, and to him the Englishman had always been a little mad.

But whatever Brent's faults or virtues, he had his code. He lived by it, and by it he meant to die. The foundation stone of that code was loyalty. Stockton had never saved

Brent's life, renounced a girl both loved, exonerated him from a false accusation, or anything so dramatic. They had simply been boyhood friends in a certain British university, years ago, and years had passed between their occasional meetings since then. Stockton had no claim on Brent, except for their old friendship. But that was a tie as solid as a log chain, and the Englishman had known it, when, in the desperation of knowing himself doomed, he had crawled to Brent's door. And Brent had given his promise, and he intended making it good. It did not occur to him that there was any other alternative. Stuart Brent was the restless black sheep of an aristocratic old California family whose founder crossed the plains in an ox wagon in '49-and he had never welshed a bet nor let down a friend.

He turned his head and stared through a window, almost hidden by its satin curtains. He was comfortable here. His luck had been phenomenal of late. To-morrow evening there was a big poker game scheduled at his favorite club, with a fat Oklahoma oil king who was ripe for a cleaning. The races began at Tia Juana within a few days, and Brent had his eye on a slim sorrel gelding that ran like the flame of a prairie fire.

Outside, the fog curled and drifted, beading the pane. Pictures formed for him there-prophetic pictures of an East different from the colorful civilized East he had touched in his roamings. Pictures not at all like the European-dominated cities he remembered, exotic colors of veranda-shaded clubs, soft-footed servants laden with cooling drinks, languorous and beautiful women, white garments and sun helmets. Shiveringly he sensed a wilder, older East; it had blown a scent of itself to him out of the fog, over a knife stained with human blood. An East not soft and warm and exotic-colored, but bleak and grim and savage, where peace was not and law was a mockery, and life hung on the tilt of a balanced blade. The East known by Stockton, and this mysterious American they called "El Borak."

Brent's world was here, the world he had promised to abandon for a blind, quixotic mission; he knew nothing of that other leaner, fiercer world; but there was no hesitation in his manner as he turned toward the door.

Chapter II

A WIND BLEW over the shoulders of the peaks where the snow lay drifted, a knife-edge wind that slashed through leather and wadded cloth in spite of the searing sun. Stuart Brent blinked his eyes against the glare of that intolerable sun, shivered at the bite of the wind. He had no coat, and his shirt was tattered. For the thousandth futile, involuntary time, he wrenched at the fetters on his wrists. They jangled, and the man riding in front of him cursed, turned and struck him heavily in the mouth. Brent reeled in his saddle, blood starting to his lips.

The saddle chafed him, and the stirrups were too short for his long legs. He was riding along a knife-edge trail, in the middle of a straggling line of some thirty men-ragged men on gaunt, ribby horses. They rode hunched in their high-peaked saddles, turbaned heads thrust forward and nodding in unison to the clop-clop of their horses" hoofs, long-barreled rifles swaying across the saddlebows. On one hand rose a towering cliff; on the other, a sheer precipice fell away into echoing depths. The skin was worn from Brent's wrists by the rusty, clumsy iron manacles that secured them; he was bruised from the kicks and blows, faint with hunger and giddy with the enormousness of the altitude. His nose bled at times without having been struck. Ahead of them loomed the backbone of the gigantic range that had risen like a rampart before them for so many days.

Dizzily he reviewed the events of the weeks that stretched between the time he had carried Dick Stockton, dying, into his flat, and this unbelievable, yet painfully real moment. The intervening period of time might have been an unfathomable and unbridgeable gulf stretching between and dividing two worlds that had nothing in common save consciousness.

He had come to India on the first ship he could catch. Official doors had opened to him at the whispered password:

93

"Remember the kites of Khoral Nulla!" His path had been smoothed by impressive-looking documents with great red seals, by cryptic orders barked over telephones, or whispered into attentive ears. He had moved smoothly northward along hitherto unguessed channels. He had glimpsed, faintly, some of the shadowy, mountainous machinery grinding silently and ceaselessly behind the scenes-the unseen, half-suspected cogwheels of the empire that girdles the world.

Mustached men with medals on their breasts had conferred with him as to his needs, and quiet men in civilian clothes had guided him on his way. But no one had asked him why he sought El Borak, or what message he bore. The password and the mention of Stockton had sufficed. His friend had been more important in the imperial scheme of things than Brent had ever realized. The adventure had seemed more and more fantastic as he progressed-a page out of the "Arabian Nights," as he blindly carried a dead man's message, the significance of which he could not even guess, to a mysterious figure lost in the mists of the hills; while, at a whispered incantation, hidden doors swung wide and enigmatic figures bowed him on his way. But all this changed in the North.

Gordon was not in Kabul. This Brent learned from the lips of no less than the ameer himself-wearing his European garments as if born to them, but with the sharp, restless eyes of a man who knows he is a pawn between powerful rivals, and whose nerves are worn thin by the constant struggle for survival. Brent sensed that Gordon was a staff on which the ameer leaned heavily. But neither king nor agents of empire could chain the American's roving foot, or direct the hawk flights of the man the Afghans called "El Borak," the "Swift."

And Gordon was gone-wandering alone into those naked hills whose bleak mysteries had long ago claimed him from his own kind. He might be gone a month, he might be gone a year. He might-and the ameer shifted uneasily at the possibility-never return. The crag-set villages were full of his blood enemies.

Not even the long arm of empire reached beyond Kabul. The ameer ruled the tribes after a fashion-with a dominance that dared not presume too far. This was the Country of the Hills, where law was hinged on the strong arm wielding the long knife.

Gordon had vanished into the Northwest. And Brent, though flinching at the grim nakedness of the Himalayas, did not hesitate or visualize an alternative. He asked for and received an escort of soldiers. With them he pushed on, trying to follow Gordon's trail through the mountain villages.

A week out of Kabul they lost all trace of him. To all effects Gordon had vanished into thin air. The wild, shaggy hillmen answered questions sullenly, or not at all, glaring at the nervous Kabuli soldiery from under black brows. The farther they got away from Kabul, the more open the hostility. Only once did a question evoke a spontaneous response, and that was a suggestion that Gordon had been murdered by hostile tribesmen. At that, sardonic laughter yelled up from the wild men-the fierce, mocking mirth of the hills. El Borak trapped by his enemies? Is the gray wolf devoured by the fat-tailed sheep? And another gust of dry, ironic laughter, as hard as the black crags that burned under a sun of liquid flame. Stubborn as his grandsire who had glimpsed a mirage of tree-fringed ocean shore across the scorching desolation of another desert, Brent groped on, at a blind venture, trying to pick up the cold scent, far past the point of safety, as the gray-faced soldiers warned him again and again. They warned him that they were far from Kabul, in a sparsely settled, rebellious, little-explored region, whose wild people were rebels to the ameer, and enemies to El Borak. They would have deserted Brent long before and fled back to Kabul, had they not feared the ameer's wrath.

Their forebodings were justified in the hurricane of rifle fire that swept their camp in a chill gray dawn. Most of them fell at the first volley that ripped from the rocks about them. The rest fought futilely, ridden over and cut down by the wild riders that materialized out of the gray. Brent knew the surprise had been the soldiers" fault, but he did not have it in his heart to curse them, even now. They had been like children, sneaking in out of the cold as soon as his back was turned, sleeping on sentry duty, and lapsing into slovenly and unmilitary habits as soon as they were out of sight of Kabul. They had not wanted to come, in the first place; a foreboding of doom had haunted them; and now they were dead, and he was a captive, riding toward a fate he could not even guess.

Four days had passed since that slaughter, but he still turned sick when he remembered it-the smell of powder and blood, the screams, the rending chop of steel. He shuddered at the memory of the man he had killed in that last rush, with his pistol muzzle almost in the bearded face that lunged at him beneath a lifted rifle butt. He had never killed a man before. He sickened as he remembered the cries of the wounded soldiers when the conquerors cut their throats. And over and over he wondered why he had been spared-why they had overpowered and fettered him, instead of killing him. His suffering had been so intense he often wished they had killed him outright.

He was allowed to ride, and he was fed grudgingly when the others ate. But the food was niggardly. He who had never known hunger was never without it now, a gnawing misery. His coat had been taken from him, and the nights were a long agony in which he almost froze on the hard ground, in the icy winds. He wearied unto death of the day-long riding over incredible trails that wound up and up until he felt as if he could reach out a hand-if his hands were free-and touch the cold, pale sky. He was kicked and beaten until the first fiery resentment and humiliation had been dissolved in a dull hurt that was only aware of the physical pain, not of the injury to his self-respect.

He did not know who his captors were. They did not deign to speak English to him, but he had picked up more than a smattering of Pashto on that long journey up the Khyber to Kabul, and from Kabul westward. Like many men who live by their wits, he had the knack of acquiring new languages. But all he learned from listening to their conversation was that their leader was called Muhammad ez Zahir, and their destiny was Rub el Harami.

Rub el Harami! Brent had heard it first as a meaningless phrase gasped from Richard Stockton's blue lips. He had heard more of it as he came northward from the hot plains of the Punjab-a city of mystery and evil, which no white man had ever visited except as a captive, and from which none had ever escaped. A plague spot, sprawled in the high, bare hills, almost fabulous, beyond the reach of the ameer--an outlaw city, whence the winds blew whispered tales too fantastic and hideous for credence, even in this Country of the Knife.

At times Brent's escort mocked him, their burning eyes and grimly smiling lips lending a sinister meaning to their taunt: "The Feringi goes to Rub el Harami!"

For the pride of race he stiffened his spine and set his jaw; he plumbed unsuspected depths of endurance-legacy of a clean, athletic life, sharpened by the hard traveling of the past weeks.

They crossed a rocky crest and dropped down an incline between ridges that tilted up for a thousand feet.

Far above and beyond them they occasionally glimpsed a notch in the rampart that was the pass over which they must cross the backbone of the range up which they were toiling. It was as they labored up a long slope that the solitary horseman appeared.

The sun was poised on the knife-edge crest of a ridge to the west, a blood-colored ball, turning a streak of the sky to flame. Against that crimson ball a horseman appeared suddenly, a centaur image, black against the blinding curtain. Below him every rider turned in his saddle, and rifle bolts clicked. It did not need the barked command of Muhammed ez Zahir to halt the troop. There was something wild and arresting about that untamed figure in the sunset that held every eye. The rider's head was thrown back, the horse's long mane streaming in the wind.

Then the black silhouette detached itself from the crimson ball and moved down toward them, details springing into being as it emerged from the blinding background. It was a man on a rangy black stallion who came down the rocky, pathless slope with the smooth curving flight of an eagle, the sure hoofs spurning the ground. Brent, himself a horseman, felt his heart leap into his throat with admiration for the savage steed.

But he almost forgot the horse when the rider pulled up before them. He was neither tall nor bulky, but a barbaric strength was evident in his compact shoulders, his deep chest, his corded wrists. There was strength, too, in the keen, dark face, and the eyes, the blackest Brent had even seen, gleamed with an inward fire such as the American had seen burn in the eyes of wild things-an indomitable wildness and an unquenchable vitality. The thin, black mustache did not hide the hard set of the mouth.

The stranger looked like a desert dandy beside the ragged men of the troop, but it was a dandyism definitely masculine, from the silken turban to the silver-heeled boots. His bright-hued robe was belted with a gold-buckled girdle that supported a Turkish saber and a long dagger. A rifle jutted its butt from a scabbard beneath his knee.

Thirty-odd pairs of hostile eyes centered on him, after suspiciously sweeping the empty ridges behind him as he galloped up before the troop and reined his steed back on its haunches with a flourish that set the gold ornaments jingling on curb chains and reins. An empty hand was flung up in an exaggerated gesture of peace. The rider, well poised and confident, carried himself with a definite swagger.

"What do you want?" growled Muhammad ez Zahir, his cocked rifle covering the stranger.

"A small thing, as Allah is my witness!" declared the other, speaking Pashto with an accent Brent had never heard before. "I am Shirkuh, of Jebel Jawur. I ride to Rub el Harami. I wish to accompany you."

"Are you alone?" demanded Muhammad.

"I set forth from Herat many days ago with a party of camel men who swore they would guide me to Rub el Harami. Last night they sought to slay and rob me. One of them died suddenly. The others ran away, leaving me without food or guides. I lost my way, and have been wandering in the mountains all last night and all this day. Just now, by the favor of Allah, I sighted your band."

"How do you know we are bound for Rub el Harami?" demanded Muhammad.

"Are you not Muhammad ez Zahir, the prince of swordsmen?" countered Shirkuh.

The Afghan's beard bristled with satisfaction. He was not impervious to flattery. But he was still suspicious.

"You know me, Kurd?"

"Who does not know Muhammad ez Zahir? I saw you in the suk of Teheran, years ago. And now men say you are high in the ranks of the Black Tigers."

"Beware how your tongue runs, Kurd!" responded Muhammad. "Words are sometimes blades to cut men's throats. Are you sure of a welcome in Rub el Harami?"

"What stranger can be sure of a welcome there?" Shirkuh laughed. "But there is Feringi blood on my sword, and a price on my head. I have heard that such men were welcome in Rub el Harami."

"Ride with us if you will," said Muhammad. "I will get you through the Pass of Nadir Khan. But what may await you at the city gates is none of my affair. I have not invited you to Rub el Harami. I accept no responsibility for you."

"I ask for no man to vouch for me," retorted Shirkuh, with a glint of anger, brief and sharp, like the flash of hidden steel struck by a flint and momentarily revealed. He glanced curiously at Brent.

"Has there been a raid over the border?" he asked.

"This fool came seeking someone," scornfully answered Muhammad. "He walked into a trap set for him."

"What will be done with him in Rub el Harami?" pursued the newcomer, and Brent's interest in the conversation suddenly became painfully intense.

"He will be placed on the slave block," answered Muhammad, "according to the age-old custom of the city. Who bids highest will have him."

And so Brent learned the fate in store for him, and cold sweat broke out on his flesh as he contemplated a life spent as a tortured drudge to some turbaned ruffian. But he held up his head, feeling Shirkuh's fierce eyes upon him.

The stranger said slowly: "It may be his destiny to serve Shirkuh, of the Jebel Jawur! I never owned a slave-but who knows? It strikes my fancy to buy this Feringi!"

Brent reflected that Shirkuh must know that he was in no danger of being murdered and robbed, or he would never so openly imply possession of money. That suggested that he knew these were picked men, carrying out someone's instructions so implicitly that they could be depended on not to commit any crime not included in those orders. That implied organization and obedience beyond the conception of any ordinary hill chief. He was convinced that these men belonged to that mysterious cult against which Stockton had warned him-the Black Tigers. Then had their capture of him been due merely to chance? It seemed improbable.

"There are rich men in Rub el Harami, Kurd," growled Muhammad. "But it may be that none will want this Feringi and a wandering vagabond like you might buy him. Who knows?"

"Only in Allah is knowledge," agreed Shirkuh, and swung his horse into line behind Brent, crowding a man out of position and laughing when the Afghan snarled at him.

The troop got into motion, and a man leaned over to strike Brent with a rifle butt. Shirkuh checked the stroke. His lips laughed, but there was menace in his eyes.

"Nay! This infidel may belong to me before many days, and I will not have his bones broken!"

The man growled, but did not press the matter, and the troop rode on. They toiled up a ridge in a long shadow cast by the crag behind which the sun had sunk, and came into a valley and the sight of the sun again, just sinking behind a mountain. As they went down the slope, they spied white turbans moving among the crags to the west, and Muhammad ez Zahir snarled in suspicion at Shirkuh.

"Are they friends of yours, you dog? You said you were alone!"

"I know them not!" declared Shirkuh. Then he dragged his rifle from its boot. "The dogs fire on us!" For a tiny tongue of fire had jetted from among the boulders in the distance, and a bullet whined overhead.

"Hill-bred dogs who grudge us the use of the well ahead!" said Muhammad ez Zahir. "Would we had time to teach them a lesson! Hold your fire, you dogs! The range is too long for either they or us to do damage."

But Shirkuh wheeled out of the line of march and rode toward the foot of the ridge. Half a dozen men broke cover, high up on the slope, and dashed away over the crest, leaning low and spurring hard. Shirkuh fired once, then took steadier aim and fired three shots in swift succession.

"You missed!" shouted Muhammad angrily. "Who could hit at such a range?"

"Nay!" yelled Shirkuh. "Look!"

One of the ragged white shapes had wavered and pitched forward on its pony's neck. The beast vanished over the ridge, its rider lolling limply in the saddle.

"He will not ride far!" exulted Shirkuh, waving his rifle over his head as he raced back to the troop. "We Kurds have eyes like mountain hawks!"

"Shooting a Pathan hill thief does not make a hero," snapped Muhammad, turning disgustedly away.

But Shirkuh merely laughed tolerantly, as one so sure of his fame that he could afford to overlook the jealousies of lesser souls.

They rode on down into the broad valley, seeing no more of the hillmen. Dusk was falling when they halted beside the well. Brent, too stiff to dismount, was roughly jerked off his horse. His legs were bound, and he was allowed to sit with his back against a boulder just far enough away from the fires they built to keep him from benefiting any from the heat. No guard was set over him at present.

Presently Shirkuh came striding over to where the prisoner gnawed at the wretched crusts they allowed him. Shirkuh walked with a horseman's roll, setting his booted legs wide. He carried an iron bowl of stewed mutton, and some chupatties.

"Eat, Feringi!" he commanded roughly, but not harshly. "A slave whose ribs jut through his hide is no good

105

to work or to fight. These niggardly Pathans would starve their grandfathers. But we Kurds are as generous as we are valiant!"

He offered the food with a gesture as of bestowing a province. Brent accepted it without thanks, and ate voraciously. Shirkuh had dominated the drama ever since he had entered it-a swashbuckler who swaggered upon the stage and would not be ignored. Even Muhammad ez Zahir was overshadowed by the overflowing vitality of the man. Shirkuh seemed a strange mixture of brutal barbarian and unsophisticated youth. There was a boyish exuberance in his swagger, and he displayed touches of naive simplicity at times. But there was nothing childish about his glittering black eyes, and he moved with a tigerish suppleness that Brent knew could be translated instantly into a blur of murderous action.

Shirkuh thrust his thumbs in his girdle now and stood looking down at the American as he ate. The light from the nearest fire of dry tamarisk branches threw his dark face into shadowy half relief and gave it somehow an older, more austere look. The shadowy half light had erased the boyishness from his countenance, replacing it with a suggestion of somberness.

"Why did you come into the hills?" he demanded abruptly.

Brent did not immediately answer; he chewed on, toying with an idea. He was in as desperate a plight as he could be in, and he saw no way out. He looked about, seeing that his captors were out of earshot. He did not see the dim shape that squirmed up behind the boulder against which he leaned. He reached a sudden decision and spoke.

"Do you know the man called El Borak?"

Was there suspicion suddenly in the black eyes?

"I have heard of him," Shirkuh replied warily:

"I came into the hills looking for him. Can you find him? If you could get a message to him, I would pay you thirty thousand rupees."

Shirkuh scowled, as if torn between suspicion and avarice.

"I am a stranger in these hills," he said. "How could I find El Borak?"

"Then help me to escape," urged Brent. "I will pay you an equal sum."

Shirkuh tugged his mustache.

"I am one sword against thirty," he growled. "How do I know I would be paid? Feringi are all liars. I am an outlaw with a price on my head. The Turks would flay me, the Russians would shoot me, the British would hang me. There is nowhere I can go except to Rub el Harami. If I helped you to escape, that door would be barred against me, too."

"I will speak to the British for you," urged Brent. "El Borak has power. He will secure a pardon for you."

He believed what he said; besides, he was in that desperate state when a man is likely to promise anything.

Indecision flickered in the black eyes, and Shirkuh started to speak, then changed his mind, turned on his heel, and strode away. A moment later the spy crouching behind the boulders glided away without having been discovered by Brent, who sat staring in despair after Shirkuh.

Shirkuh went straight to Muhammad, gnawing strips of dried mutton as he sat cross-legged on a dingy sheepskin near a small fire on the other side of the well. Shirkuh got there before the spy did.

"The Feringi has offered me money to take a word to El Borak," he said abruptly. "Also to aid him to escape. I bade him go to Jehannum, of course. In the Jebel Jawur I have heard of El Borak, but I have never seen him. Who is he?"

"A devil," growled Muhammad ez Zahir. "An American, like this dog. The tribes about the Khyber are his friends, and he is an adviser of the ameer, and an ally of the rajah, though he was once an outlaw. He has never dared come to Rub el Harami. I saw him once, three years ago, in the fight by Kalat-i-Ghilzai, where he and his cursed Afridis broke the back of the revolt that had else unseated the ameer. If we could catch him, Abd el Khafid would fill our mouths with gold."

"Perhaps this Feringi knows where to find him!" exclaimed Shirkuh, his eyes burning with a glitter that might have been avarice. "I will go to him and swear to deliver his message, and so trick him into telling me what he knows of El Borak."

"It is all one to me," answered Muhammad indifferently. "If I had wished to know why he came into the hills, I would have tortured it out of him before now. But my orders were merely to capture him and bring him alive to Rub el Harami. I could not turn aside, not even to capture El Borak. But if you are admitted into the city, perhaps Abd el Khafid will give you a troop to go hunting El Borak."

"I will try!"

"Allah grant you luck," said Muhammad. "El Borak is a dog. I would myself give a thousand rupees to see him hanging in the market place."

"If it be the will of Allah, you shall meet El Borak!" said Shirkuh, turning away.

Doubtless it was the play of the firelight on his face which caused his eyes to burn as they did, but Muhammad felt a curious chill play down his spine, though he could not reason why.

Shirkuh's booted feet crunched away through the shale, and a furtive, ragged shadow came out of the night and squatted at Muhammad's elbow.

"I spied on the Kurd and the infidel as you ordered," muttered the spy. "The Feringi offered Shirkuh thirty thousand rupees either to seek out El Borak and deliver a message to him, or to aid him to escape us. Shirkuh lusted for the gold, but he has been outlawed by all the Feringis, and he dares not close the one door open to him."

"Good," growled Muhammad in his beard. "Kurds are dogs; it is well that this one is in no position to bite. I will speak for him at the pass. He does not guess the choice that awaits him at the gates of Rub el Harami."

Brent was sunk in the dreamless slumber of exhaustion, despite the hardness of the rocky ground and the chill of the night. An urgent hand shook him awake, an urgent whisper checked his startled exclamation. He saw a vague shape bending over him, and heard the snoring of his guard a few feet away. Guarding a man bound and fettered was more or less of a formality of routine. Shirkuh's voice hissed in Brent's ear.

"Tell me the message you wished to send El Borak! Be swift, before the guard awakes. I could not take the message when we talked before, for there was a cursed spy listening behind that rock. I told Muhammad what passed between us, because I knew the spy would tell him anyway, and I wished to disarm suspicion before it took root. Tell me the word!"

Brent accepted the desperate gamble.

"Tell him that Richard Stockton died, but before he died, he said this: "The Black Tigers have a new prince; they call him Abd el Khafid, but his real name is Vladimir Jakrovitch." This man dwells in Rub el Harami, Stockton told me."

"I understand," muttered Shirkuh. "El Borak shall know."

"But what of me?" urged Brent.

"I cannot help you escape now," muttered Shirkuh. "There are too many of them. All the guards are not asleep. Armed men patrol the outskirts of the camp, and others watch the horses--my own among them."

"I cannot pay you unless I get away!" argued Brent.

"That is in the lap of Allah!" hissed Shirkuh. "I must slip back to my blankets now, before I am missed. Here is a cloak against the chill of the night."

Brent felt himself enveloped in a grateful warmth, and then Shirkuh was gone, gliding away in the night with boots that made no more noise than the moccasins of a red Indian. Brent lay wondering if he had done the right thing. There was no reason why he should trust Shirkuh. But if he had done no good, at least he could not see that he had done any harm, either to himself, El Borak, or those interests menaced by the mysterious Black Tigers. He was a drowning man, clutching at straws. At last he went to sleep again, lulled by the delicious warmth of the cloak Shirkuh had thrown over him, and hoping that he would slip away in the night and ride to find Gordon-wherever he might be wandering.

Chapter III

IT WAS SHIRKUH, however, who brought the American's breakfast to him the next morning. Shirkuh made no sign either of friendship or enmity, beyond a gruff admonition to eat heartily, as he did not wish to buy a skinny slave. But that might have been for the benefit of the guard yawning and stretching near by. Brent reflected that the cloak was sure evidence that Shirkuh had visited him in the night, but no one appeared to notice it.

As he ate, grateful at least for the good food, Brent was torn between doubts and hopes. He swung between halfhearted trust and complete mistrust of the man. Kurds were bred in deception and cut their teeth on treachery. Why should that offer of help not have been a trick to curry favor with Muhammad ez Zahir? Yet Brent realized that if Muhammad had wished to learn the reason for his presence in the hills, the Afghan would have been more likely to resort to torture than an elaborate deception. Then Shirkuh, like all Kurds, must be avaricious, and that was Brent's best chance. And if Shirkuh delivered the message, he must go further and help Brent to escape, in order to get his reward, for Brent, a slave in Rub el Harami, could not pay him thirty thousand rupees. One service necessitated the other, if Shirkuh hoped to profit by the deal. Then there was El Borak; if he got the message, he would learn of Brent's plight, and he would hardly fail to aid a fellow Feringi in adversity. It all depended now on Shirkuh.

Brent stared intently at the supple rider, etched against the sharp dawn. There was nothing of the Turanian or the Semite in Shirkuh's features. In the Iranian highlands there must be many clans who kept their ancient Aryan lineage pure. Shirkuh, in European garments, and without that Oriental mustache, would pass unnoticed in any Western crowd, but for that primordial blaze in his restless black eyes. They reflected an untamable soul. How could he expect this barbarian to deal with him according to the standards of the Western world?

They were pressing on before sunup, and their trail always led up now, higher and higher, through knife cuts in solid masses of towering sandstone, and along narrow paths that wound up and up interminably, until Brent was gasping again with the rarefied air of the high places. At high noon, when the wind was knife-edged with ice, and the sun was a splash of molten fire, they reached the Pass of Nadir Khan-a narrow cut winding tortuously for a mile between turrets of dull colored rock. A squat mud-and-stone tower stood in the mouth, occupied by ragged warriors squatting on their aerie like vultures. The troop halted until Muhammad ez Zahir was recognized. He vouched for the cavalcade, Shirkuh included, with a wave of his hand, and the rifles on the tower were lowered. Muhammad rode on into the pass, the others filing after him. Brent felt despairingly as if one prison door had already slammed behind him.

They halted for the midday meal in the corridor of the pass, shaded from the sun and sheltered from the wind. Again Shirkuh brought food to Brent, without comment or objection from the Afghans. But when Brent tried to catch his eye, he avoided the American's gaze.

After they left the pass, the road pitched down in long curving sweeps, through successively lower mountains that ran away and away like gigantic stairsteps from the crest of the range. The trail grew plainer, more traveled, but night found them still among the hills.

When Shirkuh brought food to Brent that night as usual, the American tried to engage him in conversation, under cover of casual talk for the benefit of the Afghan detailed to guard the American that night, who lolled near by, bolting chupatties.

"Is Rub el Harami a large city?" Brent asked.

"I have never been there," returned Shirkuh, rather shortly.

"Is Abd el Khafid the ruler?" persisted Brent.

"He is emir of Rub el Harami," said Shirkuh.

"And prince of the Black Tigers," spoke up the Afghan guard unexpectedly. He was in a garrulous mood, and he saw no reason for secrecy. One of his hearers would soon be a slave in Rub el Harami, the other, if accepted, a member of the clan.

"I am myself a Black Tiger," the guard boasted. "All in this troop are Black Tigers, and picked men. We are the lords of Rub el Harami."

"Then all in the city are not Black Tigers?" asked Brent.

"All are thieves. Only thieves live in Rub el Harami. But not all are Black Tigers. But it is the headquarters of the clan, and the prince of the Black Tigers is always emir of Rub el Harami."

"Who ordered my capture?" inquired Brent. "Muhammad ez Zahir?"

"Muhammad only does as he is ordered," returned the guard. "None gives orders in Rub el Harami save Abd el Khafid. He is absolute lord save where the customs of the city are involved. Not even the prince of the Black Tigers can change the customs of Rub el Harami. It was a city of thieves before the days of Genghis Khan. What its name was first, none knows; the Arabs call it Rub el Harami, the Abode of Thieves, and the name has stuck."

"It is an outlaw city?"

"It has never owned a lord save the prince of the Black Tigers," boasted the guard. "It pays no taxes to any save him—and to Shaitan."

"What do you mean, to Shaitan?" demanded Shirkuh.

"It is an ancient custom," answered the guard. "Each year a hundredweight of gold is given as an offering to Shaitan, so the city shall prosper. It is sealed in a secret cave somewhere near the city, but where no man knows, save the prince and the council of imams."

"Devil worship!" snorted Shirkuh. "It is an offense to Allah!"

"It is an ancient custom," defended the guard.

Shirkuh strode off, as if scandalized, and Brent lapsed into disappointed silence. He wrapped himself in Shirkuh's cloak as well as he could and slept.

They were up before dawn and pushing through the hills until they breasted a sweeping wall, down which the trail wound, and saw a rocky plain set in the midst of bare mountain chains, and the flat-topped towers of Rub el Harami rising before them.

They had not halted for the midday meal. As they neared the city, the trail became a well-traveled road. They overtook or met men on horses, men walking and driving laden mules. Brent remembered that it had been said that only stolen goods entered Rub el Harami. Its inhabitants were the scum of the hills, and the men they encountered looked

116

it. Brent found himself comparing them with Shirkuh. The man was a wild outlaw, who boasted of his bloody crimes, but he was a clean-cut barbarian. He differed from these as a gray wolf differs from mangy alley curs.

He eyed all they met or passed with a gaze half naive, half challenging. He was boyishly interested; he was ready to fight at the flick of a turban end, and gave the road to no man. He was the youth of the world incarnated, credulous, merry, hot-headed, generous, cruel, and arrogant. And Brent knew his life hung on the young savage's changing whims.

Rub el Harami was a walled city standing in the narrow rock-strewn plain hemmed in by bare hills. A battery of field pieces could have knocked down its walls with a dozen volleys-but the army never marched that could have dragged field pieces over the road that led to it through the Pass of Nadir Khan. Its gray walls loomed bleakly above the gray dusty waste of the small plain. A chill wind from the northern peaks brought a tang of snow and started the dust spinning. Well curbs rose gauntly here and there on the plain, and near each well stood a cluster of squalid huts. Peasants in rags bent their backs over sterile patches that yielded grudging crops-mere smudges on the dusty expanse. The low-hanging sun turned the dust to a bloody haze in the air, as the troop with its prisoner trudged on weary horses across the plain to the gaunt city.

Beneath a lowering arch, flanked by squat watchtowers, an iron-bolted gate stood open, guarded by a dozen swashbucklers whose girdles bristled with daggers. They clicked the bolts of their German rifles and stared arrogantly about them, as if itching to practice on some living target.

The troop halted, and the captain of the guard swaggered forth, a giant with bulging muscles and a henna-stained beard.

"Thy names and business!" he roared, glaring intolerantly at Brent.

"My name you know as well as you know your own," growled Muhammad ez Zahir. "I am taking a prisoner into the city, by order of Abd el Khafid."

"Pass, Muhammad ez Zahir," growled the captain. "But who is this Kurd?"

Muhammad grinned wolfishly, as if at a secret jest.

"An adventurer who seeks admission-Shirkuh, of the Jebel Jawur."

While they were speaking, a richly clad, powerfully built man on a white mare rode out of the gate and halted, unnoticed, behind the guardsmen. The henna-bearded captain turned toward Shirkuh who had dismounted to get a pebble out of his stallion's hoof.

"Are you one of the clan?" he demanded. "Do you know the secret signs?"

"I have not yet been accepted," answered Shirkuh, turning to face him. "Men tell me I must be passed upon by the council of imams."

"Aye, if you reach them! Does any chief of the city speak for you?"

"I am a stranger," replied Shirkuh shortly.

"We like not strangers in Rub el Harami," said the captain. "There are but three ways a stranger may enter the city. As a captive, like that infidel dog yonder; as one vouched for and indorsed by some established chief of the city; or"-he showed yellow fangs in an evil grin-"as the slayer of some fighting man of the city!"

He shifted the rifle to his right hand and slapped the butt with his left palm. Sardonic laughter rose about them, the dry, strident, cruel cackling of the hills. Those who laughed knew that in any kind of fight between a stranger and a man of the city every foul advantage would be taken. For a stranger to be forced into a formal duel with a Black Tiger was tantamount to signing his death warrant. Brent, rigid with sudden concern, guessed this from the vicious laughter.

But Shirkuh did not seem abashed.

"It is an ancient custom?" he asked naively, dropping a hand to his girdle.

"Ancient as Islam!" assured the giant captain, towering above him. "A tried warrior, with weapons in his hands, thou must slay!"

"Why, then-"

Shirkuh laughed, and as he laughed, he struck. His motion was as quick as the blurring stroke of a cobra. In one movement he whipped the dagger from his girdle and struck upward under the captain's bearded chin. The Afghan had no opportunity to defend himself, no chance to lift rifle or draw sword. Before he realized Shirkuh's intention, he was down, his life gushing out of his sliced jugular.

An instant of stunned silence was broken by wild yells of laughter from the lookers-on and the men of the troop. It was just such a devilish jest as the bloodthirsty hill natures appreciated. There is humor in the hills, but it is a fiendish humor. The strange youth had shown a glint of the hard wolfish sophistication that underlay his apparent callowness.

But the other guardsmen cried out angrily and surged forward, with a sharp rattle of rifle bolts. Shirkuh sprang back and tore his rifle from its saddle scabbard. Muhammad and his men looked on cynically. It was none of their affair. They had enjoyed Shirkuh's grim and bitter jest; they would equally enjoy the sight of him being shot down by his victim's comrades.

But before a finger could crook on a trigger, the man on the white mare rode forward, beating down the rifles of the guards with a riding whip.

"Stop!" he commanded. "The Kurd is in the right. He slew according to the law. The man's weapons were in his hands, and he was a tried warrior."

"But he was taken unaware!" they clamored.

"The more fool he!" was the callous retort. "The law makes no point of that. I speak for the Kurd. And I am Alafdal Khan, once of Waziristan."

"Nay, we know you, my lord!" The guardsmen salaamed profoundly.

Muhammad ez Zahir gathered up his reins and spoke to Shirkuh.

"You luck still holds, Kurd!"

"Allah loves brave men!" Shirkuh laughed, swinging into the saddle.

Muhammad ez Zahir rode under the arch, and the troop streamed after him, their captive in their midst. They traversed a short narrow street, winding between walls of mud and wood, where overhanging balconies almost touched each other over the crooked way. Brent saw women staring at them through the lattices. The cavalcade emerged into a square much like that of any other hill town, Open shops and stalls lined it, and it was thronged by a colorful crowd. But there was a difference. The crowd was too heterogeneous, for

121

one thing; then there was too much wealth in sight. The town was prosperous, but with a sinister, unnatural prosperity. Gold and silk gleamed on barefooted ruffians whose proper garb was rags, and the goods displayed in the shops seemed mute evidence of murder and pillage. This was in truth a city of thieves.

The throng was lawless and turbulent, its temper set on a hair trigger. There were human skulls nailed above the gate, and in an iron cage made fast to the wall Brent saw a human skeleton. Vultures perched on the bars. Brent felt cold sweat bead his flesh. That might well be his own fate-to starve slowly in an iron cage hung above the heads of the jeering crowd. A sick abhorrence and a fierce hatred of this vile city swept over him.

As they rode into the city, Alafdal Khan drew his mare alongside Shirkuh's stallion. The Waziri was a bull-shouldered man with a bushy purple-stained beard and wide, ox-like eyes.

"I like you, Kurd," he announced. "You are in truth a mountain lion. Take service with me. A masterless man is a broken blade in Rub el Harami."

"I thought Abd el Khafid was master of Rub el Harami," said Shirkuh.

"Aye! But the city is divided into factions, and each man who is wise follows one chief or the other. Only picked men with long years of service behind them are chosen for Abd el

Khafid's house troops. The others follow various lords, who are each responsible to the emir."

"I am my own man!" boasted Shirkuh. "But you spoke for me at the gate. What devil's custom is this, when a stranger must kill a man to enter?"

"In old times it was meant to test a stranger's valor, and make sure that each man who came into Rub el Harami was a tried warrior," said Alafdal. "For generations, however, it has become merely an excuse to murder strangers. Few come uninvited. You should have secured the patronage of some chief of the clan before you came. Then you could have entered the city peacefully."

"I knew no man in the clan," muttered Shirkuh. "There are no Black Tigers in the Jebel Jawur. But men say the clan is coming to life, after slumbering in idleness for a hundred years, and-"

A disturbance in the crowd ahead of them interrupted him. The people in the square had massed thickly about the troop, slowing their progress, and growling ominously at the sight of Brent. Curses were howled, and bits of offal and refuse thrown, and now a scarred Shinwari stooped and caught up a stone which he cast at the white man. The missile grazed Brent's ear, drawing blood, and with a curse Shirkuh drove his horse against the fellow, knocking him down. A deep roar rose from the mob, and it surged forward menacingly. Shirkuh dragged his rifle from under his knee, but Alafdal Khan caught his arm

"Nay, brother! Do not fire. Leave these dogs to me."

He lifted his voice in a bull's bellow which carried across the square.

"Peace, my children! This is Shirkuh, of Jebel Jawur, who has come to be one of us. I speak for him-I, Alafdal Khan!"

A cheer rose from the crowd whose spirit was as vagrant and changeable as a leaf tossed in the wind. Obviously the Waziri was popular in Rub el Harami, and Brent guessed why as he saw Alafdal thrust a hand into a money pouch he carried at his girdle. But before the chief could completely mollify the mob by flinging a handful of coins among them, another figure entered the central drama. It was a Ghilzai who reined his horse through the crowd-a slim man, but tall and broad-shouldered, and one who looked as though his frame were of woven steel wires. He wore a rose-colored turban; a rich girdle clasped his supple waist, and his caftan was embroidered with gilt thread. A clump of ruffians on horseback followed him.

He drew rein in front of Alafdal Khan, whose beard instantly bristled while his wide eyes dilated truculently. Shirkuh quietly exchanged his rifle for his saber.

"That is my man your Kurd rode down," said the Ghilzai, indicating the groaning ruffian now dragging his bleeding hulk away. "Do you set your men on mine in the streets, Alafdal Khan?"

The people fell tensely silent, their own passions forgotten in the rivalry of the chiefs. Even Brent could tell that this was no new antagonism, but the rankling of an old quarrel. The Ghilzai was alert, sneering, coldly provocative. Alafdal Khan was belligerent, angry, yet uneasy.

"Your man began it, Ali Shah," he growled. "Stand aside. We take a prisoner to the Adobe of the Damned."

Brent sensed that Alafdal Khan was avoiding the issue. Yet he did not lack followers. Hard-eyed men with weapons in their girdles, some on foot, some on horseback, pushed through the throng and ranged themselves behind the Waziri. It was not physical courage Alafdal lacked, but some fiber of decision.

At Alafdal's declaration, which placed him in the position of one engaged in the emir's business, and therefore not to be interfered with-a statement at which Muhammad ez Zahir smiled cynically-Ali Shah hesitated, and the tense instant might have smoldered out, had it not been for one of the Ghilzai's men-a lean Orakzai, with hashish madness in his eyes. Standing in the edge of the crowd, he rested a rifle over the shoulder of the man in front of him and fired point-blank at the Waziri chief. Only the convulsive start of the owner of the shoulder saved Alafdal Khan. The bullet tore a piece out of his turban, and before the Orakzai could fire

125

again, Shirkuh rode at him and cut him down with a stroke that split his head to the teeth.

It was like throwing a lighted match into a powder mill. In an instant the square was a seething battle ground, where the adherents of the rival chiefs leaped at each others" throats with all the zeal ordinary men generally display in fighting somebody else's battle. Muhammad ez Zahir, unable to force his way through the heaving mass, stolidly drew his troopers in a solid ring around his prisoner. He had not interfered when the stones were cast. Stones would not kill the Feringi, and he was concerned only in getting Brent to his master alive and able to talk. He did not care how bloody and battered he might be. But in this melee a chance stroke might kill the infidel. His men faced outward, beating off attempts to get at their prisoner. Otherwise they took no part in the fighting. This brawl between rival chiefs, common enough in Rub el Harami, was none of Muhammad's affair.

Brent watched fascinated. But for modern weapons it might have been a riot in ancient Babylon, Cairo, or Nineveh-the same old jealousies, same old passions, same old instinct of the common man fiercely to take up some lordling's quarrel. He saw gaudily clad horsemen curvetting and caracoling as they slashed at each other with tulwars that were arcs of fire in the setting sun, and he saw ragged rascals belaboring each other with staves and cobblestones. No more shots were fired; it seemed an unwritten law that firearms were not to be used in street fighting. Or perhaps ammunition was too precious for them to waste on each other.

But it was bloody enough while it lasted, and it littered the square with stunned and bleeding figures. Men with broken heads went down under the stamping hoofs, and some of them did not get up again. Ali Shah's retainers outnumbered Alafdal Khan's, but the majority of the crowd were for the Waziri, as evidenced by the fragments of stone and wood that whizzed about the ears of his enemies. One of these well-meant missiles almost proved their champion's undoing. It was a potsherd, hurled with more zeal than accuracy at Ali Shah. It missed him and crashed full against Alafdal's bearded chin with an impact that filled the Waziri's eyes with tears and stars.

As he reeled in his saddle, his sword arm sinking, Ali Shah spurred at him, lifting his tulwar. There was murder in the air, while the blinded giant groped dazedly, sensing his peril. But Shirkuh was between them, lunging through the crowd like a driven bolt. He caught the swinging tulwar on his saber, and struck back, rising in his stirrups to add force to the blow. His blade struck flat, but it broke the left arm Ali Shah threw up in desperation, and beat down on the Ghilzai's turban with a fury that stretched the chief bleeding and senseless on the trampled cobblestones.

127

A gratified yell went up from the crowd, and Ali Shah's men fell back, confused and intimidated. Then there rose a thunder of hoofs, and a troop of men in compact formation swept the crowd to right and left as they plunged ruthlessly through. They were tall men in black chain armor and spired helmets, and their leader was a black-bearded Yusufzai, resplendent in gold-chased steel.

"Give way!" he ordered, with the hard arrogance of authority. "Clear the suk, in the name of Abd el Khafid, emir of Rub el Harami!"

"The Black Tigers!" muttered the people, giving back, but watching Alafdal Khan expectantly.

For an instant it seemed that the Waziri would defy the riders. His beard bristled, his eyes dilated-then he wavered, shrugged his giant shoulders, and sheathed his tulwar.

"Obey the law, my children," he advised them, and, not to be cheated out of the gesture he loved, he reached into his bulging pouch and sent a golden shower over their heads.

They went scrambling after the coins, shouting, and cheering, and laughing, and somebody yelled audaciously:

"Hail, Alafdal Khan, emir of Rub el Harami!"

Alafdal's countenance was an almost comical mingling of vanity and apprehension. He eyed the Yusufzai captain sidewise half triumphantly, half uneasily, tugging at his purple beard. The captain said crisply:

"Let there be an end to this nonsense. Alafdal Khan, the emir will hold you to account if any more fighting occurs. He is weary of this quarrel."

"Ali Shah started it!" roared the Waziri heatedly.

The crowd rumbled menacingly behind him, stooping furtively for stones and sticks. Again that half-exultant, half-frightened look flitted across Alafdal's broad face. The Yusufzai laughed sardonically.

"Too much popularity in the streets may cost a man his head in the palace!" said he, and turning away, he began clearing the square.

The mob fell back sullenly, growling in their beards, not exactly flinching from the prodding lances of the riders, but retiring grudgingly and with menace in their bearing. Brent believed that all they needed to rise in bloody revolt was a determined leader. Ali Shah's men picked up their senseless chief and lifted him into his saddle; they moved off across the suk with the leader lolling drunkenly in their midst. The fallen men who were able to stand were hustled to their feet by the Black Tigers.

Alafdal glared after them in a curiously helpless anger, his hand in his purple beard. Then he rumbled like a bear and rode off with his men, the wounded ones swaying on the saddles of their companions. Shirkuh rode with him, and as he reined away, he shot a glance at Brent which the American hoped meant that he was not deserting him.

Muhammad ez Zahir led his men and captive out of the square and down a winding street, cackling sardonically in his beard as he went.

"Alafdal Khan is ambitious and fearful, which is a sorry combination. He hates Ali Shah, yet avoids bringing the feud to a climax. He would like to be emir of Rub el Harami, but he doubts his own strength. He will never do anything but guzzle wine and throw money to the multitude. The fool! Yet he fights like a hungry bear once he is roused."

A trooper nudged Brent and pointed ahead of them to a squat building with iron-barred windows.

"The Abode of the Damned, Feringi!" he said maliciously. "No prisoner ever escaped therefrom-and none ever spent more than one night there."

At the door Muhammad gave his captive in charge of a one-eyed Sudozai with a squad of brutal-looking blacks armed with whips and bludgeons. These led him up a dimly lighted corridor to a cell with a barred door. Into this they thrust him. They placed on the floor a vessel of scummy water and a flat loaf of moldy bread, and then tiled out. The key turned in the lock with a chillingly final sound.

A few last rays of the sunset's afterglow found their way through the tiny, high, thick-barred window. Brent ate and drank mechanically, a prey to sick forebodings. All his future hinged now on Shirkuh, and Brent felt it was a chance as thin as a sword edge. Stiffly he stretched himself on the musty straw heaped in one corner. As he sank to sleep, he wondered dimly if there had ever really been a trim, exquisitely tailored person named Stuart Brent who slept in a soft bed and drank iced drinks out of slim-stemmed glasses, and danced with pink-and-white visions of feminine loveliness under tinted electric lights. It was a far-off dream; this was reality-rotten straw that crawled with vermin, smelly water and stale bread, and the scent of spilled blood that still seemed to cling to his garments after the fight in the square.

Chapter IV

BRENT AWOKE WITH the light of a torch dazzling his eyes. This torch was placed in a socket in the wall, and when his eyes became accustomed to the wavering glare, he saw a tall, powerful man in a long satin caftan and a green turban with a gold brooch. From beneath this turban, wide gray eyes, as cold as a sword of ice, regarded him contemplatively.

"You are Stuart Brent."

It was a statement, not a question. The man spoke English with only a hint of an accent; but that hint was unmistakable. Brent made no reply. This was Abd el Khafid, of course, but it was like meeting a character of fable clothed in flesh. Abd el Khafid and El Borak had begun to take on the appearance in Brent's worn brain of symbolic will-o'-the-wisps, nonexistent twin phantoms luring him to his doom. But here stood half of that phantasm, living and speaking. Perhaps El Borak was equally real, after all.

Brent studied the man almost impersonally. He looked Oriental enough in that garb, with his black pointed beard. But his hands were too big for a high-caste Moslem's hands-sinewy, ruthless hands that looked as if they could grasp either a sword hilt or a scepter. The body under the caftan appeared hard and capable-not with the tigerish suppleness of Shirkuh, but strong and quick, nevertheless.

"My spies watched you all the way from San Francisco," said Abd el Khafid. "They knew when you bought a steamship ticket to India. Their reports were wired by relays to Kabul-I have my secret wireless sets and spies in every capital of Asia-and thence here. I have my wireless set hidden back in the hills, here. Inconvenient, but the people would not stand for it in the city. It was a violation of custom. Rub el Harami rests on a foundation of customs-irksome at times, but mostly useful.

"I knew you would not have immediately sailed for India had not Richard Stockton told you something before he died, and I thought at first of having you killed as soon as you stepped off the ship. Then I decided to wait a bit and try to learn just how much you knew before I had you removed. Spies sent me word that you were coming North-that apparently you had told the British only that you wished to find El Borak. I knew then that Stockton had told you to find El Borak and tell him my true identity. Stockton was a human bloodhound, but it was only through the indiscretion of a servant that he learned the secret.

"Stockton knew that the only man who could harm me was El Borak. I am safe from the English here, safe from the ameer. El Borak could cause me trouble, if he suspected my true identity. As it is, so long as he considers me merely Abd el Khafid, a Moslem fanatic from Samarkand, he will not interfere. But if he should learn who I really am, he would guess why I am here, and what I am doing.

"So I let you come up the Khyber unmolested. It was evident by this time that you intended giving the news directly to El Borak, and my spies told me El Borak had vanished in the hills. I knew when you left Kabul, searching for him, and I sent Muhammad ez Zahir to capture and bring you here. You were easy to trace-a Melakani wandering in the hills with a band of Kabuli soldiery. So you entered Rub el Harami at last the only way an infidel may enter-as a captive, destined for the slave block."

"You are an infidel," retorted Brent. "If I expose your true identity to these people-"

The strong shoulders under the caftan shrugged.

"The imams know I was born a Russian. They know likewise that I am a true Moslem-that I foreswore Christianity and publicly acknowledged Islam, years ago. I cut all ties that bound me to Feringistan. My name is Abd el Khafid. I have a right to wear this green turban. I am a hadji. I have made the pilgrimage to Mecca. Tell the people of Rub el Harami that I am a Christian. They will laugh at you. To the masses I am a Moslem like themselves; to the council of imams I am a true convert."

Brent said nothing; he was in a trap he could not break.

"You are but a fly in my web," said Abd el Khafid contemptuously. "So unimportant that I intend to tell you my full purpose. It is good practice speaking in English. Sometimes I almost forget European tongues.

"The Black Tigers compose a very ancient society. It originally grew out of the bodyguard of Genghis Khan. After his death they settled in Rub el Harami, even then an outlaw city, and became the ruling caste. It expanded into a secret society, always with its headquarters here in this city. It soon became Moslem, a clan of fanatical haters of the Feringi, and the emirs sold the swords of their followers to many leaders of jihad, the holy war.

"It flourished, then decayed. A hundred years ago the clan was nearly exterminated in a hill feud, and the organization became a shadow, limited to the rulers and officials of Rub el Harami alone. But they still held the city. Ten years ago I cut loose from my people and became a Moslem, heart and soul. In my wanderings I discovered the Black Tigers, and saw their potentialities. I journeyed to Rub el Harami, and here I stumbled upon a secret that set my brain on fire.

"But I run ahead of my tale. It was only three years ago that I gained admittance into the clan. It was during the seven years preceding that, seven years of wandering, fighting, and plotting all over Asia, that clashed more than once with El Borak, and learned how dangerous the man was-and that we must always be enemies, since our interests and ideals were so antithetical. So when I came to Rub el Harami, I simply dropped out of sight of El Borak and all the other adventurers that like him and me rove the waste places of the East. Before I came to the city, I spent months in erasing my tracks. Valdimir Jakrovitch, known also as Akbar Shah, disappeared entirely. Not even El Borak connected him with Abd el Khafid, wanderer from Samarkand. I had stepped into a completely new role and personality. If El Borak should see me, he might suspect-but he never shall, except as my captive.

"Without interference from him I began to build up the clan, first as a member of the ranks, from which I swiftly rose, then as prince of the clan, to which position I attained less than a year ago, by means and intrigues I shall not inflict upon you. I have reorganized the society, expanded it as of old, placed my spies in every country in the world. Of course

El Borak must have heard that the Black Tiger was stirring again; but to him it would mean only the spasmodic activity of a band of fanatics, without international significance.

"But he would guess its true meaning if he knew that Abd el Khafid is the man he fought up and down the length and breadth of Asia, years ago!" The man's eyes blazed, his voice vibrated. In his super-egotism he found intense satisfaction in even so small and hostile an audience as his prisoner. "Did you ever hear of the Golden Cave of Shaitan el Kabir?

"It lies within a day's ride of the city, so carefully hidden that an army of men might search for it forever, in vain. But I have seen it! It is a sight to madden a man-heaped from floor to roof with blocks of gold! It is the offerings to Shaitan-custom dating from old heathen days. Each year a hundred-weight of gold, levied on the people of the city, is melted and molded in small blocks, and carried and placed in the cave by the imams and the emir. And-"

"Do you mean to tell me that a treasure of that size exists near this city of thieves?" demanded Brent incredulously.

"Why not? Have you not heard the city's customs are unbending as iron? Only the imams know the secret of the cave; the knowledge is handed down from imam to imam, from emir to emir. The people do not know; they suppose the gold is taken by Shaitan to his infernal abode. If they knew, they would not touch it. Take gold dedicated the

Shaitan the Damned? You little know the Oriental mind. Not a Moslem in the world would touch a grain of it, even though he were starving.

"But I am free of such superstitions. Within a few days the gift to Shaitan will be placed in the cave. It will be another year then before the imams visit the cavern again. And before that time comes around, I will have accomplished my purpose. I will secretly remove the gold from the cave, working utterly alone, and will melt it down and recast it in different forms. Oh, I understand the art and have the proper equipment. When I have finished, none can recognize it as the accursed gold of Shaitan.

"With it I can feed and equip an army! I can buy rifles, ammunition, machine guns, airplanes, and mercenaries to fly them. I can arm every cutthroat in the Himalayas! These hill tribes have the makings of the finest army in the world-all they need is equipment. And that equipment I will supply. There are plenty of European sources ready to sell me whatever I want. And the gold of Shaitan will supply my needs!" The man was sweating, his eyes blazing as if madness like molten gold had entered his veins. "The world never dreamed of such a treasure-trove! The golden offerings of a thousand years heaped from floor to ceiling! And it is mine!"

"The imams will kill you!" whispered Brent, appalled.

"They will not know for nearly a year. I will invent a lie to explain my great wealth. They will not suspect until they open the cave next year. Then it will be too late. Then I will be free from the Black Tigers. I will be an emperor!"

"With my great new army I will sweep down into the plains of India. I will lead a horde of Afghans, Persians, Pathans, Arabs, Turkomen that will make up for discipline by numbers and ferocity. The Indian Moslems will rise! I will sweep the English out of the land! I will rule supreme from Samarkand to Cape Comorin!"

"Why do you tell me this?" asked Brent. "What's to prevent me from betraying you to the imams?"

"You will never see an imam," was the grim reply. "I will see that you have no opportunity to talk. But enough of this: I allowed you to come alive to Rub el Harami only because I wanted to learn what secret password Stockton gave you to use with the British officials. I know you had one, by the speed and ease with which you were passed up to Kabul. I have long sought to get one of my spies into the very vitals of the secret service. This password will enable me to do so. Tell me what it is."

Brent laughed sardonically, then. "You're going to kill me anyway. I certainly don't intend to deprive myself of this one tiny crumb of retaliation. I'm not going to put another weapon in your filthy hands."

"You're a fool!" exclaimed Abd el Khafid, with a flash of anger too sudden, too easily aroused for complete self-confidence. The man was on edge, and not so sure of himself as he seemed.

"Doubtless," agreed Brent tranquilly. "And what about it?"

"Very well!" Abd el Khafid restrained himself by an obvious effort. "I cannot touch you to-night. You are the property of the city, according to age-old custom not even I can ignore. But to-morrow you will be sold on the block to the highest bidder. No one wants a Feringi slave, except for the pleasure of torturing. They are too soft for hard work. I will buy you for a few rupees, and then there will be nothing to prevent my making you talk. Before I fling your mangled carcass out on the garbage heap for the vultures, you will have told me everything I want to know."

Abruptly he turned and stalked out of the dungeon. Brent heard his footsteps reecho hollowly on the flags of the corridor. A wisp of conversation came back faintly. Then a door slammed and there was nothing but silence and a star blinking dimly through the barred window.

In another part of the city Shirkuh lounged on a silken divan, under the glow of bronze lamps that struck sparkling glints from the rich wine brimming in golden goblets. Shirkuh drank deep, smacking his lips, desert-fashion, as a matter of politeness to his host. He seemed to have no thought in the world except the quenching of his thirst, but Alafdal Khan, on another couch, knit his brows in perplexity. He was uncovering astonishing discoveries in this wild young warrior from the western mountains-unsuspected subtleties and hidden depths.

"Why do you wish to buy this Melakani?" he demanded.

"He is necessary to us," asserted Shirkuh. With the bronze lamps throwing his face into half shadow, the boyishness was gone, replaced by a keen hawk-like hardness and maturity.

"We must have him. I will buy him in the suk tomorrow, and he will aid us in making you emir of Rub el Harami."

"But you have no money!" expostulated the Waziri.

"You must lend it to me."

"But Abd el Khafid desires him," argued Alafdal Khan. "He sent Muhammad ez Zahir out to capture him. It would be unwise to bid against the emir."

Shirkuh emptied his cup before answering.

"From what you have told me of the city," he said presently, "this is the situation. Only a certain per cent of the citizens are Black Tigers. They constitute a ruling caste and a sort of police force to support the emir. The emirs are complete despots, except when checked by customs whose roots are lost in the mists of antiquity. They rule with an iron rein over a turbulent and lawless population, composed of the dregs and scum of Central Asia."

"That is true," agreed Alafdal Khan.

"But in the past, the people have risen and deposed a ruler who trampled on tradition, forcing the Black Tigers to elevate another prince. Very well. You have told me that the number of Black Tigers in the city is comparatively small at present. Many have been sent as spies or emissaries to other regions. You yourself are high in the ranks of the clan."

"An empty honor," said Alafdal bitterly. "My advice is never asked in council. I have no authority except with my own personal retainers. And they are less than those of Abd el Khafid or Ali Shah."

"It is upon the crowd in the streets we must rely," replied Shirkuh. "You are popular with the masses. They are almost ready to rise under you, were you to declare yourself. But that will come later. They need a leader and a motive. We will supply both. But first we must secure the Feringi. With him safe in our hands, we will plan our next move in the game."

Alafdal Khan scowled, his powerful fingers knotting about the slender stem of the wineglass. Conflicting emotions of vanity, ambition, and fear played across his broad face.

"You talk high!" he complained. "You ride into Rub el Harami, a penniless adventurer, and say you can make me emir of the city! How do I know you are not an empty bag of wind? How can you make me prince of Rub el Harami?"

Shirkuh set down his wineglass and rose, folding his arms. He looked somberly down at the astounded Waziri, all naiveness and reckless humor gone out of his face. He spoke a single phrase, and Alafdal ejaculated stranglingly and lurched to his feet, spilling his wine. He reeled like a drunkard, clutching at the divan, his dilated eyes searching, with a fierce intensity, the dark, immobile face before him.

"Do you believe, now, that I can make you emir of Rub el Harami?" demanded Shirkuh.

"Who could doubt it?" panted Alafdal. "Have you not put kings on their thrones? But you are mad, to come here! One word to the mob and they would rend you limb from limb!"

"You will not speak that word," said Shirkuh with conviction. "You will not throw away the lordship of Rub el Harami."

And Alafdal nodded slowly, the fire of ambition surging redly in his eyes.

Chapter V

DAWN STREAMING GRAYLY through the barred window awakened Brent. He reflected that it might be the

142

last dawn he would see as a free man. He laughed wryly at the thought. Free? Yet at least he was still a captive, not a slave. There was a vast difference between a captive and a slave-a revolting gulf, in which, crossing, a man or woman's self-respect must be forever lost.

Presently black slaves came with a jug of cheap sour wine, and food-chupatties, rice cakes, dried dates. Royal fare compared with his supper the night before. A Tajik barber shaved him and trimmed his hair, and he was allowed the luxury of scrubbing himself pink in the prison bath.

He was grateful for the opportunity, but the whole proceeding was disgusting. He felt like a prize animal being curried and groomed for display. Some whim prompted him to ask the barber where the proceeds of his sale would go, and the man answered into the city treasury, to keep the walls repaired. A singularly unromantic usage for the price of a human being, but typical of the hard practicality of the East. Brent thought fleetingly of Shirkuh, then shrugged his shoulders. Apparently the Kurd had abandoned him to his fate.

Clad only in a loin cloth and sandals, he was led from the prison by the one-eyed Sudozai and a huge black slave. Horses were waiting for them at the gate, and he was ordered to mount. Between the slave masters he clattered up the street before the sun was up. But already the crowd was gathering in the square. The auctioning of a white man was

143

an event, and there was, furthermore, a feeling of expectancy in the air, sharpened by the fight of the day before.

In the midst of the square there stood a thick platform built solidly of stone blocks; it was perhaps four feet high and thirty feet across. On this platform the Sudozai took his stand, grasping a piece of rope which was tied loosely about Brent's neck. Behind them stood the stolid Soudanese with a drawn scimitar on his shoulder.

Before, and to one side of the block the crowd had left a space clear, and there Abd el Khafid sat his horse, amid a troop of Black Tigers, bizarre in their ceremonial armor. Ceremonial it must be, reflected Brent; it might turn a sword blade, but it would afford no protection against a bullet. But it was one of the many fantastic customs of the city, where tradition took the place of written law. The bodyguard of the emir had always worn black armor. Therefore, they would always wear it. Muhammad ez Zahir commanded them. Brent did not see Ali Shah.

Another custom was responsible for the presence of Abd el Khafid, instead of sending a servant to buy the American for him; not even the emir could bid by proxy.

As he climbed upon the block, Brent heard a cheer, and saw Alafdal Khan and Shirkuh pushing through the throng on their horses. Behind them came thirty-five warriors, well armed and well mounted. The Waziri chief was plainly nervous, but Shirkuh strutted like a peacock, even on horseback, before the admiring gaze of the throng.

At the ringing ovation given them, annoyance flitted across Abd el Khafid's broad, pale face, and that expression was followed by a more sinister darkening that boded ill for the Waziri and his ally.

The auction began abruptly and undramatically. The Sudozai began in a singsong voice to narrate the desirable physical points of the prisoner, when Abd el Khafid cut him short and offered fifty rupees.

"A hundred!" instantly yelled Shirkuh.

Abd el Khafid turned an irritated and menacing glare on him. Shirkuh grinned insolently, and the crowd hugged itself, sensing a conflict of the sort it loved.

"Three hundred!" snarled the emir, meaning to squelch this irreverent vagabond without delay.

"Four hundred!" shouted Shirkuh.

"A thousand!" cried Adb el Khafid in a passion.

"Eleven hundred!"

And Shirkuh deliberately laughed in the emir's face, and the crowd laughed with him. Abd el Khafid appeared at a disadvantage, for he was a bit confused at this unexpected opposition, and had lost his temper too easily. The fierce eyes of the crowd missed nothing of this, for it is on such points the wolf pack ceaselessly and pitilessly judges its leader. Their sympathies swung to the laughing, youthful stranger, sitting his horse with careless ease.

Brent's heart had leaped into his throat at the first sound of Shirkuh's voice. If the man meant to aid him, this was the most obvious way to take. Then his heart sank again at the determination in Abd el Khafid's angry face. The emir would never let his captive slip between his fingers. And though the Gift of Shaitan was not yet in the Russian's possession, yet doubtless his private resources were too great for Shirkuh. In a contest of finances Shirkuh was foredoomed to lose.

Brent's conclusions were not those of Abd el Khafid. The emir shot a glance at Alafdal Khan, shifting uneasily in his saddle. He saw the beads of moisture gathered on the Waziri's broad brow, and realized a collusion between the men. New anger blazed in the emir's eyes.

In his way Abd el Khafid was miserly. He was willing to squander gold like water on a main objective, but it irked him exceedingly to pay an exorbitant price to attain a minor goal. He knew-every man in the crowd knew now-that Alafdal Khan was backing Shirkuh. And all men knew that the Waziri was one of the wealthiest men in the city, and a prodigal spender. Abd el Khafid's nostrils pinched in with wrath as he realized the heights of extravagance to which he might be forced, did Shirkuh persist in this impertinent opposition to his wishes. The Gift of Shaitan was not yet in his hands, and his private funds were drained constantly by the expenses of his spy system and his various intrigues. He raised the bid in a harsh, anger-edged voice.

Brent, studying the drama with the keen, understanding eyes of a gambler, realized that Abd el Khafid had got off on the wrong foot. Shirkuh's bearing appealed to the crowd. They laughed at his sallies, which were salty and sparkling with all the age-old ribaldry of the East, and they hissed covertly at the emir, under cover of their neighbors.

The bidding mounted to unexpected heights. Abd el Khafid, white about the nostrils as he sensed the growing hostility of the crowd, did not speak except to snarl his offers. Shirkuh rolled in his saddle, slapped his thighs, yelled his bids, and defiantly brandished a leathern bag which gave out a musical tinkling.

The excitement of the crowd was at white heat. Ferocity began to edge their yells. Brent, looking down at the heaving mass, had a confused impression of dark, convulsed faces, blazing eyes, and strident voices. Alafdal Khan was sweating, but he did not interfere, not even when the bidding rose above fifty thousand rupees.

It was more than a bidding contest; it was the subtle play of two opposing wills, as hard and supple as tempered steel. Abd el Khafid realized that if he withdrew now, his prestige would never recover from the blow. In his rage he made his first mistake.

He rose suddenly in his stirrups, clapping his hands.

"Let there be an end to this madness!" he roared. "No white slave is worth this much! I declare the auction closed! I buy this dog for sixty thousand rupees! Take him to my house, slave master!"

A roar of protest rose from the throng, and Shirkuh drove his horses alongside the block and leaped off to it, tossing his rein to a Waziri.

"Is this justice?" he shouted. "Is this done according to custom? Men of Rub el Harami, I demand justice! I bid sixty-one thousand rupees. I stand ready to bid more, if necessary! When has an emir been allowed to use his authority to rob a citizen, and cheat the people? Nay, we be thieves-but shall we rob one another? Who is Abd el Khafid, to trample the customs of the city! If the customs are broken, what shall hold you together? Rub el Harami lives only so long as the ancient traditions are observed. Will you let Abd el Khafid destroy them-and you?"

A cataract of straining human voices answered him. The crowd had become a myriad-fanged, flashing-eyed mass of hate.

"Obey the customs!" yelled Shirkuh, and the crowd took up the yell.

"Obey the customs!" It was the thunder of unreined seas, the roar of a storm wind ripping through icy passes. Blindly men seized the slogan, yowling it under a forest of lean arms and clenched fists. Men go mad on a slogan; conquerors

148

have swept to empire, prophets to new world religions on a shouted phrase. All the men in the square were screaming it like a ritual now, rocking and tossing on their feet, fists clenched, froth on their lips. They no longer reasoned; they were a forest of blind human emotions, swayed by the storm wind of a shouted phrase that embodied passion and the urge to action.

Abd el Khafid lost his head. He drew his sword and cut a man who was clawing at his stirrup mouthing: "Obey the customs, emir!" and the spurt of blood edged the yells with murder lust. But as yet the mob was only a blind, raging monster without a head.

"Clear the suk!" shouted Abd el Khafid.

The lances dipped, and the Black Tigers moved forward uncertainly. A hail of stones greeted them.

Shirkuh leaped to the edge of the block, lifting his arms, shouting, cutting the volume of sound by the knifing intensity of his yell.

"Down with Abd el Khafid! Hail, Alafdal Khan, emir of Rub el Harami!"

"Hail, Alafdal Khan!" came back from the crowd like a thunderclap.

Abd el Khafid rose in his stirrups, livid.

"Fools! Are you utterly mad? Shall I call my riders to sweep the streets clear of you?"

149

Shirkuh threw back his head and laughed like a wolf howling.

"Call them!" he yelled. "Before you can gather them from the taverns and dens, we will stain the square with your blood! Prove your right to rule! You have violated one custom-redeem yourself by another! Men of Rub el Harami, is it not a tradition that an emir must be able to defend his title with the sword?"

"Aye!" roared back the mob.

"Then let Abd el Khafid fight Alafdal Khan!" shouted Shirkuh.

"Let them fight!" bellowed the mob.

Abd el Khafid's eyes turned red. He was sure of his prowess with the sword, but this revolt against his authority enraged him to the point of insanity. This was the very center of his power; here like a spider he had spun his webs, expecting attack on the fringes, but never here. Now he was caught off-guard. Too many trusted henchmen were far afield. Others were scattered throughout the city, useless to him at the moment. His bodyguard was too small to defy the crowd. Mentally he promised himself a feast of hangings and beheadings when he could bring back a sufficient force of men to Rub el Harami. In the meantime he would settle Alafdal's ambitions permanently.

"Kingmaker, eh?" he snarled in Shirkuh's face, as he leaped off his horse to the block. He whipped out his tulwar and swung it around his head, a sheen of silver in the sun. "I'll nail your head to the Herati Gate when I've finished with this ox-eyed fool!"

Shirkuh laughed at him and stepped back, herding the slave masters and their captive to the back of the block. Alafdal Khan was scrambling to the platform, his tulwar in his hand.

He was not fully straightened on the block when Abd el Khafid was on him with the fury of a tornado. The crowd cried out, fearing that the emir's whirlwind speed would envelop the powerful but slower chief. But it was this very swiftness that undid the Russian. In his wild fury to kill, Abd el Khafid forgot judgment. The stroke he aimed at Alafdal's head would have decapitated an ox; but he began it in mid-stride, and its violence threw his descending foot out of line. He stumbled, his blade cut thin air as Alafdal dodged-and then the Waziri's sword was through him.

It was over in a flash. Abd el Khafid had practically impaled himself on the Waziri's blade. The rush, the stroke, the counter-thrust, and the emir kicking his life out on the stone like a spitted rat-it all happened in a mere tick of time that left the mob speechless.

Shirkuh sprang forward like a panther in the instant of silence while the crowd held its breath and Alafdal gaped stupidly from the red tulwar in his hand to the dead man at his feet.

151

"Hail to Alafdal Khan, emir of Rub el Harami!" yelled Shirkuh, and the crowd thundered its response.

"On your horse, man, quick!" Shirkuh snarled in Alafdal's ear, thrusting him toward his steed, while seeming to bow him toward it.

The crowd was going mad with the senseless joy of a mob that sees its favorite elevated above them. As Alafdal, still dazed by the rapidity of events, clambered on his horse, Shirkuh turned on the stunned Black Tiger riders.

"Dogs!" he thundered. "Form ranks! Escort your new master to the palace, for his title to be confirmed by the council of imams!"

They were moving unwillingly forward, afraid of the crowd, when a commotion interrupted the flow of events. Ali Shah and forty armed horsemen came pushing their way through the crowd and halted beside the armored riders. The crowd bared its teeth, remembering the Ghilzai's feud with their new emir. Yet there was iron in Ali Shah. He did not flinch, but the old indecision wavered in Alafdal's eyes at the sight of his foe.

Shirkuh turned on Ali Shah with the swift suspicion of a tiger, but before anyone could speak, a wild figure dashed from among the Ghilzais and leaped on the block. It was the Shinwari Shirkuh had ridden down the day before. The man threw a lean arm out toward Shirkuh.

"He is an impostor, brothers!" he screamed. "I thought I knew him yesterday! An hour ago I remembered! He is no Kurd! He is-"

Shirkuh shot the man through the body. He staggered to a rolling fall that carried him to the edge of the block. There he lifted himself on an elbow, and pointed at Shirkuh. Blood spattered the Shinwari's beard as he croaked in the sudden silence:

"I swear by the beard of the Prophet, he is no Moslem!"

"He is El Borak!"

A shudder passed over the crowd.

"Obey the customs!" came Ali Shah's sardonic voice in the unnatural stillness. "You killed your emir because of a small custom. There stands a man who has violated the greatest one-your enemy, El Borak!"

There was conviction in his voice, yet no one had really doubted the accusation of the dying Shinwari. The amazing revelation had struck them all dumb, Brent included. But only for an instant.

The blind reaction of the crowd was as instantaneous as it had been before. The tense stillness snapped like a banjo string to a flood of sound:

"Down with the infidels! Death to El Borak! Death to Alafdal Khan!"

153

To Brent it seemed that the crowd suddenly rose like a foaming torrent and flowed over the edge of the block. Above the deafening clamor he heard the crashing of the big automatic in El Borak's hand. Blood spattered, and in an instant the edge of the block was littered by writhing bodies over which the living tripped and stumbled.

El Borak sprang to Brent, knocked his guards sprawling with the pistol barrel, and seized the dazed captive, dragged him toward the black stallion to which the Waziri still clung. The mob was swarming like wolves about Alafdal and his warriors, and the Black Tigers and Ali Shah were trying to get at them through the press. Alafdal bawled something desperate and incoherent to El Borak as he laid lustily about him with his tulwar. The Waziri chief was almost crazed with bewilderment. A moment ago he had been emir of Rub el Harami, with the crowd applauding him. Now the same crowd was trying to take him out of his saddle.

"Make for your house, Alafdal!" yelled El Borak.

He leaped into the saddle just as the man holding the horse went down with his head shattered by a cobblestone. The wild figure who had killed him leaped forward, gibbering, clawing at the rider's leg. El Borak drove a sharp silver heel into his eye, stretching him bleeding and screaming on the ground. He ruthlessly slashed off a hand that grasped at his rein, and beat back a ring of snarling faces with another swing of his saber.

"Get on behind me, Brent!" he ordered, holding the frantic horse close to the block.

It was only when he heard the English words, with their Southwestern accent, that Brent realized that this was no dream, and he had at last actually encountered the man he had sought.

Men were grasping at Brent. He beat them off with clenched fists, leaped on the stallion behind the saddle. He grasped the cantle, resisting the natural impulse to hold onto the man in front of him. El Borak would need the free use of his body if they won through that seething mass of frantic humanity which packed the square from edge to edge. It was a frothing, dark-waved sea, swirling about islands of horsemen.

But the stallion gathered itself and lunged terribly, knocking over screaming figures like tenpins. Bones snapped under its hoofs. Over the heads of the crowd Brent saw Ali Shah and his riders beating savagely at the mob with their swords, trying to reach Alafdal Khan. Ali Shah was cool no longer; his dark face was convulsed.

The stallion waded through that sea of humanity, its rider slashing right and left, clearing a red road. Brent felt hands clawing at them as they went by, felt the inexorable hoofs grinding over writhing bodies. Ahead of them the Waziris, in a compact formation, were cutting their way toward the west side of the square. Already a dozen of them had been dragged from their saddles and torn to pieces.

El Borak dragged his rifle out of its boot, and it banged redly in the snarling faces, blasting a lane through them. Along that lane the black stallion thundered, to smite with irresistible impact the mass hemming in Alafdal Khan. It burst asunder, and the black horse sped on, while its rider yelled:

"Fall in behind me! We'll make a stand at your house!"

The Waziris closed in behind him. They might have abandoned El Borak if they had had the choice. But the people included them all in their blind rage against the breakers of tradition. As they broke through the press, behind them the Black Tigers brought their rifles into play for the first time. A hail of bullets swept the square, emptying half the Waziri saddles. The survivors dashed into a narrow street.

A mass of snarling figures blocked their way. Men swarmed from the houses to cut them off. Men were surging into the alley behind them. A thrown stone numbed Brent's shoulder. El Borak was using the empty rifle like a mace. In a rush they smote the men massed in the street.

The great black stallion reared and lashed down with mallet-like hoofs, and its rider flailed with a rifle stock now splintered and smeared with blood. But behind them Alafdal's steed stumbled and fell. Alafdal's disordered turban and his dripping tulwar appeared for an instant above a sea of heads and tossing arms. His men plunged madly in to rescue him and were hemmed in by a solid mass of humanity as more men surged down the street from the square. Hamstrung horses went down, screaming. El Borak wheeled his stallion back toward the melee, and as he did so, a swarm of men burst from a narrow alleyway. One seized Brent's leg and dragged him from the horse. As they rolled in the dust, the Afghan heaved Brent below him, mouthing like an ape, and lifted a crooked knife. Brent saw it glint in the sunlight, had an instant's numb realization of doom-then El Borak, reining the rearing stallion around, leaned from the saddle and smashed the Afghan's skull with his rifle butt.

The man fell across Brent, and then from an arched doorway an ancient blunderbuss banged, and the stallion reared and fell sprawling, half its head shot away. El Borak leaped clear, hit on his feet like a cat, and hurled the broken rifle in the faces of the swarm bearing down on him. He leaped back, tearing his saber clear. It flickered like lightning, and three men fell with cleft heads. But the mob was blood-mad, heedless of death. Brainlessly they rushed against him, flailing with staves and bludgeons, bearing him by their very weight back into an arched doorway. The panels splintered inward under the impact of the hurtling bodies, and El Borak vanished from Brent's sight. The mob poured in after him.

Brent cast off the limp body that lay across him and rose. He had a brief glimpse of a dark writhing mass where the fight swirled about the fallen chief, of Ali Shah and his riders beating at the crowd with their swords-then a bludgeon, wielded from behind, fell glancingly on his head, and he fell blind and senseless into the trampled dust.

Slowly consciousness returned to Stuart Brent. His head ached dully, and his hair was stiff with clotted blood. He struggled to his elbows, though the effort made his head swim sickeningly, and stared about him.

He was lying on a stone floor littered with moldy straw. Light came in from a high-barred window. There was a door with a broad barred wicket. Other figures lay near him and one sat cross-legged, staring at him blankly. It was Alafdal Khan.

The Waziri's beard was torn, his turban gone. His features were swollen, and bruised, and skinned, one ear mangled. Three of his men lay near, one groaning. All had been frightfully beaten, and the man who groaned seemed to have a broken arm.

"They didn't kill us!" marveled Brent.

Alafdal Khan swung his great head like an ox in pain and groaned: "Cursed be the day I laid eyes on El Borak!"

One of the men crept painfully to Brent's side.

"I am Achmet, sahib," he said, spitting blood from a broken tooth. "There lie Hassan and Suleiman. Ali Shah and his men beat the dogs off us, but they had mauled us so that all were dead save these you see. Our lord is like one touched by Allah."

"Are we in the Abode of the Damned?" asked Brent.

"Nay, sahib. We are in the common jail which lies near the west wall."

"Why did they save us from the mob?"

"For a more exquisite end!" Achmet shuddered. "Does the sahib know the death the Black Tigers reserve for traitors?"

"No!" Brent's lips were suddenly dry.

"We will be flayed to-morrow night in the square. It is an old pagan custom. Rub El Harami is a city of customs."

"So I have learned!" agreed Brent grimly. "What of El Borak?"

"I do not know. He vanished into a house, with many men in pursuit. They must have overtaken and slain him."

Chapter VI

WHEN THE DOOR in the archway burst inward under the impact of Gordon's iron-hard shoulders, he tumbled backward into a dim, carpeted hallway. His pursuers, crowding after him, jammed in the doorway in a sweating, cursing crush which his saber quickly turned into a shambles. Before they could clear the door of the dead, he was racing down the hall.

He made a turn to the left, ran across a chamber where veiled women squealed and scattered, emerged into a narrow alley, leaped a low wall, and found himself in a small garden. Behind him sounded the clamor of his hunters, momentarily baffled. He crossed the garden and through a partly open door came into a winding corridor. Somewhere a slave was singing in the weird chant of the Soudan, apparently heedless of the dog-fight noises going on upon the other side of the wall. Gordon moved down the corridor, careful to keep his silver heels from clinking. Presently he came to a winding staircase and up it he went, making no noise on the richly carpeted steps. As he came out into an upper corridor, he saw a curtained door and heard beyond it a faint, musical clinking which he recognized. He glided to the partly open door and peered through the curtains. In a richly appointed room, lighted by a tinted skylight, a portly, gray-bearded man sat with his back to the door, counting coins out of a leather bag into an ebony chest. He was so intent on the business at hand that he did not seem aware of the growing clamor below. Or perhaps street riots were too common in Rub el Harami to attract the attention of a thrifty merchant, intent only on increasing his riches.

Pad of swift feet on the stair, and Gordon slipped behind the partly open door. A richly clad young man, with a scimitar in his hand, ran up the steps and hurried to the door. He thrust the curtains aside and paused on the threshold, panting with haste and excitement.

"Father!" he shouted. "El Borak is in the city! Do you not hear the din below? They are hunting him through the houses! He may be in our very house! Men are searching the lower rooms even now!"

"Let them hunt him," replied the old man. "Remain here with me, Abdullah. Shut that door and lock it. El Borak is a tiger."

As the youth turned, instead of the yielding curtain behind him, he felt the contact of a hard, solid body, and simultaneously a corded arm locked about his neck, choking his startled cry. Then he felt the light prick of a knife and he went limp with fright, his scimitar sliding from his nerveless hand. The old man had turned at his son's gasp, and now he froze, gray beneath his beard, his moneybag dangling.

Gordon thrust the youth into the room, not releasing his grip, and let the curtains close behind them.

"Do not move," he warned the old man softly.

He dragged his trembling captive across the room and into a tapestried alcove. Before he vanished into it, he spoke briefly to the merchant:

"They are coming up the stairs, looking for me. Meet them at the door and send them away. Do not play me false by even the flick of an eyelash, if you value your son's life."

The old man's eyes were dilated with pure horror. Gordon well knew the power of paternal affection. In a welter of hate, treachery, and cruelty, it was a real and vital passion, as strong as the throb of the human heart. The merchant might defy Gordon were his own life alone at stake; but the American knew he would not risk the life of his son.

Sandals stamped up the stair, and rough voices shouted. The old man hurried to the door, stumbling in his haste. He thrust his head through the curtains, in response to a bawled question. His reply came plainly to Gordon.

"El Borak? Dogs! Take your clamor from my walls! If El Borak is in the house of Nureddin el Aziz, he is in the rooms below. Ye have searched them? Then look for him elsewhere, and a curse on you!"

The footsteps dwindled down the stair, the voices faded and ceased.

Gordon pushed Abdullah out into the chamber.

"Shut the door!" the American ordered.

Nureddin obeyed, with poisonous eyes but fear-twisted face.

"I will stay in this room a while," said Gordon. "If you play me false-if any man besides yourself crosses that threshold, the first stroke of the fight will plunge my blade in Abdullah's heart."

"What do you wish?" asked Nureddin nervously.

"Give me the key to that door. No, toss it on the table there. Now go forth into the streets and learn if the Feringi, or any of the Waziris live. Then return to me. And if you love your son, keep my secret!"

The merchant left the room without a word, and Gordon bound Abdullah's wrists and ankles with strips torn from the curtains. The youth was gray with fear, incapable of resistance. Gordon laid him on a divan, and reloaded his big automatic. He discarded the tattered remnants of his robe. The white silk shirt beneath was torn, revealing his muscular breast, his close-fitting breeches smeared with blood.

Nureddin returned presently, rapping at the door and naming himself.

Gordon unlocked the door and stepped back, his pistol muzzle a few inches from Abdullah's ear. But the old man was alone when he hurried in. He closed the door and sighed with relief to see Abdullah uninjured.

"What is your news?" demanded Gordon.

"Men comb the city for you, and Ali Shah has declared himself prince of the Black Tigers. The imams have confirmed his claim. The mob has looted Alafdal Khan's house and slain every Waziri they could find. But the Feringi lives, and so likewise does Alafdal Khan and three of his men. They lie in the common jail. To-morrow night they die."

"Do your slaves suspect my presence?"

"Nay. None saw you enter."

"Good. Bring wine and food. Abdullah shall taste it before I eat."

"My slaves will think it strange to see me bearing food!"

"Go to the stair and call your orders down to them. Bid them set the food outside the door and then return downstairs."

This was done, and Gordon ate and drank heartily, sitting cross-legged on the divan at Abdullah's head, his pistol on his lap.

The day wore on. El Borak sat motionless, his eternal vigilance never relaxing. The Afghans watched him, hating and fearing him. As evening approached, he spoke to Nureddin after a silence that had endured for hours.

"Go and procure for me a robe and cloak of black silk, and a black helmet such as is worn by the Black Tigers. Bring me also boots with lower heels than these-and not silver-and a mask such as members of the clan wear on secret missions."

The old man frowned. "The garments I can procure from my own shop. But how am I to secure the helmet and mask?"

"That is thy affair. Gold can open any door, they say. Go!"

As soon as Nureddin had departed, reluctantly, Gordon kicked off his boots, and next removed his mustache, using the keen-edged dagger for a razor. With its removal vanished the last trace of Shirkuh the Kurd.

Twilight had come, to Rub el Harami. The room seemed full of a blue mist, blurring objects. Gordon had lighted a bronze lamp when Nureddin returned with the articles El Borak had ordered.

"Lay them on the table and sit down on the divan with your hands behind you," Gordon commanded.

When the merchant had done so, the American bound his wrists and ankles. Then Gordon donned the boots and the robe, placed the black lacquered steel helmet on his head, and drew the black cloak about him; lastly he put on the mask which fell in folds of black silk to his breast, with two slits over his eyes. Turning to Nureddin, he asked:

"Is there a likeness between me and another?"

"Allah preserve us! You are one with Dhira Azrail, the executioner of the Black Tigers, when he goes forth to slay at the emir's command."

"Good. I have heard much of this man who slays secretly, who moves through the night like a black jinn of destruction. Few have seen his face, men say."

"Allah defend me from ever seeing it!" said Nureddin fervently.

Gordon glanced at the skylight. Stars twinkled beyond it.

"I go now from your house, Nureddin," said he. "But lest you rouse the household in your zeal of hospitality, I must gag you and your son."

"We will smother!" exclaimed Nureddin. "We will starve in this room!"

"You will do neither one nor the other," Gordon assured him. "No man I gagged ever smothered. Has not Allah given you nostrils through which to breathe? Your servants will find you and release you in the morning."

This was deftly accomplished, and Gordon advised:

"Observe that I have not touched your moneybags, and be grateful!"

He left the room, locking the door behind him. He hoped it would be several hours before either of his captives managed to work the gag out of his mouth and arouse the household with his yells.

Moving like a black-clad ghost through the dimly lighted corridors, Gordon descended the winding stair and came into the lower hallway. A black slave sat cross-legged at the foot of the stair, but his head was sunk on his broad breast, and his snores resounded through the hall. He did not see or hear the velvet-footed shadow that glided past him. Gordon slid back the bolt on the door and emerged into the garden, whose broad leaves and petals hung motionless in the still starlight. Outside, the city was silent. Men had gone early behind locked doors, and few roamed the streets, except those patrols searching ceaselessly for El Borak.

He climbed the wall and dropped into the narrow alley. He knew where the common jail was, for in his role of Shirkuh he had familiarized himself with the general features of the town. He kept close to the wall, under the shadows of the overhanging balconies, but he did not slink. His movements were calculated to suggest a man who has no reason for concealment, but who chooses to shun conspicuousness.

The street seemed empty. From some of the roof gardens came the wail of native citterns, or voices lifted in song. Somewhere a wretch screamed agonizingly to the impact of blows on naked flesh.

Once Gordon heard the clink of steel ahead of him and turned quickly into a dark alley to let a patrol swing past. They were men in armor, on foot, but carrying cocked rifles at the ready and peering in every direction. They kept close together, and their vigilance reflected their fear of the quarry they hunted. When they rounded the first corner, he emerged from his hiding place and hurried on.

But he had to depend on his disguise before he reached the prison. A squad of armed men rounded the corner ahead of him, and no concealment offered itself. At the sound of their footsteps he had slowed his pace to a stately stride. With his cloak folded close about him, his head slightly bent as if in somber meditation, he moved on, paying no heed to the soldiers. They shrank back, murmuring:

"Allah preserve us! It is Dhira Azrail-the Arm of the Angel of Death! An order has been given!"

They hurried on, without looking back. A few moments later Gordon had reached the lowering arch of the prison door. A dozen guardsmen stood alertly under the arch, their rifle barrels gleaming bluely in the glare of a torch thrust in a niche in the wall. These rifles were instantly leveled at the figure that moved out of the shadows. Then the men hesitated, staring wide-eyed at the somber black shape standing silently before them.

"Your pardon!" entreated the captain of the guard, saluting. "We could not recognize-in the shadow-We did not know an order had been given."

A ghostly hand, half muffled in the black cloak, gestured toward the door, and the guardsmen opened it in stumbling haste, salaaming deeply. As the black figure moved through, they closed the door and made fast the chain.

"The mob will see no show in the suk after all," muttered one.

Chapter VII

IN THE CELL where Brent and his companions lay, time dragged on leaden feet. Hassan groaned with the pain of his broken arm. Suleiman cursed Ali Shah in a monotonous drone. Achmet was inclined to talk, but his comments cast no light of hope on their condition. Alafdal Khan sat like a man in a daze.

No food was given them, only scummy water that smelled. They used most of it to bathe their wounds. Brent suggested trying to set Hassan's arm, but the others showed no interest. Hassan had only another day to live. Why bother? Then there was nothing with which to make splints.

Brent mostly lay on his back, watching the little square of dry blue Himalayan sky through the barred window.

He watched the blue fade, turn pink with sunset and deep purple with twilight; it became a square of blue-black velvet, set with a cluster of white stars. Outside, in the corridor that ran between the cells, bronze lamps glowed, and he wondered vaguely how far, on the backs of groaning camels, had come the oil that filled them.

In their light a cloaked figure came down the corridor, and a scarred sardonic face was pressed to the bars. Achmet gasped, his eyes dilated.

"Do you know me, dog?" inquired the stranger.

Achmet nodded, moistening lips suddenly dry.

169

"Are we to die to-night, then?" he asked.

The head under the flowing headdress was shaken.

"Not unless you are fool enough to speak my name. Your companions do not know me. I have not come in my usual capacity, but to guard the prison to-night. Ali Shah fears El Borak might seek to aid you."

"Then El Borak lives!" ejaculated Brent, to whom everything else in the conversation had been unintelligible.

"He still lives." The stranger laughed. "But he will be found, if he is still in the city. If he has fled-well, the passes have been closed by heavy guards, and horsemen are combing the plain and the hills. If he comes here tonight, he will be dealt with. Ali Shah chose to send me rather than a squad of riflemen. Not even the guards know who I am."

As he turned away toward the rear end of the corridor, Brent asked:

"Who is that man?"

But Achmet's flow of conversation had been dried up by the sight of that lean, sardonic face. He shuddered, and drew away from his companions, sitting cross-legged with bowed head. From time to time his shoulders twitched, as if he had seen a reptile or a ghoul.

Brent sighed and stretched himself on the straw. His battered limbs ached, and he was hungry.

Presently he heard the outer door clang. Voices came faintly to him, and the door closed again. Idly he wondered if they were changing the guard. Then he heard the soft rustle of cloth. A man was coming down the corridor. An instant later he came into the range of their vision, and his appearance clutched Brent with an icy dread. Clad in black from head to foot, a spired helmet gave him an appearance of unnatural height. He was enveloped in the folds of a black cloak. But the most sinister implication was in the black mask which fell in loose folds to his breast.

Brent's flesh crawled. Why was that silent, cowled figure coming to their dungeon in the blackness and stillness of the night hours?

The others glared wildly; even Alafdal was shaken out of his daze. Hassan whimpered:

"It is Dhira Azrail!"

But bewilderment mingled with the fear in Achmet's eyes.

The scar-faced stranger came suddenly from the depths of the corridor and confronted the masked man just before the door. The lamplight fell on his face, upon which played a faint, cynical smile.

"What do you wish? I am in charge here."

The masked man's voice was muffled. It sounded cavernous and ghostly, fitting his appearance.

"I am Dhira Azrail. An order has been given. Open the door."

The scarred one salaamed deeply, and murmured: "Hearkening and obedience, my lord!"

He produced a key, turned it in the lock, pulled open the heavy door, and bowed again, humbly indicating for the other to enter. The masked man was moving past him when Achmet came to life startlingly.

"El Borak!" he screamed. "Beware! He is Dhira Azrail!"

The masked man wheeled like a flash, and the knife the other had aimed at his back glanced from his helmet as he turned. The real Dhira Azrail snarled like a wild cat, but before he could strike again, El Borak's right fist met his jaw with a crushing impact. Flesh, and bone, and consciousness gave way together, and the executioner sagged senseless to the floor.

As Gordon sprang into the cell, the prisoners stumbled dazedly to their feet. Except Achmet, who, knowing that the scarred man was Dhira Azrail, had realized that the man in the mask must be El Borak-and had acted accordingly-they did not grasp the situation until Gordon threw his mask back.

"Can you all walk?" rapped Gordon. "Good! We'll have to pull out afoot. I couldn't arrange for horses."

Alafdal Khan looked at him dully.

"Why should I go?" he muttered. "Yesterday I had wealth and power. Now I am a penniless vagabond. If I leave

172

Rub el Harami, the ameer will cut off my head. It was an ill day I met you, El Borak! You made a tool of me for your intrigues."

"So I did, Alafdal Khan." Gordon faced him squarely. "But I would have made you emir in good truth. The dice have fallen against us, but our lives remain. And a bold man can rebuild his fortune. I promise you that if we escape, the ameer will pardon you and these men."

"His word is not wind," urged Achmet, "He has come to aid us, when he might have escaped alone. Take heart, my lord!"

Gordon was stripping the weapons from the senseless executioner. The man wore two German automatics, a tulwar, and a curved knife. Gordon gave a pistol to Brent, and one to Alafdal; Achmet received the tulwar, and Suleiman the knife, and Gordon gave his own knife to Hassan. The executioner's garments were given to Brent, who was practically naked. The oriental garments felt strange, but he was grateful for their warmth.

The brief struggle had not produced any noise likely to be overheard by the guard beyond the arched door. Gordon led his band down the corridor, between rows of empty cells, until they came to the rear door. There was no guard outside, as it was deemed too strong to be forced by anything short of artillery. It was of massive metal, fastened by a huge bar set in gigantic iron brackets bolted powerfully into the stone. It took all Gordon's strength to lift it out of the brackets and lean it against the wall, but then the door swung silently open, revealing the blackness of a narrow alley into which they filed.

Gordon pulled the door to behind them. How much leeway they had he did not know. The guard would eventually get suspicious when the supposed Dhira Azrail did not emerge, but he believed it would take them a good while to overcome their almost superstitious dread of the executioner enough to investigate. As for the real Dhira Azrail, he would not recover his senses for hours.

The prison was not far from the west wall. They met no one as they hurried through winding, ill-smelling alleys until they reached the wall at the place where a flight of narrow steps led up to the parapets. Men were patrolling the wall. They crouched in the shadows below the stair and heard the tread of two sentries who met on the firing ledge, exchange muffled greetings, and passed on. As the footsteps dwindled, they glided up the steps. Gordon had secured a rope from an unguarded camel stall. He made it fast by a loose loop to a merlon. One by one they slid swiftly down. Gordon was last, and he flipped the rope loose and coiled it. They might need it again.

They crouched an instant beneath the wall. A wind stole across the plain and stirred Brent's hair. They were free, armed, and outside the devil city. But they were afoot, and the passes were closed against them. Without a word they filed after Gordon across the shadowed plain.

At a safe distance their leader halted, and the men grouped around him, a vague cluster in the starlight.

"All the roads that lead from Rub el Harami are barred against us," he said abruptly. "They've filled the passes with soldiers. We'll have to make our way through the mountains the best way we can. And the only direction in which we can hope to eventually find safety is the east."

"The Great Range bars our path to the east," muttered Alafdal Khan. "Only through the Pass of Nadir Khan may we cross it."

"There is another way," answered Gordon. "It is a pass which lies far to the north of Nadir Khan. There isn't any road leading to it, and it hasn't been used for many generations. But it has a name-the Afridis call it the Pass of Swords and I've seen it from the east. I've never been west of it before, but maybe I can lead you to it. It lies many days" march from here, through wild mountains which none of us has ever traversed. But it's our only chance. We must have horses and food. Do any of you know where horses can be procured outside the city?"

"Yonder on the north side of the plain," said Achmet, "where a gorge opens from the hills, there dwells a peasant who owns seven horses-wretched, flea-bitten beasts they are, though."

"They must suffice. Lead us to them."

The going was not easy, for the plain was littered with rocks and cut with shallow gullies. All except Gordon were stiff and sore from their beatings, and Hassan's broken arm was a knifing agony to him. It was after more than an hour and a half of tortuous travel that the low mud-and-rock pen loomed before them and they heard the beasts stamping and snorting within it, alarmed by the sounds of their approach. The cluster of buildings squatted in the widening mouth of a shallow canyon, with a shadowy background of bare hills.

Gordon went ahead of the rest, and when the peasant came yawning out of his hut, looking for the wolves he thought were frightening his property, he never saw the tigerish shadow behind him until Gordon's iron fingers shut off his wind. A threat hissed in his ear reduced him to quaking quiescence, though he ventured a wail of protest as he saw other shadowy figures saddling and leading out his beasts.

"Sahibs, I am a poor man! These beasts are not fit for great lords to ride, but they are all of my property! Allah be my witness!"

"Break his head," advised Hassan, whom pain made bloodthirsty.

But Gordon stilled their captive's weeping with a handful of gold which represented at least three times the value of his whole herd. Dazzled by this rich reward, the peasant ceased his complaints, cursed his whimpering wives and children into silence, and at Gordon's order brought forth all the food that was in his hut-leathery loaves of bread, jerked mutton, salt, and eggs. It was little enough with which to start a hard journey. Feed for the horses was slung in a bag behind each saddle, and loaded on the spare horse.

While the beasts were being saddled, Gordon, by the light of a torch held inside a shed by a disheveled woman, whittled splints, tore up a shirt for bandages, and set Hassan's arm-a sickening task, because of the swollen condition of the member. It left Hassan green-faced and gagging, yet he was able to mount with the others.

In the darkness of the small hours they rode up the pathless gorge which led into the trackless hills. Hassan was insistent on cutting the throats of the entire peasant family, but Gordon vetoed this.

"Yes, I know he'll head for the city to betray us, as soon as we, get out of sight. But he'll have to go on foot, and we'll lose ourselves in the hills before he gets there."

"There are men trained like bloodhounds in Rub el Harami," said Achmet. "They can track a wolf over bare rock."

Sunrise found them high up in the hills, out of sight of the plain, picking their way up treacherous shale-littered slopes, following dry watercourses, always careful to keep below the sky line as much as possible. Brent was already confused. They seemed lost in a labyrinth of bare hills, in which he was able to recognize general directions only by glimpses of the snow-capped peaks of the Great Range ahead.

As they rode, he studied their leader. There was nothing in Gordon's manner by which he could recognize Shirkuh the Kurd. Gone was the Kurdish accent, the boyish, reckless merry-mad swagger, the peacock vanity of dress, even the wide-legged horseman's stride. The real Gordon was almost the direct antithesis of the role he had assumed. In place of the strutting, gaudily clad, braggart youth, there was a direct, hard-eyed man, who wasted no words and about whom there was no trace of egotism or braggadocio. There was nothing of the Oriental about his countenance now, and Brent knew that the mustache alone had not accounted for the perfection of his disguise. That disguise had not depended on any mechanical device; it had been a perfection of mimicry. By no artificial means, but by completely entering into the spirit of the role he had assumed, Gordon had altered the expression of his face, his bearing, his whole personality. He had so marvelously portrayed a personality so utterly different from his own, that it seemed impossible that the two were one. Only the eyes were unchanged--the gleaming, untamed black eyes, reflecting a barbarism of vitality and character.

But if not garrulous, Gordon did not prove taciturn, when Brent began to ask questions.

"I was on another trail when I left Kabul," he said. "No need to take up your time with that now. I knew the Black Tigers had a new emir, but didn't know it was Jakrovitch, of course. I'd never bothered to investigate the Black Tigers; didn't consider them important. I left Kabul alone and picked up half a dozen Afridi friends on the way. I became a Kurd after I was well on my road. That's why you lost my trail. None knew me except my Afridis.

"But before I completed my mission, word came through the hills that a Feringi with an escort of Kabuli was looking for me. News travels fast and far through the tribes. I rode back looking for you, and finally sighted you, as a prisoner. I didn't know who'd captured you, but I saw there were too many for us to fight, so I went down to parley. As soon as I saw Muhammad ez Zahir, I guessed who they were, and told them that lie about being lost in the hills and wanting to get to Rub el Harami. I signaled my men-you saw them. They were the men who fired on us as we were coming into the valley where the well was."

"But you shot one of them!"

"I shot over their heads. Just as they purposely missed us. My shots-one, pause, and then three in succession-were a signal that I was going on with the troop, and for them to return to our rendezvous on Kalat el Jehungir and wait for

179

me. When one fell forward on his horse, it was a signal that they understood. We have an elaborate code of signals, of all kinds.

"I intended trying to get you away that night, but when you gave me Stockton's message, it changed the situation. If the new emir was Jakrovitch, I knew what it meant. Imagine India under the rule of a swine like Jakrovitch!

"I knew that Jakrovitch was after the gold in Shaitan's Cave. It couldn't be anything else. Oh, yes, I knew the custom of offering gold each year to the Devil. Stockton and I had discussed the peril to the peace of Asia if a white adventurer ever got his hands on it.

"So I knew I'd have to go to Rub el Harami. I didn't dare tell you who I was-too many men spying around all the time. When we got to the city, Fate put Alafdal Khan in my hands. A true Moslem emir is no peril to the Indian Empire. A real Oriental wouldn't touch Shaitan's gold to save his life. I meant to make Alafdal emir. I had to tell him who I was before he'd believe I had a chance of doing it.

"I didn't premeditatedly precipitate that riot in the suk. I simply took advantage of it. I wanted to get you safely out of Jakrovitch's hands before I started anything, so I persuaded Alafdal Kahn that we needed you in our plot, and he put up the money to buy you. Then during the auction Jakrovitch lost his head and played into my hands. Everything would have worked out perfectly, if it hadn't been for Ali Shah and his man, that Shinwari! It was inevitable that somebody would recognize me sooner or later, but I hoped to destroy Jakrovitch, set Alafdal solidly in power, and have an avenue of escape open for you and me before that happened."

"At least Jakrovitch is dead," said Brent.

"We didn't fail there," agreed Gordon. "Ali Shah is no menace to the world. He won't touch the gold. The organization Jakrovitch built up will fall apart, leaving only the comparatively harmless core of the Black Tigers as it was before his coming. We've drawn their fangs, as far as the safety of India is concerned. All that's at stake now are our own lives-but I'll admit I'm selfish enough to want to preserve them."

Chapter VIII

BRENT BEAT His numbed hands together for warmth. For days they had been struggling through the trackless hills. The lean horses stumbled against the blast that roared between intervals of breathless sun blaze. The riders clung to the saddles when they could, or stumbled on afoot, leading their mounts, continually gnawed by hunger. At night they huddled together for warmth, men and beasts, in the lee of some rock or cliff, only occasionally finding wood enough to build a tiny fire.

Gordon's endurance was amazing. It was he who led the way, finding water, erasing their too obvious tracks, caring for the mounts when the others were too exhausted to move. He gave his cloak and robe to the ragged Waziris, himself seeming impervious to the chill winds as to the blazing sun.

The pack horse died. There was little food left for the horses, less for the men. They had left the hills now and were in the higher reaches, with the peaks of the Great Range looming through the mists ahead of them. Life became a pain-tinged dream to Brent in which one scene stood out vividly. They sat their gaunt horses at the head of a long valley and saw, far back, white dots moving in the morning mists.

"They have found our trail," muttered Alafdal Khan. "They will not quit it while we live. They have good horses and plenty of food."

And thereafter from time to time they glimpsed, far away and below and behind them, those sinister moving dots, that slowly, slowly cut down the long lead. Gordon ceased his attempts to hide their trail, and they headed straight for the backbone of the range which rose like a rampart before them-scarecrow men on phantom horses, following a grim-faced chief.

On a midday when the sky was as clear as chilled steel, they struggled over a lofty mountain shoulder and sighted a notch that broke the chain of snow-clad summits, and beyond it, the pinnacle of a lesser, more distant peak.

"The Pass of Swords," said Gordon. "The peak beyond it is Kalat el Jehungir, where my men are waiting for me. There will be a man sweeping the surrounding country all the time with powerful field glasses. I don't know whether they can see smoke this far or not, but I'm going to send up a signal for them to meet us at the pass."

Achmet climbed the mountainside with him. The others were too weak for the attempt. High up on the giddy slope they found enough green wood to make a fire that smoked. Presently, manipulated with ragged cloak, balls of thick black smoke rolled upward against the blue. It was the old Indian technique of Gordon's native plains, and Brent knew it was a thousand-to-one shot. Yet hillmen had eyes like hawks.

They descended the shoulder and lost sight of the pass. Then they started climbing once more, over slopes and crags and along the rims of gigantic precipices. It was on one of those ledges that Suleiman's horse stumbled and screamed and went over the edge, to smash to a pulp with its rider a thousand feet below, while the others stared helplessly.

It was at the foot of the long canyon that pitched upward toward the pass that the starving horses reached the limit of their endurance. The fugitives killed one and haggled off chunks of gristly flesh with their knives. They scorched the meat over a tiny fire, scarcely tasting it as they bolted it. Bodies and nerves were numb for rest and sleep. Brent clung to one thought-if the Afridis had seen the signal, they would be waiting at the pass, with fresh horses. On fresh horses they could escape, for the mounts of their pursuers must be nearly exhausted, too.

On foot they struggled up the steep canyon. Night fell while they struggled, but they did not halt. All through the night they drove their agonized bodies on, and at dawn they emerged from the mouth of the canyon to a broad slope that tilted up to the gap of clear sky cut in the mountain wall. It was empty. The Afridis were not there. Behind them white dots were moving inexorably up the canyon.

"We'll make our last stand at the mouth of the pass," said Gordon.

His eyes swept his phantom crew with a strange remorse. They looked like dead men. They reeled on their feet, their heads swimming with exhaustion and dizziness.

"Sorry about it all," he said. "Sorry, Brent."

"Stockton was my friend," said Brent, and then could have cursed himself, had he had the strength. It sounded so trite, so melodramatic.

"Alafdal, I'm sorry," said Gordon. "Sorry for all you men."

Alafdal lifted his head like a lion throwing back his mane.

184

"Nay, el Borak! You made a king of me. I was but a glutton and a sot, dreaming dreams I was too timid and too lazy to attempt. You gave me a moment of glory. It is worth all the rest of my life."

Painfully they struggled up to the head of the pass. Brent crawled the last few yards, till Gordon lifted him to his feet. There in the mouth of the great corridor that ran between echoing cliffs, their hair blowing in the icy wind, they looked back the way they had come and saw their pursuers, dots no longer, but men on horses. There was a group of them within a mile, a larger cluster far back down the canyon. The toughest and best-mounted riders had drawn away from the others.

The fugitives lay behind boulders in the mouth of the pass. They had three pistols, a saber, a tulwar, and a knife between them. The riders had seen their quarry turn at bay; their rifles glinted in the early-morning light as they flogged their reeling horses up the slope. Brent recognized Ali Shah himself, his arm in a sling; Muhammad ez Zahir; the black-bearded Yusufzai captain. A group of grim warriors were at their heels. All were gaunt-faced from the long grind. They came on recklessly, firing as they came. Yet the men at bay drew first blood.

Alafdal Khan, a poor shot and knowing it, had exchanged his pistol for Achmet's tulwar. Now Achmet sighted and fired and knocked a rider out of his saddle almost at the limit of pistol range. In his exultation he yelled and incautiously lifted his head above the boulder. A volley of rifle fire spattered the rock with splashes of hot lead, and one bullet hit Achmet between the eyes. Alafdal snatched the pistol as it fell and began firing. His eyes were bloodshot, his aim wild. But a horse fell, pinning its rider.

Above the crackling of the Luger came the doom-like crash of Gordon's Colt. Only the toss of his horse's head saved Ali Shah. The horse caught the bullet meant for him, and Ali Shah sprang clear as it fell, rolling to cover. The others abandoned their horses and followed suit. They came wriggling up the slope, firing as they came, keeping to cover.

Brent realized that he was firing the other German pistol only when he heard a man scream and saw him fall across a boulder. Vaguely, then, he realized that he had killed another man. Alafdal Khan had emptied his pistol without doing much harm. Brent fired and missed, scored a hit, and missed again. His hand shook with weakness, and his eyes played him tricks. But Gordon was not missing. It seemed to Brent that every time the Colt crashed a man screamed and fell. The slope was littered with white-clad figures. They had not worn their black armor on that chase.

Perhaps the madness of the high places had entered Ali Shah's brain on that long pursuit. At any rate he would not wait for the rest of his men, plodding far behind him. Like a madman he drove his warriors to the assault. They came on, firing and dying in the teeth of Gordon's bullets till the slope was a shambles. But the survivors came grimly on, nearer and nearer, and then suddenly they had broken cover and were charging like a gust of hill wind.

Gordon missed Ali Shah with his last bullet and killed the man behind him, and then like ghosts rising from the ground on Judgment Day the fugitives rose and grappled with their pursuers.

Brent fired his last shot full into the face of a savage who rushed at him, clubbing a rifle. Death halted the man's charge, but the rifle stock fell, numbing Brent's shoulder and hurling him to the ground, and there, as he writhed vainly, he saw the brief madness of the fight that raged about him.

He saw the crippled Hassan, snarling like a wounded wolf, beaten down by a Ghilzai who stood with one foot on his neck and repeatedly drove a broken lance through his body. Squirming under the merciless heel, Hassan slashed blindly upward with El Borak's knife in his death agony, and the Ghilzai staggered drunkenly away, blood gushing from the great vein which had been severed behind his knee. He fell dying a few feet from his victim.

Brent saw Ali Shah shoot Alafdal Khan through the body as they came face to face, and Alafdal Khan, dying on his feet, split his enemy's head with one tremendous swing of his tulwar, so they fell together.

Brent saw Gordon cut down the black-bearded Yusufzai captain, and spring at Muhammad ez Zahir with a hate too primitive to accord his foe an honorable death. He parried Muhammad's tulwar and dashed his saber guard into the Afghan's face. Killing his man was not enough for his berserk rage; all his roused passion called for a dog's death for his enemy. And like a raging fury he battered the Afghan back and down with blows of the guard and hilt, refusing to honor him by striking with the blade, until Muhammad fell and lay with broken skull.

Gordon lurched about to face down the slope, the only man on his feet. He stood swaying on wide-braced feet among the dead, and shook the blood from his eyes. They were as red as flame burning on black water. He took a fresh grip on the bloody hilt of his saber, and glared at the horsemen spurring up the canyon-at bay at last, drunken with slaughter, and conscious only of the blind lust to slay and slay before he himself sank in the red welter of his last, grim fight.

Then hoofs rang loud on the rock behind him, and he wheeled, blades lifted-to check suddenly, a wild, bloodstained figure against the sunrise.

"El Borak!"

The pass was filled with shouting. Dimly Brent saw half a dozen horsemen sweep into view: He heard Gordon yell:

"Yar Ali Khan! You saw my signal after all! Give them a volley!"

The banging of their rifles filled the pass with thunder. Brent, twisting his head painfully, saw the demoralization of the Black Tigers. He saw men falling from their saddles, others spurring back down the canyon. Wearied from the long chase, disheartened by the fall of their emir, fearful of a trap, the tired men on tired horses fell back out of range.

Brent was aware of Gordon bending over him, heard him tell the tall Afridi he called Yar Ali Khan to see to the others; heard Yar Ali Khan say they were all dead. Then, as in a dream, Brent felt himself lifted into a saddle, with a man behind to hold him on. Wind blew his hair, and he realized they were galloping. The walls gave back the ring of the flying hoofs, and then they were through the pass, and galloping down the long slope beyond. He saw Gordon riding near him, on the steed of an Afridi who had mounted before a comrade. And before Brent fainted from sheer exhaustion, he heard Gordon say:

"Let them follow us now if they will; they'll never catch us on their worn-out nags, not in a thousand years!"

And Brent sank into the grateful oblivion of senselessness with his laughter ringing in his ears-the iron, elemental, indomitable laughter of El Borak.

THE END

THE DAUGHTER OF ERLIK KHAN

Chapter I

THE TALL ENGLISHMAN, Pembroke, was scratching lines on the earth with his hunting knife, talking in a jerky tone that indicated suppressed excitement: "I tell you, Ormond, that peak to the west is the one we were to look for. Here, I've marked a map in the dirt. This mark here represents our camp, and this one is the peak. We've marched north far enough. At this spot we should turn westward--"

"Shut up!" muttered Ormond. "Rub out that map. Here comes Gordon."

Pembroke obliterated the faint lines with a quick sweep of his open hand, and as he scrambled up he managed to shuffle his feet across the spot. He and Ormond were laughing and talking easily as the third man of the expedition came up.

Gordon was shorter then his companions, but his physique did not suffer by comparison with either the rangy Pembroke or the more closely knit Ormond. He was one of those rare individuals at once lithe and compact. His strength did not give the impression of being locked up within himself as is the case with so many strong men. He moved with a flowing ease that advertised power more subtly than does mere beefy bulk.

Though he was clad much like the two Englishmen except for an Arab headdress, he fitted into the scene as they did not. He, an American, seemed almost as much a part of these rugged uplands as the wild nomads which pasture their sheep along the slopes of the Hindu Kush. There was a certitude in his level gaze, and economy of motion in his movements, that reflected kinship with the wilderness.

"Pembroke and I were discussing that peak, Gordon," said Ormond, indicating the mountain under discussion, which reared a snow cap in the clear afternoon sky beyond a range of blue hills, hazy with distance. "We were wondering if it had a name."

"Everything in these hills has a name," Gordon answered. "Some of them don't appear on the maps, though. That peak is called Mount Erlik Khan. Less than a dozen white men have seen it."

"Never heard of it," was Pembroke's comment. "If we weren't in such a hurry to find poor old Reynolds, it might be fun having a closer look at it, what?"

"If getting your belly ripped open can be called fun," returned Gordon. "Erlik Khan's in Black Kirghiz country."

"Kirghiz? Heathens and devil worshipers? Sacred city of Yolgan and all that rot."

"No rot about the devil worship," Gordon returned. "We're almost on the borders of their country now. This is a sort of no man's land here, squabbled over by the Kirghiz and Moslem nomads from farther east. We've been lucky not to have met any of the former. They're an isolated branch off the main stalk which centers about Issik-kul, and they hate white men like poison.

"This is the closest point we approach their country. From now on, as we travel north, we'll be swinging away from it. In another week, at most, we ought to be in the territory of the Uzbek tribe who you think captured your friend."

"I hope the old boy is still alive." Pembroke sighed.

"When you engaged me as Peshawar I told you I feared it was a futile quest," said Gordon. "If that tribe did capture your friend, the chances are all against his being still alive. I'm just warning you, so you won't be too disappointed if we don't find him."

"We appreciate that, old man," returned Ormond. "We knew no one but you could get us there with our heads still on our bally shoulders."

"We're not there yet," remarked Gordon cryptically, shifting his rifle under his arm. "I saw hangel sign before we went into camp, and I'm going to see if I can bag one. I may not be back before dark."

"Going afoot?" inquired Pembroke.

"Yes; if I get one I'll bring back a haunch for supper."

And with no further comment Gordon strode off down the rolling slope, while the other men stared silently after him.

He seemed to melt rather than stride into the broad copse at the foot of the slope. The men turned, still unspeaking, and glanced at the servants going about their duties in the camp--four stolid Pathans and a slender Punjabi Moslem who was Gordon's personal servant.

The camp with its faded tents and tethered horses was the one spot of sentient life in a scene so vast and broodingly silent that it was almost daunting. To the south, stretched an unbroken rampart of hills climbing up to snowy peaks. Far to the north rose another more broken range.

Between those barriers lay a great expanse of rolling table-land, broken by solitary peaks and lesser hill ranges, and dotted thickly with copses of ash, birch, and larch. Now, in the beginning of the short summer, the slopes were covered with tall lush grass. But here no herds were watched by turbaned nomads and that giant peak far to the southwest seemed somehow aware of that fact. It brooded like a somber sentinel of the unknown.

"Come into my tent!"

Pembroke turned away quickly, motioning Ormond to follow. Neither of them noticed the burning intensity with which the Punjabi Ahmed stared after them. In the tent, the men sitting facing each other across a small folding table, Pembroke took pencil and paper and began tracing a duplicate of the map he had scratched in the dirt.

"Reynolds has served his purpose, and so has Gordon," he said. "It was a big risk bringing him, but he was the only man who could get us safely through Afghanistan. The weight that American carries with the Mohammedans is amazing. But it doesn't carry with the Kirghiz, and beyond this point we don't need him.

"That's the peak the Tajik described, right enough, and he gave it the same name Gordon called it. Using it as a guide, we can't miss Yolgan. We head due west, bearing a little to the north of Mount Erlik Khan. We don't need Gordon's guidance from now on, and we won't need him going back, because we're returning by the way of Kashmir, and we'll have a better safe-conduct even than he. Question now is, how are we going to get rid of him?"

"That's easy," snapped Ormond; he was the harder-framed, the more decisive, of the two. "We'll simply pick a quarrel with him and refuse to continue in his company. He'll tell us to go to the devil, take his confounded Punjabi, and head back for Kabul--or maybe some other wilderness. He spends most of his time wandering around countries that are taboo to most white men."

"Good enough!" approved Pembroke. "We don't want to fight him. He's too infernally quick with a gun. The

Afghans call him 'El Borak," the Swift. I had something of the sort in mind when I cooked up an excuse to halt here in the middle of the afternoon. I recognized that peak, you see. We'll let him think we're going on to the Uzbeks, alone, because, naturally, we don't want him to know we're going to Yolgan--"

"What's that?" snapped Ormond suddenly, his hand closing on his pistol butt.

In that instant, when his eyes narrowed and his nostrils expanded, he looked almost like another man, as if suspicion disclosed his true--and sinister--nature.

"Go on talking," he muttered. "Somebody's listening outside the tent."

Pembroke obeyed, and Ormond, noiselessly pushing back his camp chair, plunged suddenly out of the tent and fell on some one with a snarl of gratification. An instant later he reentered, dragging the Punjabi, Ahmed, with him. The slender Indian writhed vainly in the Englishman's iron grip.

"This rat was eavesdropping," Ormond snarled.

"Now he'll spill everything to Gordon and there'll be a fight, sure!" The prospect seemed to agitate Pembroke considerably. "What'll we do now? What are you going to do?"

Ormond laughed savagely. "I haven't come this far to risk getting a bullet in my guts and losing everything. I've killed men for less than this."

Pembroke cried out an involuntary protest as Ormond's hand dipped and the blue-gleaming gun came up. Ahmed screamed, and his cry was drowned in the roar of the shot.

"Now we'll have to kill Gordon!"

Pembroke wiped his brow with a hand that shook a trifle. Outside rose a sudden mutter of Pashto as the Pathan servants crowded toward the tent.

"He's played into our hands!" rapped Ormond, shoving the still smoking gun back into his holster. With his booted toe he stirred the motionless body at his feet as casually as if it had been that of a snake. "He's out on foot, with only a handful of cartridges. It's just as well this turned out as it did."

"What do you mean?" Pembroke's wits seemed momentarily muddled.

"We'll simply pack up and clear out. Let him try to follow us on foot, if he wants to. There are limits to the abilities of every man. Left in these mountains on foot, without food, blankets, or ammunition, I don't think any white man will ever see Francis Xavier Gordon alive again."

Chapter II

WHEN GORDON LEFT the camp he did not look behind him. Any thoughts of treachery on the part of his companions was furthest from his mind. He had no reason to suppose that they were anything except what they had represented themselves to be--white men taking a long chance to find a comrade the unmapped solitudes had swallowed up.

It was an hour or so after leaving the camp when, skirting the end of a grassy ridge, he sighted an antelope moving along the fringe of a thicket. The wind, such as there was, was blowing toward him, away from the animal. He began stalking it through the thicket, when a movement in the bushes behind him brought him around to the realization that he himself was being stalked.

He had a glimpse of a figure behind a clump of scrub, and then a bullet fanned his ear, and he fired at the flash and the puff of smoke. There was a thrashing among the foliage and then stillness. A moment later he was bending over a picturesquely clad form on the ground.

It was a lean, wiry man, young, with an ermine-edged khilat, a fur calpack, and silver-heeled boots. Sheathed knives were in his girdle, and a modern repeating rifle lay near his hand. He had been shot through the heart.

"Turkoman," muttered Gordon. "Bandit, from his looks, out on a lone scout. I wonder how far he's been trailing me."

He knew the presence of the man implied two things: somewhere in the vicinity there was a band of Turkomans;

and somewhere, probably close by, there was a horse. A nomad never walked far, even when stalking a victim. He glanced up at the rise which rolled up from the copse. It was logical to believe that the Moslem had sighted him from the crest of the low ridge, had tied his horse on the other side, and glided down into the thicket to waylay him while he stalked the antelope.

Gordon went up the slope warily, though he did not believe there were any other tribesmen within earshot--else the reports of the rifles would have brought them to the spot--and found the horse without trouble. It was a Turkish stallion with a red leather saddle with wide silver stirrups and a bridle heavy with goldwork. A scimitar hung from the saddle peak in an ornamented leather scabbard.

Swinging into the saddle, Gordon studied all quarters of the compass from the summit of the ridge. In the south a faint ribbon of smoke stood against the evening. His black eyes were keen as a hawk's; not many could have distinguished that filmy blue feather against the cerulean of the sky.

"Turkoman means bandits," he muttered. "Smoke means camp. They're trailing us, sure as fate."

Reining about, he headed for the camp. His hunt had carried him some miles east of the site, but he rode at a pace that ate up the distance. It was not yet twilight when he halted in the fringe of the larches and sat silently scanning the slope on which the camp had stood. It was bare. There was no sign of tents, men, or beasts.

His gaze sifted the surrounding ridges and clumps, but found nothing to rouse his alert suspicion. At last he walked his steed up the acclivity, carrying his rifle at the ready. He saw a smear of blood on the ground where he knew Pembroke's tent had stood, but there was no other sign of violence, and the grass was not trampled as it would have been by a charge of wild horsemen.

He read the evidence of a swift but orderly exodus. His companions had simply struck their tents, loaded the pack animals, and departed. But why? Sight of distant horsemen might have stampeded the white men, though neither had shown any sign of the white feather before; but certainly Ahmed would not have deserted his master and friend.

As he traced the course of the horses through the grass, his puzzlement increased; they had gone westward.

Their avowed destination lay beyond those mountains in the north. They knew that, as well as he. But there was no mistake about it. For some reason, shortly after he had left camp, as he read the signs, they had packed hurriedly and set off westward, toward the forbidden country identified by Mount Erlik.

Thinking that possibly they had a logical reason for shifting camp and had left him a note of some kind which he had failed to find, Gordon rode back to the camp site and began casting about it in an ever-widening circle, studying the ground. And presently he saw sure signs that a heavy body had been dragged through the grass.

Men and horses had almost obliterated the dim track, but for years Gordon's life had depended upon the keenness of his faculties. He remembered the smear of blood on the ground where Pembroke's tent had stood.

He followed the crushed grass down the south slope and into a thicket, and an instant later he was kneeling beside the body of a man. It was Ahmed, and at first glance Gordon thought he was dead. Then he saw that the Punjabi, though shot through the body and un-doubtedly dying, still had a faint spark of life in him.

He lifted the turbaned head and set his canteen to the blue lips. Ahmed groaned, and into his glazed eyes came intelligence and recognition.

"Who did this, Ahmed?" Gordon's voice grated with the suppression of his emotions.

"Ormond Sahib," gasped the Punjabi. "I listened outside their tent, because I feared they planned treachery to you. I never trusted them. So they shot me and have gone away, leaving you to die alone in the hills."

"But why?" Gordon was more mystified than ever.

"They go to Yolgan," panted Ahmed. "The Reynolds Sahib we sought never existed. He was a lie they created to hoodwink you."

"Why to Yolgan?" asked Gordon.

But Ahmed's eyes dilated with the imminence of death; in a racking convulsion he heaved up in Gordon's arms; then blood gushed from his lips and he died.

Gordon rose, mechanically dusting his hands. Immobile as the deserts he haunted, he was not prone to display his emotions. Now he merely went about heaping stones over the body to make a cairn that wolves and jackals could not tear into. Ahmed had been his companion on many a dim road; less servant than friend.

But when he had lifted the last stone, Gordon climbed into the saddle, and without a backward glance he rode westward. He was alone in a savage country, without food or proper equipage. Chance had given him a horse, and years of wandering on the raw edges of the world had given him experience and a greater familiarity with this unknown land than any other white man he knew. It was conceivable that he might live to win his way through to some civilized outpost.

But he did not even give that possibility a thought. Gordon's ideas of obligation, of debt and payment, were as direct and primitive as those of the barbarians among whom his lot had been cast for so many years. Ahmed had been his friend and had died in his service. Blood must pay for blood.

That was as certain in Gordon's mind as hunger is certain in the mind of a gray timber wolf. He did not know why the killers were going toward forbidden Yolgan, and he did not greatly care. His task was to follow them to hell if necessary and exact full payment for spilled blood. No other course suggested itself.

Darkness fell and the stars came out, but he did not slacken his pace. Even by starlight it was not hard to follow the trail of the caravan through the high grass. The Turkish horse proved a good one and fairly fresh. He felt certain of overtaking the laden pack ponies, in spite of their long start.

As the hours passed, however, he decided that the Englishmen were determined to push on all night. They evidently meant to put so much distance between them and himself that he could never catch them, following on foot as they thought him to be. But why were they so anxious to keep from him the truth of their destination?

A sudden thought made his face grim, and after that he pushed his mount a bit harder. His hand instinctively sought the hilt of the broad scimitar slung from the high-peaked horn.

His gaze sought the white cap of Mount Erlik, ghostly in the starlight, then swung to the point where he knew Yolgan lay. He had been there before, himself, had heard the deep roar of the long bronze trumpets that shaven-headed priests blow from the mountains at sunrise.

It was past midnight when he sighted fires near the willow-massed banks of a stream. At first glance he knew it was not the camp of the men he followed. The fires were too many. It was an ordu of the nomadic Kirghiz who roam the country between Mount Erlik Khan and the loose boundaries of the Mohammedan tribes. This camp lay full in the path of Yolgan and he wondered if the Englishmen had known enough to avoid it. These fierce people hated strangers. He himself, when he visited Yolgan, had accomplished the feat disguised as a native.

Gaining the stream above the camp he moved closer, in the shelter of the willows, until he could make out the dim shapes of sentries on horseback in the light of the small fires. And he saw something else--three white European tents inside the ring of round, gray felt kibitkas. He swore silently; if the Black Kirghiz had killed the white men, appropriating their belongings, it meant the end of his vengeance. He moved nearer.

It was a suspicious, slinking, wolf-like dog that betrayed him. Its frenzied clamor brought men swarming out of the felt tents, and a swarm of mounted sentinels raced toward the spot, stringing bows as they came.

Gordon had no wish to be filled with arrows as he ran. He spurred out of the willows and was among the horsemen before they were aware of him, slashing silently right and left with the Turkish scimitar. Blades swung around him, but the men were more confused than he. He felt his edge grate against steel and glance down to split a broad skull; then he was through the cordon and racing into deeper darkness while the demoralized pack howled behind him.

A familiar voice shouting above the clamor told him that Ormond, at least, was not dead. He glanced back to see a tall figure cross the firelight and recognized Pembroke's rangy frame. The fire gleamed on steel in his hands. That they were armed showed they were not prisoners, though this forbearance on the part of the fierce nomads was more than his store of Eastern lore could explain.

The pursuers did not follow him far; drawing in under the shadows of a thicket he heard them shouting gutturally to each other as they rode back to the tent. There would be no more sleep in that ordu that night. Men with naked steel in their hands would pace their horses about the encampment until dawn. It would be difficult to steal back for a long shot at his enemies. But now, before he slew them, he wished to learn what took them to Yolgan.

Absently his hand caressed the hawk-headed pommel of the Turkoman scimitar. Then he turned again eastward and rode back along the route he had come, as fast as he could push the wearying horse. It was not yet dawn when he came upon what he had hoped to find--a second camp, some ten miles west of the spot where Ahmed had been killed; dying fires reflected on one small tent and on the forms of men wrapped in cloaks on the ground.

He did not approach too near; when he could make out the lines of slowly moving shapes that were picketed horses and could see other shapes that were riders pacing about the camp, he drew back behind a thicketed ridge, dismounted and unsaddled his horse.

While it eagerly cropped the fresh grass, he sat cross-legged with his back to a tree trunk, his rifle across his knees, as motionless as an image and as imbued with the vast patience of the East as the eternal hills themselves.

Chapter III

DAWN WAS LITTLE more than a hint of grayness in the sky when the camp that Gordon watched was astir. Smoldering coals leaped up into flames again, and the scent of mutton stew filled the air. Wiry men in caps of Astrakhan fur and girdled caftans swaggered among the horse lines or squatted beside the cooking pots, questing after savory morsels with unwashed fingers. There were no women among them and scant luggage. The lightness with which they traveled could mean only one thing.

The sun was not yet up when they began saddling horses and belting on weapons. Gordon chose that moment to appear, riding leisurely down the ridge toward them.

A yell went up, and instantly a score of rifles covered him. The very boldness of his action stayed their fingers on the triggers. Gordon wasted no time, though he did not appear hurried. Their chief had already mounted, and Gordon reined up almost beside him. The Turkoman glared- -a hawk-nosed, evil-eyed ruffian with a henna-stained beard. Recognition grew like a red flame in his eyes, and, seeing this, his warriors made no move.

"Yusef Khan," said Gordon, "you Sunnite dog, have I found you at last?"

Yusef Khan plucked his red beard and snarled like a wolf. "Are you mad, El Borak?"

"It is El Borak!" rose an excited murmur from the warriors, and that gained Gordon another respite.

They crowded closer, their blood lust for the instant conquered by their curiosity. El Borak was a name known from Istanbul to Bhutan and repeated in a hundred wild tales wherever the wolves of the desert gathered.

As for Yusef Khan, he was puzzled, and furtively eyed the slope down which Gordon had ridden. He feared the white man's cunning almost as much as he hated him, and in his suspicion, hate and fear that he was in a trap, the

Turkoman was as dangerous and uncertain as a wounded cobra.

"What do you here?" he demanded. "Speak quickly, before my warriors strip the skin from you a little at a time."

"I came following an old feud." Gordon had come down the ridge with no set plan, but he was not surprised to find a personal enemy leading the Turkomans. It was no unusual coincidence. Gordon had blood-foes scattered all over Central Asia.

"You are a fool--"

In the midst of the chief's sentence Gordon leaned from his saddle and struck Yusef Khan across the face with his open hand. The blow cracked like a bull whip and Yusef reeled, almost losing his seat. He howled like a wolf and clawed at his girdle, so muddled with fury that he hesitated between knife and pistol. Gordon could have shot him down while he fumbled, but that was not the American's plan.

"Keep off!" he warned the warriors, yet not reaching for a weapon. "I have no quarrel with you. This concerns only your chief and me."

With another man that would have had no effect; but another man would have been dead already. Even the wildest tribesman had a vague feeling that the rules governing action against ordinary feringhi did not apply to El Borak.

"Take him!" howled Yusef Khan. "He shall be flayed alive!"

They moved forward at that, and Gordon laughed unpleasantly.

"Torture will not wipe out the shame I have put upon your chief," he taunted. "Men will say ye are led by a khan who bears the mark of El Borak's hand in his beard. How is such shame to be wiped out? Lo, he calls on his warriors to avenge him! Is Yusef Khan a coward?"

They hesitated again and looked at their chief whose beard was clotted with foam. They all knew that to wipe out such an insult the aggressor must be slain by the victim in single combat. In that wolf pack even a suspicion of cowardice was tantamount to a death sentence.

If Yusef Khan failed to accept Gordon's challenge, his men might obey him and torture the American to death at his pleasure, but they would not forget, and from that moment he was doomed.

Yusef Khan knew this; knew that Gordon had tricked him into a personal duel, but he was too drunk with fury to care. His eyes were red as those of a rabid wolf, and he had forgotten his suspicions that Gordon had riflemen hidden up on the ridge. He had forgotten everything except his frenzied passion to wipe out forever the glitter in those savage black eyes that mocked him.

"Dog!" he screamed, ripping out his broad scimitar. "Die at the hands of a chief!"

He came like a typhoon, his cloak whipping out in the wind behind him, his scimitar flaming above his head. Gordon met him in the center of the space the warriors left suddenly clear.

Yusef Khan rode a magnificent horse as if it were part of him, and it was fresh. But Gordon's mount had rested, and it was well-trained in the game of war. Both horses responded instantly to the will of their riders.

The fighters revolved about each other in swift curvets and gambados, their blades flashing and grating without the slightest pause, turned red by the rising sun. It was less like two men fighting on horseback than like a pair of centaurs, half man and half beast, striking for one another's life.

"Dog!" panted Yusef Khan, hacking and hewing like a man possessed of devils. "I'll nail your head to my tent pole--ahhhh!"

Not a dozen of the hundred men watching saw the stroke, except as a dazzling flash of steel before their eyes, but all heard its crunching impact. Yusef Khan's charger screamed and reared, throwing a dead man from the saddle with a split skull.

A wordless wolfish yell that was neither anger nor applause went up, and Gordon wheeled, whirling his scimitar about his head so that the red drops flew in a shower.

"Yusef Khan is dead!" he roared. "Is there one to take up his quarrel?"

They gaped at him, not sure of his intention, and before they could recover from the surprise of seeing their invincible chief fall, Gordon thrust his scimitar back in its sheath with a certain air of finality and said:

"And now who will follow me to plunder greater than any of ye ever dreamed?"

That struck an instant spark, but their eagerness was qualified by suspicion.

"Show us!" demanded one. "Show us the plunder before we slay thee."

Without answering, Gordon swung off his horse and cast the reins to a mustached rider to hold, who was so astonished that he accepted the indignity without protest. Gordon strode over to a cooking pot, squatted beside it and began to eat ravenously. He had not tasted food in many hours.

"Shall I show you the stars by daylight?" he demanded, scooping out handfuls of stewed mutton, "Yet the stars are there, and men see them in the proper time. If I had the loot would I come asking you to share it? Neither of us can win it without the other's aid."

"He lies," said one whom his comrades addressed as Uzun Beg. "Let us slay him and continue to follow the caravan we have been tracking."

"Who will lead you?" asked Gordon pointedly.

They scowled at him, and various ruffians who considered themselves logical candidates glanced furtively at one another. Then all looked back at Gordon, unconcernedly wolfing down mutton stew five minutes after having slain the most dangerous swordsman of the black tents.

His attitude of indifference deceived nobody. They knew he was dangerous as a cobra that could strike like lightning in any direction. They knew they could not kill him so quickly that he would not kill some of them, and naturally none wanted to be first to die.

That alone would not have stopped them. But that was combined with curiosity, avarice roused by his mention of plunder, vague suspicion that he would not have put himself in a trap unless he held some sort of a winning hand, and jealousy of the leaders of each other.

Uzun Beg, who had been examining Gordon's mount, exclaimed angrily: "He rides Ali Khan's steed!"

"Aye," Gordon assented tranquilly. "Moreover this is Ali Khan's sword. He fired at me from ambush, so he lies dead."

There was no answer. There was no feeling in that wolf pack except fear and hate, and respect for courage, craft, and ferocity.

211

"Where would you lead us?" demanded one named Orkhan Shan, tacitly recognizing Gordon's dominance. "We be all free men and sons of the sword."

"Ye be all sons of dogs," answered Gordon. "Men without grazing lands or wives, outcasts, denied by thine own people--outlaws whose lives are forfeit, and who must roam in the naked mountains. You followed that dead dog without question. Now ye demand this and that of me!"

Then ensued a medley of argument among themselves, in which Gordon seemed to take no interest. All his attention was devoted to the cooking pot. His attitude was no pose; without swagger or conceit the man was so sure of himself that his bearing was no more self-conscious among a hundred cutthroats hovering on the hair line of murder than it would have been among friends.

Many eyes sought the gun butt at his hip. Men said his skill with the weapon was sorcery; an ordinary revolver became in his hand a living engine of destruction that was drawn and roaring death before a man could realize that Gordon's hand had moved.

"Men say thou hast never broken thy word," suggested Orkhan. "Swear to lead us to this plunder, and it may be we shall see."

"I swear no oaths," answered Gordon, rising and wiping his hands on a saddle cloth. "I have spoken. It is enough. Follow me, and many of you will die. Aye, the jackals will feed full. You will go up to the paradise of the prophet and your brothers will forget your names. But to those that live, wealth like the rain of Allah will fall upon them."

"Enough of words!" exclaimed one greedily. "Lead us to this rare loot."

"You dare not follow where I would lead," he answered. "It lies in the land of the Kara Kirghiz."

"We dare, by Allah!" they barked angrily. "We are already in the land of the Black Kirghiz, and we follow the caravan of some infidels, whom, inshallah, we shall send to hell before another sunrise."

"Bismillah," said Gordon. "Many of you shall eat arrows and edged steel before our quest is over. But if you dare stake your lives against plunder richer than the treasures of Hind, come with me. We have far to ride."

A few minutes later the whole band was trotting westward. Gordon led, with lean riders on either hand; their attitude suggested that he was more prisoner then guide, but he was not perturbed. His confidence in his destiny had again been justified, and the fact that he had not the slightest idea of how to redeem his pledge concerning treasure disturbed him not at all. A way would be opened to him, somehow, and at present he did not even bother to consider it.

Chapter IV

THE FACT THAT Gordon knew the country better than the Turkomans did aided him in his subtle policy to gain ascendency over them. From giving suggestions to giving orders and being obeyed is a short step, when delicately taken.

He took care that they kept below the sky lines as much as possible. It was not easy to hide the progress of a hundred men from the alert nomads; but these roamed far and there was a chance that only the band he had seen were between him and Yolgan.

But Gordon doubted this when they crossed a track that had been made since he rode eastward the night before. Many riders had passed that point, and Gordon urged greater speed, knowing that if they were spied by the Kirghiz instant pursuit was inevitable.

In the late afternoon they came in sight of the ordu beside the willow-lined stream. Horses tended by youngsters grazed near the camp, and farther away the riders watched the sheep which browsed through the tall grass.

Gordon had left all his men except half a dozen in a thicket-massed hollow behind the next ridge, and he now lay among a cluster of boulders on a slope overlooking the valley. The encampment was beneath him, distinct in every detail, and he frowned. There was no sign of the white tents.

The Englishmen had been there. They were not there now. Had their hosts turned on them at last, or had they continued alone toward Yolgan?

The Turkomans, who did not doubt that they were to attack and loot their hereditary enemies, began to grow impatient.

"Their fighting men are less than ours," suggested Uzun Beg, "and they are scattered, suspecting nothing. It is long since an enemy invaded the land of the Black Kirghiz. Send back for the others, and let us attack. You promised us plunder."

"Flat-faced women and fat-tailed sheep?" Gordon jeered.

"Some of the women are fair to look at," the Turkoman maintained. "And we could feast full on the sheep. But these dogs carry gold in their wagons to trade to merchants from Kashmir. It comes from Mount Erlik Khan."

Gordon remembered that he had heard tales of a gold mine in Mount Erlik before, and he had seen some crudely cast ingots the owners of which swore they had them from the Black Kirghiz. But gold did not interest him just then.

"That is a child's tale," he said, at least half believing what he said. "The plunder I will lead you to is real, would you throw it away for a dream? Go back to the others and bid them stay hidden. Presently I will return."

They were instantly suspicious, and he saw it.

"Return thou, Uzun Beg," he said, "and give the others my message. The rest of you come with me."

That quieted the hair-trigger suspicions of the five, but Uzun Beg grumbled in his beard as he strode back down the slope, mounted and rode eastward. Gordon and his companions likewise mounted behind the crest and, keeping below the sky line, they followed the ridge around as it slanted toward the southwest.

It ended in sheer cliffs, as if it had been sliced off with a knife, but dense thickets hid them from the sight of the camp as they crossed the space that lay between the cliffs and the next ridge, which ran to a bend in the stream, a mile below the ordu.

This ridge was considerably higher than the one they had left, and before they reached the point where it began to slope downward toward the river, Gordon crawled to the crest and scanned the camp again with a pair of binoculars that had once been the property of Yusef Khan.

The nomads showed no sign that they suspected the presence of enemies, and Gordon turned his glasses farther eastward, located the ridge beyond which his men were concealed, but saw no sign of them. But he did see something else.

Miles to the east a knife-edge ridge cut the sky, notched with a shallow pass. As he looked he saw a string of black dots moving through that notch. It was so far away that even the powerful glasses did not identify them, but he knew what the dots were--mounted men, many of them.

Hurrying back to his five Turkomans, he said nothing, but pressed on, and presently they emerged from behind the ridge and came upon the stream where it wound out of sight of the encampment. Here was the logical crossing for any road leading to Yolgan, and it was not long before he found what he sought.

In the mud at the edges of the stream were the prints of shod hoofs and at one spot the mark of a European boot. The Englishmen had crossed here; beyond the ford their trail lay west, across the rolling table-land.

Gordon was puzzled anew. He had supposed that there was some particular reason why this clan had received the Englishmen in peace. He had reasoned that Ormond would persuade them to escort him to Yolgan. Though the clans made common cause against invaders, there were feuds among themselves, and the fact that one tribe received a man in peace did not mean that another tribe would not cut his throat.

Gordon had never heard of the nomads of this region showing friendship to any white man. Yet the Englishmen had passed the night in that ordu and now plunged boldly on as if confident of their reception. It looked like utter madness.

As he meditated, a distant sputter of rifle fire jerked his head up. He splashed across the stream and raced up the slope that hid them from the valley, with the Turkomans at his heels working the levers of their rifles. As he topped the slope he saw the scene below him crystal-etched in the blue evening.

The Turkomans were attacking the Kirghiz camp. They had crept up the ridge overlooking the valley, and then swept down like a whirlwind. The surprise had been almost, but not quite, complete. Outriding shepherds had been shot down and the flocks scattered, but the surviving nomads had made a stand within the ring of their tents and wagons.

Ancient matchlocks, bows, and a few modern rifles answered the fire of the Turkomans. These came on swiftly, shooting from the saddle, only to wheel and swerve out of close range again.

The Kirghiz were protected by their cover, but even so the hail of lead took toll. A few saddles were emptied, but the Turkomans were hard hit on their prancing horses, as the riders swung their bodies from side to side.

Gordon gave his horse the rein and came galloping across the valley, his scimitar glittering in his hand. With his enemies gone from the camp, there was no reason for attacking the Kirghiz now as he had planned. But the distance was too great for shouted orders to be heard.

The Turkomans saw him coming, sword in hand, and mistook his meaning. They thought he meant to lead a charge, and in their zeal they anticipated him.

They were aided by the panic which struck the Kirghiz as they saw Gordon and his five Turkomans sweep down the slope and construed it as an attack in force on their flank.

Instantly they directed all their fire at the newcomers, emptying the clumsy matchlocks long before Gordon was even within good rifle range. And as they did, the Turkomans charged home with a yell that shook the valley, preceded by a withering fire as they blazed away over their horses' ears.

This time no ragged volleys could stop them. In their panic the tribesmen had loosed all their firearms at once, and the charge caught them with matchlocks and muskets empty. A straggling rifle fire met the oncoming raiders and knocked a few out of their saddles, and a flight of arrows accounted for a few more, but then the charge burst on the makeshift barricade and crumpled it. The howling Turkomans rode their horses in among the tents, flailing right and left with scimitars already crimson.

For an instant hell raged in the ordu, then the demoralized nomads broke and fled as best they could, being cut down and trampled by the conquerors. Neither women nor children were spared by the blood-mad Turks. Such as could slipped out of the ring and ran wailing for the river. An instant later the riders were after them like wolves.

219

Yet, winged by the fear of death, a disorderly mob reached the shore first, broke through the willows and plunged screaming over the low bank, trampling each other in the water. Before the Turkomans could rein their horses over the bank, Gordon arrived, with his horse plastered with sweat and snorting foam.

Enraged at the wanton slaughter, Gordon was an incarnation of berserk fury. He caught the first man's bridle and threw his horse back on its haunches with such violence that the beast lost its footing and fell, sprawling, throwing its rider. The next man sought to crowd past, giving tongue like a wolf, and him Gordon smote with the flat of his scimitar. Only the heavy fur cap saved the skull beneath, and the man pitched, senseless, from his saddle. The others yelled and reined back suddenly.

Gordon's wrath was like a dash of ice-cold water in their faces, shocking their blood-mad nerves into stinging sensibility. From among the tents cries still affronted the twilight, with the butcherlike chopping of merciless sword blows, but Gordon gave no heed. He could save no one in the plundered camp, where the howling warriors were ripping the tents to pieces, overturning the wagons and setting the torch in a hundred places.

More and more men with burning eyes and dripping blades were streaming toward the river, halting as they saw El Borak barring their way. There was not a ruffian there who looked half as formidable as Gordon did in that instant. His lips snarled and his eyes were black coals of hell's fire.

There was no play acting about it. His mask of immobility had fallen, revealing the sheer primordial ferocity of the soul beneath. The dazed Turkomans, still dizzy from the glutting of their blood lust, weary from striking great blows, and puzzled by his attitude, shrank back from him.

"Who gave the order to attack?" he yelled, and his voice was like the slash of a saber.

He trembled in the intensity of his passion. He was a blazing flame of fury and death, without control or repression. He was as wild and brute-savage in that moment as the wildest barbarian in that raw land.

"Uzun Beg!" cried a score of voices, and men pointed at the scowling warrior. "He said that you had stolen away to betray us to the Kirghiz, and that we should attack before they had time to come upon us and surround us. We believed him until we saw you riding over the slope."

With a wordless fierce yell like the scream of a striking panther, Gordon hurled his horse like a typhoon on Uzun Beg, smiting with his scimitar. Uzun Beg catapulted from his saddle with his skull crushed, dead before he actually realized that he was menaced.

El Borak wheeled on the others and they reined back from him, scrambling in terror.

"Dogs! Jackals! Noseless apes! Forgotten of God!" he lashed them with words that burned like scorpions. "Sons of nameless curs! Did I not bid you keep hidden? Is my word wind--a leaf to be blown away by the breath of a dog like Uzun Beg? Now you have lapped up needless blood, and the whole countryside will be riding us down like jackals. Where is your loot? Where is the gold with which the wagons were laden?"

"There was no gold," muttered a tribesman, mopping blood from a sword cut.

They flinched from the savage scorn and anger in Gordon's baying laughter.

"Dogs that nuzzle in the dung heaps of hell! I should leave you to die."

"Slay him!" mouthed a tribesman. "Shall we eat of an infidel? Slay him and let us go back whence we came. There is no loot in this naked land."

The proposal was not greeted with enthusiasm. Their rifles were all empty, some even discarded in the fury of sword strokes. They knew the rifle under El Borak's knee was loaded and the pistol at his hip. Nor did any of them care to ride into the teeth of that reddened scimitar that swung like a live thing in his right hand.

Gordon saw their indecision and mocked them. He did not argue or reason as another man might have done. And if he had, they would have killed him. He beat down opposition with curses, abuses, and threats that were convincing because he meant every word he spat at them. They submitted because they were a wolf pack, and he was the grimmest wolf of them all.

Not one man in a thousand could have bearded them as he did and lived. But there was a driving elemental power about him that shook resolution and daunted anger--something of the fury of an unleashed torrent or a roaring wind that hammered down will power by sheer ferocity.

"We will have no more of thee," the boldest voiced the last spark of rebellion. "Go thy ways, and we will go ours."

Gordon barked a bitter laugh. "Thy ways lead to the fires of Jehannum!" he taunted bitterly. "Ye have spilled blood, and blood will be demanded in payment. Do you dream that those who have escaped will not flee to the nearest tribes and raise the countryside? You will have a thousand riders about your ears before dawn."

"Let us ride eastward," one said nervously. "We will be out of this land of devils before the alarm is raised."

Again Gordon laughed and men shivered. "Fools! You cannot return. With the glasses I have seen a body of horsemen following our trail. Ye are caught in the fangs of the vise. Without me you cannot go onward; if you stand still or go back, none of you will see another sun set."

Panic followed instantly which was more difficult to fight down than rebellion.

"Slay him!" howled one. "He has led us into a trap!"

"Fools!" cried Orkhan Shah, who was one of the five Gordon had led to the ford. "It was not he who tricked you into charging the Kirghiz. He would have led us on to the loot he promised. He knows this land and we do not. If ye slay him now, ye slay the only man who may save us!"

That spark caught instantly, and they clamored about Gordon.

"The wisdom of the sahibs is thine! We be dogs who eat dirt! Save us from our folly! Lo, we obey thee! Lead us out of this land of death, and show us the gold whereof thou spokest!"

Gordon sheathed his scimitar and took command without comment. He gave orders and they were obeyed. Once these wild men, in their fear, turned to him, they trusted him implicitly. They knew he was somehow using them ruthlessly in his own plans, but that was nothing more than any one of them would have done had he been able. In that wild land only the ways of the wolf pack prevailed.

As many Kirghiz horses as could be quickly caught were rounded up. On some of them food and articles of clothing from the looted camp were hastily tied. Half a dozen Turkomans had been killed, nearly a dozen wounded. The dead were left where they had fallen. The most badly wounded were tied to their saddles, and their groans made the night hideous. Darkness had fallen as the desperate band rode over the slope and plunged across the river. The wailing of the Kirghiz women, hidden in the thickets, was like the dirging of lost souls.

Chapter V

GORDON DID NOT attempt to follow the trail of the Englishman over the comparatively level table-land. Yolgan was his destination and he believed he would find them there, but there was desperate need to escape the tribesmen who he was certain were following them, and who would be lashed to fiercer determination by what they would find in the camp by the river.

Instead of heading straight across the table-land, Gordon swung into the hills that bordered it on the south and began following them westward. Before midnight one of the wounded men died in his saddle, and some of the others were semidelirious. They hid the body in a crevice and went on. They moved through the darkness of the hills like ghosts; the only sounds were the clink of hoofs on stone and the groans of the wounded.

An hour before dawn they came to a stream which wound between limestone ledges, a broad shallow stream with a solid rock bottom. They waded their horses along it for three miles, then climbed out again on the same side.

Gordon knew that the Kirghiz, smelling out their trail like wolves, would follow them to the bank and expect some such ruse as an effort to hide their tracks. But he hoped that the nomads would be expecting them to cross the stream and plunge into the mountains on the other side and would therefore waste time looking for tracks along the south bank.

He now headed westward in a more direct route. He did not expect to throw the Kirghiz entirely off the scent. He was only playing for time. If they lost his trail, they would search in any direction first except toward Yolgan, and to Yolgan he must go, since there was now no chance of catching his enemies on the road.

Dawn found them in the hills, a haggard, weary band. Gordon bade them halt and rest and, while they did so, he climbed the highest crag he could find and patiently scanned the surrounding cliffs and ravines with his binoculars, while he chewed tough strips of dried mutton which the tribesmen carried between saddle and saddlecloth to keep warm and soft. He alternated with cat naps of ten or fifteen minutes' duration, storing up concentrated energy as men of the outlands learn to do, and between times watching the ridges for signs of pursuit.

He let the men rest as long as he dared, and the sun was high when he descended the rock and stirred them into wakefulness. Their steel-spring bodies had recovered some of their resilience, and they rose and saddled with alacrity, all except one of the wounded men, who had died in his sleep. They lowered his body into a deep fissure in the rocks and went on, more slowly, for the horses felt the grind more than the men.

All day they threaded their way through wild gorges overhung by gloomy crags. The Turkomans were crowded by the grim desolation and the knowledge that a horde of bloodthirsty barbarians were on their trail. They followed Gordon without question as he led them, turning and twisting, along dizzy heights and down into the abysmal gloom of savage gorges, then up turreted ridges again and around windswept shoulders.

He had used every artifice known to him to shake off pursuit and was making for his set goal as fast as possible. He did not fear encountering any clans in these bare hills; they grazed their flocks on the lower levels. But he was as familiar with the route he was following as his men thought.

He was feeling his way, mostly by the instinct for direction that men who live in the open possess, but he would have been lost a dozen times but for glimpses of Mount Erlik Khan shouldering up above the surrounding hills in the distance.

As they progressed westward he recognized other landmarks, seen from new angles, and just before sunset he glimpsed a broad shallow valley, across the pine-grown slopes of which he saw the walls of Yolgan looming against the crags behind it.

Yolgan was built at the foot of a mountain, overlooking the valley through which a stream wandered among masses of reeds and willows. Timber was unusually dense. Rugged mountains, dominated by Erlik's peak to the south, swept around the valley to the south and west, and in the north it was blocked by a chain of hills. To the east it was open, sloping down from a succession of uneven ridges. Gordon and his men had followed the ranges in their flight, and now they looked down on the valley from the south.

El Borak led the warriors down from the higher crags and hid them on one of the many gorges debouching on the lower slopes, not more than a mile and a half from the city itself. It ended in a cul-de-sac and suggested a trap, but the horses were ready to fall from exhaustion, the men's canteens were empty, and a spring gurgling out of the solid rock decided Gordon.

He found a ravine leading out of the gorge and placed men on guard there, as well as at the gorge mouth. It would serve as an avenue of escape if need be. The men gnawed the scraps of food that remained, and dressed their wounds as best they could. When he told them he was going on a solitary scout they looked at him with lack-luster eyes, in the grip of the fatalism that is the heritage of the Turkish races.

They did not mistrust him, but they felt like dead men already. They looked like ghouls, with their dusty, torn garments, clotted with dried blood, and sunken eyes of hunger and weariness. They squatted or lay about, wrapped in their tattered cloaks, unspeaking.

Gordon was more optimistic than they. Perhaps they had not completely eluded the Kirghiz, but he believed it would take some time for even those human bloodhounds to ferret them out, and he did not fear discovery by the inhabitants of Yolgan. He knew they seldom wandered into the hills.

Gordon had neither slept nor eaten as much as his men, but his steely frame was more enduring than theirs, and he was animated by a terrific vitality that would keep his brain clear and his body vibrant long after another man had dropped in his tracks.

It was dark when Gordon strode on foot out of the gorge, the stars hanging over the peaks like points of chilled silver. He did not strike straight across the valley, but kept to the line of marching hills. So it was no great coincidence that he discovered the cave where men were hidden.

It was situated in a rocky shoulder that ran out into the valley, and which he skirted rather than clamber over. Tamarisk grew thickly about it, masking the mouth so effectually that it was only by chance that he glimpsed the reflection of a fire against a smooth inner wall.

Gordon crept through the thickets and peered in. It was a bigger cave than the mouth indicated. A small fire was going, and three men squatted by it, eating and conversing in guttural Pashto. Gordon recognized three of the camp servants of the Englishmen. Farther back in the cave he saw the horses and heaps of camp equipment. The mutter of conversation was unintelligible where he crouched, and even as he wondered where the white men and the fourth servant were, he heard someone approaching.

He drew back farther into the shadows and waited, and presently a tall figure loomed in the starlight. It was the other Pathan, his arms full of firewood.

As he strode toward the natural camp which led up the cave mouth, he passed so close to Gordon's hiding place that the American could have touched him with an extended arm. But he did not extend an arm; he sprang on the man's back like a panther on a buck.

The firewood was knocked in all directions and the two men rolled together down a short grassy slope, but Gordon's fingers were digging into the Pathan's bull throat, strangling his efforts to cry out, and the struggle made no noise that could have been heard inside the cave above the crackle of the tamarisk chunks.

The Pathan's superior height and weight were futile against the corded sinews and wrestling skills of his opponent. Heaving the man under him, Gordon crouched on his breast and throttled him dizzy before he relaxed his grasp and let life and intelligence flow back into his victim's dazed brain.

The Pathan recognized his captor and his fear was the greater, because he thought he was in the hands of a ghost. His eyes glimmered in the gloom and his teeth shone in the black tangle of his beard.

"Where are the Englishmen?" demanded Gordon softly. "Speak, you dog, before I break your neck!"

"They went at dusk toward the city of devils!" gasped the Pathan.

"Prisoners?"

"Nay; one with a shaven head guided them. They bore their weapons and were not afraid."

"What are they doing here?"

"By Allah, I do not know!"

"Tell me all you do know," commanded Gordori. "But speak softly. If your mates hear and come forth, you will suddenly cease to be. Begin where I went forth to shoot the stag. After that, Ormond killed Ahmed. That I know."

"Aye; it was the Englishman. I had naught to do with it. I saw Ahmed lurking outside Pembroke Sahib's tent. Presently Ormond Sahib came forth and dragged him in the tent. A gun spoke, and when we went to look, the Punjabi lay dead on the floor of the tent.

"Then the sahibs bade us strike the tents and load the pack horses, and we did so without question. We went westward in great haste. When the night was not yet half over, we sighted a camp of pagans, and my brothers and I were much afraid. But the sahibs went forward, and when the accursed ones came forth with arrows on string, Ormond Sahib held up a strange emblem which glowed in the light of the torches, whereupon the heathens dismounted and bowed to the earth.

"We abode in their camp that night. In the darkness someone came to the camp and there was fighting and a man slain, and Ormond Sahib said it was a spying Turkoman, and that there would be fighting, so at dawn we left the pagans and went westward in haste, across the ford. When we met other heathen, Ormond showed them the talisman, and they did us honor. All day we hastened, driving the beasts hard, and when night fell we did not halt, for Ormond Sahib was like one mad. So before the night was half gone, we came into this valley, and the sahibs hid us in this cave.

"Here we abode until a pagan passed near the cavern this morning, driving sheep. Then Ormond Sahib called to him and showed him the talisman and made it known that he wished speech with the priest of the city. So the man went, and presently he returned with the priest who could speak Kashmiri. He and the sahibs talked long together, but what they said I know not. But Ormond Sahib killed the man who had gone to fetch the priest, and he and the priest hid the body with stones.

"Then after more talk, the priest went away, and the sahibs abode in the cave all day. But at dusk another man came to them, a man with a shaven head and camel's hair robes, and they went with him toward the city. They bade us eat and then saddle and pack the animals, and be ready to move with great haste between midnight and dawn. That is all I know, as Allah is my witness."

Gordon made no reply. He believed the man was telling the truth, and his bewilderment grew. As he meditated on the tangle, he unconsciously relaxed his grip, and the Pathan chose that instant to make his break for freedom. With a convulsive heave he tore himself partly free of Gordon's grasp, whipped from his garments a knife he had been unable to reach before, and yelled loudly as he stabbed.

Gordon avoided the thrust by a quick twist of his body; the edge slit his shirt and the skin beneath, and stung by its bite and his peril, he caught the Pathan's bull neck in both hands and put all his strength into a savage wrench. The man's spinal column snapped like a rotten branch, and Gordon flung himself over backward into the thicker shadows as a man bulked black in the mouth of the cavern. The fellow called a cautious query, but Gordon waited for no more. He was already gone like a phantom into the gloom.

The Pathan repeated his call and then, getting no response, summoned his mates in some trepidation. With weapons in their hands they stole down the ramp, and presently one of them stumbled over the body of their companion. They bent over it, muttering affrightedly.

"This is a place of devils," said one. "The devils have slain Akbar."

"Nay," said another. "It is the people of this valley. They mean to slay us one by one." He grasped his rifle and stared fearsomely into the shadows that hemmed them in. "They have bewitched the sahibs and led them away to be slain," he muttered.

"We will be next," said the third. "The sahibs are dead. Let us load the animals and go away quickly. Better die in the hills than wait like sheep for our throats to be cut."

A few minutes later they were hurrying eastward through the pines as fast as they could urge the beasts.

Of this Gordon knew nothing. When he left the slope below the cave he did not follow the trend of the hills as before, but headed straight through the pines toward the lights of Yolgan. He had not gone far when he struck a road from the east leading toward the city. It wound among the pines, a slightly less dark thread in a bulwark of blackness.

He followed it to within easy sight of the great gate which stood open in the dark and massive walls of the town. Guards leaned carelessly on their matchlocks. Yolgan feared no attack. Why should it? The wildest of the Mohammedan tribes shunned the land of the devil worshipers. Sounds of barter and dispute were wafted by the night wind through the gate.

Somewhere in Yolgan, Gordon was sure, were the men he was seeking. That they intended returning to the cave he had been assured. But there was a reason why he wished to enter Yolgan, a reason not altogether tied up with vengeance. As he pondered, hidden in the deep shadow, he heard the soft clop of hoofs on the dusty road behind him. He slid farther back among the pines; then with a sudden thought he turned and made his way beyond the first turn, where he crouched in the blackness beside the road.

Presently a train of laden pack mules came along, with men before and behind and at either side. They bore no torches, moving like men who knew their path. Gordon's eyes had so adjusted themselves to the faint starlight of the road that he was able to recognize them as Kirghiz herdsmen in their long cloaks and round caps. They passed so close to him that their body-scent filled his nostrils.

He crouched lower in the blackness, and as the last man moved past him, a steely arm hooked fiercely about the Kirghiz's throat, choking his cry. An iron fist crunched against his jaw and he sagged senseless in Gordon's arms. The others were already out of sight around the bend of the trail, and the scrape of the mules' bulging packs against the branches along the road was enough to drown the slight noises of the struggle.

235

Gordon dragged his victim in under the black branches and swiftly stripped him, discarding his own boots and kaffiyeh and donning the native's garments, with pistol and scimitar buckled on under the long cloak. A few minutes later he was moving along after the receding column, leaning on his staff as with the weariness of long travel. He knew the man behind him would not regain consciousness for hours.

He came up with the tail of the train, but lagged behind as a straggler might. He kept close enough to the caravan to be identified with it, but not so close as to tempt conversation or recognition by the other members of the train. When they passed through the gate none challenged him. Even in the flare of the torches under the great gloomy arch he looked like a native, with his dark features fitting in with his garments and the lambskin cap.

As he went down the torch-lighted street, passing unnoticed among the people who chattered and argued in the markets and stalls, he might have been one of the many Kirghiz shepherds who wandered about, gaping at the sights of the city which to them represented the last word in the metropolitan.

Yolgan was not like any other city in Asia. Legend said it was built long ago by a cult of devil worshipers who, driven from their distant homeland, had found sanctuary in this unmapped country, where an isolated branch of the Black Kirghiz, wilder than their kinsmen, roamed as masters. The people of the city were a mixed breed, descendants of these original founders and the Kirghiz.

Gordon saw the monks who were the ruling caste in Yolgan striding through the bazaars--tall, shaven-headed men with Mongolian features. He wondered anew as to their exact origin. They were not Tibetans. Their religion was not a depraved Buddhism. It was unadulterated devil worship. The architecture of their shrines and temples differed from any he had ever encountered anywhere.

But he wasted no time in conjecture, nor in aimless wandering. He went straight to the great stone building squatted against the side of the mountain at the foot of which Yolgan was built. Its great blank curtains of stone seemed almost like part of the mountain itself.

No one hindered him. He mounted a long flight of steps that were at least a hundred feet wide, bending over his staff as with the weariness of a long pilgrimage. Great bronze doors stood open, unguarded, and he kicked off his sandals and came into a huge hall the inner gloom of which was barely lighted by dim brazen lamps in which melted butter was burned.

Shaven-headed monks moved through the shadows like dusky ghosts, but they gave him no heed, thinking him merely a rustic worshiper come to leave some humble offering at the shrine of Erlik, Lord of the Seventh Hell.

At the other end of the hall, view was cut off by a great divided curtain of gilded leather that hung from the lofty roof to the floor. Half a dozen steps that crossed the hall led up to the foot of the curtain, and before it a monk sat cross-legged and motionless as a statue, arms folded and head bent as if in communion with unguessed spirits.

Gordon halted at the foot of the steps, made as if to prostrate himself, then retreated as if in sudden panic. The monk showed no interest. He had seen too many nomads from the outer world overcome by superstitious awe before the curtain that hid the dread effigy of Erlik Khan. The timid Kirghiz might skulk about the temple for hours before working up nerve enough to make his devotions to the deity. None of the priests paid any attention to the man in the caftan of a shepherd who slunk away as if abashed.

As soon as he was confident that he was not being watched, Gordon slipped through a dark doorway some distance from the gilded curtain and groped his way down a broad unlighted hallway until he came to a flight of stairs. Up this he went with both haste and caution and came presently into a long corridor along which winked sparks of light, like fireflies in a runnel.

He knew these lights were tiny lamps in the small cells that lined the passage, where the monks spent long hours in contemplation of dark mysteries, or pored over forbidden volumes, the very existence of which is not suspected by the outer world. There was a stair at the nearer end of the corridor, and up this he went, without being discovered by the monks in their cells. The pin points of light in the chambers did not serve to illuminate the darkness of the corridor to any extent.

As Gordon approached a crook in the stair he renewed his caution, for he knew there would be a man on guard at the head of the steps. He knew also that he would be likely to be asleep. The man was there--a half-naked giant with the wizened features of a deaf mute. A broad-tipped tulwar lay across his knees and his head rested on it as he slept.

Gordon stole noiselessly past him and came into an upper corridor which was dimly lighted by brass lamps hung at intervals. There were no doorless cells here, but heavy bronze-bound teak portals flanked the passage. Gordon went straight to one which was particularly ornately carved and furnished with an unusual fretted arch by way of ornament. He crouched there listening intently, then took a chance and rapped softly on the door. He rapped nine times, with an interval between each three raps.

There was an instant's tense silence, then an impulsive rush of feet across a carpeted floor, and the door was jerked open. A magnificent figure stood framed in the soft light. It was a woman, a lithe, splendid creature whose vibrant figure exuded magnetic vitality. The jewels that sparkled in the girdle about her supple hips were no more scintillant than her eyes.

Instant recognition blazed in those eyes, despite his native garments. She caught him in a fierce grasp. Her slender arms were strong as pliant steel.

"El Borak! I knew you would come!"

Gordon stepped into the chamber and closed the door behind him. A quick glance showed him there was no one there but themselves. Its thick Persian rugs, silk divans, velvet hangings, and gold-chased lamps struck a vivid contrast with the grim plainness of the rest of the temple. Then he turned his full attention again to the woman who stood before him, her white hands clenched in a sort of passionate triumph.

"How did you know I would come, Yasmeena?" he asked.

"You never failed a friend in need," she answered.

"Who is in need?"

"I!"

"But you are a goddess!"

"I explained it all in my letter!" she exclaimed bewilderedly.

Gordon shook his head. "I have received no letter."

"Then why are you here?" she demanded in evident puzzlement.

"It's a long story," he answered. "Tell me first why Yasmeena, who had the world at her feet and threw it away for weariness to become a goddess in a strange land, should speak of herself as one in need."

"In desperate need, El Borak." She raked back her dark locks with a nervously quick hand. Her eyes were shadowed with weariness and something more, something which Gordon had never seen there before--the shadow of fear.

"Here is food you need more than I," she said as she sank down on a divan and with a dainty foot pushed toward him a small gold table on which were chupaties, curried rice, and broiled mutton, all in gold vessels, and a gold jug of kumiss.

He sat down without comment and began to eat with unfeigned gusto. In his drab camel's-hair caftan, with the wide sleeves drawn back from his corded brown arms, he looked out of place in that exotic chamber.

Yasmeena watched him broodingly, her chin resting on her hand, her somber eyes enigmatic.

"I did not have the world at my feet, El Borak," she said presently. "But I had enough of it to sicken me. It became a wine which had lost its savor. Flattery became like an insult; the adulation of men became an empty repetition without meaning. I grew maddeningly weary of the flat fool faces that smirked eternally up at me, all wearing the same sheep expressions and animated by the same sheep thoughts. All except a few men like you, El Borak, and you were wolves in the flock. I might have loved you, El Borak, but there is something too fierce about you; your soul is a whetted blade on which I feared I might cut myself."

He made no reply, but tilted the golden jug and gulped down enough stinging kumiss to have made an ordinary man's head swim at once. He had lived the life of the nomads so long that their tastes had become his.

"So I became a princess, wife of a prince of Kashmir," she went on, her eyes smoldering with a marvelous shifting of clouds and colors. "I thought I knew the depths of men's swinishness. I found I had much to learn. He was a beast. I fled from him into India, and the British protected me when his ruffians would have dragged me back to him. He still offers many thousand rupees to anyone who will bring me alive to him, so that he may soothe his vanity by having me tortured to death."

"I have heard a rumor to that effect," answered Gordon.

A recurrent thought caused his face to darken. He did not frown, but the effect was subtly sinister.

"That experience completed my distaste for the life I knew," she said, her dark eyes vividly introspective. "I remembered that my father was a priest of Yolgan who fled away for love of a stranger woman. I had emptied the cup and the bowl was dry. I remembered Yolgan through the tales my father told me when I was a babe, and a great yearning rose in me to lose the world and find my soul. All the gods

I knew had proved false to me. The mark of Erlik was upon me--" she parted her pearl-sewn vest and displayed a curious starlike mark between her firm breasts.

"I came to Yolgan as well you know, because you brought me, in the guise of a Kirghiz from Issik-kul. As you know, the people remembered my father, and though they looked on him as a traitor, they accepted me as one of them, and because of an old legend which spoke of the star on a woman's bosom, they hailed me as a goddess, the incarnation of the daughter of Erlik Khan.

"For a while after you went away I was content. The people worshipped me with more sincerity than I had ever seen displayed by the masses of civilization. Their curious rituals were strange and fascinating. Then I began to go further into their mysteries; I began to sense the essence of the formula--" She paused, and Gordon saw the fear grow in her eyes again.

"I had dreamed of a calm retreat of mystics, inhabited by philosophers. I found a haunt of bestial devils, ignorant of all but evil. Mysticism? It is black shamanism, foul as the tundras which bred it. I have seen things that made me afraid. Yes, I, Yasmeena, who never knew the meaning of the word, I have learned fear. Yogok, the high priest, taught me. You warned me against Yogok before you left Yolgan. Well had I heeded you. He hates me. He knows I am not divine, but he fears my power over the people. He would have slain me long ago had he dared.

"I am wearied to death of Yolgan. Erlik Khan and his devils have proved no less an illusion than the gods of India and the West. I have not found the perfect way. I have found only awakened desire to return to the world I cast away.

"I want to go back to Delhi. At night I dream of the noise and smells of the streets and bazaars. I am half Indian, and all the blood of India is calling me. I was a fool. I had life in my hands and did not recognize it."

"Why not go back, then?" asked Gordon.

She shuddered. "I cannot. The gods of Yolgan must remain in Yolgan forever. Should one depart, the people believe the city would perish. Yogok would be glad to see me go, but he fears the fury of the people too much either to slay me or aid me to escape. I knew there was but one man who might help me. I wrote a letter to you and smuggled it out by a Tajik trader. With it I sent my sacred emblem--a jeweled gold star-- which would pass you safely through the country of the nomads. They would not harm a man bearing it. He would be safe from all but the priests of the city. I explained that in my letter."

"I never got it," Gordon answered. "I'm here after a couple of scoundrels whom I was guiding into the Uzbek country, and who for no apparent reason murdered my servant Ahmed and deserted me in the hills. They're in Yolgan now, somewhere."

"White men?" she exclaimed. "That is impossible! They could never have got through the tribes--"

"There's only one key to the puzzle," he interrupted. "Somehow your letter fell into their hands. They used your star to let them through. They don't mean to rescue you, because they got in touch with Yogok as soon as they reached the valley. There's only one thing I can think of--they intend kidnapping you to sell to your former husband."

She sat up straight; her white hands clenched on the edge of the divan and her eyes flashed. In that instant she looked as splendid and as dangerous as a cobra when it rears up to strike.

"Back to that pig? Where are these dogs? I will speak a word to the people and they shall cease to be!"

"That would betray yourself," returned Gordon. "The people would kill the stranger, and Yogok, too, maybe, but they'd learn that you'd been trying to escape from Yolgan. They allow you the freedom of the temple, don't they?"

"Yes; with shaven-headed skulkers spying on my every move, except when I am on this floor, from which only a single stair leads down. That stair is always guarded."

"By a guard who sleeps," said Gordon. "That's bad enough, but if the people found you were trying to escape, they might shut you up in a little cell for the rest of your life. People are particularly careful of their deities."

She shuddered, and her fine eyes flashed the fear an eagle feels for a cage. "Then what are we to do?"

"I don't know--yet. I have nearly a hundred Turkoman ruffians hidden up in the hills, but just now they're more hindrance than help. There's not enough of them to do much good in a pitched battle, and they're almost sure to be discovered tomorrow, if not before. I brought them into this mess, and it's up to me to get them out--or as many as I can. I came here to kill these Englishmen, Ormond and Pembroke. But that can wait now. I'm going to get you out of here, but I don't dare move until I know where Yogok and the Englishmen are. Is there anyone in Yolgan you can trust?"

"Any of the people would die for me, but they won't let me go. Only actual harm done me by the monks would stir them up against Yogok. No; I dare trust none of them."

"You say that stair is the only way up onto this floor?"

"Yes. The temple is built against the mountain, and galleries and corridors on the lower floors go back far into the mountain itself. But this is the highest floor, and is reserved entirely for me. There's no escape from it except down through the temple, swarming with monks. I keep only one servant here at night, and she is at present sleeping in a chamber some distance from this and is senseless with bhang as usual."

"Good enough!" grunted Gordon. "Here, take this pistol. Lock the door after I go through and admit no one but myself. You'll recognize me by the nine raps, as usual."

"Where are you going?" she demanded, staring up and mechanically taking the weapon he tendered her, butt first.

"To do a little spying," he answered. "I've got to know what Yogok and the others are doing. If I tried to smuggle you out now, we might run square into them. I can't make plans until I know some of theirs. If they intend sneaking you out tonight, as I think they do, it might be a good idea to let them do it, and then swoop down with the Turkomans and take you away from them, when they've got well away from the city. But I don't want to do that unless I have to. Bound to be shooting and a chance of your getting hit by a stray bullet. I'm going now; listen for my rap."

Chapter VI

THE MUTE GUARD still slumbered on the stair as Gordon glided past him. No lights glinted now as he descended into the lower corridor. He knew the cells were all empty, for the monks slept in chambers on a lower level.

As he hesitated, he heard sandals shuffling down the passage in the pitch blackness.

Stepping into one of the cells he waited until the unseen traveler was opposite him, then he hissed softly. The tread halted and a voice muttered a query.

"Art thou Yatub?" asked Gordon in the gutturals of the Kirghiz. Many of the lower monks were pure Kirghiz in blood and speech.

"Nay," came the answer. "I am Ojuh. Who art thou?"

"No matter; call me Yogok's dog if thou wilt. I am a watcher. Have the white men come into the temple yet?"

"Aye. Yogok brought them by the secret way, lest the people suspect their presence. If thou art close to Yogok, tell me--what is his plan?"

"What is thine own opinion?" asked Gordon.

An evil laugh answered him, and he could feel the monk leaning closer in the darkness to rest an elbow on the jamb.

"Yogok is crafty," he murmured. "When the Tajik whom Yasmeena bribed to bear her letter showed it to Yogok, our master bade him do as she had instructed him. When the man for whom she sent came for her, Yogok planned to slay both him and her, making it seem to the people that the white man had slain their goddess."

"Yogok is not forgiving," said Gordon at a venture.

"A cobra is more so." The monk laughed. "Yasmeena has thwarted him too often in the matter of sacrifices for him to allow her to depart in peace."

"Yet such is now his plan!" asserted Gordon.

"Nay; thou art a simple man, for one who calls himself a watcher. The letter was meant for El Borak. But the Tajik was greedy and sold it to these sahibs and told them of Yogok. They will not take her to India. They will sell her to a prince in Kashmir who will have her beaten to death with a slipper. Yogok himself will guide them through the hills by the secret route. He is in terror of the people, but his hate for Yasmeena overcomes him."

Gordon had heard all he wished to know, and he was in a sudden rush to be gone. He had abandoned his tentative plan of letting Ormond get the girl outside the city before rescuing her. With Yogok guiding the Englishmen through hidden passes, he might find it impossible to overtake them.

The monk, however, was in no hurry to conclude the conversation. He began speaking again, and then Gordon saw a light moving like a glowworm in the blackness, and he heart a swift patter of bare feet and a man breathing heavily. He drew farther back into the cell.

It was another monk who came up the corridor, carrying a small brass lamp that lighted his broad, thin-lipped face and made him look something like a Mongolian devil.

As he saw the monk outside the cell, he began hastily: "Yogok and the white men have gone to Yasmeena's chamber. The girl, her servant who spied upon her, has told us that the white devil El Borak is in Yolgan. He talked with Yasmeena less than half an hour agone. The girl sped to Yogok as swiftly as she dared, but she dared not stir until he had left Yasmeena's chamber. He is somewhere in the temple. I gather men to search. Come with me, thou, and thou also--"

He swung the lamp about so that it shone full on Gordon, crouching in the cell. As the man blinked to see the garments of a shepherd instead of the familiar robes of a monk, Gordon lashed out for his jaw, quick and silent as the stroke of a python. The monk went down like a man shot in the head, and even as the lamp smashed on the floor, Gordon had leaped and grappled with the other man in the sudden darkness.

A single cry rang to the vaulted roof before it was strangled in the corded throat. The monk was hard to hold as a snake, and he kept groping for a knife, but as they crashed into the stone wall, Gordon smashed his opponent's head savagely against it. The man went limp and Gordon flung him down beside the other senseless shape.

The next instant Gordon was racing up the stairway. It was only a few steps from the cell where he had hidden, its upper portion dim in the subdued light of the upper corridor. He knew no one had gone up or down while he talked with the monk. Yet the man with the lamp had said that Yogok and the others had gone to Yasmeena's chamber, and that her treacherous servant girl had come to them.

He rounded the crook with reckless haste, his scimitar ready, but the slumping figure at the stairhead did not rise to oppose him. There was a new sag in the mute's shoulders as he huddled on the steps. He had been stabbed in the back, so fiercely that the spinal column had been severed with one stroke.

Gordon wondered why the priest should kill one of his own servants, but he did not pause; premonition gripping his heart, he hurled himself down the corridor and in through the arched doorway, which was unbolted. The chamber was empty. Cushions from the divan were strewn on the floor. Yasmeena was not to be seen.

Gordon stood like a statue in the center of the room, his scimitar in his hand. The blue sheen of the light on steel was no more deadly than the glitter on his black eyes. His gaze swept the room, lingering no longer on a slight bulge in the hangings on the rear wall than anywhere else.

He turned toward the door, took a step--then wheeled and raced across the chamber like a gust of wind, slashing and hacking at the tapestry before the man hiding there realized he was discovered. The keen edge ribboned the velvet arras and blood spurted; out of the tatters a figure toppled to the floor--a shaven monk, literally cut to pieces.

He had dropped his knife and could only grovel and moan, clutching at his spurting arteries.

"Where is she?" snarled Gordon, panting with passion as he crouched over his hideous handiwork. "Where is she?"

But the man only whimpered and yammered and died without speaking.

Gordon ran to the walls and began ripping the hangings away. Somewhere he knew there must be a secret door. But the walls showed blank, resisting his most violent efforts. He could not follow Yasmeena by the route her abductors had obviously carried her. He must escape the city and hasten to the cave, where the servants were hidden, and to which the Englishmen would undoubtedly return. He was sweating with the violence of his rage, which almost submerged caution. He ripped off the camel's hair robe, feeling in his frenzy that it cramped and hampered him.

But the action brought a thought born of cold reason. The garments of the senseless monks in the corridor below would furnish him with a disguise which would aid him to pass unhindered through the temple, where he knew scores of shaven-headed murderers were hunting him.

He ran silently from the chamber, passed the sprawling corpse, rounded the turn of the stair--then he stopped short. The lower corridor was a blaze of light, and at the foot of the stairs stood a mass of monks, holding torches and swords. He saw rifles in the hands of a dozen.

Details sprang out in startling clarity in the instant that the monks yelled and raised their rifles. Beyond them he saw a round-faced slant-eyed girl crouching by the wall. She grasped a rope which hung down the wall and jerked, and Gordon felt the stairs give way beneath him. The rifles roared in a ragged volley as he shot down the black opening which gaped beneath his feet, and the bullets whined over his head. A fierce cry of triumph rose from the monks.

Chapter VII

AFTER GORDON LEFT HER, Yasmeena made fast the door and returned to her divan. She idly studied the big pistol he had left with her, fascinated by the blue gleam of the light on its dully polished steel.

Then she tossed it aside and lay back with her eyes closed. There was a certain sophistication or innate mysticism in her which refused to let her put much faith in material weapons. Hers was that overrefinement of civilization which instinctively belittles physical action. With all her admiration for Gordon, he was, after all, to her, a barbarian who put his trust in lead and steel.

She undervalued the weapon he had left with her, and so it was out of her reach when the noise of a swishing tapestry roused her. She turned and stared at the rear wall with eyes suddenly dilated. Behind the hanging she knew-- or thought she knew--was solid stone wall, built hard against the sheer mountainside.

But now that hanging lifted, grasped in a yellow clawlike hand. The hand was followed by a face--an evil, leering, grayish face, with slanted eyes and lank hair falling over a narrow forehead. A thin gash of a mouth gaped, revealing pointed teeth.

She was so astounded that she sat frozen, unable to supply the simple explanation of the phenomenon, until the man entered the room with a slithering silence repulsively suggestive of a snake. Then she saw that a black opening gaped in the wall behind the lifted arras, and two faces were framed in it--white men's faces, hard and inexorable as stone.

She sprang up then and snatched for the revolver, but it was at the other end of the divan. She ran around for it, but the slant-eyed man, with a motion incredibly quick, was before her and crushed her cruelly in his lean arms, clapping a hand over her mouth. He heeded the twisting and writhing of her supple body no more than the struggles of a child.

"Swift!" he ordered in harsh gutturals. "Bind her!"

The white men had followed him into the chamber, but it was a monk who obeyed, adding a velvet gag. One of the white men picked up the pistol.

"See to the mute who slumbers on the stairs," her captor ordered. "He is not our man, but a creature set by the people to guard her. Even a mute can speak by gestures sometimes."

The evil-faced monk bowed deeply and, unbolting the door, went out, thumbing a long knife. Another monk stood in the secret entrance.

"You did not know of the hidden door," jeered the slant-eyed man. "You fool! The mountain below this temple is honeycombed with tunnels. You have been spied on constantly. The girl whom you thought drunk on bhang watched tonight while you talked with El Borak. That will not alter my plans any, though, except that I have set my monks to slay El Borak.

"Then we will show the people his body and tell them that you have returned to your father in the Seventh Hell because Yolgan has been polluted by the presence of a Feringhi. In the meantime these sahibs will be well on their way to Kashmir with you, my lovely goddess! Daughter of Erlik! Bah!"

"We're wasting time, Yogok," broke in Ormond roughly. "Once in the hills, you say, we won't meet any of the Kirghiz, but I want to be far from Yolgan by daylight."

The priest nodded and motioned to the monk who came forward and lifted Yasmeena onto a litter he carried. Pembroke took the other end. At that moment the other monk glided back into the chamber, wiping blood from his curved blade.

Yogok directed him to hide behind the hangings. "El Borak might return before the others find him."

Then they passed through the hidden door into darkness lighted by a butter lamp in Yogok's hand. The priest slid to the heavy section of stone that formed part of the wall and made it fast with a bronze bar. Yasmeena saw by the small light of the lamp that they were in a narrow corridor which slanted downward at a pitch which grew steeper until it ended in a long narrow stair cut out of solid rock.

At the bottom of this stair they struck a level tunnel which they followed for some time, the Englishmen and the monk alternating with the litter. It ended at last in a wall of rock, in the center of which was a stone block which worked on a pivot. This turned, they emerged into a cave, at the mouth of which stars were visible through a tangle of branches.

When Yogok pushed the block back in place its rough exterior looked like part of a solid wall. He extinguished the lamp and a moment later was pushing aside the massed willows which masked the cave mouth. As they emerged into the starlight, Yasmeena saw that these willows stood on the bank of a stream.

When her captors had pushed through the trees, waded the shallow channel, and ascended the farther bank, she saw a cluster of lights off to her right. Those lights were Yolgan. They had followed tunnels out into the solid rock of the mountain and had come out at its foot less than half a mile from the city. Directly ahead of her the forest lifted in rows of black ramparts, and off to the left the hills climbed in marching lines.

Her captors set off through the starlight, their apparent objective a jutting shoulder less than half a mile to the east. The distance was covered in silence. The nervousness of the white men was no more evident than that of Yogok. Each man was thinking what his fate would be if the common people of Yolgan discovered them kidnapping their goddess.

Yogok's fear was greater than that of the Englishmen. He had covered his tracks with corpses--the shepherd who had brought him Ormond's message, the mute guardian of the stairs; his teeth chattered as he conjured up possibilities. El Borak must die without speaking, also; that, he had drilled into the monks.

"Faster! Faster!" he urged, a note of panic in his voice as he glared at the black forest walls about him. In the moan of the night wind he seemed to hear the stealthy tread of pursuers.

"Here's the cave," grunted Ormond. "Set her down; no use lugging her up that slope. I'll go get the servants and the horses. We'll mount her on one of the pack animals. Have to leave some of our stuff behind, anyhow. Ohai, Akbar!" he called softly.

There was no answer. The fire had gone out in the cave and the mouth gaped black and silent.

"Have they gone to sleep?" Ormond swore irritably. "I'll jolly well wake 'em. Wait!"

He ran lightly up the rough camp and vanished in the cave. A moment later his voice reached them, echoing hollowly between the rocky walls. The echoes did not disguise the sudden fear in his voice.

Chapter VIII

WHEN GORDON FELL through the treacherous stairs, he shot downward in utter blackness to land on solid stone. Not one man in a hundred could have survived the fall with unsmashed bones, but El Borak was all knit wires and steel springs. He landed on all fours, catlike, with bent joints absorbing the shock. Even so his whole body was numbed, and his limbs crumpled under him, letting his frame dash violently against the stone.

He lay there half stunned for a space, then pulled himself together, cursing the stinging and tingling of his hands and feet, and felt himself for broken bones.

Thankful to find himself intact, he groped for and found the scimitar which he had cast from him as he fell. Above him the trap had closed. Where he was he had no idea, but it was dark as a Stygian vault. He wondered how far he had fallen, and felt that it was farther than anyone would ever believe, supposing he escaped to tell of it. He felt about in the darkness and found that he was in a square cell of no great dimensions. The one door was locked on the outside.

His investigations took him only a matter of seconds, and it was while he was feeling the door that he heard someone fumbling at it on the other side. He drew back, believing that those who dropped him into the cell would scarcely have had time to reach it by a safer way. He believed it was someone who had heard the sound of his fall and was coming to investigate, doubtless expecting to find a corpse on the floor.

The door was cast open and light blinded him, but he cut at the vague figure which loomed in the open door. Then his eyes could see and they saw a monk lying on the floor of a narrow lamp-lighted corridor with his shaven head split to the temples. The passage was empty except for the dead man.

The floor of the corridor sloped slightly, and Gordon went down it, because to go up it would obviously be returning toward his enemies. He momentarily expected to hear them howling on his heels, but evidently they considered that his fall through the trap, riddled, as they thought, with bullets, was sufficient and were in no hurry to verify their belief. Doubtless it was the duty of the monk he had killed to finish off victims dropped through the trap on the stairs.

The corridor made a sharp turn to the right and the lamps no longer burned along the walls. Gordon took one of them and went on, finding that the pitch of the slope grew steeper until he was forced to check his descent with a hand braced against the wall. These walls were solid rock, and he knew he was in the mountain on which the temple was built.

He did not believe any of the inhabitants of Yolgan knew of these tunnels except the monks; certainly Yasmeena was ignorant of them. Thought of the girl made him wince. Heaven alone knew where she was, just then, but he could not aid her until he had escaped himself from these rat-runs.

Presently the passage turned at right angles into a broader tunnel which ran level, and he followed it hastily but cautiously, holding his lamp high. Ahead of him he saw the tunnel end at last against a rough stone wall in which a door was set in the shape of a ponderous square block. This, he discovered, was hung on a pivot, and it revolved with ease, letting him through into a cave beyond.

As Yasmeena had seen the stars among the branches not long before, Gordon now discovered them. He put out his lamp, halted an instant to let his eyes get used to the sudden darkness, and then started toward the cavern mouth.

Just as he reached it, he crouched back. Somebody was splashing through the water outside, thrashing through the willows. The man came panting up the short steep slope, and Gordon saw the evil face of Yogok in the starlight before the man became a shapeless blob of blackness as he plunged into the cavern.

The next instant El Borak sprang, bearing his man to the floor. Yogok let out one hair-raising yell, and then Gordon found his throat and crouched over him, savagely digging and twisting his fingers in the priest's neck.

"Where is Yasmeena?" he demanded.

A gurgle answered him. He relaxed his grip a trifle and repeated the question. Yogok was mad with fear of his attack in the dark, but somehow--probably by the body-scent or the lack of it--he divined that his captor was a white man.

"Are you El Borak?" he gasped.

"Who else? Where is Yasmeena?" Gordon emphasized his demand by a wrench which brought a gurgle of pain from Yogok's thin lips.

"The Englishmen have her!" he panted.

"Where are they?"

"Nay; I know not! Ahhh! Mercy, sahib! I will tell!"

Yogok's eyes glimmered white with fear in the darkness. His lean body was shaking as with an ague.

"We took her to a cave where the sahibs' servants were hidden. They were gone, with the horses. The Englishmen accused me of treachery. They said I had made away with their servants and meant to murder them. They lied. By Erlik, I know not what became of their cursed Pathans! The Englishmen attacked me, but I fled while a servant of mine fought with them."

Gordon hauled him to his feet, faced him toward the cave mouth and bound his hands behind him with his own girdle.

"We're going back," he said grimly. "One yelp out of you and I'll let out your snake's soul. Guide me as straight to Ormond's cave as you know."

"Nay; the dogs will slay me!"

"I'll kill you if you don't," Gordon assured him, pushing Yogok stumbling before him.

The priest was not a back-to-the-wall fighter. Confronted by two perils he chose the more remote. They waded the stream and on the other side Yogok turned to the right. Gordon jerked him back.

"I know where I am now," he growled. "And I know where the cave is. It's in that jut of land to the left. If there's a path through the pines, show it to me."

Yogok surrendered and hurried through the shadows, conscious of Gordon's grasp on his collar and the broad edge of Gordon's scimitar glimmering near. It was growing toward the darkness that precedes dawn as they came to the cave which loomed dark and silent among the trees.

"They are gone!" Yogok shivered.

"I didn't expect to find them here," muttered Gordon. "I came here to pick up their trail. If they thought you'd set the natives on them, they'd pull out on foot. What worries me is what they did with Yasmeena."

"Listen!"

Yogok started convulsively as a low moan smote the air.

Gordon threw him and lashed together his hands and feet. "Not a sound out of you!" he warned, and then stole up the ramp, sword ready.

At the mouth he hesitated unwilling to show himself against the dim starlight behind him. Then he heard the moan again and knew it was not feigned. It was a human being in mortal agony.

He felt his way into the darkness and presently stumbled over something yielding, which evoked another moan. His hands told him it was a man in European clothing.

Something warm and oozy smeared his hands as he groped. Feeling in the man's pockets he found a box of matches and struck one, cupping it in his hands.

A livid face with glassy eyes stared up at him.

"Pembroke!" muttered Gordon.

The sound of his name seemed to rouse the dying man. He half rose on an elbow, blood trickling from his mouth with the effort.

"Ormond!" he whispered ghastily. "Have you come back? Damn you, I'll do for you yet--"

"I'm not Ormond," growled the American. "I'm Gordon. It seems somebody has saved me the trouble of killing you. Where's Yasmeena?"

"He took her away." The Englishman's voice was scarcely intelligible, choked by the flow of blood. "Ormond, the dirty swine! We found the cave empty--knew old Yogok had betrayed us. We jumped him. He ran away. His damned monk stabbed me. Ormond took Yasmeena and the monk and went away. He's mad. He's going to try to cross the mountains on foot, with the girl, and the monk to guide him. And he left me to die, the swine, the filthy swine!"

The dying man's voice rose to a hysterical shriek; he heaved himself up, his eyes glaring; then a terrible shudder ran through his body and he was dead.

Gordon rose, struck another match and swept a glance over the cave. It was utterly bare. Not a firearm in sight.

Ormond had evidently robbed his dying partner. Ormond, starting through the mountains with a captive woman, and a treacherous monk for a guide, on foot and with no provisions--surely the man must be mad.

Returning to Yogok he unbound his legs, repeating Pembroke's tale in a few words. He saw the priest's eyes gleam in the starlight.

"Good! They will all die in the mountains! Let them go!"

"We're following them," Gordon answered. "You know the way the monk will lead Ormond. Show it to me."

A restoration of confidence had wakened insolence and defiance.

"No! Let them die!"

With a searing curse Gordon caught the priest's throat and jammed his head back between his shoulders, until his eyes were glaring at the stars.

"Damn you!" he ground between his teeth, shaking the man as a dog shakes a rat. "If you try to balk me now I'll kill you the slowest way I know. Do you want me to drag you back to Yolgan and tell the people what you plotted against the daughter of Erlik Khan? They'll kill me, but they'll flay you alive!"

Yogok knew Gordon would not do that, not because the American feared death, but because to sacrifice himself would be to remove Yasmeena's last hope. But Gordon's glaring eyes made him cold with fear; he sensed the abysmal rage that gripped the white man and knew that El Borak was on the point of tearing him limb from limb. In that moment there was no bloody deed of which Gordon was not capable.

"Stay, sahib!" Yogok gasped. "I will guide you."

"And guide me right!" Gordon jerked him savagely to his feet. "They have been gone less than an hour. If we don't overtake them by sunrise, I'll know you've led me astray, and I'll tie you head down to a cliff for the vultures to eat alive."

Chapter IX

IN THE DARKNESS before dawn Yogok led Gordon up into the hills by a narrow trail that wound among ravines and windy crags, climbing ever southward. The eternal lights of Yolgan fell away behind them, growing smaller and smaller with distance.

They left half a mile to the east of the gorge where the Turkomans were concealed. Gordon ardently wished to get his men out of that ravine before dawn, but he dared not take the time now. His eyes burned from lack of sleep and moments of giddiness assailed him, but the fire of his driving energy burned fiercer than ever. He urged the priest to greater and greater speed until sweat dripped like water from the man's trembling limbs.

"He'll practically have to drag the girl. She'll fight him every step of the way. And he'll have to beat the monk every now and then to make him point out the right path. We ought to be gaining on them at every step."

Full dawn found them climbing a ledge that pitched up around a gigantic shoulder where the wind staggered them. Then, off to the left, sounded a sudden rattle of rifle fire. The wind brought it in snatches. Gordon turned, loosing his binoculars. They were high above the ridges and hills that rimmed the valley.

He could see Yolgan in the distance, like a huddle of toy blocks. He could see the gorges that debouched into the valley spread out like the fingers of a hand. He saw the gorge in which his Turkomans had taken refuge. Black dots which he knew were men were scattered among the boulders at the canyon mouth and up on the rims of the walls; tiny white puffs spurted.

Even before he brought his glasses into play he knew that the pursuing Kirghiz had at last smelled his men out. The Turkomans were bottled in the gorge. He saw puffs of smoke jetting from the rocks that from the mountainside overhung the ravine leading out of the canyon. Strings of dots moved out of the gates of Yolgan, which were men coming to investigate the shooting. Doubtless the Kirghiz had sent riders to bring the men of the city.

Yogok shrieked and fell down flat on the ledge. Gordon felt his cap tugged from his head as if by an invisible hand, and there came to him the flat sharp crack of a rifle.

He dropped behind a boulder and began scanning the narrow, sheer-walled plateau upon which the ledge debouched. Presently a head and part of a shoulder rose above a shelf of rock, and then a rifle came up and spoke flatly. The bullet knocked a chip out of the boulder near Gordon's elbow.

Ormond had been making even poorer time than Gordon hoped, and seeing his pursuers gaining, had turned to make a fight of it. That he recognized Gordon was evident from his mocking shouts. There was a hint of hysteria in them.

Yogok was too helpless with terror to do anything but hug the ledge and moan. Gordon began working his way toward the Englishman. Evidently Ormond did not know that he had no firearm. The sun was not yet above the peaks when it turned to fire, and the light and atmosphere of those altitudes make for uncertain shooting.

Ormond blazed away as Gordon flitted from ridge to boulder and from rock to ledge, and sometimes his lead whispered perilously close. But Gordon was gliding ever nearer, working his way so that the sun would be behind him when it rose. Something about that silent shadowy figure that he could not hit began to shake Ormond's nerve; it was more like being stalked by a leopard than by a human being.

Gordon could not see Yasmeena, but presently he saw the monk. The man took advantage of a moment when Ormond was loading his rifle. He sprang up from behind the ledge with his hands tied behind his back, and scudded across the rock like a rabbit. Ormond, like a man gone mad, jerked a pistol and put a bullet between his shoulders, and he stumbled and slid screaming over the thousand-foot edge.

Gordon broke cover, too, and came ripping across the treacherous rock like a gust of hill wind. As he came the sun burst up over a ridge behind him, full in Ormond's eyes. The Englishman yelled incoherently, trying to shade his eyes with his left arm, and began firing half blindly. The bullets ripped past Gordon's head or knocked up splinters of stone at his speeding feet. Panic had Ormond, and he was firing without proper aim.

Then the hammer clicked on an empty chamber. Another stride and Gordon would reach him with that hovering arc of steel that the sun turned crimson. Ormond hurled the pistol blindly, yelling "You damned werewolf! I'll cheat you yet!" and bounded far out, arms outspread.

His feet struck the sloping lip of a fissure and he shot down and vanished so suddenly it was like the unreality of a dream.

Gordon reached the crevice and glared down into echoing darkness. He could see nothing, but the chasm seemed bottomless. With an angry shrug he turned away, disappointed.

Behind the stony shelf Gordon found Yasmeena lying with her arms bound, where Ormond had flung her down. Her soft slippers hung in tatters, and the bruises and abrasions on her tender flesh told of Ormond's brutal attempts to force her at top speed along the rocky path.

Gordon cut her cords and she caught his arms with all her old fierceness of passion. There was no fear in her eyes now, only wild excitement.

"They said you were dead!" she cried. "I knew they lied! They cannot kill you any more than they can kill the mountains or the wind that blows across them. You have Yogok. I saw him. He knows the secret paths better than the monk Ormond killed. Let us go, while the Kirghiz are killing the Turkomans! What if we have no supplies? It is summer. We shall not freeze. We can starve for a while if need be. Let us go!"

"I brought those men to Yolgan with me for my own purposes, Yasmeena," he replied. "Even for you I can't desert them."

She nodded her splendid head. "I expected that from you, El Borak."

Ormond's rifle lay nearby but there were no cartridges for it. He cast it over the precipice and, taking Yasmeena's hand, led her back to the ledge where Yogok lay yammering.

Gordon hauled him erect and pointed to the gorge where the white puffs spurted.

"Is there a way to reach that gorge without returning to the valley? Your life depends on it."

"Half these gorges have hidden exits," answered Yogok, shivering. "That one has. But I cannot guide you along that route with my arms tied."

Gordon unbound his hands, but tied the girdle about the priest's waist and retained the other end in his hand. "Lead on," he ordered.

Yogok led them back along the ledge they had just traversed to a point where, halfway along it, it was cut by a great natural causeway of solid stone. They made their way along it, with dizzy depths echoing on either hand, to a broad ledge which skirted a deep canyon. They followed this ledge around a colossal crag and after a while Yogok plunged into a cave which opened upon the narrow path.

This they traversed in semidarkness relieved by light which filtered in from a ragged crevice in the roof. The cave wound steeply downward, following a fault in the rock, and they came out at last in a triangular cleft between towering walls. The narrow slit which was the cave mouth opened in a side of the cleft and was masked from outer view by a spur of rock that looked like part of a solid wall. Gordon had looked into that cleft the day before and failed to discover the cave.

The sound of firing had grown louder as they advanced along the twisting cave, and now it filled the defile with thundering echoes. They were in the gorge of the Turkomans. Gordon saw the wiry warriors crouching among the boulders at the mouth, firing at the fur-capped heads which appeared among the rocks of the outer slopes.

He shouted before they saw him, and they nearly shot him before they recognized him. He went toward them, dragging Yogok with him, and the warriors stared in silent amazement at the shivering priest and the girl in her tattered finery. She scarcely noticed them; they were wolves whose fangs she did not fear; all her attention was centered on Gordon. When a bullet whined near her she did not flinch.

Men crouched at the mouth of the ravine, firing into it. Bullets hummed back up the gut.

"They stole up in the darkness," grunted Orkhan, binding up a bleeding bullet hole in his forearm. "They had the gorge mouth surrounded before our sentries saw them. They cut the throat of the sentry we had stationed down the ravine and came stealing up it. Had not others in the gorge seen them and opened fire, they would have cut all our throats while we slept. Aye, they were like cats that see in the dark. What shall we do, El Borak? We are trapped. We cannot climb these walls. There is the spring, and grass for the horses and we have slept, but we have no food left and our ammunition will not last forever."

Gordon took a yataghan from one of the men and handed it to Yasmeena.

"Watch Yogok," he directed. "Stab him if he seeks to escape."

And from the flash of her eyes he knew that she at last realized the value of direct action in its proper place, and that she would not hesitate to carry out his order. Yogok looked like a singed serpent in his fury, but he feared Yasmeena as much as he did Gordon.

El Borak collected a rifle and a handful of cartridges on his way to the boulder-strewn gorge mouth. Three Turkomans lay dead among the rocks and others were wounded. The Kirghiz were working their way up the outer slope on foot from rock to rock, trying to get in to close quarters where their superior numbers would count, but not willing to sacrifice too many lives to get there. Up from the city a ragged line of men was streaming through the pines.

"We've got to get out of this trap before the monks come up with the Kirghiz and lead them up in the hills and down through that cave," Gordon muttered.

He could see them already toiling up the first ridges of the hills, shouting frantically to the tribesmen as they came. Working in fierce haste he told off half a dozen men on the best horses, and mounting Yogok and Yasmeena on spare steeds, he ordered the priest to lead the Turkomans back through the cave. To Orkhan Shah he gave instructions to follow Yasmeena's orders, and so imbued with trust was the Turkoman that he made no objections to obeying a woman.

Three of the men remaining with him Gordon stationed at the ravine, and with the other three he held the mouth of the canyon. They began firing as the others urged their horses down the defile. The men on the lower slopes sensed that the volleys were diminishing and came storming up the acclivities, only to take cover again as they were swept by a hail of lead, the deadly accuracy of which made up for its lack of volume. Gordon's presence heartened his men and they put new spirit in their rifle work.

When the last rider had disappeared into the cleft, Gordon waited until he thought the fugitives had time enough to traverse the winding cave, and then he fell back swiftly, picked up the men at the ravine, and raced for the hidden exit. The men outside suspected a trap in the sudden cessation of the firing, and they held back for long minutes, during which time Gordon and his men were galloping through the twisting cavern, their hoofs filling the narrow gut with thunder.

The others awaited them on the ledge skirting the ravine and Gordon sent them hurrying on. He cursed because he could not be at two places at once--at the head of the column bullying Yogok, and at the rear watching for the first of the pursuers to ride out on the ledge. But Yasmeena, flourishing the knife at the priest's throat, was guarantee against treachery at the front. She had sworn to sink the blade in his breast if the Kirghiz came within rifle range, and Yogok sweated with fear and himself urged the band onward.

They moved around the corner of the crag and out across the ridge, a knife-edged causeway half a mile in length, with a sheet of rock slanting steeply down for a thousand feet oh either hand.

Gordon waited alone at the angle of the ledge. When his party was moving like insects along the crest of the ridge, the first of the Kirghiz came racing out on the ledge. Sitting his horse behind a jutting spur of rock, Gordon lined his sights carefully and fired. It was a long range, even for him; so long that he missed the first rider and hit the horse instead.

The stricken beast reared high, screaming, and plunged backward. The screams and plunges of the maddened animal, before it toppled over the edge, put the horses in confusion behind it. Three more got out of control and were carried over the cliff with their riders, and the other Kirghiz retreated into the cave. After a while they tried again, but a bullet spattering on the rock sent them scurrying back.

A glance over his shoulder showed Gordon his horsemen just dropping off the ridge onto the farther ledge. He reined about and sent his horse flying along the path. If he loitered, the Kirghiz might venture out again, find no one opposing them, and reach the bend of the trail in time to pick him off the causeway.

Most of his hardened band had dismounted, leading their horses at a walk. Gordon rode at a gallop with death yawning on either hand if the horse slipped or put a single foot wrong. But the beast was sure-footed as a mountain sheep.

Gordon's head swam from lack of sleep as he glanced down into the blue haze of the abyss, but he did not slacken his pace. When he dropped down the slope onto the ledge where Yasmeena stood, white-faced and her nails biting into her pink palms, the Kirghiz had not yet appeared.

Gordon pushed his riders as hard as he dared, making them from time to time change to the spare horses, to save the animals as much as possible. Nearly a dozen of these still remained. Many of the men were giddy with dizziness caused by hunger and the altitude. He himself was mad for sleep and kept himself awake only by an effort of will that made the hills reel to his gaze.

He kept his grip on clarity of purpose as only a man toughened by a savagely hard life can do, and led them on, following the paths Yogok pointed out. They skirted ledges that hovered over ravines the bottoms of which were lost in shadowy gloom. They plunged through defiles like a knife cut where sheer walls rose up to the skies on either hand.

Behind them from time to time they heard faint yells, and once, when they toiled up over the shoulder of a breathtaking crag on a path where the horses fought for footing, they saw their pursuers far below and behind them. The Kirghiz and monks were not maintaining such a suicidal pace; hate is seldom as desperate as the will to live.

The snowy crest of Mount Erlik loomed higher and higher before them, and Yogok, when questioned, swore that the way to safety lay through the mountain. More he would not say; he was green with fear, and his mind held to but one thought--to keep the trail that would buy his life. He feared his captors no more than he feared that his pursuing subjects would overtake them and learn of his duplicity in regard to their goddess.

They pushed on like men already dead, beginning to stagger with weakness and exhaustion. The horses drooped and stumbled. The wind was like whetted steel. Darkness was gathering when they followed the backbone of a giant ridge which ran like a natural causeway to the sheer slope of Mount Erlik Khan.

The mountain towered gigantically above them, a brutish mass of crags and dizzy escarpments and colossal steeps, with the snow-clad pinnacle, glimpsed between the great spurs, dominating all. The ridge ended at a ledge high up among the cliffs, and in the sheer rock there stood a bronze door, thickly carved with inscriptions that Gordon could not decipher. It was heavy enough to have resisted an attack of artillery.

"This is sacred to Erlik," said Yogok, but he showed about as much reverence as one of the Mohammedans. "Push against the door. Nay; fear not. On my life, there is no trap."

"On your life it is," Gordon assured him grimly, and himself set a shoulder to the door, almost falling as he dismounted.

Chapter X

THE PONDEROUS PORTAL swung inward with a smoothness that showed the antique hinges had recently been oiled. A makeshift torch revealed the entrance to a tunnel, cut in solid rock. A few feet from the door the tunnel opened out like the neck of a bottle, and the flickering torch, held at the entrance, only hinted at the vastness of its dimensions.

"This tunnel runs clear through the mountain," said Yogok. "By dawn we can be out of reach of those who follow, because even if they climb over the mountain by the most direct route, they must go by foot and it will take them all the rest of the night and all of another day. If they skirt the mountain and work their way through the passes of the surrounding hills, it will take them even longer; and their horses are weary, too.

"That is the way I was going to guide Ormond. I was not going to take him through the mountain. But it is the only way of escape for you. There is food here. At certain seasons of the year the monks work here. In that cell there are lamps."

He pointed to a small chamber cut in the rock just inside the doorway. Gordon lighted several of the butter lamps, and gave them to the Turkomans to carry. He dared not follow the course which caution suggested and ride ahead to investigate before he led his men into the tunnel. The pursuers were too close behind them. He must bar the big door and plunge on, trusting the priest's desire to save his own skin.

When the men were all in the tunnel, Yogok directed the barring of the door--giant bronze bars, thick as a man's leg. It took half a dozen of the weakened Turkomans to lift one, but once they were in place, Gordon was certain that nothing short of siege guns could force the ton-heavy door, with its massive bronze sills and jambs set deep in the living rock.

He made Yogok ride between him and Orkhan, the Turkoman holding a lamp. There was no use trusting Yogok, even though the priest was getting some satisfaction out of the thought that he was at least ridding himself of the 'goddess' he feared and hated, although it meant foregoing his vengeance on her.

Even with all his faculties occupied in a savage battle to keep from falling senseless with exhaustion, Gordon found space to be amazed at what the light showed him. He had never dreamed of the existence of such a place. Thirty men could have ridden abreast in the cavernlike passage, and the roof soared out of sight in some places; in others stalactites reflected the light in a thousand scintillant colors.

The floors and walls were as even as man-shaped marble, and Gordon wondered how many centuries had been required for the hand-cutting and smoothing of them. Cells appeared at irregular intervals, cut in the rock at the sides, and presently he saw marks of pick work, and then caught glints of dull yellow.

The light showed him the incredible truth. The tales of Mount Erlik Khan were true. The walls were patterned with veins of gold that could be dug out of the rock with a knife point.

The Turkomans, who smelled loot as vultures smell carrion, woke suddenly out of their daze of fatigue and began to take an almost painfully intense interest.

"This is where the monks get their gold, sahib," said Orkhan, his eyes blazing in the lamplight. "Let me twist the old one's toe for a space, and he will tell us where they have hidden that which they have dug out of the walls."

But 'the old one' did not need persuasion. He pointed out a square-hewn chamber in which stood stacks of peculiarly shaped objects that were ingots of virgin gold. In other, larger cells were the primitive contrivances with which they smelted the ore and cast the metal.

"Take what ye will," said Yogok indifferently. "A thousand horses could not carry away the gold we have cast and stored, and we have scarcely dipped into the richness of the veins."

Thin lips were licked greedily, drooping mustaches twisted in emotion, and eyes that burned like hawks' were turned questioningly on Gordon.

"Ye have spare horses," he suggested, and that was enough for them.

After that nothing could have convinced them that everything which had passed had not been planned by Gordon in order to lead them to the gold which was the plunder he had promised them. They loaded the extra ponies until he interfered, to save the animals' strength. Then they hacked off chunks of the soft gold and stuffed their pouches and belts and girdles, and even so they had scarcely diminished the stacks. Some of the raiders lifted up their voices and wept when they saw how much they must leave behind.

"Assuredly," they promised each other, "we shall return with wagons and many horses and secure every crumb of it, inshallah!"

"Dogs!" swore Gordon. "Ye have each man a fortune beyond your dreams. Are ye jackals to feast on carrion until your bellies burst? Will ye loiter here until the Kirghiz cross the mountain and cut us off? What of the gold then, you crop-eared rogues?"

Of more interest to the American was a cell where barley was stored in leather sacks, and he made the tribesmen load some of the horses with food instead of gold. They grumbled, but they obeyed him. They would obey him now, if he ordered them to ride with him into Jehannum.

Every nerve in his body shrieked for sleep, submerging hunger; but he gnawed a handful of raw barley and flogged his failing powers with the lash of his driving will. Yasmeena drooped in her saddle wearily, but her eyes shone unclouded in the lamplight, and Gordon was dully aware of a deep respect for her that dwarfed even his former admiration.

They rode on through that glittering, dream-palace cavern, the tribesmen munching barley and babbling ecstatically of the joys their gold would buy, and at last they came to a bronze door which was a counterpart of the one at the other end of the tunnel. It was not barred. Yogok maintained that none but the monks had visited Mount Erlik in centuries. The door swung inward at their efforts and they blinked in the glow of a white dawn.

They were looking out on a small ledge from which a narrow trail wound along the edge of a giant escarpment. On one side the land fell away sheer for thousands of feet, so that a stream at the bottom looked like a thread of silver, and on the other a sheer cliff rose for some five hundred feet.

The cliff limited the view to the left, but to the right Gordon could see some of the mountains which flanked Mount Erlik Khan, and the valley far below them wandered southward away to a pass in the distance, a notch in the savage rampart of the hills.

"This is life for you, El Borak," said Yogok, pointing to the pass. "Three miles from the spot where we now stand this trail leads down into the valley where there is water and game and rich grass for the horses. You can follow it southward beyond the pass for three days' journey when you will come into country you know well. It is inhabited by marauding tribes, but they will not attack a party as large as yours. You can be through the pass before the Kirghiz round the mountain, and they will not follow you through it. That is the limit of their country. Now let me go."

"Not yet; I'll release you at the pass. You can make your way back here easily and wait for the Kirghiz, and tell them any lie you want to about the goddess."

Yogok glared angrily at Gordon. The American's eyes were bloodshot, the skin stretched taut over the bones of his face. He looked like a man who had been sweated in hell's fires, and he felt the same way. There was no reason for Yogok's strident objections, except a desire to get out of the company of those he hated as quickly as possible.

In Gordon's state a man reverts to primitive instincts, and the American held his thrumming nerves in an iron grip to keep from braining the priest with his gun butt. Dispute and importunities were like screaming insults to his struggling brain.

While the priest squawked, and Gordon hesitated between reasoning with him or knocking him down, the Turkomans, inspired by the gold and food, and eager for the trail, began to crowd past him. Half a dozen had emerged on the ledge when Gordon noticed them, and ordering Orkhan to bring Yogok along, he rode past those on the ledge, intending to take the lead as usual. But one of the men was already out to the path, and could neither turn back nor hug the wall close enough to let Gordon by.

The American, perforce, called to him to go ahead, and he would follow, and even as Gordon set his horse to the trail a volley of boulders came thundering down from above.

They hit the wretched Turkoman and swept him and his horse off the trail as a broom sweeps a spider from a wall. One of the stones, bouncing from the ledge, hit Gordon's horse and broke its leg, and the beast screamed and toppled over the side after the other.

Gordon threw himself clear as it fell, landed half over the edge, and clawed a desperate way to safety with Yasmeena's screams the the yells of the Turkomans ringing in his ears. There was nothing seen to shoot at, but some of them loosed their rifles anyway, and the volley was greeted by a wild peal of mocking laughter from the cliffs above.

In no way unnerved by his narrow escape, Gordon drove his men back into the shelter of the cave. They were like wolves in a trap, ready to strike blind right and left, and a dozen tulwars hovered over Yogok's head.

"Slay him! He has led us into a trap! Allah!"

Yogok's face was a green, convulsed mask of fear. He squalled like a tortured cat.

"Nay! I led you swift and sure! The Kirghiz could not have reached this side of the mountain by this time!"

"Were there monks hiding in these cells?" asked Gordon. "They could have sneaked out when they saw us coming in. Is that a monk up there?"

"Nay; as Erlik is my witness! We work the gold three moons a year; at other times it is death to go near Mount Erlik. I know not who it is."

Gordon ventured out on the path again and was greeted by another shower of stones, which he barely avoided, and a voice yelled high above him:

"You Yankee dog, how do you like that? I've got you now, damn you! Thought I was done for when I fell into that fissure, didn't you? Well, there was a ledge a few feet down that I landed on. You couldn't see it because the sun wasn't high enough to shine down into it. If I'd had a gun I'd have killed you when you looked down. I climbed out after you left."

"Ormond!" snarled Gordon.

"Did you think I hadn't wormed anything out of that monk?" the Englishman yelled. "He told me all about the paths and Mount Erlik after I'd caved in some of his teeth with a gun barrel. I saw old Yogok with you and knew he'd lead you to Erlik. I got here first. I'd have barred the door and locked you out to be butchered by the fellows who're chasing you, but I couldn't lift the bars. But anyway, I've got you trapped. You can't leave the cave; if you do I'll mash you like insects on the path. I can see you on it, and you can't see me. I'm going to keep you here until the Kirghiz come up. I've still got Yasmeena's symbol. They'll listen to me.

"I'll tell them Yogok is helping you to kidnap her; they'll kill you all except her. They'll take her back, but I don't care now. I don't need that Kashmiri's money. I've got the secret of Mount Erlik Khan!"

Gordon fell back into the doorway and repeated what the Englishman had said. Yogok turned a shade greener in his fear, and all stared silently at El Borak. His bloodshot gaze traveled over them as they stood blinking, disheveled, and haggard, with lamps paled by the dawn, like ghouls caught above earth by daybreak. Grimly he marshaled his straying wits. Gordon had never reached the ultimate limits of his endurance; always he had plumbed a deeper, hidden reservoir of vitality below what seemed the last.

"Is there another way out of here?" he demanded.

Yogok shook his head, chattering again with terror. "No way that men and horses can go."

"What do you mean?"

The priest moved back into the darkness and held a lamp close to the flank of the wall where the tunnel narrowed for the entrance. Rusty bits of metal jutted from the rock.

"Here was once a ladder," he said. "It led far up to a crevice in the wall where long ago one sat to watch the southern pass for invaders. But none has climbed it for many years, and the handholds are rusty and rotten. The crevice opens on the sheer of the outer cliffs, and even if a man reached it, he could scarcely climb down the outside."

"Well, maybe I can pick Ormond off from the crevice," muttered Gordon, his head swimming with the effort of thinking.

Standing still was making infinitely harder his fight to keep awake. The muttering of the Turkomans was a meaningless tangle of sound, and Yasmeena's dark anxious eyes seemed to be looking at him from a vast distance. He thought he felt her arms cling to him briefly, but could not be sure. The lights were beginning to swim in a thick mist.

Beating himself into wakefulness by striking his own face with his open hand, he began to climb, a rifle slung to his back. Orkhan was plucking at him, begging to be allowed to make the attempt in his stead, but Gordon shook him off. In his dazed brain was a conviction that the responsibility was his own. He went up like an automaton, slowly, all his muddled faculties concentrating grimly on the task.

Fifty feet up, the light of the lamps ceased to aid him, and he groped upward in the gloom, feeling for the rusty bolts set in the wall. They were so rotten that he dared not put his full weight on any one of them. In some places they were missing and he clung with his fingers in the niches where they had been. Only the slant of the rock enabled him to accomplish the climb at all, and it seemed endless, a hell-born eternity of torture.

The lamps below him were like fireflies in the darkness, and the roof with its clustering stalactites was only a few yards above his head. Then he saw a gleam of light, and an instant later he was crouching in a cleft that opened on the outer air. It was only a couple of yards wide, and not tall enough for a man to stand upright.

He crawled along it for some thirty feet and then looked out on a rugged slant that pitched down to a crest of cliffs, a hundred feet below. He could not see the ledge where the door opened, nor the path that led from it, but he saw a figure crouching among the boulders along the lip of the cliff, and he unslung his rifle.

Ordinarily he could not have missed at that range. But his bloodshot eyes refused to line the sights. Slumber never assails a weary man so fiercely as in the growing light of dawn. The figure among the rocks below merged and blended fantastically with the scenery, and the sights of the rifle were mere blurs.

Setting his teeth, Gordon pulled the trigger, and the bullet smashed on the rock a foot from Ormond's head. The Englishman dived out of sight among the boulders.

In desperation Gordon slung his rifle and threw a leg over the lip of the cleft. He was certain that Ormond had no firearm. Down below the Turkomans were clamoring like a wolf pack, but his numbed faculties were fully occupied with the task of climbing down the ribbed pitch. He stumbled and fumbled and nearly fell, and at last he did slip and came sliding and tumbling down until his rifle caught on a projection and held him dangling by the strap.

In a red mist he saw Ormond break cover, with a tulwar that he must have found in the cavern, and in a panic lest the Englishman climb up and kill him as he hung helplessly, Gordon braced his feet and elbows against the rock and wrenched savagely, breaking the rifle strap. He plunged down like a plummet, hit the slope, clawed at rocks and knobs, and brought up on shalving stone a dozen feet from the cliff edge, while his rifle, tumbling before him, slid over and was gone.

The fall jolted his numbed nerves back into life again, knocked some of the cobwebs out of his dizzy brain. Ormond was within a few steps of him when he scrambled up, drawing his scimitar. The Englishman was as savage and haggard in appearance as was Gordon, and his eyes blazed with a frenzy that almost amounted to madness.

"Steel to steel now, El Borak!" Ormond gritted. "We'll see if you're the swordsman they say you are!"

Ormond came with a rush and Gordon met him, fired above his exhaustion by his hate and the stinging frenzy of battle. They fought back and forth along the cliff edge, with a foot to spare between them and eternity sometimes, until the clangor of the swords wakened the eagles to shrill hysteria.

Ormond fought like a wild man, yet with all the craft the sword masters of his native England had taught him. Gordon fought as he had learned to fight in grim and merciless battles in the hills and the steppes and the deserts. He fought as an Afghan fights, with the furious intensity of onslaught that gathers force like a rising hurricane as it progresses.

Beating on his blade like a smith on an anvil, Gordon drove the Englishman staggering before him, until the man swayed dizzily with his heels over the edge of the cliff.

"Swine!" gasped Ormond with his last breath, and spat in his enemy's face and slashed madly at his head.

"This for Ahmed!" roared Gordon, and his scimitar whirled past Ormond's blade and crunched home.

The Englishman reeled outward, his features suddenly blotted out by blood and brains, and pitched backward into the gulf without a sound.

Gordon sat down on a boulder, suddenly aware of the quivering of his leg muscles. He sat there, his gory blade across his knees and his head sunk in his hands, his brain a black blank, until shouts welling up from below roused him to consciousness.

"Ohai, El Borak! A man with a cleft head has fallen past us into the valley! Art thou safe? We await orders!"

He lifted his head and glanced at the sun which was just rising over the eastern peaks, turning to crimson flame the snow of Mount Erlik Khan. He would have traded all the gold of the monks of Yolgan to be allowed to lie down and sleep for an hour, and climbing up on his stiffened legs that

291

trembled with his weight was a task of appalling magnitude. But his labor was not yet done; there was no rest for him this side of the pass.

Summoning the shreds of strength, he shouted down to the raiders.

"Get upon the horses and ride, sons of nameless dogs! Follow the trail and I will come along the cliff. I see a place beyond the next bend where I can climb down to the trail. Bring Yogok with you; he has earned his release, but the time is not yet."

"Hurry, El Borak," floated up Yasmeena's golden call. "It is far to Delhi, and many mountains lie between!"

Gordon laughed and sheathed his scimitar, and his laugh sounded like the ghastly mirth of a hyena; below him the Turkomans had taken the road and were already singing a chant improvised in his honor, naming 'Son of the Sword' the man who staggered along the cliffs above them, with a face like a grinning skull and feet that left smears of blood on the rock.

Chapter XI

IT WAS THE stealthy clink of steel on stone that wakened Gordon. In the dim starlight a shadowy bulk loomed over him and something glinted in the lifted hand.

Gordon went into action like a steel spring uncoiling. His left hand checked the descending wrist with its curved knife, and simultaneously he heaved upward and locked his right hand savagely on a hairy throat.

A gurgling gasp was strangled in that throat and Gordon, resisting the other's terrific plunges, hooked a leg about his knee and heaved him over and underneath. There was no sound except the rasp and thud of straining bodies. Gordon fought, as always, in grim silence. No sound came from the straining lips of the man beneath. His right hand writhed in Gordon's grip while his left tore futilely at the wrist whose iron fingers drove deeper and deeper into the throat they grasped. That wrist felt like a mass of woven steel wires to the weakening fingers that clawed at it. Grimly Gordon maintained his position, driving all the power of his compact shoulders and corded arms into his throttling fingers. He knew it was his life or that of the man who had crept up to stab him in the dark. In that unmapped corner of the Afghan mountains all fights were to the death. The tearing fingers relaxed. A convulsive shudder ran through the great body straining beneath the American. It went limp.

THE END

HAWK OF THE HILLS

I

TO A MAN standing in the gorge below, the man clinging to the sloping cliff would have been invisible, hidden from sight by the jutting ledges that looked like irregular stone steps from a distance. From a distance, also, the rugged wall looked easy to climb; but there were heart-breaking spaces between those ledges--stretches of treacherous shale, and steep pitches where clawing fingers and groping toes scarcely found a grip.

One misstep, one handhold lost and the climber would have pitched backward in a headlong, rolling fall three hundred feet to the rocky canyon bed. But the man on the cliff was Francis Xavier Gordon, and it was not his destiny to dash out his brains on the floor of a Himalayan gorge.

He was reaching the end of his climb. The rim of the wall was only a few feet above him, but the intervening space was the most dangerous he had yet covered. He paused to shake the sweat from his eyes, drew a deep breath through his nostrils, and once more matched eye and muscle against the brute treachery of the gigantic barrier. Faint yells welled up from below, vibrant with hate and edged with blood lust. He did not look down. His upper lip lifted in a silent snarl, as a panther might snarl at the sound of his hunters' voices. That was all. His fingers clawed at the stone until blood oozed from under his broken nails. Rivulets of gravel started beneath his boots and streamed down the ledges. He was almost there--but under his toe a jutting stone began to give way. With an explosive expansion of energy that brought a tortured gasp from him, he lunged upward, just as his foothold tore from the soil that had held it. For one sickening instant he felt eternity yawn beneath him--then his upflung fingers hooked over the rim of the crest. For an instant he hung there, suspended, while pebbles and stones went rattling down the face of the cliff in a miniature avalanche. Then with a powerful knotting and contracting of iron biceps, he lifted his weight and an instant later climbed over the rim and stared down.

He could make out nothing in the gorge below, beyond the glimpse of a tangle of thickets. The jutting ledges obstructed the view from above as well as from below. But he knew his pursuers were ranging those thickets down there, the men whose knives were still reeking with the blood of his friends. He heard their voices, edged with the hysteria of murder, dwindling westward. They were following a blind lead and a false trail.

Gordon stood up on the rim of the gigantic wall, the one atom of visible life among monstrous pillars and abutments of stone; they rose on all sides, dwarfing him, brown insensible giants shouldering the sky. But Gordon gave no thought to the somber magnificence of his surroundings, or of his own comparative insignificance.

Scenery, however awesome, is but a background for the human drama in its varying phases. Gordon's soul was a maelstrom of wrath, and the distant, dwindling shout below him drove crimson waves of murder surging through his brain. He drew from his boot the long knife he had placed there when he began his desperate climb. Half-dried blood stained the sharp steel, and the sight of it gave him a fierce satisfaction. There were dead men back there in the valley into which the gorge ran, and not all of them were Gordon's Afridi friends. Some were Orakzai, the henchmen of the traitor Afdal Khan--the treacherous dogs who had sat down in seeming amity with Yusef Shah, the Afridi chief, his three headmen and his American ally, and who had turned the friendly conference suddenly into a holocaust of murder.

Gordon's shirt was in ribbons, revealing a shallow sword cut across the thick muscles of his breast, from which blood oozed slowly. His black hair was plastered with sweat, the scabbards at his hips empty. He might have been a statue on the cliffs, he stood so motionless, except for the steady rise and fall of his arching chest as he breathed deep through expanded nostrils. In his black eyes grew a flame like fire on deep black water. His body grew rigid; muscles swelled in knotted cords on his arms, and the veins of his temples stood out.

Treachery and murder! He was still bewildered, seeking a motive. His actions until this moment had been largely instinctive, reflexes responding to peril and the threat of destruction. The episode had been so unexpected--so totally lacking in apparent reason. One moment a hum of friendly conversation, men sitting cross-legged about a fire while tea boiled and meat roasted; the next instant knives sinking home, guns crashing, men falling in the smoke--Afridi men; his friends, struck down about him, with their rifles laid aside, their knives in their scabbards.

Only his steel-trap coordination had saved him--that instant, primitive reaction to danger that is not dependent upon reason or any logical thought process. Even before his conscious mind grasped what was happening, Gordon was on his feet with both guns blazing. And then there was no time for consecutive thinking, nothing but desperate hand-to-hand-fighting, and flight on foot--a long run and a hard climb. But for the thicket-choked mouth of a narrow gorge they would have had him, in spite of everything.

Now, temporarily safe, he could pause and apply reasoning to the problem of why Afdal Khan, chief of the Khoruk Orakzai, plotted thus foully to slay the four chiefs of his neighbors, the Afridis of Kurram, and their feringhi friend. But no motive presented itself. The massacre seemed utterly wanton and reasonless. At the moment Gordon did not greatly care. It was enough to know that his friends were dead, and to know who had killed them.

Another tier of rock rose some yards behind him, broken by a narrow, twisting cleft. Into this he moved. He did not expect to meet an enemy; they would all be down there in the gorge, beating up the thickets for him; but he carried the long knife in his hand, just in case.

It was purely an instinctive gesture, like the unsheathing of a panther's claws. His dark face was like iron; his black eyes burned redly; as he strode along the narrow defile he was more dangerous than any wounded panther. An urge painful in its intensity beat at his brain like a hammer that would not ease; revenge! revenge! revenge! All the depths of his being responded to the reverberation. The thin veneer of civilization had been swept away by a red tidal wave. Gordon had gone back a million years into the red dawn of man's beginning; he was as starkly primitive as the colossal stones that rose about him.

Ahead of him the defile twisted about a jutting shoulder to come, as he knew, out upon a winding mountain path. That path would lead him out of the country of his enemies, and he had no reason to expect to meet any of them upon it. So it was a shocking surprise to him when he rounded the granite shoulder and came face to face with a tall man who lolled against a rock, with a pistol in his hand.

That pistol was leveled at the American's breast.

Gordon stood motionless, a dozen feet separating the two men. Beyond the tall man stood a finely caparisoned Kabuli stallion, tied to a tamarisk.

"Ali Bahadur!" muttered Gordon, the red flame in his black eyes.

"Aye!" Ali Bahadur was clad in Pathan elegance. His boots were stitched with gilt thread, his turban was of rose-colored silk, and his girdled khalat was gaudily striped. He was a handsome man, with an aquiline face and dark, alert eyes, which just now were lighted with cruel triumph. He laughed mockingly.

"I was not mistaken, El Borak. When you fled into the thicket-choked mouth of the gorge, I did not follow you as the others did. They ran headlong into the copse, on foot, bawling like bulls. Not I. I did not think you would flee on down the gorge until my men cornered you. I believed that as soon as you got out of their sight you would climb the wall, though no man has ever climbed it before. I knew you would climb out on this side, for not even Shaitan the Damned could scale those sheer precipices on the other side of the gorge.

"So I galloped back up the valley to where, a mile north of the spot where we camped, another gorge opens and runs westward. This path leads up out of that gorge and crosses the ridge and here turns southwesterly--as I knew you knew.

My steed is swift! I knew this point was the only one at which you could reach this trail, and when I arrived, there were no boot prints in the dust to tell me you had reached it and passed on ahead of me. Nay, hardly had I paused when I heard stones rattling down the cliff, so I dismounted and awaited your coming! For only through that cleft could you reach the path."

"You came alone," said Gordon, never taking his eyes from the Orakzai. "You have more guts than I thought."

"I knew you had no guns," answered Ali Bahadur. "I saw you empty them and throw them away and draw your knife as you fought your way through my warriors. Courage? Any fool can have courage. I have wits, which is better."

"You talk like a Persian," muttered Gordon. He was caught fairly, his scabbards empty, his knife arm hanging at his side. He knew Ali would shoot at the slightest motion.

"My brother Afdal Khan will praise me when I bring him your head!" taunted the Orakzai. His Oriental vanity could not resist making a grandiose gesture out of his triumph. Like many of his race, swaggering dramatics were his weakness; if he had simply hidden behind a rock and shot Gordon when he first appeared, Ali Bahadur might be alive today.

"Why did Afdal Khan invite us to a feast and then murder my friends?" Gordon demanded. "There has been peace between the clans for years."

"My brother has ambitions," answered Ali Bahadur. "The Afridis stood in his way, though they knew it not. Why should my brother waste men in a long war to remove them? Only a fool gives warning before he strikes."

"And only a dog turns traitor," retorted Gordon.

"The salt had not been eaten," reminded Ali. "The men of Kurram were fools, and thou with them!" He was enjoying his triumph to the utmost, prolonging the scene as greatly as he dared. He knew he should have shot already.

There was a tense readiness about Gordon's posture that made his flesh crawl, and Gordon's eyes were red flame when the sun struck them. But it glutted Ali's vanity deliriously to know that El Borak, the grimmest fighter in all the North, was in his power--held at pistol muzzle, poised on the brink of Jehannum into which he would topple at the pressure of a finger on the trigger. Ali Bahadur knew Gordon's deadly quickness, how he could spring and kill in the flicker of an eyelid.

But no human thews could cross the intervening yards quicker than lead spitting from a pistol muzzle. And at the first hint of movement, Ali would bring the gratifying scene to a sudden close.

Gordon opened his mouth as if to speak, then closed it. The suspicious Pathan was instantly tense. Gordon's eyes flickered past him, then back instantly, and fixed on his face with an increased intensity. To all appearances Gordon had seen something behind Ali-- something he did not wish Ali to see, and was doing all in his power to conceal the fact that he had seen something, to keep Ali from turning his head. And turn his head Ali did; he did it involuntarily, in spite of himself. He had not completed the motion before he sensed the trick and jerked his head back, firing as he did so, even as he caught the blur that was the lightninglike motion of Gordon's right arm.

Motion and shot were practically simultaneous. Ali went to his knees as if struck by sudden paralysis, and flopped over on his side. Gurgling and choking he struggled to his elbows, eyes starting from his head, lips drawn back in a ghastly grin, his chin held up by the hilt of Gordon's knife that jutted from his throat. With a dying effort he lifted the pistol with both hands, trying to cock it with fumbling thumbs. Then blood gushed from his blue lips and the pistol slipped from his hands. His fingers clawed briefly at the earth, then spread and stiffened, and his head sank down on his extended arms.

Gordon had not moved from his tracks. Blood oozed slowly from a round blue hole in his left shoulder. He did not seem to be aware of the wound. Not until Ali Bahadur's brief, spasmodic twitchings had ceased did he move. He snarled, the thick, blood-glutted snarl of a jungle cat, and spat toward the prostrate Orakzai.

He made no move to recover the knife he had thrown with such deadly force and aim, nor did he pick up the smoking pistol. He strode to the stallion which snorted and trembled at the reek of spilt blood, untied him and swung into the gilt-stitched saddle.

As he reined away up the winding hill path he turned in the saddle and shook his fist in the direction of his enemies--a threat and a ferocious promise; the game had just begun; the first blood had been shed in a feud that was to litter the hills with charred villages and the bodies of dead men, and trouble the dreams of kings and viceroys.

II

GEOFFREY WILLOUGHBY SHIFTED himself in his saddle and glanced at the gaunt ridges and bare stone crags that rose about him, mentally comparing the members of his escort with the features of the landscape.

Physical environment inescapably molded its inhabitants. With one exception his companions were as sullen, hard, barbarous and somber as the huge brown rocks that frowned about them. The one exception was Suleiman, a Punjabi Moslem, ostensibly his servant, actually a valuable member of the English secret service.

Willoughby himself was not a member of that service. His status was unique; he was one of those ubiquitous Englishmen who steadily build the empire, moving obscurely behind the scenes, and letting other men take the credit-- men in bemedaled uniforms, or loud-voiced men with top hats and titles.

Few knew just what Willoughby's commission was, or what niche he filled in the official structure; but the epitome of the man and his career was once embodied in the request of a harried deputy commissioner: "Hell on the border; send Willoughby!" Because of his unadvertised activities, troops did not march and cannons did not boom on more occasions than the general public ever realized. So it was not really surprising--except to those die-hards who refuse to believe that maintaining peace on the Afghan Border is fundamentally different from keeping order in Trafalgar Square--that Willoughby should be riding forth in the company of hairy cutthroats to arbitrate a bloody hill feud at the request of an Oriental despot.

Willoughby was of medium height and stockily, almost chubbily, built, though there were unexpected muscles under his ruddy skin. His hair was taffy-colored, his eyes blue, wide and deceptively ingenuous. He wore civilian khakis and a huge sun helmet. If he was armed the fact was not apparent. His frank, faintly freckled face was not unpleasant, but it displayed little evidence of the razor-sharp brain that worked behind it.

He jogged along as placidly as if he were ambling down a lane in his native Suffolk, and he was more at ease than the ruffians who accompanied him--four wild-looking, ragged tribesmen under the command of a patriarch whose stately carriage and gray-shot pointed beard did not conceal the innate savagery reflected in his truculent visage. Baber Ali, uncle of Afdal Khan, was old, but his back was straight as a trooper's, and his gaunt frame was wolfishly hard. He was his nephew's right-hand man, possessing all Afdal Khan's ferocity, but little of his subtlety and cunning.

They were following a trail that looped down a steep slope which fell away for a thousand feet into a labyrinth of gorges. In a valley a mile to the south, Willoughby sighted a huddle of charred and blackened ruins.

"A village, Baber?" he asked.

Baber snarled like an old wolf.

"Aye! That was Khuttak! El Borak and his devils burned it and slew every man able to bear arms."

Willoughby looked with new interest. It was such things as that he had come to stop, and it was El Borak he was now riding to see.

"El Borak is a son of Shaitan," growled old Baber.

"Not a village of Afdal Khan's remains unburned save only Khoruk itself. And of the outlying towers, only my sangar remains, which lies between this spot and Khoruk. Now he has seized the cavern called Akbar's Castle, and that is in Orakzai territory. By Allah, for an hour we have been riding in country claimed by us Orakzai, but now it has become a no man's land, a border strewn with corpses and burned villages, where no man's life is safe. At any moment we may be fired upon."

"Gordon has given his word," reminded Willoughby.

"His word is not wind," admitted the old ruffian grudgingly.

They had dropped down from the heights and were traversing a narrow plateau that broke into a series of gorges at the other end. Willoughby thought of the letter in his pocket, which had come to him by devious ways. He had memorized it, recognizing its dramatic value as a historical document.

Geoffrey Willoughby,

Ghazrael Fort:

If you want to parley, come to Shaitan's Minaret, alone. Let your escort stop outside the mouth of the gorge. They won't be molested, but if any Orakzai follows you into the gorge, he'll be shot.

Francis X. Gordon.

Concise and to the point. Parley, eh? The man had assumed the role of a general carrying on a regular war, and left no doubt that he considered Willoughby, not a disinterested arbiter, but a diplomat working in the interests of the opposing side.

"We should be near the Gorge of the Minaret," said Willoughby.

Baber Ali pointed. "There is its mouth."

"Await me here."

Suleiman dismounted and eased his steed's girths. The Pathans climbed down uneasily, hugging their rifles and scanning the escarpments. Somewhere down that winding gorge Gordon was lurking with his vengeful warriors. The Orakzai were afraid. They were miles from Khoruk, in the midst of a region that had become a bloody debatable ground through slaughter on both sides. They instinctively looked toward the southwest where, miles away, lay the crag-built village of Kurram.

Baber twisted his beard and gnawed the corner of his lip. He seemed devoured by an inward fire of anger and suspicion which would not let him rest.

"You will go forward from this point alone, sahib?"

Willoughby nodded, gathering up his reins.

"He will kill you!"

"I think not."

Willoughby knew very well that Baber Ali would never have thus placed himself within Gordon's reach unless he placed full confidence in the American's promise of safety.

"Then make the dog agree to a truce!" snarled Baber, his savage arrogance submerging his grudging civility. "By Allah, this feud is a thorn in the side of Afdal Khan--and of me!"

"We'll see." Willoughby nudged his mount with his heels and jogged on down the gorge, not an impressive figure at all as he slumped carelessly in his saddle, his cork helmet bobbing with each step of the horse. Behind him the Pathans watched eagerly until he passed out of sight around a bend of the canyon.

Willoughby's tranquillity was partly, though not altogether, assumed. He was not afraid, nor was he excited. But he would have been more than human had not the anticipation of meeting El Borak stirred his imagination to a certain extent and roused speculations.

The name of El Borak was woven in the tales told in all the caravanserais and bazaars from Teheran to Bombay. For three years rumors had drifted down the Khyber of intrigues and grim battles fought among the lonely hills, where a hard-eyed white man was hewing out a place of power among the wild tribesmen.

The British had not cared to interfere until this latest stone cast by Gordon into the pool of Afghan politics threatened to spread ripples that might lap at the doors of foreign palaces. Hence Willoughby, jogging down the winding Gorge of the Minaret. Queer sort of renegade,

Willoughby reflected. Most white men who went native were despised by the people among whom they cast their lot. But even Gordon's enemies respected him, and it did not seem to be on account of his celebrated fighting ability alone. Gordon, Willoughby vaguely understood, had grown up on the southwestern frontier of the United States, and had a formidable reputation as a gun fanner before he ever drifted East.

Willoughby had covered a mile from the mouth of the gorge before he rounded a bend in the rocky wall and saw the Minaret looming up before him--a tall, tapering spirelike crag, detached, except at the base, from the canyon wall. No one was in sight. Willoughby tied his horse in the shade of the cliff and walked toward the base of the Minaret where he halted and stood gently fanning himself with his helmet, and idly wondering how many rifles were aimed at him from vantage points invisible to himself. Abruptly Gordon was before him.

It was a startling experience, even to a man whose nerves were under as perfect control as Willoughby's. The Englishman indeed stopped fanning himself and stood motionless, holding the helmet lifted. There had been no sound, not even the crunch of rubble under a boot heel to warn him. One instant the space before him was empty, the next it was filled by a figure vibrant with dynamic life. Boulders strewn at the foot of the wall offered plenty of

cover for a stealthy advance, but the miracle of that advance-
-to Willoughby, who had never fought Yaqui Indians in
their own country--was the silence with which Gordon had
accomplished it.

"You're Willoughby, of course." The Southern accent
was faint, but unmistakable.

Willoughby nodded, absorbed in his scrutiny of the
man before him. Gordon was not a large man, but he was
remarkably compact, with a squareness of shoulders and
a thickness of chest that reflected unusual strength and
vitality. Willoughby noted the black butts of the heavy
pistols jutting from his hips, the knife hilt projecting from
his right boot. He sought the hard bronzed face in vain for
marks of weakness or degeneracy. There was a gleam in the
black eyes such as Willoughby had never before seen in any
man of the so-called civilized races.

No, this man was no degenerate; his plunging into
native feuds and brawls indicated no retrogression. It was
simply the response of a primitive nature seeking its most
natural environment. Willoughby felt that the man before
him must look exactly as an untamed, precivilization Anglo-
Saxon must have looked some ten thousand years before.

"I'm Willoughby," he said. "Glad you found it
convenient to meet me. Shall we sit down in the shade?"

"No. There's no need of taking up that much time.
Word came to me that you were at Ghazrael, trying to get in

touch with me. I sent you my answer by a Tajik trader. You got it, or you wouldn't be here. All right; here I am. Tell me what you've got to say and I'll answer you."

Willoughby discarded the plan he had partly formulated. The sort of diplomacy he'd had in mind wouldn't work here. This man was no dull bully, with a dominance acquired by brute strength alone, nor was he a self-seeking adventurer of the politician type, lying and bluffing his way through. He could not be bought off, nor frightened by a bluff. He was as real and vital and dangerous as a panther, though Willoughby felt no personal fear.

"All right, Gordon," he answered candidly. "My say is soon said. I'm here at the request of the Amir, and the Raj. I came to Fort Ghazrael to try to get in touch with you, as you know. My companion Suleiman helped. An escort of Orakzai met me at Ghazrael, to conduct me to Khoruk, but when I got your letter I saw no reason to go to Khoruk. They're waiting at the mouth of the gorge to conduct me back to Ghazrael when my job's done. I've talked with Afdal Khan only once, at Ghazrael. He's ready for peace. In fact it was at his request that the Amir sent me out here to try to settle this feud between you and him."

"It's none of the Amir's business," retorted Gordon. "Since when did he begin interfering with tribal feuds?"

"In this case one of the parties appealed to him," answered Willoughby. "Then the feud affects him personally.

It's needless for me to remind you that one of the main caravan roads from Persia traverses this region, and since the feud began, the caravans avoid it and turn up into Turkestan. The trade that ordinarily passes through Kabul, by which the Amir acquires much rich revenue, is being deflected out of his territory."

"And he's dickering with the Russians to get it back." Gordon laughed mirthlessly. "He's tried to keep that secret, because English guns are all that keep him on his throne. But the Russians are offering him a lot of tempting bait, and he's playing with fire--and the British are afraid he'll scorch his fingers--and theirs!"

Willoughby blinked. Still, he might have known that Gordon would know the inside of Afghan politics at least as well as himself.

"But Afdal Khan has expressed himself, both to the Amir and to me, as desiring to end this feud," argued Willoughby. "He swears he's been acting on the defensive all along. If you don't agree to at least a truce the Amir will take a hand himself. As soon as I return to Kabul and tell him you refuse to submit to arbitration, he'll declare you an outlaw, and every ruffian in the hills will be whetting his knife for your head. Be reasonable, man. Doubtless you feel you had provocation for your attacks on Afdal Khan. But you've done enough damage. Forget what's passed--"

"Forget!"

Willoughby involuntarily stepped back as the pupils of Gordon's eyes contracted like those of an angry leopard.

"Forget!" he repeated thickly. "You ask me to forget the blood of my friends! You've heard only one side of this thing. Not that I give a damn what you think, but you'll hear my side, for once. Afdal Khan has friends at court. I haven't. I don't want any."

So a wild Highland chief might have cast his defiance in the teeth of the king's emissary, thought Willoughby, fascinated by the play of passion in the dark face before him.

"Afdal Khan invited my friends to a feast and cut them down in cold blood--Yusef Shah, and this three chiefs--all sworn friends of mine, do you understand? And you ask me to forget them, as you might ask me to throw aside a worn-out scabbard! And why? So the Amir can grab his taxes off the fat Persian traders; so the Russians won't have a chance to inveigle him into some treaty the British wouldn't approve of; so the English can keep their claws sunk in on this side of the border, too!

"Well, here's my answer: You and the Amir and the Raj can all go to hell together. Go back to Amir and tell him to put a price on my head. Let him send his Uzbek guards to help the Orakzai--and as many Russians and Britishers and whatever else he's able to get. This feud will end when I kill Afdal Khan. Not before."

313

"You're sacrificing the welfare of the many to avenge the blood of the few," protested Willoughby.

"Who says I am? Afdal Khan? He's the Amir's worst enemy, if the Amir only knew it, getting him embroiled in a war that's none of his business. In another month I'll have Afdal Khan's head, and the caravans will pass freely over this road again. If Afdal Khan should win-- Why did this feud begin in the first place? I'll tell you! Afdal wants full control of the wells in this region, wells which command the caravan route, and which have been in the hands of the Afridis for centuries. Let him get possession of them and he'll fleece the merchants before they ever get to Kabul. Yes, and turn the trade permanently into Russian territory."

"He wouldn't dare--"

"He dares anything. He's got backing you don't even guess. Ask him how it is that his men are all armed with Russian rifles! Hell! Afdal's howling for help because I've taken Akbar's Castle and he can't dislodge me. He asked you to make me agree to give up the Castle, didn't he? Yes, I thought so. And if I were fool enough to do it, he'd ambush me and my men as we marched back to Kurram. You'd hardly have time to get back to Kabul before a rider would be at your heels to tell the Amir how I'd treacherously attacked Afdal Khan and been killed in self-defense, and how Afdal had been forced to attack and burn Kurram! He's trying to gain by outside intervention what he's lost in battle, and to

314

catch me off my guard and murder me as he did Yusef Shah. He's making monkeys out of the Amir and you. And you want me to let him make a monkey out of me--and a corpse too--just because a little dirty trade is being deflected from Kabul!"

"You needn't feel so hostile to the British--" Willoughby began.

"I don't; nor to the Persians, nor the Russians, either. I just want all hands to attend to their own business and leave mine alone."

"But this blood-feud madness isn't the proper thing for a white man," pleaded Willoughby. "You're not an Afghan. You're an Englishman, by descent, at least--"

"I'm Highland Scotch and black Irish by descent," grunted Gordon. "That's got nothing to do with it. I've had my say. Go back and tell the Amir the feud will end --when I've killed Afal Khan."

And turning on his heel he vanished as noiselessly as he had appeared.

Willoughby started after him helplessly. Damn it all, he'd handled this matter like an amateur! Reviewing his arguments he felt like kicking himself; but any arguments seemed puerile against the primitive determination of El Borak. Debating with him was like arguing with a wind, or a flood, or a forest fire, or some other elemental fact. The man didn't fit into any ordered classification; he was

315

as untamed as any barbarian who trod the Himalayas, yet there was nothing rudimentary or underdeveloped about his mentality.

Well, there was nothing to do at present but return to Fort Ghazrael and send a rider to Kabul, reporting failure. But the game was not played out. Willoughby's own stubborn determination was roused. The affair began to take on a personal aspect utterly lacking in most of his campaigns; he began to look upon it not only as a diplomatic problem, but also as a contest of wits between Gordon and himself. As he mounted his horse and headed back up the gorge, he swore he would terminate that feud, and that it would be terminated his way, and not Gordon's.

There was probably much truth in Gordon's assertions. Of course, he and the Amir had heard only Afdal Khan's side of the matter; and of course, Afdal Khan was a rogue. But he could not believe that the chief's ambitions were as sweeping and sinister as Gordon maintained. He could not believe they embraced more than a seizing of local power in this isolated hill district. Petty exactions on the caravans, now levied by the Afridis; that was all.

Anyway, Gordon had no business allowing his private wishes to interfere with official aims, which, faulty as they might be, nevertheless had the welfare of the people in view. Willoughby would never have let his personal feelings stand in the way of policy, and he considered that to do so was reprehensible in others. It was Gordon's duty to forget the murder of his friends--again Willoughby experienced that sensation of helplessness. Gordon would never do that. To expect him to violate his instinct was as sensible as expecting a hungry wolf to turn away from raw meat.

Willoughby had returned up the gorge as leisurely as he had ridden down it. Now he emerged from the mouth and saw Suleiman and the Pathans standing in a tense group, staring eagerly at him. Baber Ali's eyes burned like a wolf's. Willoughby felt a slight shock of surprise as he met the fierce intensity of the old chief's eyes. Why should Baber so savagely desire the success of his emissary? The Orakzai had been getting the worst of the war, but they were not whipped, by any means. Was there, after all, something behind the visible surface--some deep-laid obscure element or plot that involved Willoughby's mission? Was there truth in Gordon's accusations of foreign entanglements and veiled motives?

Babar took three steps forward, and his beard quivered with his eagerness.

"Well?" His voice was harsh as the rasp of a sword against its scabbard. "Will the dog make peace?"

Willoughby shook his head. "He swears the feud will end only when he has slain Afdal Khan."

"Thou hast failed!"

The passion in Baber's voice startled Willoughby. For an instant he thought the chief would draw his long knife and leap upon him. Then Baber Ali deliberately turned his back on the Englishman and strode to his horse. Freeing it with a savage jerk he swung into the saddle and galloped away without a backward glance. And he did not take the trail Willoughby must follow on his return to Fort Ghazrael; he rode north, in the direction of Khoruk. The implication was unmistakable; he was abandoning Willoughby to his own resources, repudiating all responsibility for him.

Suleiman bent his head as he fumbled at his mount's girths, to hide the tinge of gray that crept under his brown skin. Willoughby turned from staring after the departing chief, to see the eyes of the four tribesmen fixed unwinkingly upon him--hard, murky eyes from under shocks of tangled hair.

He felt a slight chill crawl down his spine. These men were savages, hardly above the mental level of wild beasts. They would act unthinkingly, blindly following the instincts implanted in them and their kind throughout long centuries of merciless Himalayan existence. Their instincts were to murder and plunder all men not of their own clan. He was an alien. The protection spread over him and his companion by their chief had been removed.

By turning his back and riding away as he had, Baber Ali had tacitly given permission for the feringhi to be slain.

Baber Ali was himself far more of a savage than was Afdal Khan; he was governed by his untamed emotions, and prone to do childish and horrible things in moments of passion. Infuriated by Willoughby's failure to bring about a truce, it was characteristic of him to vent his rage and disappointment on the Englishman.

Willoughby calmly reviewed the situation in the time he took to gather up his reins. He could never get back to Ghazrael without an escort. If he and Suleiman tried to ride away from these ruffians, they would undoubtedly be shot in the back. There was nothing else to do but try and bluff it out. They had been given their orders to escort him to the Gorge of the Minaret and back again to Fort Ghazrael. Those orders had not been revoked in actual words. The tribesmen might hesitate to act on their own initiative, without positive orders.

He glanced at the low-hanging sun, nudged his horse.

"Let's be on our way. We have far to ride."

He pushed straight at the cluster of men who divided sullenly to let him through. Suleiman followed him. Neither looked to right nor left, nor showed by any sign that they expected the men to do other than follow them. Silently the Pathans swung upon their horses and trailed after them, rifle butts resting on thighs, muzzles pointing upward.

Willoughby slouched in his saddle, jogging easily along. He did not look back, but he felt four pairs of beady eyes fixed on his broad back in sullen indecision. His matter-of-fact manner baffled them, exerted a certain dominance over their slow minds. But he knew that if either he or Suleiman showed the slightest sign of fear or doubt, they would be shot down instantly. He whistled tunelessly between his teeth, whimsically feeling as if he were riding along the edge of a volcano which might erupt at any instant.

They pushed eastward, following trails that wandered down into valleys and up over rugged slants. The sun dipped behind a thousand-foot ridge and the valleys were filled with purple shadows. They reached the spot where, as they passed it earlier in the day, Baber Ali had indicated that they would camp that night.

There was a well there. The Pathans drew rein without orders from Willoughby. He would rather have pushed on, but to argue would have roused suspicions of fear on his part.

The well stood near a cliff, on a broad shelf flanked by steep slopes and ravine-cut walls. The horses were unsaddled, and Suleiman spread Willoughby's blanket rolls at the foot of the wall. The Pathans, stealthy and silent as wild things, began gathering dead tamarisk for a fire. Willoughby sat down on a rock near a cleft in the wall, and began tracing a likeness of Gordon in a small notebook, straining his eyes in the last of the twilight. He had a knack in that line, and the habit had proved valuable in the past, in the matter of uncovering disguises and identifying wanted men.

He believed that his calm acceptance of obedience as a matter of course had reduced the Pathans to a state of uncertainty, if not actual awe. As long as they were uncertain, they would not attack him.

The men moved about the small camp, performing various duties. Suleiman bent over the tiny fire, and on the other side of it a Pathan was unpacking a bundle of food. Another tribesman approached the fire from behind the Punjabi, bringing more wood.

Some instinct caused Willoughby to look up, just as the Pathan with the arm load of wood came up behind Suleiman. The Punjabi had not heard the man's approach; he did not look around. His first intimation that there was any one behind him was when the tribesman drew a knife and sank it between his shoulders.

It was done too quickly for Willoughby to shout a warning. He caught the glint of the firelight on the blade as it was driven into Suleiman's back. The Punjabi cried out and fell to his knees, and the man on the other side of the fire snatched a flint-lock pistol from among his rags and shot him through the body. Suleiman drew his revolver and fired once, and the tribesman fell into the fire, shot through the head.

Suleiman slipped down in a pool of his own blood, and lay still.

It all happened while Willoughby was springing to his feet. He was unarmed. He stood frozen for an instant, helpless. One of the men picked up a rifle and fired at him point-blank. He heard the bullet smash on a rock behind him. Stung out of his paralysis he turned and sprang into the cleft of the wall. An instant later he was running as fleetly down the narrow gap as his build would allow, his heels winged by the wild howls of triumph behind him.

Willoughby would have cursed himself as he ran, could he have spared the breath. The sudden attack had been brutish, blundering, without plan or premeditation. The tribesman had unexpectedly found himself behind Suleiman and had reacted to his natural instincts. Willoughby realized that if he had had a revolver he could probably have defeated the attack, at least upon his own life. He had never needed one before; had always believed diplomacy a better weapon than a firearm. But twice today diplomacy had failed miserably. All the faults and weaknesses of his system seemed to be coming to light at once. He had made a pretty hash of this business from the start.

But he had an idea that he would soon be beyond self-censure or official blame. Those bloodthirsty yells, drawing nearer behind him, assured him of that.

Suddenly Willoughby was afraid, horribly afraid. His tongue seemed frozen to his palate and a clammy sweat beaded his skin. He ran on down the dark defile like a man running in a nightmare, his ears straining for the expected sound of sandaled feet pattering behind him, the skin between his shoulders crawling in expectation of a plunging knife. It was dark. He caromed into boulders, tripped over loose stones, tearing the skin of his hands on the shale.

Abruptly he was out of the defile, and a knife-edge ridge loomed ahead of him like the steep roof of a house, black against the blue-black star-dotted sky. He struggled up it, his breath coming in racking gasps. He knew they were close behind him, although he could see nothing in the dark.

But keen eyes saw his dim bulk outlined against the stars when he crawled over the crest. Tongues of red flame licked in the darkness below him; reports banged flatly against the rocky walls. Frantically he hauled himself over and rolled down the slope on the other side. But not all the way. Almost immediately he brought up against something hard yet yielding. Vaguely, half blind from sweat and exhaustion, he saw a figure looming over him, some object lifted in menace outlined against the stars. He threw up an arm but it did not check the swinging rifle stock. Fire burst in glittering sparks about him, and he did not hear the crackling of the rifles that ran along the crest of the ridge.

III

IT WAS THE smashing reverberation of gunfire, reechoing between narrow walls, which first impressed itself on Willoughby's sluggish reviving consciousness. Then he was aware of his throbbing head. Lifting a hand to it, he discovered it had been efficiently bandaged. He was lying on what felt like a sheepskin coat, and he felt bare, cold rock under it. He struggled to his elbows and shook his head violently, setting his teeth against the shooting pain that resulted.

He lay in darkness, yet, some yards away, a white curtain shimmered dazzlingly before him. He swore and batted his eyes, and as his blurred sight cleared, things about him assumed their proper aspect. He was in a cave, and that white curtain was the mouth, with moonlight streaming across it. He started to rise and a rough hand grabbed him and jerked him down again, just as a rifle cracked somewhere outside and a bullet whined into the cave and smacked viciously on the stone wall.

"Keep down, sahib!" growled a voice in Pashtu. The Englishman was aware of men in the cave with him. Their eyes shone in the dark as they turned their heads toward him.

His groggy brain was functioning now, and he could understand what he saw. The cave was not a large one, and it opened upon a narrow plateau, bathed in vivid moonlight and flanked by rugged slopes. For about a hundred yards before the cave mouth the plain lay level and almost bare of rocks, but beyond that it was strewn with boulders and cut by gullies. And from those boulders and ravines white puffs bloomed from time to time, accompanied by sharp reports. Lead smacked and spattered about the entrance and whined venomously into the cavern. Somewhere a man was breathing in panting gasps that told Willoughby he was badly wounded. The moon hung at such an angle that it drove a white bar down the middle of the cave for some fifteen feet; and death lurked in that narrow strip, for the men in the cave.

They lay close to the walls on either side, hidden from the view of the besiegers and partially sheltered by broken rocks. They were not returning the fire. They lay still, hugging their rifles, the whites of their eyes gleaming in the darkness as they turned their heads from time to time.

Willoughby was about to speak, when on the plain outside a kalpak was poked cautiously around one end of a boulder. There was no response from the cave. The defenders knew that in all probability that sheepskin cap was stuck on a gun muzzle instead of a human head.

"Do you see the dog, sahib?" whispered a voice in the gloom, and Willoughby started as the answer came. For though it was framed in almost accentless Pashtu, it was the voice of a white man--the unmistakable voice of Francis Xavier Gordon.

"I see him. He's peeking around the other end of that boulder--trying to get a better shot at us, while his mate distracts our attention with that hat. See? Close to the ground, there--just about a hand's breadth of his head. Ready? All right--now!"

Six rifles cracked in a stuttering detonation, and instantly, a white-clad figure rolled from behind the boulder, flopped convulsively and lay still, a sprawl of twisted limbs in the moonlight. That, considered Willoughby, was damned good shooting, if no more than one of the six bullets hit the exposed head. The men in the cave had phosphorus rubbed in their sights, and they were not wasting ammunition.

The success of the fusillade was answered by a chorus of wrathful yells from outside, and a storm of lead burst against the cave. Plenty of it found its way inside, and hot metal splashing from a glancing slug stung Willoughby's arm through the sleeve. But the marksmen were aiming too high to do any damage, unwilling as they were to expose themselves to the fire from the cavern. Gordon's men were grimly silent; they neither wasted lead on unseen enemies, not indulged in the jeers and taunts so dear to the Afghan fighting man.

When the storm subsided to a period of vengeful waiting, Willoughby called in a low voice: "Gordon! Oh, I say there, Gordon!"

An instant later a dim form crawled to his side.

"Coming to at last, Willoughby? Here, take a swig of this."

A whiskey flask was pressed into his hand.

"No, thanks, old chap. I think you have a man who needs it worse than I." Even as he spoke he was aware that he no longer heard the stertorous breathing of the wounded man.

"That was Ahmed Khan," said Gordon. "He's gone; died while they were shooting in here a moment ago. Shot through the body as we were making for this cave."

"That's the Orakzai out there?" asked Willoughby.

"Who else?"

The throbbing in his head irritated the Englishman; his right forearm was painfully bruised, and he was thirsty.

"Let me get this straight, Gordon--am I a prisoner?"

"That depends on the way you look at it. Just now we're all hemmed up in this cave. Sorry about your broken head. But the fellow who hit you didn't know but what you were an Orakzai. It was dark."

"What the devil happened, anyway?" demanded Willoughby. "I remember them killing Suleiman, and

327

chasing me--then I got that clout on the head and went out. I must have been unconscious for hours."

"You were. Six of my men trailed you all the way from the mouth of the Gorge of the Minaret. I didn't trust Baber Ali, though it didn't occur to me that he'd try to kill you. I was well on my way back to Akbar's Castle when one of the men caught up with me and told me that Baber Ali had ridden off in the direction of his sangar and left you with his four tribesmen. I believed they intended murdering you on the road to Ghazrael, and laying it onto me. So I started after you myself.

"When you pitched camp by Jehungir's Well my men were watching from a distance, and I wasn't far away, riding hard to catch up with you before your escort killed you. Naturally I wasn't following the open trail you followed. I was coming up from the south. My men saw the Orakzai kill Suleiman, but they weren't close enough to do anything about it.

"When you ran into the defile with the Orakzai pelting after you, my men lost sight of you all in the darkness and were trying to locate you when you bumped into them. Khoda Khan knocked you stiff before he recognized you. They fired on the three men who were chasing you, and those fellows took to their heels. I heard the firing, and so did somebody else; we arrived on the scene just about the same time."

"Eh? What's that? Who?"

"Your friend, Baber Ali, with thirty horsemen! We slung you on a horse, and it was a running fight until moonrise. We were trying to get back to Akbar's Castle, but they had fresher horses and they ran us down. They got us hemmed out there on that plain and the only thing we could do was to duck in here and make our stand. So here we are, and out there he is, with thirty men--not including the three ruffians who killed your servant. He shot them in their tracks. I heard the shots and their death howls as we rode for the hills."

"I guess the old villain repented of his temper," said Willoughby. "What a cursed pity he didn't arrive a few minutes earlier. It would have saved Suleiman, poor devil. Thanks for pulling me out of a nasty mess, old fellow. And now, if you don't mind, I'll be going."

"Where?"

"Why, out there! To Ghazrael. First to Baber Ali, naturally. I've got a few things to tell that old devil."

"Willoughby, are you a fool?" Gordon demanded harshly.

"To think you'd let me go? Well, perhaps I am. I'd forgotten that as soon as I return to Kabul, you'll be declared an outlaw, won't you? But you can't keep me here forever, you know--"

"I don't intend to try," answered Gordon with a hint of anger. "If your skull wasn't already cracked I'd feel inclined to bash your head for accusing me of imprisoning you. Shake the cobwebs out of your brain. If you're an example of a British diplomat, Heaven help the empire!

"Don't you know you'd instantly be filled with lead if you stepped out there? Don't you know that Baber Ali wants your head right now more than he does mine?

"Why do you think he hasn't sent a man riding a horse to death to tell Afdal Khan he's got El Borak trapped in a cave miles from Akbar's Castle? I'll tell you: Baber Ali doesn't want Afdal to know what a mess he's made of things.

"It was characteristic of the old devil to ride off and leave you to be murdered by his ruffians; but when he cooled off a little, he realized that he'd be held responsible. He must have gotten clear to his sangar before he realized that. Then he took a band of horsemen and came pelting after you to save you, in the interest of his own skin, of course, but he got there too late--too late to keep them from killing Suleiman, and too late to kill you."

"But what--"

"Look at it from his viewpoint, man! If he'd gotten there in time to keep anyone from being killed, it would have been all right. But with Suleiman killed by his men, he dares not leave you alive. He knows the English will hold him responsible for Suleiman's death, if they learn the true circumstances. And he knows what it means to murder a British subject--especially one as important in the secret

330

service as I happen to know Suleiman was. But if he could put you out of the way, he could swear I killed you and Suleiman. Those men out there are all Baber's personal following--hard-bitten old wolves who'll cut any throat and swear any lie he orders. If you go back to Kabul and tell your story, Baber will be in bad with the Amir, the British, and Afdal Khan. So he's determined to shut your mouth, for good and all."

Willoughby was silent for a moment; presently he said frankly: "Gordon, if I didn't have such a high respect for your wits, I'd believe you. It all sounds reasonable and logical. But damn it, man, I don't know whether I'm recognizing logic or simply being twisted up in a web of clever lies. You're too dangerously subtle, Gordon, for me to allow myself to believe anything you say, without proof."

"Proof?" retorted Gordon grimly, "Listen!" Wriggling toward the cave mouth he took shelter behind a broken rock and shouted in Pashtu: "Ohai, Baber Ali!"

The scattered firing ceased instantly, and the moonlit night seemed to hold its breath. Baber Ali's voice came back, edged with suspicion.

"Speak, El Borak! I hearken."

"If I gave you the Englishmen will you let me and my men go in peace?" Gordon called.

"Aye, by the beard of Allah!" came the eager answer.

331

"But I fear he will return to Kabul and poison the Amir against me!"

"Then kill him and throw his head out," answered Baber Ali with an oath. "By Allah, it is no more than I will do for him, the prying dog!"

In the cave Willoughby murmured: "I apologize, Gordon!"

"Well?" The old Pathan was growing impatient. "Are you playing with me, El Borak? Give me the Englishman!"

"Nay, Baber Ali, I dare not trust your promise," replied Gordon.

A bloodthirsty yell and a burst of frenzied firing marked the conclusion of the brief parley, and Gordon hugged the shelter of the shattered boulders until the spasm subsided. Then he crawled back to Willoughby.

"You see?"

"I see! It looks like I'm in this thing to the hilt with you! But why Baber Ali should have been so enraged because I failed to arrange a truce--"

"He and Afdal intended taking advantage of any truce you arranged, to trap me, just as I warned you. They were using you as a cat's-paw. They know they're licked, unless they resort to something of the sort."

There followed a period of silence, in which Willoughby was moved to inquire: "What now? Are we to stay here until they starve us out? The moon will set before many hours. They'll rush us in the dark."

"I never walk into a trap I can't get out of," an-swered Gordon. "I'm just waiting for the moon to dip behind that crag and get its light out of the cave. There's an exit I don't believe the Orakzai know about. Just a narrow crack at the back of the cave. I enlarged it with a hunting knife and rifle barrel before you recovered consciousness. It's big enough for a man to slip through now. It leads out onto a ledge fifty feet above a ravine. Some of the Orakzai may be down there watching the ledge, but I doubt it. From the plain out there it would be a long, hard climb around to the back of the mountain. We'll go down on a rope made of turbans and belts, and head for Akbar's Castle. We'll have to go on foot. It's only a few miles away, but the way we'll have to go is over the mountains, and a devil's own climb."

Slowly the moon moved behind the crag, and the silver sword no longer glimmered along the rocky floor. The men in the cavern could move about without being seen by the men outside, who waited the setting of the moon with the grim patience of gray wolves.

"All right, let's go," muttered Gordon. "Khoda Khan, lead the way. I'll follow when you're all through the cleft. If anything happens to me, take the sahib to Akbar's Castle. Go over the ridges; there may be ambushes already planted in the valleys."

"Give me a gun," requested Willoughby. The rifle of the dead Ahmed Khan was pressed into his hand. He followed the shadowy, all-but-invisible file of Afridis as they glided into the deeper darkness in the recesses of the tunnel-like cavern. Their sandals made no noise on the rocky floor, but the crunch of his boots seemed loud to the Englishman. Behind them Gordon lay near the entrance, and once he fired a shot at the boulders on the plain.

Within fifty feet the cavern floor began to narrow and pitch upward. Above them a star shone in utter blackness, marking the crevice in the rock. It seemed to Willoughby that they mounted the slanting incline for a long way; the firing outside sounded muffled, and the patch of moonlight that was the cave mouth looked small with distance. The pitch became steeper, mounting up until the taller of the Afridis bent their heads to avoid the rocky roof. An instant later they reached the wall that marked the end of the cavern and glimpsed the sky through the narrow slit.

One by one they squeezed through, Willoughby last. He came out on the ledge in the starlight that overhung a ravine which was a mass of black shadows. Above them the great black crags loomed, shutting off the moonlight; everything on that side of the mountain was in shadow.

His companions clustered at the rim of the shelf as they swiftly and deftly knotted together girdles and unwound turbans to make a rope. One end was tossed over the ledge and man after man went down swiftly and silently, vanishing into the black ravine below. Willoughby helped a stalwart tribesman called Muhammad hold the rope as Khoda Khan went down. Before he went, Khoda Khan thrust his head back through the cleft and whistled softly, a signal to carry only to El Borak's alert ears.

Khoda Khan vanished into the darkness below, and Muhammad signified that he could hold the rope alone while Willoughby descended. Behind them an occasional muffled shot seemed to indicate that the Orakzai were yet unaware that their prey was escaping them.

Willoughby let himself over the ledge, hooked a leg about the rope and went down, considerably slower and more cautiously than the men who had preceded him. Above him the huge Afridi braced his legs and held the rope as firmly as though it were bound to a tree.

Willoughby was halfway down when he heard a murmur of voices on the ledge above which indicated that Gordon had come out of the cave and joined Muhammad. The Englishman looked down and made out the dim figures of the others standing below him on the ravine floor. His feet were a yard above the earth when a rifle cracked in the shadows and a red tongue of flame spat upward. An explosive grunt sounded above him and the rope went slack in his hands. He hit the ground, lost his footing and fell headlong, rolling aside as Muhammad came tumbling down. The giant struck the earth with a thud, wrapped about with the rope he had carried with him in his fall. He never moved after he landed.

Willoughby struggled up, breathless, as his companions charged past him. Knives were flickering in the shadows, dim figures reeling in locked combat. So the Orakzai had known of this possible exit! Men were fighting all around him. Gordon sprang to the rim of the ledge and fired downward without apparent aim, but a man grunted and fell, his rifle striking against Willoughby's boot. A dim, bearded face loomed out of the darkness, snarling like a ghoul. Willoughby caught a swinging tulwar on his rifle barrel, wincing at the jolt that ran through his fingers, and fired full into the beared face.

"El Borak!" howled Khoda Khan, hacking and slashing at something that snarled and gasped like a wild beast.

"Take the sahib and go!" yelled Gordon.

Willoughby realized that the fall of Muhammad with the rope had trapped Gordon on the ledge fifty feet above them.

"Nay!" shrieked Khoda Khan. "We will cast the rope up to thee--"

"Go, blast you!" roared Gordon. "The whole horde will be on your necks any minute! Go!"

The next instant Willoughby was seized under each arm and hustled at a stumbling run down the dark gorge. Men panted on each side of him, and the dripping tulwars in their hands smeared his breeches. He had a vague glimpse of three figures sprawling at the foot of the cliff, one horribly mangled. No one barred their path as they fled; Gordon's Afridis were obeying his command; but they had left their leader behind, and they sobbed curses through their teeth as they ran.

IV

GORDON WASTED NO TIME. He knew he could not escape from the ledge without a rope, by climbing either up or down, and he did not believe his enemies could reach the ledge from the ravine. He squirmed back through the cleft and ran down the slant of the cavern, expecting any instant to see his besiegers pouring into the moonlit mouth. But it stood empty, and the rifles outside kept up their irregular monotone. Obviously, Baber Ali did not realize that his victims had attempted an escape by the rear. The muffled shots he must surely have heard had imparted no meaning to him, or perhaps he considered they but constituted some trickery of El Borak's. Knowledge that an opponent is full of dangerous ruses is often a handicap, instilling an undue amount of caution.

Anyway, Baber Ali had neither rushed the cavern nor sent any appreciable number of men to reinforce the lurkers on the other side of the mountain, for the volume of his firing was undiminished. That meant he did not know of the presence of his men behind the cave. Gordon was inclined to believe that what he had taken for a strategically placed force had been merely a few restless individuals skulking along the ravine, scouting on their own initiative. He had actually seen only three men, had merely assumed the presence of others. The attack, too, had been ill-timed and poorly executed. It had neither trapped them all on the ledge nor in the ravine. The shot that killed Muhammad had doubtless been aimed at himself.

Gordon admitted his mistake; confused in the darkness as to the true state of things, he had ordered instant flight when his companions might safely have lingered long enough to tie a stone to the end of the rope and cast it back up to him. He was neatly trapped and it was largely his own fault.

But he had one advantage: Baber did not know he was alone in the cavern. And there was every reason to believe that Willoughby would reach Akbar's Castle unpursued. He fired a shot into the plain and settled himself comfortably behind the rocks near the cave mouth, his rifle at his shoulder.

The moonlit plateau showed no evidence of the attackers beyond the puffs of grayish-white smoke that bloomed in woolly whorls from behind the boulders. But there was a tense expectancy in the very air. The moon was visible below the overhanging crag; it rested a red, bent horn on the solid black mass of a mountain wall. In a few moments the plain would be plunged in darkness and then it was inevitable that Baber would rush the cavern.

Yet Baber would know that in the darkness following the setting of the moon the captives might be expected to make a break for liberty. It was certain that he already had a wide cordon spread across the plain, and the line would converge quickly on the cave mouth. The longer Gordon waited after moonset, the harder it would be to slip through the closing semicircle.

He began wrenching bullets out of cartridges with his fingers and teeth and emptying the powder into his rifle barrel, even while he studied the terrain by the last light of the sinking moon. The plateau was roughly fan-shaped, widening rapidly from the cliff-flanked wall in which opened the cave mouth. Perhaps a quar-ter of a mile across the plain showed the dark mouth of a gorge, in which he knew were tethered the horses of the Orakzai. Probably at least one man was guarding them.

The plain ran level and bare for nearly a hundred yards before the cavern mouth, but some fifty feet away, on the right, there was a deep narrow gully which began abruptly in the midst of the plain and meandered away toward the right-hand cliffs. No shot had been fired from this ravine. If an Orakzai was hidden there he had gone into it while

Gordon and his men were at the back of the cavern. It had been too close to the cave for the besiegers to reach it under the guns of the defenders.

As soon as the moon set Gordon intended to emerge and try to work his way across the plain, avoiding the Orakzai as they rushed toward the cave. It would be touch and go, the success depending on accurate timing and a good bit of luck. But there was no other alternative. He would have a chance, once he got among the rocks and gullies. His biggest risk would be that of getting shot as he ran from the cavern, with thirty rifles trained upon the black mouth. And he was providing against that when he filled his rifle barrel to the muzzle with loose powder from the broken cartridges and plugged the muzzle solidly with a huge misshapen slug he found on the cave floor.

He knew as soon as the moon vanished they would come wriggling like snakes from every direction, to cover the last few yards in a desperate rush--they would not fire until they could empty their guns point-blank into the cavern and storm in after their volley with naked steel. But thirty pairs of keen eyes would be fixed on the entrance and a volley would meet any shadowy figure seen darting from it.

The moon sank, plunging the plateau into darkness, relieved but little by the dim light of the stars. Out on the plateau Gordon heard sounds that only razor-keen ears could have caught, much less translated: the scruff of leather on stone, the faint clink of steel, the rattle of a pebble underfoot.

Rising in the black cave mouth he cocked his rifle, and poising himself for an instant, hurled it, butt first, as far to the left as he could throw it. The clash of the steel-shod butt on stone was drowned by a blinding flash of fire and a deafening detonation as the pent-up charge burst the heavy barrel asunder and in the intensified darkness that followed the flash Gordon was out of the cave and racing for the ravine on his right.

No bullet followed him, though rifles banged on the heels of that amazing report. As he had planned, the surprising explosion from an unexpected quarter had confused his enemies, wrenched their attention away from the cave mouth and the dim figure that flitted from it. Men howled with amazement and fired blindly and unreasoningly in the direction of the flash and roar. While they howled and fired, Gordon reached the gully and plunged into it almost without checking his stride--to collide with a shadowy figure which grunted and grappled with him.

In an instant Gordon's hands locked on a hairy throat, stifling the betraying yell. They went down together, and a rifle, useless in such desperate close quarters, fell from the Pathan's hand. Out on the plain pandemonium had burst, but Gordon was occupied with the blood-crazy savage beneath him.

The man was taller arid heavier than himself and his sinews were like rawhide strands, but the advantage was with the tigerish white man. As they rolled on the gully floor the Pathan strove in vain with both hands to tear away the fingers that were crushing the life from his corded throat, then still clawing at Gordon's wrist with his left hand, began to grope in his girdle for a knife. Gordon released his throat with his left hand, and with it caught the other's right wrist just as the knife came clear.

The Pathan heaved and bucked like a wild man, straining his wolfish muscles to the utmost, but in vain. He could not free his knife wrist from Gordon's grasp nor tear from his throat the fingers that were binding his neck back until his bearded chin jutted upward. Desperately, he threw himself sidewise, trying to bring his knee up to the American's groin, but his shift in position gave Gordon the leverage he had been seeking.

Instantly El Borak twisted the Pathan's wrist with such savage strength that a bone cracked and the knife fell from the numb fingers. Gordon released the broken wrist, snatched a knife from his own boot and ripped upward-- again, again, and yet again.

Not until the convulsive struggles ceased and the body went limp beneath him did Gordon release the hairy throat. He crouched above his victim, listening. The fight had been swift, fierce and silent, enduring only a matter of seconds.

The unexpected explosion had loosed hysteria in the attackers. The Orakzai were rushing the cave, not in stealth and silence, but yelling so loudly and shooting so wildly they did not seem to realize that no shots were answering them.

Nerves hung on hair triggers can be snapped by an untoward occurrence. The rush of the warriors across the plain sounded like the stampede of cattle. A man bounded up the ravine a few yards from where Gordon crouched, without seeing the American in the pit-like blackness. Howling, cursing, shooting blindly, the hillmen stormed to the cave mouth, too crazy with excitement and confused by the darkness to see the dim figure that glided out of the gully behind them and raced silently away toward the mouth of the distant gorge.

V

WILLOUGHBY ALWAYS REMEMBERED that flight over the mountains as a sort of nightmare in which he was hustled along by ragged goblins through black defiles, up tendon-straining slopes and along knife-edge ridges which fell away on either hand into depths that turned him faint with nausea. Protests, exhortations and fervent profanity did not serve to ease the flying pace at which his escort was trundling him, and presently he had no breath for protests.

He did not even have time to be grateful that the expected pursuit did not seem to be materializing.

He gasped like a dying fish and tried not to look down. He had an uncomfortable feeling that the Afridis blamed him for Gordon's plight and would gladly have heaved him off a ridge but for their leaders' parting command.

But Willoughby felt that he was just as effectually being killed by overexertion. He had never realized that human beings could traverse such a path--or rather such a pathless track--as he was being dragged over. When the moon sank the going was even harder, but he was grateful, for the abysses they seemed to be continually skirting were but floating gulfs of blackness beneath them, which did not induce the sick giddiness resulting from yawning chasms disclosed by the merciless moonlight.

His respect for Gordon's physical abilities increased to a kind of frantic awe, for he knew the American was known to be superior in stamina and endurance even to these long-legged, barrel-chested, iron-muscled mountaineers who seemed built of some substance that was tireless. Willoughby wished they would tire. They hauled him along with a man at each arm, and one to pull, and another to push when necessary, but even so the exertion was killing him. Sweat bathed him, drenching his garments. His thighs trembled and the calves of his legs were tied into agonizing knots.

He reflected in dizzy fragments that Gordon deserved whatever domination he had achieved over these iron-jawed barbarians. But mostly he did not think at all. His faculties were all occupied in keeping his feet and gulping air. The veins in his temples were nearly bursting and things were swimming in a bloody haze about him when he realized his escort, or captors--or torturers--had slowed to a walk. He voiced an incoherent croak of gratitude and shaking the sweat out of his dilated eyes, he saw that they were treading a path that ran over a natural rock bridge which spanned a deep gorge. Ahead of him, looming above a cluster of broken peaks, he saw a great black bulk heaving up against the stars like a misshapen castle.

The sharp challenge of a rifleman rang staccato from the other end of the span and was answered by Khoda Khan's bull-like bellow. The path led upon a jutting ledge and half a dozen ragged, bearded specters with rifles in their hands rose from behind a rampart of heaped-up boulders.

Willoughby was in a state of collapse, able only to realize that the killing grind was over. The Afridis half carried, half dragged him within the semicircular rampart and he saw a bronze door standing open and a doorway cut in solid rock that glowed luridly. It required an effort to realize that the glow came from a fire burning somewhere in the cavern into which the doorway led.

This, then, was Akbar's Castle. With each arm across a pair of brawny shoulders Willoughby tottered through the cleft and down a short narrow tunnel, to emerge into a broad natural chamber lighted by smoky torches and a small fire over which tea was brewing and meat cooking. Half a dozen men sat about the fire, and some forty more slept on the stone floor, wrapped in their sheepskin coats. Doorways opened from the huge main chamber, openings of other tunnels or cell-like niches, and at the other end there were stalls occupied by horses, a surprising number of them. Saddles, blanket rolls, bridles and other equipage, with stands of rifles and stacks of ammunition cases, littered the floor near the walls.

The men about the fire rose to their feet looking inquiringly at the Englishman and his escort, and the men on the floor awoke and sat up blinking like ghouls surprised by daylight. A tall broad-shouldered swashbuckler came striding out of the widest doorway opening into the cavern. He paused before the group, towering half a head taller than any other man there, hooked his thumbs in his girdle and glared balefully.

"Who is this feringhi?" he snarled suspiciously. "Where is El Borak?"

Three of the escort backed away apprehensively, but Khoda Khan, held his ground and answered: "This is the sahib Willoughby, whom El Borak met at the Minaret of

Shaitan, Yar Ali Khan. We rescued him from Baber Ali, who would have slain him. We were at bay in the cave where Yar Muhammad shot the gray wolf three summers ago. We stole out by a cleft, but the rope fell and left El Borak on a ledge fifty feet above us, and--"

"Allah!" It was a blood-curdling yell from Yar Ali Khan who seemed transformed into a maniac. "Dogs! You left him to die! Accursed ones! Forgotten of God! I'll--"

"He commanded us to bring this Englishman to Akbar's Castle," maintained Khoda Khan doggedly, "We tore our beards and wept, but we obeyed!"

"Allah!" Yar Ali Khan became a whirlwind of energy. He snatched up rifle, bandoleer and bridle. "Bring out the horses and saddle them!" he roared and a score of men scurried. "Hasten! Forty men with me to rescue El Borak! The rest hold the Castle. I leave Khoda Khan in command."

"Leave the devil in command of hell," quoth Khoda Khan profanely. "I ride with you to rescue El Borak--or I empty my rifle into your belly."

His three comrades expressed similar intentions at the top of their voices--after fighting and running all night, they were wild as starving wolves to plunge back into hazard in behalf of their chief.

"Go or stay, I care not!" howled Yar Ali Khan, tearing out a fistful of his beard in his passion. "If Borak is slain I will requite thee, by the prophet's beard and my feet! Allah rot me if I ram not a rifle stock down thy accursed gullets--dogs, jackals, noseless abominations, hasten with the horses!"

"Yar Ali Khan!" It was a yell from beyond the arch whence the tall Afridi had first emerged. "One comes riding hard up the valley!"

Yar Ali Khan yelled bloodthirstily and rushed into the tunnel, brandishing his rifle, with everybody pelting after him except the men detailed to saddle the horses.

Willoughby had been forgotten by the Pathans in the madhouse brewed by Gordon's lieutenant. He limped after them, remembering tales told of this gaunt giant and his berserk rages. The tunnel down which the ragged horde was streaming ran for less than a hundred feet when it widened to a mouth through which the gray light of dawn was stealing. Through this the Afridis were pouring and Willoughby, following them, came out upon a broad ledge a hundred feet wide and fifty deep, like a gallery before a house.

Around its semicircular rim ran a massive man-made wall, shoulder-high, pierced with loopholes slanting down. There was an arched opening in the wall, closed by a heavy bronze door, and from that door, which now stood open, a row of broad shallow steps niched in solid stone led down to a trail which in turn looped down a three-hundred-foot slope to the floor of a broad valley.

The cliffs in which the cave sat closed the western end of the valley, which opened to the east. Mists hung in the valley and out of them a horseman came flying, growing ghostlike out of the dimness of the dawn--a man on a great white horse, riding like the wind.

Yar Ali Khan glared wildly for an instant, then started forward with a convulsive leap of his whole body, flinging his rifle high above his head.

"El Borak!" he roared.

Electrified by his yell, the men surged to the wall and those saddling the mounts inside abandoned their task and rushed out onto the ledge. In an instant the wall was lined with tense figures, gripping their rifles and glaring into the white mists rolling beyond the fleeing rider, from which they momentarily expected pursuers to appear.

Willoughby, standing to one side like a spectator of a drama, felt a tingle in his veins at the sight and sound of the wild rejoicing with which these wild men greeted the man who had won their allegiance. Gordon was no bluffing adventurer; he was a real chief of men; and that, Willoughby realized, was going to make his own job that much harder.

No pursuers materialized out of the thinning mists. Gordon urged his mount up the trail, up the broad steps, and as he rode through the gate, bending his head under the arch, the roar of acclaim that went up would have stirred the blood of a king. The Pathans swarmed around him, catching at his hands, his garments, shouting praise to Allah that he was alive and whole. He grinned down at them, swung off

349

and threw his reins to the nearest man, from whom Yar Ali Khan instantly snatched them jealously, with a ferocious glare at the offending warrior.

Willoughby stepped forward. He knew he looked like a scarecrow in his stained and torn garments, but Gordon looked like a butcher, with blood dried on his shirt and smeared on his breeches where he had wiped his hands. But he did not seem to be wounded. He smiled at Willoughby for the first time.

"Tough trip, eh?"

"We've been here only a matter of minutes," Willoughby acknowledged.

"You took a short cut. I came the long way, but I made good time on Baber Ali's horse," said Gordon.

"You mentioned possible ambushes in the valleys--"

"Yes. But on horseback I could take that risk. I was shot at once, but they missed me. It's hard to aim straight in the early-morning mists."

"How did you get away?"

"Waited until the moon went down, then made a break for it. Had to kill a man in the gully before the cave. We were all twisted together when I let him have the knife and that's where this blood came from. I stole Baber's horse while the Orakzai were storming the empty cave. Stampeded the herd down a canyon. Had to shoot the fellow guarding it. Baber'll guess where I went, of course. He'll be after me as quickly as he and his men can catch their horses. I suspect they'll lay siege to the Castle, but they'll only waste their time."

Willoughby stared about him in the growing light of dawn, impressed by the strength of the stronghold. One rifleman could hold the entrance through which he had been brought. To try to advance along that narrow bridge that spanned the chasm behind the Castle would be suicide for an enemy. And no force on earth could march up the valley on this side and climb that stair in the teeth of Gordon's rifles. The mountain which contained the cave rose up like a huge stone citadel above the surrounding heights. The cliffs which flanked the valley were lower than the fortified ledge; men crawling along them would be exposed to a raking fire from above. Attack could come from no other direction.

"This is really in Afdal Khan's territory," said Gordon. "It used to be a Mogul outpost, as the name implies. It was first fortified by Akbar himself. Afdal Khan held it before I took it. It's my best safeguard for Kurram.

"After the outlying villages were burned on both sides, all my people took refuge in Kurram, just as Afdal's did in Khoruk. To attack Kurram, Afdal would have to pass Akbar's Castle and leave me in his rear. He doesn't dare do that. That's why he wanted a truce--to get me out of the Castle. With me ambushed and killed, or hemmed up in Kurram, he'd be free to strike at Kurram with all his force, without being afraid I'd burn Khoruk behind him or ambush him in my country.

"He's too cautious of his own skin. I've repeatedly challenged him to fight me man to man, but he pays no attention. He hasn't stirred out of Khoruk since the feud started, unless he had at least a hundred men with him--as many as I have in my entire force, counting these here and those guarding the women and children in Kurram."

"You've done a terrible amount of damage with so small a band," said Willoughby.

"Not difficult if you know the country, have men who trust you, and keep moving. Geronimo almost whipped an army with a handful of Apaches, and I was raised in his country. I've simply adopted his tactics. The possession of this Castle was all I needed to assure my ultimate victory. If Afdal had the guts to meet me, the feud would be over. He's the chief; the others just follow him. As it is I may have to wipe out the entire Khoruk clan. But I'll get him."

The dark flame flickered in Gordon's eyes as he spoke, and again Willoughby felt the impact of an inexorable determination, elemental in its foundation. And again he swore mentally that he would end the feud himself, in his own way, with Afdal Khan alive; though how, he had not the faintest idea at present.

Gordon glanced at him closely and advised: "Better get some sleep. If I know Baber Ali, he'll come straight to the Castle after me. He knows he can't take it, but he'll try anyway. He has at least a hundred men who follow him and take orders from nobody else--not even Afdal Khan. After the shooting starts there won't be much chance for sleeping. You look a bit done up."

Willoughby realized the truth of Gordon's comment. Sight of the white streak of dawn stealing over the ash-hued peaks weighted his eyelids with an irresistible drowsiness. He was barely able to stumble into the cave, and the smell of frying mutton exercised no charm to keep him awake. Somebody steered him to a heap of blankets and he was asleep before he was actually stretched upon them.

Gordon stood looking down at the sleeping man enigmatically and Yar Ali Khan came up as noiselessly and calmly as a gaunt gray wolf; it would have been hard to believe he was the hurricane of emotional upset which had stormed all over the cavern a short hour before.

"Is he a friend, sahib?"

"A better friend than he realizes," was Gordon's grim, cryptic reply. "I think Afdal Khan's friends will come to curse the day Geoffrey Willoughby ever came into the hills."

VI

AGAIN IT WAS the spiteful cracking of rifles which awakened Willoughby. He sat up, momentarily confused and unable to remember where he was or how he came there. Then he recalled the events of the night; he was in the stronghold of an outlaw chief, and those detonations must mean the siege Gordon had predicted. He was alone in the great cavern, except for the horses munching fodder beyond the bars at the other end. Among them he recognized the big white stallion that had belonged to Baber Ali.

The fire had died to a heap of coals and the daylight that stole through a couple or arches, which were the openings of tunnels connecting with the outer air, was augmented by half a dozen antique-looking bronze lamps.

A pot of mutton stew simmered over the coals and a dish full of chupatties stood near it. Willoughby was aware of a ravenous hunger and he set to without delay. Having eaten his fill and drunk deeply from a huge gourd which hung nearby, full of sweet, cool water, he rose and started toward the tunnel through which he had first entered the Castle.

Near the mouth he almost stumbled over an incongruous object--a large telescope mounted on a tripod, and obviously modern and expensive. A glance out on the ledge showed him only half a dozen warriors sitting against the rampart, their rifles across their knees. He glanced at the ribbon of stone that spanned the deep gorge and shivered as he remembered how he had crossed it in the darkness. It looked scarcely a foot wide in places. He turned back, crossed the cavern and traversed the other tunnel.

He halted in the outer mouth. The wall that rimmed the ledge was lined with Afridis, kneeling or lying at the loopholes. They were not firing. Gordon leaned idly against the bronze door, his head in plain sight of anyone who might be in the valley below. He nodded a greeting as Willoughby advanced and joined him at the door. Again the Englishman found himself a member of a besieged force, but this time the advantage was all with the defenders.

Down in the valley, out of effectual rifle range, a long skirmish line of men was advancing very slowly on foot, firing as they came, and taking advantage of every bit of cover. Farther back, small in the distance, a large herd of horses grazed, watched by men who sat cross-legged in the shade of the cliff. The position of the sun indicated that the day was well along toward the middle of the afternoon.

"I've slept longer than I thought," Willoughby remarked. "How long has this firing been going on?"

"Ever since noon. They're wasting Russian cartridges scandalously. But you slept like a dead man. Baber Ali didn't get here as quickly as I thought he would. He evidently stopped to round up more men. There are at least a hundred down there."

To Willoughby the attack seemed glaringly futile. The men on the ledge were too well protected to suffer from the long-range firing. And before the attackers could get near enough to pick out the loopholes, the bullets of the Afridis would be knocking them over like tenpins. He glimpsed men crawling among the boulders on the cliffs, but they were at the same disadvantage as the men in the valley below-- Gordon's rifle-men had a vantage point above them.

"What can Baber Ali hope for?" he asked.

"He's desperate. He knows you're up here with me and he's taking a thousand-to-one chance. But he's wasting his time. I have enough ammunition and food to stand a six-month siege; there's a spring in the cavern."

"Why hasn't Afdal Khan kept you hemmed up here with part of his men while he stormed Kurram with the rest of his force?"

"Because it would take his whole force to storm Kurram; its defenses are almost as strong as these. Then he has a dread of having me at his back. Too big a risk that his men couldn't keep me cooped up. He's got to reduce Akbar's Castle before he can strike at Kurram."

"The devil!" said Willoughby irritably, brought back to his own situation. "I came to arbitrate this feud and now I find myself a prisoner. I've got to get out of here--got to get back to Ghazrael."

"I'm as anxious to get you out as you are to go," answered Gordon. "If you're killed I'm sure to be blamed for it. I don't mind being outlawed for the things I have done, but I don't care to shoulder something I didn't do."

"Couldn't I slip out of here tonight? By way of the bridge--"

"There are men on the other side of the gorge, watching for just such a move. Baber Ali means to close your mouth if human means can do it."

"If Afdal Khan knew what's going on he'd come and drag the old ruffian off my neck," growled Willoughby. "Afdal knows he can't afford to let his clan kill an Englishman. But Baber will take good care Afdal doesn't know, of course. If I could get a letter to him--but of course that's impossible."

"We can try it, though," returned Gordon. "You write the note. Afdal knows your handwriting, doesn't he? Good! Tonight I'll sneak out and take it to his nearest outpost. He keeps a line of patrols among the hills a few miles beyond Jehungir's Well."

"But if I can't slip out, how can you--"

"I can do it all right, alone. No offense, but you Englishmen sound like a herd of longhorn steers at your stealthiest. The Orakzai are among the crags on the other side of the Gorge of Mekram. I won't cross the bridge. My men will let me down a rope ladder into the gorge tonight before moonrise. I'll slip up to the camp of the nearest outpost, wrap the note around a pebble and throw it among them. Being Afdal's men and not Baber's, they'll take it to him. I'll come back the way I went, after moonset. It'll be safe enough."

"But how safe will it be for Afdal Khan when he comes for me?"

"You can tell Afdal Khan he won't be harmed if he plays fair," Gordon answered. "But you'd better make some arrangements so you can see him and know he's there before you trust yourself outside this cave. And there's the pinch, because Afdal won't dare show himself for fear I'd shoot him. He's broken so many pacts himself he can't believe anybody would keep one. Not where his hide is concerned. He trusted me to keep my word in regard to Baber and your escort, but would he trust himself to my promise?"

Willoughby scowled, cramming the bowl of his pipe. "Wait!" he said suddenly. "I saw a big telescope in the cavern, mounted on a tripod--is it in working order?"

"I should say it is. I imported that from Germany, by the way of Turkey and Persia. That's one reason Akbar's Castle has never been surprised. It carries for miles."

"Does Afdal Khan know of it?"

"I'm sure he does."

"Good!"

Seating himself on the ledge, Willoughby drew forth pencil and notebook, propped the latter against his knee, and wrote in his clear concise hand:

AFDAL KHAN: I am at Akbar's Castle, now being besieged by your uncle, Baber Ali. Baber was so unreasonably incensed at my failure to effect a truce that he allowed my servant Suleiman to be murdered, and now intends murdering me, to stop my mouth.

I don't have to remind you how fatal it would be to the interests of your party for this to occur. I want you to come to Akbar's Castle and get me out of this. Gordon assures me you will not be molested if you play fair, but here is a way by which you need not feel you are taking any chances: Gordon has a large telescope through which I can identify you while you are still out of rifle range. In the Gorge of Mekram, and southwest of the Castle, there is a mass of boulders split off from the right wall and well out of rifle range from the Castle. If you were to come and stand on those boulders, I could identify you easily.

Naturally, I will not leave the Castle until I know you are present to protect me from your uncle. As soon as I have identified you, I will come down the gorge alone. You can watch me all the way and assure yourself that no treachery is intended. No one but myself will leave the Castle. On your part I do not wish any of your men to advance beyond the boulders and I will not answer for their safety if they should, as I intend to safeguard Gordon in this matter as well as yourself.

GEOFFREY WILLOUGHBY

He handed the letter over for Gordon to read. The American nodded. "That may bring him. I don't know. He's kept out of my sight ever since the feud started."

Then ensued a period of waiting, in which the sun seemed sluggishly to crawl toward the western peaks. Down in the valley and on the cliffs the Orakzai kept up their fruitless firing with a persistency that convinced Willoughby of the truth of Gordon's assertion that ammunition was being supplied them by some European power.

The Afridis were not perturbed. They lounged at ease by the wall, laughed, joked, chewed jerked mutton and fired through the slanting loopholes when the Orakzai crept too close. Three still white-clad forms in the valley and one on the cliffs testified to their accuracy. Willoughby realized that Gordon was right when he said the clan which held Akbar's Castle was certain to win the war eventually. Only a desperate old savage like Baber Ali would waste time and men trying to take it. Yet the Orakzai had originally held it. How Gordon had gained possession of it Willoughby could not imagine.

The sun dipped at last; the Himalayan twilight deepened into black-velvet, star-veined dusk. Gordon rose, a vague figure in the starlight.

"Time for me to be going."

He had laid aside his rifle and buckled a tulwar to his hip. Willoughby followed him into the great cavern, now dim and shadowy in the light of the bronze lamps, and through the narrow tunnel and the bronze door.

Yar Ali Khan, Khoda Khan, and half a dozen others followed them. The light from the cavern stole through the tunnel, vaguely etching the moving figures of the men. Then the bronze door was closed softly and Willoughby's companions were shapeless blurs in the thick soft darkness around him. The gorge below was a floating river of blackness. The bridge was a dark streak that ran into the unknown and vanished. Not even the keenest eyes of the hills, watching from beyond the gorge, could have even discerned the jut of the ledge under the black bulk of the Castle, much less the movements of the men upon it.

The voices of the men working at the rim of the ledge were lowering the rope ladder--a hundred and fifty feet of it--into the gorge. Gordon's face was a light were lowering the rope ladder--a hundred and fifty feet of it--into the gorge. Gordon's face was a light blur in the darkness. Willoughby groped for his hand and found him already swinging over the rampart onto the ladder, one end of which was made fast to a great iron ring set in the stone of the ledge.

"Gordon, I feel like a bounder, letting you take this risk for me. Suppose some of those devils are down there in the gorge?"

"Not much chance. They don't know we have this way of coming and going. If I can steal a horse, I'll be back in the Castle before dawn. If I can't, and have to make the whole trip there and back on foot, I may have to hide out in the hills tomorrow and get back into the Castle the next night. Don't worry about me. They'll never see me. Yar Ali Khan, watch for a rush before the moon rises."

"Aye, sahib." The bearded giant's undisturbed manner reassured Willoughby.

The next instant Gordon began to melt into the gloom below. Before he had climbed down five rungs the men crouching on the rampart could no longer see him. He made no sound in his descent. Khoda Khan knelt with a hand on the ropes, and as soon as he felt them go slack, he began to haul the ladder up. Willoughby leaned over the edge, straining his ears to catch some sound from below--scruff of leather, rattle of shale--he heard nothing.

Yar Ali Khan muttered, his beard brushing Willoughby's ear: "Nay, sahib, if such ears as yours could hear him, every Orakzai on this side of the mountain would know a man stole down the gorge! You will not hear him--nor will they. There are Lifters of the Khyber who can steal rifles out of the tents of the British soldiers, but they are blundering cattle compared to El Borak. Before dawn a wolf will howl in the gorge, and we will know El Borak has returned and will let down the ladder for him."

But like the others, the huge Afridi leaned over the rampart listening intently for some fifteen minutes after the ladder had been drawn up. Then with a gesture to the others he turned and opened the bronze door a crack. They stole through hurriedly. Somewhere in the blackness across the gorge a rifle cracked flatly and lead spanged a foot or so above the lintel. In spite of the rampart some quick eye among the crags had caught the glow of the opened door. But it was blind shooting. The sentries left on the ledge did not reply.

Back on the ledge that overlooked the valley, Willoughby noted an air of expectancy among the warriors at the loopholes. They were momentarily expecting the attack of which Gordon had warned them.

"How did Gordon ever take Akbar's Castle?" Willoughby asked Khoda Khan, who seemed more ready to answer questions than any of the other taciturn warriors.

The Afridi squatted beside him near the open bronze gate, rifle in hand, the butt resting on the ledge. Over them was the blue-black bowl of the Himalayan night, flecked with clusters of frosty silver.

"He sent Yar Ali Khan with forty horsemen to make a feint at Baber Ali's sangar," answered Khoda Khan promptly.

"Thinking to trap us, Afdal drew all his men out of Akbar's Castle except three. Afdal believed three men could hold it against an army, and so they could--against an army. Not against El Borak. While Baber Ali and Afdal were striving to pin Yar Ali Khan and us forty riders between them, and we were leading the dogs a merry chase over the hills, El Borak rode alone down this valley. He came disguised as a Persian trader, with his turban awry and his rich garments dusty and rent. He fled down the valley shouting that thieves had looted his caravan and were pursuing him to take from him his purse of gold and his pouch of jewels.

"The accursed ones left to guard the Castle were greedy, and they saw only a rich and helpless merchant, to be looted. So they bade him take refuge in the cavern and opened the gate to him. He rode into Akbar's Castle crying praise to Allah--with empty hands, but a knife and pistols under his khalat. Then the accursed ones mocked him and set on him to strip him of his riches--by Allah they found they caught a tiger in the guise of a lamb! One he slew with the knife, the other two he shot. Alone he took the stronghold against which armies have thundered in vain! When we forty-one horsemen evaded the Orakzai and doubled back, as it had been planned, lo! the bronze gate was open to us and we were lords of Akbar's Castle! Ha! The forgotten of God charge the stair!"

From the shadows below there welled up the sudden, swift drum of hoofs and Willoughby glimpsed movement in the darkness of the valley. The blurred masses resolved themselves into dim figures racing up the looping trail: At the same time a rattle of rifle fire burst out behind the Castle, from beyond the Gorge of Mekram. The Afridis displayed no excitement. Khoda Khan did not even close the bronze gate. They held their fire until the hoofs of the foremost horses were ringing on the lower steps of the stair. Then a burst of flame crowned the wall, and in its flash Willoughby saw wild bearded faces, horses tossing heads and manes.

In the darkness following the volley there rose screams of agony from men and beasts, mingled with the thrashing and kicking of wounded horses and the grating of shod hoofs on stone as some of the beasts slid backward down the stair. Dead and dying piled in a heaving, agonized mass, and the stairs became a shambles as again and yet again the rippling volleys crashed.

Willoughby wiped a damp brow with a shaking hand, grateful that the hoofbeats were receding down the valley. The gasps and moans and cries which welled up from the ghastly heap at the foot of the stairs sickened him.

"They are fools," said Khoda Khan, levering fresh cartridges into his rifle. "Thrice in past attacks have they charged the stair by darkness, and thrice have we broken them. Baber Ali is a bull rushing blindly to his destruction."

Rifles began to flash and crack down in the valley as the baffled besiegers vented their wrath in blind discharges. Bullets smacked along the wall of the cliff, and Khoda Khan closed the bronze gate.

"Why don't they attack by way of the bridge?" Willoughby wondered.

"Doubtless they did. Did you not hear the shots? But the path is narrow and one man behind the rampart could keep it clear. And there are six men there, all skilled marksmen."

Willoughby nodded, remembering the narrow ribbon of rock flanked on either hand by echoing depths.

"Look, sahib, the moon rises."

Over the eastern peaks a glow began which grew to a soft golden fire against which the peaks stood blackly outlined. Then the moon rose, not the mellow gold globe promised by the forerunning luster, but a gaunt, red, savage moon, of the high Himalayas.

Khoda Khan opened the bronze gate and peered down the stair, grunting softly in gratification. Willoughby, looking over his shoulder, shuddered. The heap at the foot of the stairs was no longer a merciful blur, for the moon outlined it in pitiless detail. Dead horses and dead men lay in a tangled gory mound with rifles and sword blades thrust out of the pile like weeds growing out of a scrap heap. There must have been at least a dozen horses and almost as many men in that shambles.

"A shame to waste good horses thus," muttered Khoda Khan. "Baber Ali is a fool." He closed the gate.

Willoughby leaned back against the wall, drawing a heavy sheepskin coat about him. He felt sick and futile. The men down in the valley must feel the same way, for the firing was falling off, becoming spasmodic. Even Baber Ali must realize the futility of the siege by this time. Willoughby smiled bitterly to himself. He had come to arbitrate a hill feud--and down there men lay dead in heaps. But the game was not yet played out. The thought of Gordon stealing through those black mountains out there somewhere discouraged sleep. Yet he did slumber at last, despite himself.

It was Khoda Khan who shook him awake. Willoughby looked up blinking. Dawn was just whitening the peaks. Only a dozen men squatted at the loopholes. From the cavern stole the reek of coffee and frying meat.

"Your letter has been safely delivered, sahib."

"Eh? What's that? Gordon's returned?"

Willoughby rose stiffly, relieved that Gordon had not suffered on his account. He glanced over the wall. Down the valley the camp of the raiders was veiled by the morning mists, but several strands of smoke oozed toward the sky. He did not look down the stair; he did not wish to see the cold faces of the dead in the white dawn light.

He followed Khoda Khan into the great chamber where some of the warriors were sleeping and some preparing breakfast. The Afridi gestured toward a cell-like niche where a man lay. He had his back to the door, but the black, close-cropped hair and dusty khakis were unmistakable.

"He is weary," said Khoda Khan. "He sleeps."

Willoughby nodded. He had begun to wonder if Gordon ever found it necessary to rest and sleep like ordinary men.

"It were well to go upon the ledge and watch for Afdal Khan," said Khoda Khan. "We have mounted the telescope there, sahib. One shall bring your breakfast to you there. We have no way of knowing when Afdal will come."

Out on the ledge the telescope stood on its tripod, projecting like a cannon over the rampart. He trained it on the mass of boulders down the ravine. The Gorge of Mekram ran from the north to the southwest. The boulders, called the Rocks, were more than a mile of the southwest of the Castle. Just beyond them the gorge bent sharply. A man could reach the Rocks from the southwest without being spied from the Castle, but he could not approach beyond them without being seen. Nor could anyone leave the Castle from that side and approach the Rocks without being seen by anyone hiding there.

The Rocks were simply a litter of huge boulders which had broken off from the canyon wall. Just now, as Willoughby looked, the mist floated about them, making them hazy and indistinct. Yet as he watched them they became more sharply outlined, growing out of the thinning mist. And on the tallest rock there stood a motionless figure. The telescope brought it out in vivid clarity. There was no mistaking that tall, powerful figure. It was Afdal Khan who stood there, watching the Castle with a pair of binoculars.

"He must have got the letter early in the night, or ridden hard to get here this early," muttered Willoughby. "Maybe he was at some spot nearer than Khoruk. Did Gordon say?"

"No, sahib."

"Well, no matter. We won't wake Gordon. No, I won't wait for breakfast. Tell El Borak that I'm grateful for all the trouble he's taken in my behalf and I'll do what I can for him when I get back to Ghazrael. But he'd better decide to let this thing be arbitrated. I'll see that Afdal doesn't try any treachery."

"Yes, sahib."

They tossed the rope ladder into the gorge and it unwound swiftly as it tumbled down and dangled within a foot of the canyon floor. The Afridis showed their heads above the ramparts without hesitation, but when Willoughby mounted the rampart and stood in plain sight, he felt a peculiar crawling between his shoulders.

But no rifle spoke from the crags beyond the gorge. Of course, the sight of Afdal Khan was sufficient guarantee of his safety. Willoughby set a foot in the ladder and went down, refusing to look below him. The ladder tended to swing and spin after he had progressed a few yards and from time to time he had to steady himself with a hand against the cliff wall. But altogether it was not so bad, and presently he heaved a sigh of relief as he felt the rocky floor under his feet. He waved his arms, but the rope was already being drawn up swiftly. He glanced about him. If any bodies had fallen from the bridge in the night battle, they had been removed. He turned and walked down the gorge, toward the appointed rendezvous.

Dawn grew about him, the white mists changing to rosy pink, and swiftly dissipating. He could make out the outlines of the Rocks plainly now, without artificial aid, but he no longer saw Afdal Khan. Doubtless the suspicious chief was watching his approach from some hiding place. He kept listening for distant shots that would indicate Baber Ali was renewing the siege, but he heard none. Doubtless Baber Ali had already received orders from Afdal Khan, and he visualized Afdal's amazement and rage when he learned of his uncle's indiscretions.

He reached the Rocks--a great heap of rugged, irregular stones and broken boulders, towering thirty feet in the air in places.

He halted and called: "Afdal Khan!"

"This way, sahib," a voice answered. "Among the Rocks."

Willoughby advanced between a couple of jagged boulders and came into a sort of natural theater, made by the space inclosed between the overhanging cliff and the mass of detached rocks. Fifty men could have stood there without being crowded, but only one man was in sight--a tall, lusty man in early middle life, in turban and silken khalat. He stood with his head thrown back in unconscious arrogance, a broad tulwar in his hand.

The faint crawling between his shoulders that had accompanied Willoughby all the way down the gorge, in spite of himself, left him at the sight. When he spoke his voice was casual.

"I'm glad to see you, Afdal Khan."

"And I am glad to see you, sahib!" the Orakzai answered with a chill smile. He thumbed the razor-edge of his tulwar. "You have failed in the mission for which I brought you into these hills--but your death will serve me almost as well."

Had the Rocks burst into a roar about him the surprise would have been no more shocking. Willoughby literally staggered with the impact of the stunning revelation.

"What? My death? Afdal, are you mad?"

"What will the English do to Baber Ali?" demanded the chief.

"They'll demand that he be tried for the murder of Suleiman," answered Willoughby.

"And the Amir would hang him, to placate the British!" Afdal Khan laughed mirthlessly. "But if you were dead, none would ever know! Bah! Do you think I would let my uncle be hanged for slaying that Punjabi dog? Baber was a fool to let his men take the Indian's life. I would have prevented it, had I known. But now it is done and I mean to protect him. El Borak is not so wise as I thought or he would have known that I would never let Baber be punished."

"It means ruin for you if you murder me," reminded Willoughby--through dry lips, for he read the murderous gleam in the Orakzai's eyes.

"Where are the witnesses to accuse me? There is none this side of the Castle save you and I. I have removed my men from the crags near the bridge. I sent them all into the valley--partly because I feared lest one might fire a hasty shot and spoil my plan, partly because I do not trust my own men any farther than I have to. Sometimes a man can be bribed or persuaded to betray even his chief.

"Before dawn I sent men to comb the gorge and these Rocks to make sure no trap had been set for me. Then I came here and sent them away and remained here alone. They do not know why I came. They shall never know. Tonight, when the moon rises, your head will be found in a sack at the foot of the stair that leads down from Akbar's Castle and there will be a hundred men to swear it was thrown down by El Borak.

"And because they will believe it themselves, none can prove them liars. I want them to believe it themselves, because I know how shrewd you English are in discovering lies. I will send your head to Fort Ali Masjid, with fifty men to swear El Borak murdered you. The British will force the Amir to send an army up here, with field pieces, and shell El Borak out of my Castle. Who will believe him if he has the opportunity to say he did not slay you?"

"Gordon was right!" muttered Willoughby helplessly. "You are a treacherous dog. Would you mind telling me just why you forced this feud on him?"

"Not at all, since you will be dead in a few moments, I want control of the wells that dominate the caravan routes. The Russians will pay me a great deal of gold to help them smuggle rifles and ammunition down from Persia and Turkestan, into Afghanistan and Kashmir and India. I will help them, and they will help me. Some day they will make me Amir of Afghanistan."

"Gordon was right," was all Willoughby could say. "The man was right! And this truce you wanted--I suppose it was another trick?"

"Of course! I wanted to get El Borak out of my Castle."

"What a fool I've been," muttered Willoughby.

"Best make your peace with God then berate yourself, sahib," said Afdal Khan, beginning to swing the heavy tulwar to and fro, turning the blade so the edge gleamed in the early light. "There are only you and I and Allah to see--and Allah hates infidels! Steel is silent and sure--one stroke, swift and deadly, and your head will be mine to use as I wish--"

He advanced with the noiseless stride of the hillman. Willoughby set his teeth and clenched his hands until the nails bit into the palms. He knew it was useless to run; the Orakzai would overtake him within half a dozen strides. It was equally futile to leap and grapple with his bare hands, but it was all he could do; death would smite him in mid-leap and there would be a rush of darkness and an end of planning and working and all things hoped for--

"Wait a minute, Afdal Khan!"

The voice was moderately pitched, but if it had been a sudden scream the effect could have been no more startling. Afdal Khan started violently and whirled about. He froze in his tracks and the tulwar slipped from his fingers. His face went ashen and slowly his hands rose above his shoulders. Gordon stood in a cleft of the cleft, and a heavy pistol, held hip-high, menaced the chief's waistline. Gordon's expression was one of faint amusement, but a hot flame leaped and smoldered in his black eyes.

"El Borak!" stammered Afdal Khan dazedly. "El Borak!" Suddenly he cried out like a madman. "You are a ghost--a devil! The Rocks were empty--my men searched them--"

"I was hiding on a ledge on the cliff above their heads," Gordon answered. "I entered the Rocks after they left. Keep your hands away from your girdle, Afdal Khan. I could have shot you any time within the last hour, but I wanted Willoughby to know you for the rogue you are."

"But I saw you in the cave," gasped Willoughby, "asleep in the cave--"

"You saw an Afridi, Ali Shah, in some of my clothes, pretending to be sleeping," answered Gordon, never taking his eyes off Afdal Khan. "I was afraid if you knew I wasn't in the Castle, you'd refuse to meet Afdal, thinking I was up to something. So after I tossed your note into the Orakzai camp, I came back to the Castle while you were asleep, gave my men their orders and hid down the gorge.

"You see I knew Afdal wouldn't let Baber be punished for killing Suleiman. He couldn't if he wanted to. Baber has too many followers in the Khoruk clan. And the only way of keeping the Amir's favor without handing Baber over for trial, would be to shut your mouth. He could always lay it onto me, then. I knew that note would bring him to meet you--and I knew he'd come prepared to kill you."

"He might have killed me," muttered Willoughby.

"I've had a gun trained on him ever since you came within range. If he'd brought men with him, I'd have shot him before you left the Castle. When I saw he meant to wait here alone, I waited for you to find out for yourself what kind of a dog he is. You've been in no danger."

"I thought he arrived early, to have come from Khoruk."

"I knew he wasn't at Khoruk when I left the Castle last night," said Gordon. "I knew when Baber found us safe in the Castle he'd make a clean breast of everything to Afdal--and that Afdal would come to help him. Afdal was camped half a mile back in the hills--surrounded by a mob of fighting men, as usual, and under cover. If I could have got a shot at him then, I wouldn't have bothered to deliver your note. But this is as good a time as any."

Again the flames leaped up the black eyes and sweat beaded Afdal Khan's swarthy skin.

"You're not going to kill him in cold blood?" Willoughby protested.

"No. I'll give him a better chance than he gave Yusef Khan."

Gordon stepped to the silent Pathan, pressed his muzzle against his ribs and drew a knife and revolver from Afdal Khan's girdle. He tossed the weapons up among the rocks and sheathed his own pistol. Then he drew his tulwar with a soft rasp of steel against leather. When he spoke his voice was calm, but Willoughby saw the veins knot and swell on his temples.

"Pick up your blade, Afdal Khan. There is no one here save the Englishman, you, I and Allah--and Allah hates swine!"

Afdal Khan snarled like a trapped panther; he bent his knees, reaching one hand toward the weapon--he crouched there motionless for an instant eyeing Gordon with a wide, blank glare--then all in one motion he snatched up the tulwar and came like a Himalayan hill gust.

Willoughby caught his breath at the blinding ferocity of that onslaught. It seemed to him that Afdal's hand hardly touched the hilt before he was hacking at Gordon's head. But Gordon's head was not there. And Willoughby, expecting to see the American overwhelmed in the storm of steel that played about him began to recall tales he had heard of El Borak's prowess with the heavy, curved Himalayan blade.

Afdal Khan was taller and heavier than Gordon, and he was as quick as a famished wolf. He rained blow on blow with all the strength of his corded arm, and so swiftly Willoughby could follow the strokes only by the incessant clangor of steel on steel. But that flashing tulwar did not connect; each murderous blow rang on Gordon's blade or swished past his head as he shifted. Not that the American fought a running fight. Afdal Khan moved about much more than did Gordon. The Orakzai swayed and bent his body agilely to right and left, leaped in and out, and circled his antagonist, smiting incessantly.

377

Gordon moved his head frequently to avoid blows, but he seldom shifted his feet except to keep his enemy always in front of him. His stance was as firm as that of a deep-rooted rock, and his blade was never beaten down. Beneath the heaviest blows the Pathan could deal, it opposed an unyielding guard.

The man's wrist and forearm must be made of iron, thought Willoughby, staring in amazement. Afdal Khan beat on El Borak's tulwar like a smith on an anvil, striving to beat the American to his knee by the sheer weight of his attack; cords of muscle stood out on Gordon's wrist as he met the attack. He did not give back a foot. His guard never weakened.

Afdal Khan was panting and perspiration streamed down his dark face. His eyes held the glare of a wild beast. Gordon was not even breathing hard. He seemed utterly unaffected by the tempest beating upon him. And desperation flooded Afdal Khan's face, as he felt his own strength waning beneath his maddened efforts to beat down that iron guard.

"Dog!" he gasped, spat in Gordon's face and lunged in terrifically, staking all on one stroke, and throwing his sword arm far back before he swung his tulwar in an arc that might have felled an oak.

Then Gordon moved and the speed of his shift would have shamed a wounded catamount. Willoughby could not follow his motion--he only saw that Afdal Khan's mighty swipe had cleft only empty air, and Gordon's blade was a blinding flicker in the rising sun. There was a sound as of a cleaver sundering a joint of beef and Afdal Khan staggered. Gordon stepped back with a low laugh, merciless as the ring of flint, and a thread of crimson wandered down the broad blade in his hand.

Afdal Khan's face was livid; he swayed drunkenly on his feet, his eyes dilated; his left hand was pressed to his side, and blood spouted between the fingers; his right arm fought to raise the tulwar that had become an imponderable weight.

"Allah!" he croaked. "Allah--" Suddenly his knees bent and he fell as a tree falls.

Willoughby bent over him in awe.

"Good heavens, he's shorn half asunder! How could a man live even those few seconds, with a wound like that?"

"Hillmen are hard to kill," Gordon answered, shaking the red drops from his blade. The crimson glare had gone out of his eyes; the fire that had for so long burned consumingly in his soul had been quenched at last, though it had been quenched in blood.

"You can go back to Kabul and tell the Amir the feud's over," he said. "The caravans from Persia will soon be passing over the road again."

"What about Baber Ali?"

"He pulled out last night, after his attack on the Castle failed. I saw him riding out of the valley with most of his men. He was sick of the siege. Afdal's men are still in the valley but they'll leg it for Khoruk as soon as they hear what's happened to Afdal. The Amir will make an outlaw out of Baber Ali as soon as you get back to Kabul. I've got no more to fear from the Khoruk clan; they'll be glad to agree to peace."

Willoughby glanced down at the dead man. The feud had ended as Gordon had sworn it would. Gordon had been in the right all along; but it was a new and not too pleasing experience to Willoughby to be used as a pawn in a game--as he himself had used so many men and women.

He laughed wryly. "Confound you, Gordon, you've bamboozled me all the way through! You let me believe that only Baber Ali was besieging us, and that Afdal Khan would protect me against his uncle! You set a trap to catch Afdal Khan, and you used me as bait! I've got an idea that if I hadn't thought of that letter-and-telescope combination, you'd have suggested it yourself."

"I'll give you an escort to Ghazrael when the rest of the Orakzai clear out," offered Gordon.

"Damn it, man, if you hadn't saved my life so often in the past forty-eight hours, I'd be inclined to use bad language! But Afdal Khan was a rogue and deserved what he got. I can't say that I relish your methods, but they're effective! You ought to be in the secret service. A few years at this rate and you'll be Amir of Afghanistan!"

THE END

THE LOST VALLEY OF ISKANDER

IT WAS THE stealthy clink of steel on stone that wakened Gordon. In the dim starlight a shadowy bulk loomed over him and something glinted in the lifted hand. Gordon went into action like a steel spring uncoiling. His left hand checked the descending wrist with its curved knife, and simultaneously he heaved upward and locked his right hand savagely on a hairy throat.

A gurgling gasp was strangled in that throat and Gordon, resisting the other's terrific plunges, hooked a leg about his knee and heaved him over and underneath. There was no sound except the rasp and thud of straining bodies. Gordon fought, as always, in grim silence. No sound came from the straining lips of the man beneath. His right hand writhed in Gordon's grip while his left tore futilely at the wrist whose iron fingers drove deeper and deeper into the throat they grasped. That wrist felt like a mass of woven steel wires to the weakening fingers that clawed at it. Grimly Gordon maintained his position, driving all the power of his compact shoulders and corded arms into his throttling fingers. He knew it was his life or that of the man who had crept up to stab him in the dark. In that unmapped corner of the Afghan mountains all fights were to the death. The tearing fingers relaxed. A convulsive shudder ran through the great body straining beneath the American. It went limp.

I. The Oiled Silk Package

GORDON SLID OFF the corpse, in the deeper shadow of the great rocks among which he had been sleeping. Instinctively he felt under his arm to see if the precious package for which he had staked his life was still safe. Yes, it was there, that flat bundle of papers wrapped in oiled silk, that meant life or death to thousands. He listened. No sound broke the stillness. About him the slopes with their ledges and boulders rose gaunt and black in the starlight. It was the darkness before the dawn.

But he knew that men moved about him, out there among the rocks. His ears, whetted by years in wild places, caught stealthy sounds—the soft rasp of cloth over stones, the faint shuffle of sandalled feet. He could not see them, and he knew they could not see him, among the clustered boulders he had chosen for his sleeping site.

His left hand groped for his rifle, and he drew his revolver with his right. That short, deadly fight had made no more noise than the silent knifing of a sleeping man might have made. Doubtless his stalkers out yonder were awaiting some signal from the man they had sent in to murder their victim.

Gordon knew who these men were. He knew their leader was the man who had dogged him for hundreds of miles, determined he should not reach India with that silk-wrapped packet. Francis Xavier Gordon was known by repute from Stamboul to the China Sea. The Muhammadans called him El Borak, the Swift, and they feared and respected him. But in Gustav Hunyadi, renegade and international adventurer, Gordon had met his match. And he knew now that Hunyadi, out there in the night, was lurking with his Turkish killers. They had ferreted him out, at last.

Gordon glided out from among the boulders as silently as a great cat. No hillman, born and bred among those crags, could have avoided loose stones more skillfully or picked his way more carefully. He headed southward, because that was the direction in which lay his ultimate goal. Doubtless he was completely surrounded.

His soft native sandals made no noise, and in his dark hillman's garb he was all but invisible. In the pitch-black shadow of an overhanging cliff, he suddenly sensed a human presence ahead of him. A voice hissed, a European tongue framing the Turki words: "Ali! Is that you? Is the dog dead? Why did you not call me?"

Gordon struck savagely in the direction of the voice. His pistol barrel crunched glancingly against a human skull, and a man groaned and crumpled. All about rose a sudden clamor of voices, the rasp of leather on rock. A stentorian voice began shouting, with a note of panic.

Gordon cast stealth to the winds. With a bound he cleared the writhing body before him, and sped off down the slope. Behind him rose a chorus of yells as the men in hiding glimpsed his shadowy figure racing through the starlight. Jets of orange cut the darkness, but the bullets whined high and wide. Gordon's flying shape was sighted but an instant, then the shadowy gulfs of the night swallowed it up. His enemies raved like foiled wolves in their bewildered rage. Once again their prey had slipped like an eel through their fingers and was gone.

So thought Gordon as he raced across the plateau beyond the clustering cliffs. They would be hot after him, with hillmen who could trail a wolf across naked rocks, but with the start he had—. Even with the thought the earth gaped blackly before him. Even his steel-trap quickness could not save him. His grasping hands caught only thin air as he plunged downward, to strike his head with stunning force at the bottom.

When he regained his senses a chill dawn was whitening the sky. He sat up groggily and felt his head, where a large lump was clotted with dried blood. It was only by chance that his neck was not broken. He had fallen into a ravine, and during the precious time he should have employed in flight, he was lying senseless among the rocks at the bottom.

Again he felt for the packet under his native shirt, though he knew it was fastened there securely. Those papers were his death-warrant, which only his skill and wit could prevent being executed. Men had laughed when Francis Xavier Gordon had warned them that the devil's own stew was bubbling in Central Asia, where a satanic adventurer was dreaming of an outlaw empire.

To prove his assertion, Gordon had gone into Turkestan, in guise of a wandering Afghan. Years spent in the Orient had given him the ability to pass himself for a native anywhere. He had secured proof no one could ignore or deny, but he had been recognized at last. He had fled for his life, and for more than his life, then. And Hunyadi, the renegade who plotted the destruction of nations, was hot on his heels. He had followed Gordon across the steppes, through the foothills, and up into the mountains where he had thought at last to throw him off. But he had failed. The Hungarian was a human bloodhound. Wary, too, as shown by his sending his craftiest slayer in to strike a blow in the dark.

Gordon found his rifle and began the climb out of the ravine. Under his left arm was proof that would make certain officials wake up and take steps to prevent the atrocious thing that Gustav Hunyadi planned. The proof was in the form of letters to various Central Asian chiefs, signed and sealed with the Hungarian's own hand. They revealed his whole plot to embroil Central Asia in a religious war and send howling hordes of fanatics against the Indian border. It was a plan for plundering on a staggering scale. That package must reach Fort Ali Masjid! With all his iron will Francis Xavier Gordon was determined it should. With equal resolution Gustav Hunyadi was determined it should not. In the clash of two such indomitable temperaments, kingdoms shake and death reaps a red harvest.

Dirt crumbled and pebbles rattled down as Gordon worked his way up the sloping side of the ravine. But presently he clambered over the edge and cast a quick look about him. He was on a narrow plateau, pitched among giant slopes which rose somberly above it. To the south showed the mouth of a narrow gorge, walled by rocky cliffs. In that direction he hurried.

He had not gone a dozen steps when a rifle cracked behind him. Even as the wind of the bullet fanned his cheek, Gordon dropped flat behind a boulder, a sense of futility tugging at his heart. He could never escape Hunyadi. This chase would end only when one of them was dead. In the increasing light he saw figures moving among the boulders along the slopes of the northwest of the plateau. He had lost his chance of escaping under cover of darkness, and now it looked like a finish fight.

He thrust forward his rifle barrel. Too much to hope that that blind blow in the dark had killed Hunyadi. The man had as many lives as a cat. A bullet splattered on the boulder close to his elbow. He had seen a tongue of flame lick out, marking the spot where the sniper lurked. He watched those rocks, and when a head and part of an arm and shoulder came up with a rifle, Gordon fired. It was a long shot, but the man reared upright and pitched forward across the rock that had sheltered him.

More bullets came, spattering Gordon's refuge. Up on the slopes, where the big boulders poised breathtakingly, he saw his enemies moving like ants, wriggling from ledge to ledge. They were spread out in a wide ragged semi-circle, trying to surround him again. He did not have enough ammunition to stop them. He dared shoot only when fairly certain of scoring a hit. He dared not make a break for the gorge behind him. He would be riddled before he could reach it. It looked like trail's end for him, and while Gordon had faced death too often to fear it greatly, the thought that those papers would never reach their destination filled him with black despair.

A bullet whining off his boulder from a new angle made him crouch lower, seeking the marksman. He glimpsed a white turban, high up on the slope, above the others. From that position the Turk could drop bullets directly into Gordon's covert.

The American could not shift his position, because a dozen other rifles nearer at hand were covering it; and he could not stay where he was. One of those dropping slugs would find him sooner or later. But the Ottoman decided that he saw a still better position, and risked a shift, trusting to the long uphill range. He did not know Gordon as Hunyadi knew him.

The Hungarian, further down the slope, yelled a fierce command, but the Turk was already in motion, headed for another ledge, his garments flapping about him. Gordon's bullet caught him in mid-stride. With a wild cry he staggered, fell headlong and crashed against a poised boulder. He was a heavy man, and the impact of his hurtling body toppled the rock from its unstable base. It rolled down the slope, dislodging others as it came. Dirt rattled in widening streams about it.

Men began recklessly to break cover. Gordon saw Hunyadi spring up and run obliquely across the slope, out of the path of the sliding rocks. The tall supple figure was unmistakable, even in Turkish garb. Gordon fired and missed, as he always seemed to miss the man, and then there was no time to fire again. The whole slope was in motion now, thundering down in a bellowing, grinding torrent of stones and dirt and boulders. The Turks were fleeing after Hunyadi, screaming: "Ya Allah!"

Gordon sprang up and raced for the mouth of the gorge. He did not look back. He heard above the roaring, the awful screams that marked the end of men caught and crushed and ground to bloody shreds under the rushing tons of shale and stone. He dropped his rifle. Every ounce of extra burden counted now. A deafening roar was in his ears as he gained the mouth of the gorge and flung himself about the beetling jut of the cliff. He crouched there, flattened against the wall, and through the gorge mouth roared a welter of dirt and rocks, boulders bouncing and tumbling, rebounding thunderously from the sides and hurtling on down the sloping pass. Yet, it was a only a trickle of the avalanche which was diverted into the gorge. The main bulk of it thundered on down the mountain.

II. The Rescue of Bardylis of Attalus

GORDON PULLED AWAY from the cliff that had sheltered him. He stood knee deep in loose dirt and broken stones. A flying splinter of stone had cut his face. The roar of the landslide was followed by an unearthly silence. Looking back on to the plateau, he saw a vast litter of broken earth, shale and rocks. Here and there an arm or a leg protruded, bloody and twisted, to mark where a human victim had been caught by the torrent. Of Hunyadi and the survivors there was no sign.

But Gordon was a fatalist where the satanic Hungarian was concerned. He felt quite sure that Hunyadi had survived, and would be upon his trail again as soon as he could collect his demoralized followers. It was likely that he would recruit the natives of these hills to his service. The man's power among the followers of Islam was little short of marvelous.

So Gordon turned hurriedly down the gorge. Rifle, pack of supplies, all were lost. He had only the garments on his body and the pistol at his hip. Starvation in these barren mountains was a haunting threat, if he escaped being butchered by the wild tribes which inhabited them. There was about one chance in ten thousand of his ever getting out alive. But he had known it was a desperate quest when he started, and long odds had never balked Francis Xavier Gordon, once of El Paso, Texas, and now for years soldier of fortune in the outlands of the world.

The gorge twisted and bent between tortuous walls. The split-off arm of the avalanche had quickly spent its force there, but Gordon still saw the slanting floor littered with boulders which had stumbled down from the higher levels. And suddenly he stopped short, his pistol snapping to a level.

On the ground before him lay a man such as he had never seen in the Afghan mountains or elsewhere. He was young, but tall and strong, clad in short silk breeches, tunic and sandals, and girdled with a broad belt which supported a curved sword.

His hair caught Gordon's attention. Blue eyes, such as the youth had, were not uncommon in the hills. But his hair was yellow, bound to his temples with a band of red cloth, and falling in a square-cut mane nearly to his shoulders. He was clearly no Afghan. Gordon remembered tales he had heard of a tribe living somewhere in these mountains who were neither Afghans nor Muhammadans. Had he stumbled upon a member of that legendary race?

The youth was vainly trying to draw his sword. He was pinned down by a boulder which had evidently caught him as he raced for the shelter of the cliff.

"Slay me and be done with it, you Moslem dog!" he gritted in Pushtu.

"I won't harm you," answered Gordon. "I'm no Moslem. Lie still. I'll help you if I can. I have no quarrel with you."

The heavy stone lay across the youth's leg in such a way that he could not extricate the member.

"Is your leg broken?" Gordon asked.

"I think not. But if you move the stone it will grind it to shreds."

Gordon saw that he spoke the truth. A depression on the under side of the stone had saved the youth's limb, while imprisoning it. If he rolled the boulder either way, it would crush the member.

"I'll have to lift it straight up," he grunted.

"You can never do it," said the youth despairingly. "Ptolemy himself could scarecely lift it, and you are not nearly so big as he."

Gordon did not pause to inquire who Ptolemy might be, nor to explain that strength is not altogether a matter of size alone. His own thews were like masses of knit steel wires.

Yet he was not at all sure that he could lift that boulder, which, while not so large as many which rolled down the gorge, was yet bulky enough to make the task look dubious. Straddling the prisoner's body, he braced his legs wide, spread his arms and gripped the big stone. Putting all his corded sinews and his scientific knowledge of weight-lifting into his effort, he uncoiled his strength in a smooth, mighty expansion of power.

His heels dug into the dirt, the veins in his temples swelled, and unexpected knots of muscles sprang out on his straining arms. But the great stone came up steadily without a jerk or waver, and the man on the ground drew his leg clear and rolled away.

Gordon let the stone fall and stepped back, shaking the perspiration from his face. The other worked his skinned, bruised leg gingerly, then looked up and extended his hand in a curiously unOriental gesture.

"I am Bardylis of Attalus," he said. "My life is yours!"

"Men call me El Borak," answered Gordon, taking his hand. They made a strong contrast: the tall, rangy youth in his strange garb, with his white skin and yellow hair, and the American, shorter, more compactly built, in his tattered Afghan garments, and his sun-darkened skin. Gordon's hair was straight and black as an Indian's, and his eyes were black as his hair.

"I was hunting on the cliffs," said Bardylis. "I heard shots and was going to investigate them, when I heard the roar of the avalanche and the gorge was filled with flying rocks. You are no Pathan, despite your name. Come to my village. You look like a man who is weary and has lost his way."

"Where is your village?"

"Yonder, down the gorge and beyond the cliffs." Bardylis pointed southward. Then, looking over Gordon's shoulder, he cried out. Gordon wheeled. High up on the beetling gorge wall, a turbaned head was poked from behind a ledge. A dark face stared down wildly. Gordon ripped out his pistol with a snarl, but the face vanished and he heard a frantic voice yelling in guttural Turki. Other voices answered, among which the American recognized the strident accents of Gustav Hunyadi. The pack was at his heels again. Undoubtedly they had seen Gordon take refuge in the gorge, and as soon as the boulders ceased tumbling, had traversed the torn slope and followed the cliffs where they would have the advantage of the man below.

But Gordon did not pause to ruminate. Even as the turbaned head vanished, he wheeled with a word to his companion, and darted around the next bend in the canyon. Bardylis followed without question, limping on his bruised leg, but moving with sufficient alacrity. Gordon heard his pursuers shouting on the cliff above and behind him, heard them crashing recklessly through stunted bushes, dislodging pebbles as they ran, heedless of everything except their desire to sight their quarry.

Although the pursuers had one advantage, the fugitives had another. They could follow the slightly slanting floor of the gorge more swiftly than the others could run along the uneven cliffs, with their broken edges and jutting ledges. They had to climb and scramble, and Gordon heard their maledictions growing fainter in the distance behind him. When they emerged from the further mouth of the gorge, they were far in advance of Hunyadi's killers.

But Gordon knew that the respite was brief. He looked about him. The narrow gorge had opened out onto a trail which ran straight along the crest of a cliff that fell away sheer three hundred feet into a deep valley, hemmed in on all sides by gigantic precipices. Gordon looked down and saw a stream winding among dense trees far below, and further on, what seemed to be stone buildings among the groves.

Bardylis pointed to the latter.

"There is my village!" he said excitedly. "If we could get into the valley we would be safe! This trail leads to the pass at the southern end, but it is five miles distant!"

Gordon shook his head. The trail ran straight along the top of the cliff and afforded no cover. "They'll run us down and shoot us like rats at long range, if we keep to this path."

"There is one other way!" cried Bardylis. "Down the cliff, at this very point! It is a secret way, and none but a man of my people has ever followed it, and then only when hard pressed. There are handholds cut into the rock. Can you climb down?"

"I'll try," answered Gordon, sheathing his pistol. To try to go down those towering cliffs looked like suicide, but it was sure death to try to outrun Hunyadi's rifles along the trail. At any minute he expected the Magyar and his men to break cover.

"I will go first and guide you," said Bardylis rapidly, kicking off his sandals and letting himself over the cliff edge. Gordon did likewise and followed him. Clinging to the sharp lip of the precipice, Gordon saw a series of small holes pitting the rock. He began the descent slowly, clinging like a fly to a wall. It was hair-raising work, and the only thing that made it possible at all was the slight convex slant of the hill at that point. Gordon had made many a desperate climb during his career, but never one which put such strain on nerve and thew. Again and again only the grip of a finger stood between him and death. Below him Bardylis toiled downward, guiding and encouraging him, until the youth finally dropped to the earth and stood looking tensely up at the man above him.

Then he shouted, with a note of strident fear in his voice. Gordon, still twenty feet from the bottom, craned his neck upward. High above him he saw a bearded face peering down at him, convulsed with triumph. Deliberately the Turk sighted downward with a pistol, then laid it aside and caught up a heavy stone, leaning far over the edge to aim its downward course. Clinging with toes and nails, Gordon drew and fired upward with the same motion. Then he flattened himself desperately against the cliff and clung on.

The man above screamed and pitched headfirst over the brink. The rock rushed down, striking Gordon a glancing blow on the shoulder, then the writhing body hurtled past and struck with a sickening concussion on the earth below. A voice shouting furiously high above announced the presence of Hunyadi at last, and Gordon slid and tumbled recklessly the remaining distance, and, with Bardylis, ran for the shelter of the trees.

A glance backward and upward showed him Hunyadi crouching on the cliff, leveling a rifle, but the next instant Gordon and Bardylis were out of sight, and Hunyadi, apparently dreading an answering shot from the trees, made a hasty retreat with the four Turks who were the survivors of his party.

III. The Sons of Iskander

"YOU SAVED MY life when you showed me that path," said Gordon.

Bardylis smiled. "Any man of Attalus could have shown you the path, which we call the Road of the Eagles. But only a hero could have followed it. From what land comes my brother?"

"From the west," answered Gordon; "from the land of America, beyond Frankistan and the sea."

Bardylis shook his head. "I have never heard of it. But come with me. My people are yours henceforth."

As they moved through the trees, Gordon scanned the cliffs in vain for some sign of his enemies. He felt certain that neither Hunyadi, bold as he was, nor any of his companions would try to follow them down "the Road of the Eagles." They were not mountaineers. They were more at home in the saddle than on a hill path. They would seek some other way into the valley. He spoke his thoughts to Bardylis.

"They will find death," answered the youth grimly. "The Pass of the King, at the southern end of the valley, is the only entrance. Men guard it with matchlocks night and day. The only strangers who enter the Valley of Iskander are traders and merchants with pack-mules."

Gordon inspected his companion curiously, aware of a certain tantalizing sensation of familiarity he could not place.

"Who are your people?" he asked. "You are not an Afghan. You do not look like a Oriental at all."

"We are the Sons of Iskander," answered Bardylis. "When the great conqueror came through these mountains long ago, he built the city we call Attalus, and left hundreds of his soldiers and their women in it. Iskander marched westward again, and after a long while word came that he was dead and his empire divided. But the people of Iskander abode here, unconquered. Many times we have slaughtered the Afghan dogs who came against us."

Light came to Gordon, illuminating that misplaced familiarity. Iskander—Alexander the Great, who conquered this part of Asia and left colonies behind him. This boy's profile was classic Grecian, such as Gordon had seen in sculptured marble, and the names he spoke were Grecian. Undoubtedly he was the descendant of some Macedonian soldier who had followed the Great Conqueror on his invasion of the East.

To test the matter, he spoke to Bardylis in ancient Greek, one of the many languages, modern and obsolete, he had picked up in his varied career. The youth cried out with pleasure.

"You speak our tongue!" he exclaimed, in the same language. "Not in a thousand years has a stranger come to us with our own speech on his lips. We converse with the Moslems in their own tongue, and they know nothing of ours. Surely, you too, are a Son of Iskander?"

Gordon shook his head, wondering how he could explain his knowledge of the tongue to this youth who knew nothing of the world outside the hills.

"My ancestors were neighbors of the people of Alexander," he said at last. "So, many of my people speak their language."

They were approaching the stone roofs which shone through the trees, and Gordon saw that Bardylis's "village" was a substantial town, surrounded by a wall. It was so plainly the work of long dead Grecian architects that he felt like a man who wandered into a past and forgotten age.

Outside the walls, men tilled the thin soil with primitive implements, and herded sheep and cattle. A few horses grazed along the bank of the stream which meandered through the valley. All the men, like Bardylis, were tall and fair-haired. They dropped their work and came running up, staring at the black-haired stranger in hostile surprise, until Bardylis reassured them.

"It is the first time any but a captive or a trader has entered the valley in centuries," said Bardylis to Gordon. "Say nothing till I bid you. I wish to surprise my people with your knowledge. Zeus, they will gape when they hear a stranger speak to them in their own tongue!"

The gate in the wall hung open and unguarded, and Gordon noticed that the wall itself was in a poor state of repair. Bardylis remarked that the guard in the narrow pass at the end of the valley was sufficient protection, and that no hostile force had ever reached the city itself. They passed through and walked along a broad paved street, in which yellow-haired people in tunics, men, women and children, went about their tasks much like the Greeks of two thousand years ago, among buildings which were duplicates of the structures of ancient Athens.

A crowd quickly formed about them, but Bardylis, bursting with glee and importance, gave them no satisfaction. He went straight toward a large edifice near the center of the town and mounting the broad steps, came into a large chamber where several men, more richly dressed than the common people, sat casting dice on a small table before them. The crowd swarmed in after them, and thronged the doorway eagerly. The chiefs ceased their dice game, and one, a giant with a commanding air, demanded: "What do you wish, Bardylis? Who is this stranger?"

"A friend of Attalus, Ptolemy, king of the valley of Iskander," answered Bardylis. "He speaks the tongue of Iskander!"

"What tale is this?" harshly demanded the giant.

"Let them hear, brother!" Bardylis directed triumphantly.

"I come in peace," said Gordon briefly, in archaic Greek. "I am called El Borak, but I am no Moslem."

A murmur of surprise went up from the throng, and Ptolemy fingered his chin and scowled suspiciously. He was a magnificently built man, clean-shaven like all his tribesmen, and handsome, but his visage was moody.

He listened impatiently while Bardylis related the circumstances of his meeting with Gordon, and when he told of the American lifting the stone that pinned him down, Ptolemy frowned and involuntarily flexed his own massive thews. He seemed ill-pleased at the approval with which the people openly greeted the tale. Evidently these descendants of Grecian athletes had as much admiration for physical perfection as had their ancient ancestors, and Ptolemy was vain of his prowess.

"How could he lift such a stone?" the king broke in. "He is of no great size. His head would scarcely top my chin."

"He is mighty beyond his stature, O king," retorted Bardylis. "Here is the bruise on my leg to prove I tell the truth. He lifted the stone I could not move, and he came down the Road of the Eagles, which few even among the Altaians have dared. He has traveled far and fought men, and now he would feast and rest."

"See to it then," grunted Ptolemy contemptuously, turning back to his dice game. "If he is a Moslem spy, your head shall answer for it."

"I stake my head gladly on his honesty, O king!" answered Bardylis proudly. Then, taking Gordon's arm, he said softly, "Come my friend. Ptolemy is short of patience and scant of courtesy. Pay no heed to him. I will take you to the house of my father."

As they pushed their way through the crowd, Gordon's gaze picked out an alien countenance among the frank, blond faces—a thin, swarthy visage, whose black eyes gleamed avidly on the American. The man was a Tajik, with a bundle on his back. When he saw he was being scrutinized he smirked and bobbed his head. There was something familiar about the gesture.

"Who is that man?" Gordon asked.

"Abdullah, a Moslem dog whom we allow to enter the valley with beads and mirrors and such trinkets as our women love. We trade ore and wine and skins for them."

403

Gordon remembered the fellow now—a shifty character who used to hang around Peshawur, and was suspected of smuggling rifles up the Khyber Pass. But when he turned and looked back, the dark face had vanished in the crowd. However, there was no reason to fear Abdullah, even if the man recognized him. The Tajik could not know of the papers he carried. Gordon felt that the people of Attalus were friendly to the friend of Bardylis, though the youth had plainly roused Ptolemy's jealous vanity by his praise of Gordon's strength.

Bardylis conducted Gordon down the street to a large stone house with a pillared portico, where he proudly displayed his friend to his father, a venerable patriarch called Perdiccas, and his mother, a tall, stately woman, well along in years. The Attalans certainly did not keep their women in seclusion like the Moslems. Gordon saw Bradylis's sisters, robust blond beauties, and his young brother. The American could scarcely suppress a smile at the strangeness of it all, being ushered into the every-day family life of two thousand years ago. These people were definitely not barbarians. They were lower, undoubtedly, in the cultural scale than their Hellenic ancestors, but they were still more highly civilized than their fierce Afghan neighbors.

The interest in their guest was genuine, but none save Bardylis showed much interest in the world outside their valley. Presently the youth led Gordon into an inner chamber and set food and wine before him. The American ate and drank ravenously, suddenly aware of the lean days that had preceded this feast. While he ate, Bardylis talked, but he did not speak of the men who had been pursuing Gordon. Evidently he supposed them to have been Afghans of the surrounding hills, whose hostility was proverbial. Gordon learned that no man of Attalus had ever been more than a day's journey away from the valley. The ferocity of the hill tribes all about them had isolated them from the world completely.

When Gordon at last expressed a desire for sleep, Bardylis left him alone, assuring him that he would not be disturbed. The American was somewhat disturbed to find that there was no door to his chamber, merely a curtain drawn across an archway. Bardylis had said there were no thieves in Attalus, but caution was so much a natural part of Gordon that he found himself a prey to uneasiness. The room opened onto a corridor, and the corridor, he believed, gave onto an outer door. The people of Attalus apparently did not find it necessary to safeguard their dwellings. But though a native could sleep in safety, that might not apply to a stranger.

Finally Gordon drew aside the couch which formed the main piece of furniture for the chamber, and making sure no spying eyes were on him, he worked loose one of the small stone blocks which composed the wall. Taking the silk-bound packet from his shirt, he thrust it into the aperture, pushed back the stone as far as it would go, and replaced the couch.

Stretching himself, then, upon the couch, he fell to evolving plans for escape with his life and those papers which meant so much to peace of Asia. He was safe enough in the valley, but he knew Hunyadi would wait for him outside with the patience of a cobra. He could not stay here forever. He would scale the cliffs some dark night and bolt for it. Hunyadi would undoubtedly have all the tribes in the hills after him, but he would trust to luck and his good right arm, as he had so often before. The wine he had drunk was potent. Weariness after the long flight weighted his limbs. Gordon's meditations merged into dream. He slept deeply and long.

IV. The Duel with Ptolemy the Kind

WHEN GORDON AWOKE he was in utter darkness. He knew that he had slept for many hours, and night had fallen. Silence reigned over the house, but he had been awakened by the soft swish of the curtains over the doorway.

He sat up on his couch and asked: "Is that you, Bardylis?"

A voice grunted, "Yes." Even as he was electrified by the realization that the voice was not that of Bardylis, something crashed down on his head, and a deeper blackness, shot with fire-sparks, engulfed him.

When he regained consciousness, a torch dazzled his eyes, and in its glow he saw three men—burly, yellow-haired men of Attalus with faces more stupid and brutish than any he had yet seen. He was lying on a stone slab in a bare chamber, whose crumbling, cob-webbed walls were vaguely illumined by the gutturing torch. His arms were bound, but not his legs. The sound of a door opening made him crane his neck, and he saw a stooped, vulture-like figure enter the room. It was Abdullah, the Tajik.

He looked down on the American with his rat-like features twisted in a venomous grin.

"Low lies the terrible El Borak!" he taunted. "Fool! I knew you the instant I saw you in the palace of Ptolemy."

"You have no feud with me," growled Gordon.

"A friend of mine has," answered the Tajik. "That is nothing to me, but it shall gain me profit. It is true you have never harmed me, but I have always feared you. So when I saw you in the city, I gathered my goods and hastened to depart, not knowing what you did here. But beyond the pass I met the Feringhi Hunyadi, and he asked me if I had seen you in the valley of Iskander whither you had fled to escape him. I answered that I had, and he urged me to help him

407

steal into the valley and take from you certain documents he said you stole from him.

"But I refused, knowing that these Attalan devils would kill me if I tried to smuggle a stranger into Iskander, and Hunyadi went back into the hills with his four Turks, and the horde of ragged Afghans he has made his friends and allies. When he had gone I returned to the valley, telling the guardsmen at the pass that I feared the Pathans.

"I persuaded these three men to aid me in capturing you. None will know what became of you, and Ptolemy will not trouble himself about you, because he is jealous of your strength. It is an old tradition that the king of Attalus must be the strongest man in the city. Ptolemy would have killed you himself, in time. But I will attend to that. I do not wish to have you on my trail, after I have taken from you the papers Hunyadi wishes. He shall have them ultimately—if he is willing to pay enough!" He laughed, a high, cackling laugh, and turned to the stolid Attalans. "Did you search him?"

"We found nothing," a giant rumbled.

Abdullah tck-tck'ed his teeth in annoyance.

"You do not know how to search a Feringhi. Here, I will do it myself."

He ran a practiced hand over his captive, scowling as his search was unrewarded. He tried to feel under the American's armpits, but Gordon's arms were bound so closely to his sides that this was impossible.

Abdulla frowned worriedly, and drew a curved dagger.

"Cut loose his arms," he directed, "then all three of you lay hold on him; it is like letting a leopard out of his cage."

Gordon made no resistance and was quickly spread-eagled on the slab, with a big Attalan at each arm and one on his legs. They held him closely, but seemed skeptical of Abdullah's repeated warnings concerning the stranger's strength.

The Tajik again approached his prisoner, lowering his knife as he reached out. With a dynamic release of coiled steel muscles, Gordon wrenched his legs free from the grasp of the careless Attalan and drove his heels into Abdullah's breast. Had his feet been booted they would have caved in Tajik's breast bone. As it was, the merchant shot backward with an agonized grunt, and struck the floor flat on his shoulders.

Gordon had not paused. That same terrific lunge had torn his left arm free, and heaving up on the slab, he smashed his left fist against the jaw of the man who gripped his right arm. The impact was that of a caulking hammer, and the Attalan went down like a butchered ox. The other two lunged in, hands grasping. Gordon threw himself over the slab to the floor on the other side, and as one of the warriors lunged around it, he caught the Attalan's wrist, wheeled, jerking the arm over his shoulder, and hurled the man bodily over his head. The Attalan struck the floor head-first with an impact that knocked wind and consciousness out of him together.

The remaining kidnapper was more wary. Seeing the terrible strength and blinding speed of his smaller foe, he drew a long knife and came in cautiously, seeking an opportunity for a mortal thrust. Gordon fell back, putting the slab between himself and that glimmering blade, while the other circled warily after him. Suddenly the American stooped and ripped a similar knife from the belt of the man he had first felled. As he did so, the Attalan gave a roar, cleared the slab with a lion-like bound, and slashed in mid-air at the stooping American.

Gordon crouched still lower and the gleaming blade whistled over his head. The man hit the floor feet-first, off balance, and tumbled forward, full into the knife that swept up in Gordon's hand. A strangled cry was wrung from the Attalan's lips as he felt himself impaled on the long blade, and he dragged Gordon down with him in his death struggles.

Tearing free from his weakening embrace, Gordon rose, his garments smeared with his victim's blood, the red knife in his hand. Abdullah staggered up with a croaking cry, his face green with pain. Gordon snarled like a wolf and sprang toward him, all his murderous passion fully roused. But the sight of that dripping knife and the savage mask of Gordon's face galvanized the Tajik. With a scream he sprang for the door, knocking the torch from its socket as he passed. It hit the floor, scattering sparks, and plunging the room into darkness, and Gordon caromed blindly into the wall.

When he righted himself and found the door, the room was empty except for himself and the Attalans, dead or senseless.

Emerging from the chamber, he found himself in a narrow street, with the stars fading for dawn. The building he had just quilted was dilapidated and obviously deserted. Down the narrow way he saw the house of Perdiccas. So he had not been carried far. Evidently his abductors had anticipated no interference. He wondered how much of a hand Bardylis had had in the plot. He did not like to think that the youth had betrayed him. But in any event, he would have to return to the house of Perdiccas, to obtain the packet he had concealed in the wall. He went down the street, still feeling a bit sick and giddy from that blow that had knocked him senseless, now that the fire of battle had cooled in his veins. The street was deserted. It seemed, indeed, more like an alley than a street, running between the back of the houses.

As he approached the house, he saw someone running toward him. It was Bardylis, and he threw himself on Gordon with a cry of relief that was not feigned.

"Oh, my brother!" he exclaimed. "What has happened? I found your chamber empty a short time ago, and blood on your couch. Are you unhurt? Nay, there is a cut upon your scalp!"

Gordon explained in a few words, saying nothing of the letters. He allowed Bardylis to suppose that Abdullah had been a personal enemy, bent on revenge. He trusted the youth now, but there was no need to disclose the truth of the packet.

Bardylis whitened with fury. "What a shame upon my house!" he cried. "Last night that dog Abdullah made my father a present of a great jug of wine, and we all drank except yourself, who were slumbering. I know now the wine was drugged. We slept like dogs.

"Because you were our guest, I posted a man at each outer door last night, but they fell asleep because of the wine they had drunk. A few minutes ago, searching for you, I found the servant who was posted at the door which opens into this alley from the corridor that runs past your chamber. His throat had been cut. It was easy for them to creep along that corridor and into your chamber while we slept."

Back in the chamber, while Bardylis went to fetch fresh garments, Gordon retrieved the packet from the wall and stowed it under his belt. In his waking hours he preferred to keep it on his person.

Bardylis returned then with the breeches, sandals and tunic of the Attalans, and while Gordon donned them, gazed in admiration at the American's bronzed and sinewy torso, devoid as it was of the slightest trace of surplus flesh.

Gordon had scarcely completed his dressing when voices were heard without, the tramp of men resounded through the hall, and a group of yellow-haired warriors appeared at the doorway, with swords at their sides. Their leader pointed at Gordon, and said: "Ptolemy commands that this man appear at once before him, in the hall of justice."

"What is this?" exclaimed Bardylis. "El Borak is my guest!"

"It is not my part to say," answered the chief. "I but carry out the commands of our king."

Gordon laid a restraining hand on Bardylis's arm. "I will go. I want to see what business Ptolemy has with me."

"I, too, will go," said Bardylis, with a snap of his jaws. "What this portends I do not know. I do know that El Borak is my friend."

The sun was not yet rising as they strode down the white street toward the palace, but people were already moving about, and many of them followed the procession.

Mounting the broad steps of the palace, they entered a wide hall, flanked with lofty columns. At the other end there were more steps, wide and curving, leading up to a dais on which, in a throne-like marble chair, sat the king of Attalus, sullen as ever. A number of his chiefs sat on stone benches on either side of the dais, and the common people ranged themselves along the wall, leaving a wide space clear before the throne.

In this open space crouched a vulture-like figure. It was Abdullah, his eyes shining with hate and fear, and before him lay the corpse of the man Gordon had killed in the deserted house. The other two kidnappers stood nearby, their bruised features sullen and ill at ease.

Gordon was conducted into the open space before the dais, and the guards fell back on either side of him. There was little formality. Ptolemy motioned to Abdullah and said: "Make your charge."

Abdullah sprang up and pointed a skinny finger in Gordon's face.

"I accuse this man of murder!" he screeched. "This morning before dawn he attacked me and my friends while we slept, and slew him who lies there. The rest of us barely escaped with our lives!"

A mutter of surprise and anger rose from the throng. Ptolemy turned his somber stare on Gordon.

"What have you to say?"

"He lies," answered the American impatiently. "I killed that man, yes—"

He was interrupted by a fierce cry from the people, who began to surge menacingly forward, to be thrust back by the guards.

"I only defended my life," said Gordon angrily, not relishing his position of defendant. "That Tajik dog and three others, that dead man and those two standing there, slipped into my chamber last night as I slept in the house of Perdiccas, knocked me senseless and carried me away to rob and kill me."

"Aye!" cried Bardylis wrathfully. "And they slew one of my father's servants while he slept."

At that the murmur of the mob changed, and they halted in uncertainty.

"A lie!" screamed Abdullah, fired to recklessness by avarice and hate. "Bardylis is bewitched! El Borak is a wizard! How else could he speak your tongue?"

The crowd recoiled abruptly, and some made furtive signs to avert conjury. The Attalans were as superstitious as their ancestors. Bardylis had drawn his sword, and his friends rallied about him, clean-cut, rangy youngsters, quivering like hunted dogs in their eagerness.

"Wizard or man!" roared Bardylis, "he is my brother, and no man touches him save at peril of his head!"

"He is a wizard!" screamed Abdullah, foam dabbling his beard. "I know him of old! Beware of him! He will bring madness and ruin upon Attalus! On his body he bears a scroll with magic inscriptions, wherein lies his necromantic power! Give that scroll to me, and I will take it afar from Attalus and destroy it where it can do no harm. Let me prove I do not lie! Hold him while I search him, and I will show you."

"Let no man dare touch El Borak!" challenged Bardylis. Then from his throne rose Ptolemy, a great menacing image of bronze, somber and awe-inspiring. He strode down the steps, and men shrank back from his bleak eyes. Bardylis stood his ground, as if ready to defy even his terrible king, but Gordon drew the lad aside. El Borak was not one to stand quietly by while someone else defended him.

"It is true," he said without heat, "that I have a packet of papers in my garments. But it is also true that it has nothing to do with witchcraft, and that I will kill the man who tries to take it from me."

At that Ptolemy's brooding impassiveness vanished in a flame of passion.

"Will you defy even me?" he roared, his eyes blazing, his great hands working convulsively. "Do you deem yourself already king of Attalus? You black-haired dog, I will kill you with my naked hands! Back, and give us space!"

His sweeping arms hurled men right and left, and roaring like a bull, he hurled himself on Gordon. So swift and violent was his attack that Gordon was unable to avoid it. They met breast to breast, and the smaller man was hurled backward, and to his knee. Ptolemy plunged over him, unable to check his velocity, and then, locked in a death-grapple they ripped and tore, while the people surged yelling about them.

Not often did El Borak find himself opposed by a man stronger than himself. But the king of Attalus was a mass of whale-bone and iron, and nerved to blinding quickness. Neither had a weapon. It was man to man, fighting as the primitive progenitors of the race fought. There was no science about Ptolemy's onslaught. He fought like a tiger or a lion, with all the appalling frenzy of the primordial. Again and again Gordon battered his way out of a grapple that threatened to snap his spine like a rotten branch. His blinding blows ripped and smashed in a riot of destruction. The tall king of Attalus swayed and trembled before them like a tree in a storm, but always came surging back like a typhoon, lashing out with great strokes that drove Gordon staggering before him, rending and tearing with mighty fingers.

Only his desperate speed and the savage skill of boxing and wrestling that was his had saved Gordon so long. Naked to the waist, battered and bruised, his tortured body quivered with the punishment he was enduring. But Ptolemy's great chest was heaving. His face was a mask of raw beef, and his torso showed the effects of a beating that would have killed a lesser man.

Gasping a cry that was half curse, half sob, he threw himself bodily on the American, bearing him down by sheer weight. As they fell he drove a knee savagely at Gordon's groin, and tried to fall with his full weight on the smaller man's breast. A twist of his body sent the knee sliding harmlessly along his thigh, and Gordon writhed from under the heavier body as they fell.

The impact broke their holds, and they staggered up simultaneously. Through the blood and sweat that streamed into his eyes, Gordon saw the king towering above him, reeling, arms spread, blood pouring down his mighty breast. His belly went in as he drew a great laboring breath. And into the relaxed pit of his stomach Gordon, crouching, drove his left with all the strength of his rigid arm, iron shoulders and knotted calves behind it. His clenched fist sank to the wrist in Ptolemy's solar plexus. The king's breath went out of him in an explosive grunt. His hands dropped and he swayed like a tall tree under the axe. Gordon's right, hooking up in a terrible arc, met his jaw with a sound like a cooper's mallet, and Ptolemy pitched headlong and lay still.

V. The Death of Hunyadi

IN THE STUPEFIED silence that followed the fall of the king, while all eyes, dilated with surprise, were fixed on the prostrate giant and the groggy figure that weaved above him, a gasping voice shouted from outside the palace. It grew louder, mingled with a clatter of hoofs which stopped at the outer steps. All wheeled toward the door as a wild figure staggered in, spattering blood.

"A guard from the pass!" cried Bardylis.

"The Moslems!" cried the man, blood spurting through his fingers which he pressed to his shoulder. "Three hundred Afghans! They have stormed the pass! They are led by a feringhi and four turki who have rifles that fire many times without reloading! These men shot us down from afar off as we strove to defend the pass. The Afghans have entered the valley—" He swayed and fell, blood trickling from his lips. A blue bullet hole showed in his shoulder, near the base of his neck.

No clamor of terror greeted this appalling news. In the utter silence that followed, all eyes turned toward Gordon, leaning dizzily against the wall, gasping for breath.

"You have conquered Ptolemy," said Bardylis. "He is dead or senseless. While he is helpless, you are king. That is the law. Tell us what to do."

Gordon gathered his dazed wits and accepted the situation without demur or question. If the Afghans were in the valley, there was no time to waste. He thought he could hear the distant popping of firearms already. "How many men are able to bear arms?" he panted.

"Three hundred and fifty," answered one of the chiefs.

"Then let them take their weapons and follow me," he said. "The walls of the city are rotten. If we try to defend them, with Hunyadi directing the siege, we will be trapped like rats. We must win with one stroke, if at all."

Someone brought him a sheathed and belted scimitar and he buckled it about his waist. His head was still swimming and his body numb, but from some obscure reservoir he drew a fund of reserve power, and the prospect of a final showdown with Hunyadi fired his blood. At his directions men lifted Ptolemy and placed him on a couch. The king had not moved since he dropped, and Gordon thought it probable that he had a concussion of the brain. That poleax smash that had felled him would have split the skull of a lesser man.

Then Gordon remembered Abdullah, and looked about for him, but the Tajik had vanished.

At the head of the warriors of Attalus, Gordon strode down the street and through the ponderous gate. All were armed with long curved swords; some had unwieldy matchlocks, ancient weapons captured from the hill tribes. He knew the Afghans would be no better armed, but the rifles of Hunyadi and his Turks would count heavily.

He could see the horde swarming up the valley, still some distance away. They were on foot. Lucky for the Attalans that one of the pass-guards had kept a horse near him. Otherwise the Afghans would have been at the very walls of the town before the word came of their invasion.

The invaders were drunk with exultation, halting to fire outlying huts and growing stuff, and to shoot cattle, in sheer wanton destructiveness. Behind Gordon rose a deep rumble of rage, and looking back at the blazing blue eyes, and tall, tense figures, the American knew he was leading no weaklings to battle.

He led them to a long straggling heap of stones which ran waveringly clear across the valley, marking an ancient fortification, long abandoned and crumbling down. It would afford some cover. When they reached it the invaders were still out of rifle fire. The Afghans had ceased their plundering and came on at an increased gait, howling like wolves.

Gordon ordered his men to lie down behind the stones, and called to him the warriors with the matchlocks—some thirty in all.

"Pay no heed to the Afghans," he instructed them. "Shoot at the men with the rifles. Do not shoot at random, but wait until I give the word, then all fire together."

The ragged horde were spreading out somewhat as they approached, loosing their matchlocks before they were in range of the grim band waiting silently along the crumbled wall. The Attalans quivered with eagerness, but Gordon gave no sign. He saw the tall, supple figure of Hunyadi, and the bulkier shapes of his turbaned Turks, in the center of

421

the ragged crescent. The men came straight on, apparently secure in the knowledge that the Attalans had no modern weapons, and that Gordon had lost his rifle. They had seen him climbing down the cliff without it. Gordon cursed Abdullah, whose treachery had lost him his pistol.

Before they were in range of the matchlocks, Hunyadi fired, and the warrior at Gordon's side slumped over, drilled through the head. A mutter of rage and impatience ran along the line, but Gordon quieted the warriors, ordering them to lie closer behind the rocks. Hunyadi tried again, and the Turks blazed away, but the bullets whined off the stones. The men moved nearer and behind them the Afghans howled with bloodthirsty impatience, rapidly getting out of hand.

Gordon had hoped to lure Hunyadi into reach of his matchlocks. But suddenly, with an earth-shaking yell, the Afghans stormed past the Hungarian in a wave, knives flaming like the sun on water. Hunyadi yelped explosively, unable to see or shoot at his enemies, for the backs of his reckless allies. Despite his curses, they came on with a roar.

Gordon, crouching among the stones, glared at the gaunt giants rushing toward him until he could make out the fanatical blaze of their eyes, then he roared: "Fire."

A thunderous volley ripped out along the wall, ragged, but terrible at that range. A storm of lead blasted the oncoming line, and men went down in windrows. Lost to all caution, the Attalans leaped the wall and hewed into the staggering Afghans with naked steel. Cursing as Hunyadi had cursed, Gordon drew his scimitar and followed them.

No time for orders now, no formation, no strategy. Attalan and Afghan, they fought as men fought a thousand years ago, without order or plan, massed in a straining, grunting, hacking mob, where naked blades flickered like lightning. Yard-long Khyber knives clanged and ground against the curved swords of the Attalans. The rending of flesh and bone beneath the chopping blades was like the sound of butchers' cleavers. The dying dragged down the living and the warriors stumbled among the mangled corpses. It was a shambles where no quarter was asked and none given, and the feuds and hates of a thousand years glutted in slaughter.

No shots were fired in that deadly crush, but about the edges of the battle circled Hunyadi and the Turks, shooting with deadly accuracy. Man to man, the stalwart Attalans were a match for the hairy hillmen, and they slightly outnumbered the invaders. But they had thrown away the advantage of their position, and the rifles of the Hungarian's own party were dealing havoc in their disordered ranks. Two of the Turks were down, one hit by a matchlock ball in that first and only volley, and another disembowelled by a dying Attalan.

As Gordon hewed his way through the straining knots and flailing blades, he met one of the remaining Turks face to face. The man thrust a rifle muzzle in his face, but the hammer fell with a click on an empty shell, and the next instant Gordon's scimitar ripped through his belly and stood out a foot behind his back. As the American twisted his blade free, the other Turk fired a pistol, missed, and hurled the empty weapon fruitlessly. He rushed in, slashing with a saber at Gordon's head. El Borak parried the singing blade, and his scimitar cut the air like a blue beam, splitting the Turk's skull to the chin.

Then he saw Hunyadi. The Hungarian was groping in his belt, and Gordon knew he was out of ammunition.

"We've tried hot lead, Gustav," challenged Gordon, "and we both still live. Come and try cold steel!"

With a wild laugh the Hungarian ripped out his blade in a bright shimmer of steel that caught the morning sun. He was a tall man, Gustav Hunyadi, black sheep son of a noble Magyar house, supple and lithe as a catamount, with dancing, reckless eyes and lips that curved in a smile as cruel as a striking sword.

"I match my life against a little package of papers, El Borak!" the Hungarian laughed as the blades met.

On each side the fighting lulled and ceased, as the warriors drew back with heaving chests and dripping swords, to watch their leaders settle the score.

The curved blades sparkled in the sunlight, ground together, leaped apart, licked in and out like living things.

Well for El Borak then that his wrist was a solid mass of steel cords, that his eye was quicker and surer than a falcon's, and his brain and thews bound together with a coordination keen as razor-edged steel. For into his play Hunyadi brought all the skill of a race of swordsmen, all the craft taught by masters of the blade of Europe and Asia, and all the savage cunning he had learned in wild battles on the edges of the world.

He was taller and had the longer reach. Again and again his blade whispered at Gordon's throat. Once it touched his arm, and a trickle of crimson began. There was no sound except the rasp of feet on the sward, the rapid whisper of the blades, the deep panting of the men. Gordon was the harder pressed. That terrible fight with Ptolemy was taking its toll. His legs trembled, his sight kept blurring. As if through a mist he saw the triumphant smile growing on the thin lips of the Magyar.

And a wild surge of desperation rose in Gordon's soul, nerving him for a last rush. It came with the unexpected fury of a dying wolf, with a flaming fan of steel, a whirlwind of blades—and then Hunyadi was down, clutching at the earth with twitching hands, Gordon's narrow curved blade through him.

The Hungarian rolled his glazing eyes up at his conqueror, and his lips distorted in a ghastly smile. "To the mistress of all true adventures!" he whispered, choking on his own blood. "To the Lady Death!"

He sank back and lay still, his pallid face turned to the sky, blood oozing from his lips.

The Afghans began slinking furtively away, their morale broken, like a pack of wolves whose leader is down. Suddenly, as if waking from a dream, the Attalans gave tongue and pelted after them. The invaders broke and fled, while the infuriated Attalans followed, stabbing and hacking at their backs, down the valley and out through the pass.

Gordon was aware that Bardylis, blood-stained but exultant, was beside him, supporting his trembling frame that seemed on the point of collapse. The American wiped the bloody sweat from his eyes, and touched the packet under his girdle. Many men had died for that. But many more would have died had it not been saved, including helpless women and children.

Bardylis muttered apprehensively, and Gordon looked up to see a gigantic figure approaching leisurely from the direction of the city, through whose gate the rejoicing women were already streaming. It was Ptolemy, his features grotesquely swollen and blackened from Gordon's iron fists. He strode serenely through the heaps of corpses, and reached the spot where the companions stood.

Bardylis gripped his notched sword, and Ptolemy, seeing the gesture, grinned with his pulped lips. He was holding something behind him.

"I do not come in anger, El Borak," he said calmly. "A man who can fight as you have fought is neither wizard, thief nor murderer. I am no child to hate a man who has bested me in fair fight—and then saved my kingdom while I lay senseless. Will you take my hand?"

Gordon grasped it with an honest surge of friendship toward this giant, whose only fault, after all, was his vanity.

"I did not recover my senses in time for the battle," said Ptolemy. "I only saw the last of it. But if I did not reach the field in time to smite the Moslem dogs, I have at least rid the valley of one rat I found hiding in the palace." He casually tossed something at Gordon's feet. The severed head of Abdullah, the features frozen in a grin of horror, stared up at the American.

"Will you live in Attalus and be my brother, as well as the brother of Bardylis?" asked Ptolemy, with a glance down the valley, toward the pass through which the warriors were harrying the howling Afghans.

"I thank you, king," said Gordon, "but I must go to my own people, and it is still a long road to travel. When I have rested for a few days, I must be gone. A little food, to carry with me on my journey is all I ask from the people

427

of Attalus, who are men as brave and valiant as their royal ancestors."

SON OF THE WHITE WOLF

Chapter I: The Battle Standard

THE COMMANDER OF the Turkish outpost of El Ashraf was awakened before dawn by the stamp of horses and jingle of accoutrements. He sat up and shouted for his orderly. There was no response, so he rose, hurriedly jerked on his garments, and strode out of the mud hut that served as his headquarters. What he saw rendered him momentarily speechless.

His command was mounted, in full marching formation, drawn up near the railroad that it was their duty to guard. The plain to the left of the track where the tents of the troopers had stood now lay bare. The tents had been loaded on the baggage camels which stood fully packed and ready to move out. The commandant glared wildly, doubting his own senses, until his eyes rested on a flag borne by a trooper. The waving pennant did not display the familiar crescent. The commandant turned pale.

"What does this mean?" he shouted, striding forward. His lieutenant, Osman, glanced at him inscrutably. Osman was a tall man, hard and supple as steel, with a dark keen face.

"Mutiny, effendi," he replied calmly. "We are sick of this war we fight for the Germans. We are sick of Djemal Pasha and those other fools of the Council of Unity and Progress, and, incidentally, of you. So we are going into the hills to build a tribe of our own."

"Madness!" gasped the officer, tugging at his revolver. Even as he drew it, Osman shot him through the head.

The lieutenant sheathed the smoking pistol and turned to the troopers. The ranks were his to a man, won to his wild ambition under the very nose of the officer who now lay there with his brains oozing.

"Listen!" he commanded.

In the tense silence they all heard the low, deep reverberation in the west.

"British guns!" said Osman. "Battering the Turkish Empire to bits! The New Turks have failed. What Asia needs is not a new party, but a new race! There are thousands of fighting men between the Syrian coast and the Persian highlands, ready to be roused by a new word, a new prophet! The East is moving in her sleep. Ours is the duty to awaken her!

"You have all sworn to follow me into the hills. Let us return to the ways of our pagan ancestors who worshipped the White Wolf on the steppes of High Asia before they bowed to the creed of Mohammed!

"We have reached the end of the Islamic Age. We abjure Allah as a superstition fostered by an epileptic Meccan camel driver. Our people have copied Arab ways too long. But we hundred men are Turks! We have burned the Koran. We bow not toward Mecca, nor swear by their false Prophet. And now follow me as we planned-to establish ourselves in a strong position in the hills and to seize Arab women for our wives."

"Our sons will be half Arab," someone protested.

"A man is the son of his father," retorted Osman. "We Turks have always looted the harims of the world for our women, but our sons are always Turks.

"Come! We have arms, horses, supplies. If we linger we shall be crushed with the rest of the army between the British on the coast and the Arabs the Englishman Lawrence is bringing up from the south. Onto El Awad! The sword for the men-captivity, for the women!"

His voice cracked like a whip as he snapped the orders that set the lines in motion. In perfect order they moved off through the lightening dawn toward the range of sawedged hills in the distance. Behind them the air still vibrated with the distant rumble of the British artillery. Over them waved a banner that bore the head of a white wolf-the battle-standard of most ancient Turan.

Chapter II: Massacre

WHEN FRAULEIN OLGA VON BRUCKMANN, known as a famous German secret agent, arrived at the tiny Arab hill-village of El Awad, it was in a drizzling rain, that made the dusk a blinding curtain over the muddy town.

With her companion, an Arab named Ahmed, she rode into the muddy street, and the villagers crept from their hovels to stare in awe at the first white woman most of them had ever seen.

A few words from Ahmed and the shaykh salaamed and showed her to the best mud hut in the village. The horses were led away to feed and shelter, and Ahmed paused long enough to whisper to his companion:

"El Awad is friendly to the Turks. Have no fear. I shall be near, in any event."

"Try and get fresh horses," she urged. "I must push on as soon as possible."

"The shaykh swears there isn't a horse in the village in fit condition to be ridden. He may be lying. But at any rate our own horses will be rested enough to go on by dawn. Even with fresh horses it would be useless to try to go any farther tonight. We'd lose our way among the hills, and in this region there's always the risk of running into Lawrence's Bedouin raiders."

Olga knew that Ahmed knew she carried important secret documents from Baghdad to Damascus, and she knew from experience that she could trust his loyalty. Removing only her dripping cloak and riding boots, she stretched herself on the dingy blankets that served as a bed. She was worn out from the strain of the journey.

She was the first white woman ever to attempt to ride from Baghdad to Damascus. Only the protection accorded a trusted secret agent by the long arm of the German-Turkish government, and her guide's zeal and craft, had brought her thus far in safety.

She fell asleep, thinking of the long weary miles still to be traveled, and even greater dangers, now that she had come into the region where the Arabs were fighting their Turkish masters. The Turks still held the country, that summer of 1917, but lightninglike raids flashed across the desert, blowing up trains, cutting tracks and butchering the inhabitants of isolated posts. Lawrence was leading the tribes northward, and with him was the mysterious American, El Borak, whose name was one to hush children.

She never knew how long she slept, but she awoke suddenly and sat up, in fright and bewilderment. The rain still beat on the roof, but there mingled with it shrieks of pain or fear, yells and the staccato crackling of rifles. She sprang up, lighted a candle and was just pulling on her boots when the door was hurled open violently.

Ahmed reeled in, his dark face livid, blood oozing through the fingers that clutched his breast.

"The village is attacked!" he cried chokingly. "Men in Turkish uniform! There must be some mistake! They know El Awad is friendly! I tried to tell their officer we are friends, but he shot me! We must get away, quick!"

A shot cracked in the open door behind him and a jet of fire spurted from the blackness. Ahmed groaned and crumpled. Olga cried out in horror, staring wide-eyed at the figure who stood before her. A tall, wiry man in Turkish uniform blocked the door. He was handsome in a dark, hawklike way, and he eyed her in a manner that brought the blood to her cheeks.

"Why did you kill that man?" she demanded. "He was a trusted servant of your country."

"I have no country," he answered, moving toward her. Outside the firing was dying away and women's voices were lifted piteously. "I go to build one, as my ancestor Osman did."

"I don't know what you're talking about," she retorted. "But unless you provide me with an escort to the nearest post, I shall report you to your superiors, and-"

He laughed wildly at her. "I have no superiors, you little fool! I am an empire builder, I tell you! I have a hundred armed men at my disposal. I'll build a new race in these hills." His eyes blazed as he spoke.

"You're mad!" she exclaimed.

"Mad? It's you who are mad not to recognize the possibilities as I have! This war is bleeding the life out of Europe. When it's over, no matter who wins, the nations will lie prostrate. Then it will be Asia's turn!

"If Lawrence can build up an Arab army to fight for him, then certainly I, an Ottoman, can build up a kingdom among my own peoples! Thousands of Turkish soldiers have deserted to the British. They and more will desert again to me, when they hear that a Turk is building anew the empire of ancient Turan."

"Do what you like," she answered, believing he had been seized by the madness that often grips men in time of war when the world seems crumbling and any wild dream looks possible. "But at least don't interfere with my mission. If you won't give me an escort, I'll go on alone."

"You'll go with me!" he retorted, looking down at her with hot admiration.

Olga was a handsome girl, tall, slender but supple, with a wealth of unruly golden hair. She was so completely feminine that no disguise would make her look like a man, not even the voluminous robes of an Arab, so she had attempted none. She trusted instead to Ahmed's skill to bring her safely through the desert.

"Do you hear those screams? My men are supplying themselves with wives to bear soldiers for the new empire.

435

Yours shall be the signal honor of being the first to go into Sultan Osman's seraglio!"

"You do not dare!" She snatched a pistol from her blouse.

Before she could level it he wrenched it from her with brutal strength.

"Dare!" He laughed at her vain struggles. "What do I not dare? I tell you a new empire is being born tonight! Come with me! There's no time for love-making now. Before dawn we must be on the march for Sulaiman's Walls. The star of the White Wolf rises!"

Chapter III: The Call of Blood

THE SUN WAS not long risen over the saw-edged mountains to the east, but already the heat was glazing the cloudless sky to the hue of white-hot steel. Along the dim road that split the immensity of the desert a single shape moved. The shape grew out of the heat-hazes of the south and resolved itself into a man on a camel.

The man was no Arab. His boots and khakis, as well as the rifle-butt jutting from beneath his knee, spoke of the West. But with his dark face and hard frame he did not look out of place, even in that fierce land. He was Francis Xavier Gordon, El Borak, whom men loved, feared or hated, according to their political complexion, from the Golden Horn to the headwaters of the Ganges.

He had ridden most of the night, but his iron frame had not yet approached the fringes of weariness. Another mile, and he sighted a yet dimmer trail straggling down from a range of hills to the east. Something was coming along this trail-a crawling something that left a broad dark smear on the hot flints.

Gordon swung his camel into the trail and a moment later bent over the man who lay there gasping stertorously. It was a young Arab, and the breast of his abba was soaked in blood.

"Yusef!" Gordon drew back the wet abba, glanced at the bared breast, then covered it again. Blood oozed steadily from a blue-rimmed bullet-hole. There was nothing he could do. Already the Arab's eyes were glazing. Gordon stared up the trail, seeing neither horse nor camel anywhere. But the dark smear stained the stones as far as he could see.

"My God, man, how far have you crawled in this condition?"

"An hour-many hours-I do not know!" panted Yusef. "I fainted and fell from the saddle. When I came to I was lying in the trail and my horse was gone. But I knew you would be coming up from the south, so I crawled-crawled! Allah, how hard are thy stones!"

Gordon set a canteen to his lips and Yusef drank noisily, then clutched Gordon's sleeve with clawing fingers.

"El Borak, I am dying and that is no great matter, but there is the matter of vengeance-not for me, ya sidi, but for innocent ones. You know I was on furlough to my village, El Awad. I am the only man of El Awad who fights for Arabia. The elders are friendly to the Turks. But last night the Turks burned El Awad! They marched in before midnight and the people welcomed them-while I hid in a shed.

"Then without warning they began slaying! The men of El Awad were unarmed and helpless. I slew one soldier myself. Then they shot me and I dragged myself away-found my horse and rode to tell the tale before I died. Ah, Allah, I have tasted of perdition this night!"

"Did you recognize their officer?" asked Gordon.

"I never saw him before. They called this leader of theirs Osman Pasha. Their flag bore the head of a white wolf. I saw it by the light of the burning huts. My people cried out in vain that they were friends.

"There was a German woman and a man of Hauran who came to El Awad from the east, just at nightfall. I think they were spies. The Turks shot him and took her captive. It was all blood and madness."

"Mad indeed!" muttered Gordon. Yusef lifted himself on an elbow and groped for him, a desperate urgency in his weakening voice.

"El Borak, I fought well for the Emir Feisal, and for Lawrence effendi, and for you! I was at Yenbo, and Wejh, and Akaba. Never have I asked a reward! I ask now: justice and vengeance! Grant me this plea: Slay the Turkish dogs who butchered my people!"

Gordon did not hesitate.

"They shall die," he answered.

Yusef smiled fiercely, gasped: "Allaho akbat!" then sank back dead.

Within the hour Gordon rode eastward. The vultures had already gathered in the sky with their grisly foreknowledge of death, then flapped sullenly away from the cairn of stones he had piled over the dead man, Yusef.

Gordon's business in the north could Wait. One reason for his dominance over the Orientals was the fact that in some ways his nature closely resembled theirs. He not only understood the cry for vengeance, but he sympathized with it. And he always kept his promise.

But he was puzzled. The destruction of a friendly village was not customary, even by the Turks, and certainly they would not ordinarily have mishandled their own spies. If they were deserters they were acting in an unusual manner, for most deserters made their way to Feisal. And that wolf's head banner?

Gordon knew that certain fanatics in the New Turks party were trying to erase all signs of Arab culture from their

439

civilization. This was an impossible task, since that civilization itself was based on Arabic culture; but he had heard that in Istambul the radicals even advocated abandoning Islam and reverting to the paganism of their ancestors. But he had never believed the tale.

The sun was sinking over the mountains of Edom when Gordon came to ruined El Awad, in a fold of the bare hills. For hours before he had marked its location by black dots dropping in the blue. That they did not rise again told him that the village was deserted except for the dead.

As he rode into the dusty street several vultures flapped heavily away. The hot sun had dried the mud, curdled the red pools in the dust. He sat in his saddle a while, staring silently.

He was no stranger to the handiwork of the Turk. He had seen much of it in the long fighting up from Jeddah on the Red Sea. But even so, he felt sick. The bodies lay in the street, headless, disemboweled, hewn asunder-bodies of children, old women and men. A red mist floated before his eyes, so that for a moment the landscape seemed to swim in blood. The slayers were gone; but they had left a plain road for him to follow.

What the signs they had left did not show him, he guessed. The slayers had loaded their female captives on baggage camels, and had gone eastward, deeper into the hills. Why they were following that road he could not guess, but he knew where it led-to the long-abandoned Walls of Sulaiman, by way of the Well of Achmet.

Without hesitation he followed. He had not gone many miles before he passed more of their work-a baby, its brains oozing from its broken head. Some kidnapped woman had hidden her child in her robes until it had been wrenched from her and brained on the rocks, before her eyes.

The country became wilder as he went. He did not halt to eat, but munched dried dates from his pouch as he rode. He did not waste time worrying over the recklessness of his action-one lone American dogging the crimson trail of a Turkish raiding party.

He had no plan; his future actions would depend on the circumstances that arose. But he had taken the death-trail and he would not turn back while he lived. He was no more foolhardy than his grandfather who single-handedly trailed an Apache war-party for days through the Guadalupes and returned to the settlement on the Pecos with scalps hanging from his belt.

The sun had set and dusk was closing in when Gordon topped a ridge and looked down on the plain whereon stands the Well of Achmet with its straggling palm grove. To the right of that cluster stood the tents, horse lines and camel lines of a well-ordered force. To the left stood a hut used by travelers as a khan. The door was shut and a sentry stood before it. While he watched, a man came from the tents with a bowl of food which he handed in at the door.

Gordon could not see the occupant, but he believed it was the German girl of whom Yusef had spoken, though why they should imprison one of their own spies was one of the mysteries of this strange affair. He saw their flag, and could make out a splotch of white that must be the wolf's head. He saw, too, the Arab women, thirty-five or forty of them herded into a pen improvised from bales and pack-saddles. They crouched together dumbly, dazed by their misfortunes.

He had hidden his camel below the ridge, on the western slope, and he lay concealed behind a clump of stunted bushes until night had fallen. Then he slipped down the slope, circling wide to avoid the mounted patrol, which rode leisurely about the camp. He lay prone behind a boulder till it had passed, then rose and stole toward the hut. Fires twinkled in the darkness beneath the palms and he heard the wailing of the captive women.

The sentry before the door of the hut did not see the cat-footed shadow that glided up to the rear wall. As Gordon drew close he heard voices within. They spoke in Turkish.

One window was in the back wall. Strips of wood had been fastened over it, to serve as both pane and bars. Peering between them, Gordon saw a slender girl in a travel-worn riding habit standing before a dark-faced man in a

442

Turkish uniform. There was no insignia to show what his rank had been. The Turk played with a riding whip and his eyes gleamed with cruelty in the light of a candle on a camp table.

"What do I care for the information you bring from Baghdad?" he was demanding. "Neither Turkey nor Germany means anything to me. But it seems you fail to realize your own position. It is mine to command, you to obey! You are my prisoner, my captive, my slave! It's time you learned what that means. And the best teacher I know is the whip!"

He fairly spat the last word at her and she paled.

"You dare not subject me to this indignity!" she whispered weakly.

Gordon knew this man must be Osman Pasha. He drew his heavy automatic from its scabbard under his armpit and aimed at the Turk's breast through the crack in the window. But even as his finger closed on the trigger he changed his mind. There was the sentry at the door, and a hundred other armed men, within hearing, whom the sound of a shot would bring on the run. He grasped the window bars and braced his legs.

"I see I must dispel your illusions," muttered Osman, moving toward the girl who cowered back until the wall stopped her. Her face was white. She had dealt with many dangerous men in her hazardous career, and she was not easily frightened. But she had never met a man like Osman.

His face was a terrifying mask of cruelty; the ferocity that gloats over the agony of a weaker thing shone in his eyes.

Suddenly he had her by the hair, dragging her to him, laughing at her scream of pain. Just then Gordon ripped the strips off the window. The snapping of the wood sounded loud as a gun-shot and Osman wheeled, drawing his pistol, as Gordon came through the window.

The American hit on his feet, leveled automatic checking Osman's move. The Turk froze, his pistol lifted shoulder high, muzzle pointing at the roof. Outside the sentry called anxiously.

"Answer him!" grated Gordon below his breath. "Tell him everything is all right. And drop that gun!"

The pistol fell to the floor and the girl snatched it up.

"Come here, Fraulein!"

She ran to him, but in her haste she crossed the line of fire. In that fleeting moment when her body shielded his, Osman acted. He kicked the table and the candle toppled and went out, and simultaneously he dived for the floor. Gordon's pistol roared deafeningly just as the hut was plunged into darkness. The next instant the door crashed inward and the sentry bulked against the starlight, to crumple as Gordon's gun crashed again and yet again.

With a sweep of his arm Gordon found the girl and drew her toward the window. He lifted her through as if she had been a child, and climbed through after her. He did not know whether his blind slug had struck Osman or not. The man was crouching silently in the darkness, but there was no time to strike a match and see whether he was living or dead. But as they ran across the shadowy plain, they heard Osman's voice lifted in passion.

By the time they reached the crest of the ridge the girl was winded. Only Gordon's arm about her waist, half dragging, half carrying her, enabled her to make the last few yards of the steep incline. The plain below them was alive with torches and shouting men. Osman was yelling for them to run down the fugitives, and his voice came faintly to them on the ridge.

"Take them alive, curse you! Scatter and find them! It's El Borak!" An instant later he was yelling with an edge of panic in his voice: "Wait. Come back! Take cover and make ready to repel an attack! He may have a horde of Arabs with him!"

"He thinks first of his own desires, and only later of the safety of his men," muttered Gordon. "I don't think he'll ever get very far. Come on."

He led the way to the camel, helped the girl into the saddle, then leaped up himself. A word, a tap of the camel wand, and the beast ambled silently off down the slope.

"I know Osman caught you at El Awad," said Gordon. "But what's he up to? What's his game?"

"He was a lieutenant stationed at El Ashraf," she answered. "He persuaded his company to mutiny, kill their commander and desert. He plans to fortify the Walls of Sulaiman, and build a new empire. I thought at first he was mad, but he isn't. He's a devil."

"The Walls of Sulaiman?" Gordon checked his mount and sat for a moment motionless in the starlight.

"Are you game for an all-night ride?" he asked presently.

"Anywhere! As long as it is far away from Osman!" There was a hint of hysteria in her voice.

"I doubt if your escape will change his plans. He'll probably lie about Achmet all night under arms expecting an attack. In the morning he will decide that I was alone, and pull out for the Walls.

"Well, I happen to know that an Arab force is there, waiting for an order from Lawrence to move on to Ageyli. Three hundred Juheina camel-riders, sworn to Feisal. Enough to eat Osman's gang. Lawrence's messenger should reach them some time between dawn and noon. There is a chance we can get there before the Juheina pull out. If we can, we'll turn them on Osman and wipe him out, with his whole pack.

"It won't upset Lawrence's plans for the Juheina to get to Ageyli a day late, and Osman must be destroyed. He's a mad dog running loose."

"His ambition sounds mad," she murmured. "But when he speaks of it, with his eyes blazing, it's easy to believe he might even succeed."

"You forget that crazier things have happened in the desert," he answered, as he swung the camel eastward. "The world is being made over here, as well as in Europe. There's no telling what damage this Osman might do, if left to himself. The Turkish Empire is falling to pieces, and new empires have risen out of the ruins of old ones.

"But if we can get to Sulaiman before the Juheina march, we'll check him. If we find them gone, we'll be in a pickle ourselves. It's a gamble, our lives against his. Are you game?"

"Till the last card falls!" she retorted. His face was a blur in the starlight, but she sensed rather than saw his grim smile of approval.

The camel's hoofs made no sound as they dropped down the slope and circled far wide of the Turkish camp. Like ghosts on a ghost-camel they moved across the plain under the stars. A faint breeze stirred the girl's hair. Not until the fires were dim behind them and they were again climbing a hill-road did she speak.

"I know you. You're the American they call El Borak, the Swift. You came down from Afghanistan when the war began. You were with King Hussein even before Lawrence came over from Egypt. Do you know who I am?"

"Yes."

"Then what's my status?" she asked. "Have you rescued me or captured me? Am I a prisoner?"

"Let us say companion, for the time being," he suggested. "We're up against a common enemy. No reason why we shouldn't make common cause, is there?"

"None!" she agreed, and leaning her blond head against his hard shoulder, she went soundly to sleep.

A gaunt moon rose, pushing back the horizons, flooding craggy slopes and dusty plains with leprous silver. The vastness of the desert seemed to mock the tiny figures on their tiring camel, as they rode blindly on toward what Fate they could not guess.

Chapter IV: Wolves of the Desert

OLGA AWOKE As dawn was breaking. She was cold and stiff, in spite of the cloak Gordon had wrapped about her, and she was hungry. They were riding through a dry gorge with rock-strewn slopes rising on either hand, and the camel's gait had become a lurching walk. Gordon halted it, slid off without making it kneel, and took its rope.

"It's about done, but the Walls aren't far ahead. Plenty of water there-food, too, if the Juheina are still there. There are dates in that pouch."

If he felt the strain of fatigue he did not show it as he strode along at the camel's head. Olga rubbed her chill hands and wished for sunrise.

"The Well of Harith," Gordon indicated a walled enclosure ahead of them. "The Turks built that wall, years ago, when the Walls of Sulaiman were an army post. Later they abandoned both positions."

The wall, built of rocks and dried mud, was in good shape, and inside the enclosure there was a partly ruined hut. The well was shallow, with a mere trickle of water at the bottom.

"I'd better get off and walk too," Olga suggested.

"These flints would cut your boots and feet to pieces. It's not far now. Then the camel can rest all it needs."

"And if the Juheina aren't there-" She left the sentence unfinished.

He shrugged his shoulders.

"Maybe Osman won't come up before the camel's rested."

"I believe he'll make a forced march," she said, not fearfully, but calmly stating an opinion. "His beasts are good. If he drives them hard, he can get here before midnight. Our camel won't be rested enough to carry us, by that time. And we couldn't get away on foot, in this desert."

He laughed, and respecting her courage, did not try to make light of their position.

"Well," he said quietly, "let's hope the Juheina are still there!"

If they were not, she and Gordon were caught in a trap of hostile, waterless desert, fanged with the long guns of predatory tribesmen.

Three miles further east the valley narrowed and the floor pitched upward, dotted by dry shrubs and boulders. Gordon pointed suddenly to a faint ribbon of smoke feathering up into the sky.

"Look! The Juheina are there!"

Olga gave a deep sigh of relief. Only then did she realize how desperately she had been hoping for some such sign. She felt like shaking a triumphant fist at the rocky waste about her, as if at a sentient enemy, sullen and cheated of its prey.

Another mile and they topped a ridge and saw a large enclosure surrounding a cluster of wells. There were Arabs squatting about their tiny cooking fires. As the travelers came suddenly into view within a few hundred yards of them, the Bedouins sprang up, shouting. Gordon drew his breath suddenly between clenched teeth.

"They're not Juheina! They're Rualla! Allies of the Turks!"

Too late to retreat. A hundred and fifty wild men were on their feet, glaring, rifles cocked.

Gordon did the next best thing and went leisurely toward them. To look at him one would have thought that he had expected to meet these men here, and anticipated nothing but a friendly greeting. Olga tried to imitate his tranquility, but she knew their lives hung on the crook of a trigger finger. These men were supposed to be her allies, but her recent experience made her distrust Orientals. The sight of these hundreds of wolfish faces filled her with sick dread.

They were hesitating, rifles lifted, nervous and uncertain as surprised wolves, then:

"Allah!" howled a tall, scarred warrior. "It is El Borak!"

Olga caught her breath as she saw the man's finger quiver on his rifle-trigger. Only a racial urge to gloat over his victim kept him from shooting the American then and there.

"El Borak!" The shout was a wave that swept the throng.

Ignoring the clamor, the menacing rifles, Gordon made the camel kneel and lifted Olga off. She tried, with fair success, to conceal her fear of the wild figures that crowded about them, but her flesh crawled at the bloodlust burning redly in each wolfish eye.

Gordon's rifle was in its boot on the saddle, and his pistol was out of sight, under his shirt. He was careful not to reach for the rifle-a move which would have brought a hail of bullets-but having helped the girl down, he turned

451

and faced the crowd casually, his hands empty. Running his glance over the fierce faces, he singled out a tall stately man in the rich garb of a shaykh, who was standing somewhat apart.

"You keep poor watch, Mitkhal ion Ali," said Gordon. "If I had been a raider your men would be lying in their blood by this time."

Before the shaykh could answer, the man who had first recognized Gordon thrust himself violently forward, his face convulsed with hate.

"You expected to find friends here, El Borak!" he exulted. "But you come too late! Three hundred Juheina dogs rode north an hour before dawn! We saw them go, and came up after they had gone. Had they known of your coming, perhaps they would have stayed to welcome you!"

"It's not to you I speak, Zangi Khan, you Kurdish dog," retorted Gordon contemptuously, "but to the Rualla-honorable men and fair foes!"

Zangi Khan snarled like a wolf and threw up his rifle, but a lean Bedouin caught his arm.

"Wait!" he growled. "Let El Borak speak. His words are not wind."

A rumble of approval came from the Arabs. Gordon had touched their fierce pride and vanity. That would not save his life, but they were willing to listen to him before they killed him.

"If you listen he will trick you with cunning words!" shouted the angered Zangi Khan furiously. "Slay him now, before he can do us harm!"

"Is Zangi Khan shaykh of the Rualla that he gives commands while Mitkhal stands silent?" asked Gordon with biting irony.

Mitkhal reacted to his taunt exactly as Gordon knew he would.

"Let El Borak speak!" he ordered. "I command here, Zangi Khan! Do not forget that."

"I do not forget, ya sidi," the Kurd assured him, but his eyes burned red at the rebuke. "I but spoke in zeal for your safety."

Mitkhal gave him a slow, searching glance which told Gordon that there was no love lost between the two men. Zangi Khan's reputation as a fighting man meant much to the younger warriors. Mitkhal was more fox than wolf, and he evidently feared the Kurd's influence over his men. As an agent of the Turkish government Zangi's authority was theoretically equal to Mitkhal's.

Actually this amounted to little, but Mitkhal's tribesmen took orders from their shaykh only. But it put Zangi in a position to use his personal talents to gain an ascendency-an ascendency Mitkhal feared would relegate him to a minor position.

"Speak, El Borak," ordered Mitkhal. "But speak swiftly. It may be," he added, "Allah's will that the moments of your life are few."

"Death marches from the west," said Gordon abruptly. "Last night a hundred Turkish deserters butchered the people of El Awad."

"Wallah!" swore a tribesman. "El Awad was friendly to the Turks!"

"A lie!" cried Zangi Khan. "Or if true, the dogs of deserters slew the people to curry favor with Feisal."

"When did men come to Feisal with the blood of children on their hands?" retorted Gordon. "They have foresworn Islam and worship the White Wolf. They carried off the young women and the old women, the men and the children they slew like dogs."

A murmur of anger rose from the Arabs. The Bedouins had a rigid code of warfare, and they did not kill women or children. It was the unwritten law of the desert, old when Abraham came up out of Chaldea.

But Zangi Khan cried out in angry derision, blind to the resentful looks cast at him. He did not understand that particular phase of the Bedouins" code, for his people had no such inhibition. Kurds in war killed women as well as men.

"What are the women of El Awad to us?" he sneered.

"Your heart I know already," answered Gordon with icy contempt. "It is to the Rualla that I speak."

"A trick!" howled the Kurd. "A lie to trick us!"

"It is no lie!" Olga stepped forward boldly. "Zangi Khan, you know that I am an agent of the German government. Osman Pasha, leader of these renegades burned El Awad last night, as El Borak has said. Osman murdered Ahmed ibn Shalaan, my guide, among others. He is as much our enemy as he is an enemy of the British."

She looked to Mitkhal for help, but the shaykh stood apart, like an actor watching a play in which he had not yet received his cue.

"What if it is the truth?" Zangi Khan snarled, muddled by his hate and fear of El Borak's cunning. "What is El Awad to us?"

Gordon caught him up instantly.

"This Kurd asks what is the destruction of a friendly village! Doubtless, naught to him! But what does it mean to you, who have left your herds and families unguarded? If you let this pack of mad dogs range the land, how can you be sure of the safety of your wives and children?"

"What would you have, El Borak?" demanded a grey-bearded raider.

"Trap these Turks and destroy them. I'll show you how."

It was then that Zangi Khan lost his head completely.

455

"Heed him not!" he screamed. "Within the hour we must ride northward! The Turks will give us ten thousand British pounds for his head!"

Avarice burned briefly in the men's eyes, to be dimmed by the reflection that the reward, offered for El Borak's head, would be claimed by the shaykh and Zangi. They made no move and Mitkhal stood aside with an air of watching a contest that did not concern himself.

"Take his head!" screamed Zangi, sensing hostility at last, and thrown into a panic by it.

His demoralization was completed by Gordon's taunting laugh.

"You seem to be the only one who wants my head, Zangi! Perhaps you can take it!"

Zangi howled incoherently, his eyes glaring red, then threw up his rifle, hip-high. Just as the muzzle came up, Gordon's automatic crashed thunderously. He had drawn so swiftly not a man there had followed his motion. Zangi Khan reeled back under the impact of hot lead, toppled sideways and lay still.

In an instant a hundred cocked rifles covered Gordon.

Confused by varying emotions, the men hesitated for the fleeting instant it took Mitkhal to shout:

"Hold! Do not shoot!"

He strode forward with the air of a man ready to take the center of the stage at last, but he could not disguise the gleam of satisfaction in his shrewd eyes.

"No man here is kin to Zangi Khan," he said offhandedly. "There is no cause for blood feud. He had eaten the salt, but he attacked our prisoner whom he thought unarmed."

He held out his hand for the pistol, but Gordon did not surrender it.

"I'm not your prisoner," said he. "I could kill you before your men could lift a finger. But I didn't come here to fight you. I came asking aid to avenge the children and women of my enemies. I risk my life for your families. Are you dogs, to do less?"

The question hung in the air unanswered, but he had struck the right chord in their barbaric bosoms, that were always ready to respond to some wild deed of reckless chivalry. Their eyes glowed and they looked at their shaykh expectantly.

Mitkhal was a shrewd politician. The butchery at El Awad meant much less to him than it meant to his younger warriors. He had associated with so-called civilized men long enough to lose much of his primitive integrity. But he always followed the side of public opinion, and was shrewd enough to lead a movement he could not check. Yet, he was not to be stampeded into a hazardous adventure.

"These Turks may be too strong for us," he objected.

"I'll show you how to destroy them with little risk," answered Gordon. "But there must be covenants between us, Mitkhal."

"These Turks must be destroyed," said Mitkhal, and he spoke sincerely there, at least. "But there are too many blood feuds between us, El Borak, for us to let you get out of our hands."

Gordon laughed.

"You can't whip the Turks without my help and you know it. Ask your young men what they desire!"

"Let El Borak lead us!" shouted a young warrior instantly. A murmur of approval paid tribute to Gordon's widespread reputation as a strategist.

"Very well!" Mitkhal took the tide. "Let there be truce between us-with conditions! Lead us against the Turks. If you win, you and the woman shall go free. If we lose, we take your head!"

Gordon nodded, and the warriors yelled in glee. It was just the sort of a bargain that appealed to their minds, and Gordon knew it was the best he could make.

"Bring bread and salt!" ordered Mitkhal, and a giant black slave moved to do his bidding. "Until the battle is lost or won there is truce between us, and no Rualla shall harm you, unless you spill Rualla blood."

Then he thought of something else and his brow darkened as he thundered:

"Where is the man who watched from the ridge?"

A terrified youth was pushed forward. He was a member of a small tribe tributary to the more important Rualla.

"Oh, shaykh," he faltered, "I was hungry and stole away to a fire for meat-"

"Dog!" Mitkhal struck him in the face. "Death is thy portion for failing in thy duty."

"Wait!" Gordon interposed. "Would you question the will of Allah? If the boy had not deserted his post he would have seen us coming up the valley, and your men would have fired on us and killed us. Then you would not have been warned of the Turks, and would have fallen prey to them before discovering they were enemies. Let him go and give thanks to Allah Who sees all!"

It was the sort of sophistry that appeals to the Arab mind. Even Mitkhal was impressed.

"Who knows the mind of Allah?" he conceded. "Live, Musa, but next time perform the will of Allah with vigilance and a mind to orders. And now, El Borak, let us discuss battle-plans while food is prepared."

Chapter V: Treachery

IT WAS NOT yet noon when Gordon halted the Rualla beside the Well of Harith. Scouts sent westward reported no

459

sign of the Turks, and the Arabs went forward with the plans made before leaving the Walls-plans outlined by Gordon and agreed to by Mitkhal. First the tribesmen began gathering rocks and hurling them into the well.

"The water's still beneath," Gordon remarked to Olga. "But it'll take hours of hard work to clean out the well so that anybody can get to it. The Turks can't do it under our rifles. If we win, we'll clean it out ourselves, so the next travelers won't suffer."

"Why not take refuge in the sangar ourselves?" she asked.

"Too much of a trap. That's what we're using it for. We'd have no chance with them in open fight, and if we laid an ambush out in the valley, they'd simply fight their way through us. But when a man's shot at in the open, his first instinct is to make for the nearest cover. So I'm hoping to trick them into going into the sangar. Then we'll bottle them up and pick them off at our leisure. Without water they can't hold out long. We shouldn't lose a dozen men, if any."

"It seems strange to see you solicitous about the lives of these Rualla, who are your enemies, after all," she laughed.

"Instinct, maybe. No man fit to lead wants to lose any more of them then he can help. Just now these men are my allies, and it's up to me to protect them as well as I can. I'll admit I'd rather be fighting with the Juheina. Feisal's messenger must have started for the Walls hours before I supposed he would."

"And if the Turks surrender, what then?"

"I'll try to get them to Lawrence-all but Osman Pasha." Gordon's face darkened. "That man hangs if he falls into my hands."

"How will you get them to Lawrence? The Rualla won't take them."

"I haven't the slightest idea. But let's catch our hare before we start broiling him. Osman may whip the daylights out of us."

"It means your head if he does," she warned with a shudder.

"Well, it's worth ten thousand pounds to the Turks," he laughed, and moved to inspect the partly ruined hut. Olga followed him.

Mitkhal, directing the blocking of the well, glanced sharply at them, then noted that a number of men were between them and the gate, and turned back to his overseeing.

"Hsss, El Borak!" It was a tense whisper, just as Gordon and Olga turned to leave the hut. An instant later they located a tousled head thrust up from behind a heap of rubble. It was the boy Musa who obviously had slipped into the hut through a crevice in the back wall.

"Watch from the door and warn me if you see anybody coming," Gordon muttered to Olga. "This lad may have something to tell."

"I have, effendi!" The boy was trembling with excitement. "I overheard the shaykh talking secretly to his black slave, Hassan. I saw them walk away among the palms while you and the woman were eating, at the Walls, and I crept after them, for I feared they meant you mischief-and you saved my life.

"El Borak, listen! Mitkah means to slay you, whether you win this battle for him or not! He was glad you slew the Kurd, and he is glad to have your aid in wiping out these Turks. But he lusts for the gold the other Turks will pay for your head. Yet he dares not break his word and the covenant of the salt openly. So, if we win the battle, Hassan is to shoot you, and swear you fell by a Turkish bullet!"

The boy rushed on with his story:

"Then Mitkhal will say to the people: "El Borak was our guest and ate our salt. But now he is dead, through no fault of ours, and there is no use wasting the reward. So we will take off his head and take it to Damascus and the Turks will give us ten thousand pounds." '

Gordon smiled grimly at Olga's horror. That was typical Arab logic.

"It didn't occur to Mitkhal that Hassan might miss his first shot and not get a chance to shoot again, I suppose?" he suggested.

"Oh, yes, effendi, Mitkhal thinks of everything. If you kill Hassan, Mitkhal will swear you broke the covenant yourself, by spilling the blood of a Rualla, or a Rualla's servant, which is the same thing, and will feel free to order you beheaded."

There was genuine humor in Gordon's laugh.

"Thanks, Musa! If I saved your life, you've paid me back. Better get out now, before somebody sees you talking to us."

"What shall we do?" exclaimed Olga, pale to the lips.

"You're in no danger," he assured her.

She colored angrily.

"I wasn't thinking of that! Do you think I have less gratitude than that Arab boy? That shaykh means to murder you, don't you understand? Let's steal camels and run for it!"

"Run where? If we did, they'd be on our heels in no time, deciding I'd lied to them about everything. Anyway, we wouldn't have a chance. They're watching us too closely. Besides, I wouldn't run if I could. I started to wipe out Osman Pasha, and this is the best chance I see to do it. Come on. Let's get out in the sangar before Mitkhal gets suspicious."

As soon as the well was blocked the men retired to the hillsides. Their camels were hidden behind the ridges, and the men crouched behind rocks and among the stunted shrubs along the slopes. Olga refused Gordon's offer to send her with an escort back to the Walls, and stayed with him taking up a position behind a rock, Osman's pistol in her belt. They lay flat on the ground and the heat of the sun-baked flints seeped through their garments.

Once she turned her head, and shuddered to see the blank black countenance of Hassan regarding them from some bushes a few yards behind them: The black slave, who knew no law but his master's command, was determined not to let Gordon out of his sight.

She spoke of this in a low whisper to the American.

"Sure," he murmured. "I saw him. But he won't shoot till he knows which way the fight's going, and is sure none of the men are looking."

Olga's flesh crawled in anticipation of more horrors. If they lost the fight the enraged Ruallas would tear Gordon to pieces, supposing he survived the encounter. If they won, his reward would be a treacherous bullet in the back.

The hours dragged slowly by. Not a flutter of cloth, no lifting of an impudent head betrayed the presence of the wild men on the slopes. Olga began to feel her nerves quiver. Doubts and forebodings gnawed maddeningly at her.

"We took position too soon! The men will lose patience. Osman can't get here before midnight. It took us all night to reach the Well."

"Bedouins never lose patience when they smell loot," he answered. "I believe Osman will get here before sundown. We made poor time on a tiring camel for the last few hours of that ride. I believe Osman broke camp before dawn and pushed hard."

Another thought came to torture her.

"Suppose he doesn't come at all? Suppose he has changed his plans and gone somewhere else? The Rualla will believe you lied to them!"

"Look!"

The sun hung low in the west, a fiery, dazzling ball. She blinked, shading her eyes.

Then the head of a marching column grew out of the dancing heat-waves: lines of horsemen, grey with dust, files of heavily laden baggage camels, with the captive women riding them. The standard hung loose in the breathless air; but once, when a vagrant gust of wind, hot as the breath of perdition, lifted the folds, the white wolf's head was displayed.

Crushing proof of idolatry and heresy! In their agitation the Rualla almost betrayed themselves. Even Mitkhal turned pale.

"Allah! Sacrilege! Forgotten of God. Hell shall be thy portion!"

"Easy!" hissed Gordon, feeling the semi-hysteria that ran down the lurking lines. "Wait for my signal. They may halt to water their camels at the Well."

Osman must have driven his people like a fiend all day. The women drooped on the loaded camels; the dust-caked faces of the soldiers were drawn. The horses reeled with weariness. But it was soon evident that they did not intend halting at the Well with their goal, the Walls of Sulaiman, so near. The head of the column was even with the sangar when Gordon fired. He was aiming at Osman, but the range was long, the sun-glare on the rocks dazzling. The man behind Osman fell, and at the signal the slopes came alive with spurting flame.

The column staggered. Horses and men went down and stunned soldiers gave back a ragged fire that did no harm. They did not even see their assailants save as bits of white cloth bobbing among the boulders.

Perhaps discipline had grown lax during the grind of that merciless march. Perhaps panic seized the tired Turks. At any rate the column broke and men fled toward the sangar without waiting for orders. They would have abandoned the baggage camels had no Osman ridden among them. Cursing and striking with the flat of his saber, he made them drive the beasts in with them.

"I hoped they'd leave the camels and women outside," grunted Gordon. "Maybe they'll drive them out when they find there's no water."

The Turks took their positions in good order, dismounting and ranging along the wall. Some dragged the Arab women off the camels and drove them into the hut. Others improvised a pen for the animals with stakes and ropes between the back of the hut and the wall. Saddles were piled in the gate to complete the barricade.

The Arabs yelled taunts as they poured in a hail of lead, and a few leaped up and danced derisively, waving their rifles. But they stopped that when a Turk drilled one of them cleanly through the head. When the demonstrations ceased, the besiegers offered scanty targets to shoot at.

However, the Turks fired back frugally and with no indication of panic, now that they were under cover and fighting the sort of a fight they understood. They were well protected by the wall from the men directly in front of them, but those facing north could be seen by the men on the south ridge, and vice versa. But the distance was too great for consistently effective shooting at these marks by the Arabs.

"We don't seem to be doing much damage," remarked Olga presently.

"Thirst will win for us," Gordon answered. "All we've got to do is to keep them bottled up. They probably have enough water in their canteens to last through the rest of the day. Certainly no longer. Look, they're going to the well now."

The well stood in the middle of the enclosure, in a comparatively exposed area, as seen from above. Olga saw men approaching it with canteens in their hands, and the Arabs, with sardonic enjoyment, refrained from firing at them. They reached the well, and then the girl saw the change come over them. It ran through their band like an electric shock. The men along the walls reacted by firing wildly. A furious yelling rose, edged with hysteria, and men began to run madly about the enclosure. Some toppled, hit by shots dropping from the ridges.

"What are they doing?" Olga started to her knees, and was instantly jerked down again by Gordon. The Turks were running into the hut. If she had been watching Gordon she would have sensed the meaning of it, for his dark face grew suddenly grim.

"They're dragging the women out!" she exclaimed. "I see Osman waving his saber. What? Oh, God! They're butchering the women!"

Above the crackle of shots rose terrible shrieks and the sickening chack of savagely driven blows. Olga turned sick and hid her face. Osman had realized the trap into which he had been driven, and his reaction was that of a mad dog. Recognizing defeat in the blocked well, facing the ruin of his crazy ambitions by thirst and Bedouin bullets, he was taking this vengeance on the whole Arab race.

On all sides the Arabs rose howling, driven to frenzy by the sight of that slaughter. That these women were of another tribe made no difference. A stern chivalry was the foundation of their society, just as it was among the frontiersmen of early America. There was no sentimentalism about it. It was real and vital as life itself.

The Rualla went berserk when they saw women of their race falling under the swords of the Turks. A wild yell shattered the brazen sky, and recklessly breaking cover, the Arabs pelted down the slopes, howling like fiends. Gordon could not check them, nor could Mitkhal. Their shouts fell on deaf ears. The walls vomited smoke and flame as withering volleys raked the oncoming hordes. Dozens fell, but enough were left to reach the wall and sweep over it in a wave that neither lead nor steel could halt.

And Gordon was among them. When he saw he could not stop the storm he joined it. Mitkhal was not far behind him, cursing his men as he ran. The shaykh had no stomach for this kind of fighting, but his leadership was at stake. No man who hung back in this charge would ever be able to command the Rualla again.

Gordon was among the first to reach the wall, leaping over the writhing bodies of half a dozen Arabs. He had not blazed away wildly as he ran like the Bedouins, to reach the wall with an empty gun. He held his fire until the flame spurts from the barrier were almost burning his face, and then emptied his rifle in a point-blank fusilade that left a bloody gap where there had been a line of fierce dark faces an instant before. Before the gap could be closed he had swarmed over and in, and the Rualla poured after him.

As his feet hit the ground a rush of men knocked him against the wall and a blade, thrusting for his life, broke against the rocks. He drove his shortened butt into a snarling face, splintering teeth and bones, and the next instant a surge of his own men over the wall cleared a space about him. He threw away his broken rifle and drew his pistol.

The Turks had been forced back from the wall in a dozen places now, and men were fighting all over the sangar. No quarter was asked-none given. The pitiful headless bodies sprawled before the blood-stained but had turned the Bedouins into hot-eyed demons. The guns were empty now, all but Gordon's automatic. The yells had died down to grunts, punctuated by death-howls. Above these sounds rose the chopping impact of flailing blades, the crunch of fiercely driven rifle butts. So grimly had the Bedouins suffered in that brainless rush, that now they were outnumbered, and the Turks fought with the fury of desperation.

It was Gordon's automatic, perhaps, that tipped the balance. He emptied it without haste and without hesitation, and at that range he could not miss. He was aware of a dark shadow forever behind him, and turned once to see black Hassan following him, smiting methodically right and left with a heavy scimitar already dripping crimson. Even in the fury of the strife, Gordon grinned. The literal-minded Soudanese was obeying instructions to keep at El Borak's heels. As long as the battle hung in doubt, he was Gordon's protector-ready to become his executioner the instant the tide turned in their favor.

"Faithful servant," called Gordon sardonically. "Have a care lest these Turks cheat you of my head!"

Hassan grinned, speechless. Suddenly blood burst from his thick lips and he buckled at the knees. Somewhere in that rush down the hill his black body had stopped a bullet. As he struggled on all fours a Turk ran in from the side and brained him with a rifle-butt. Gordon killed the Turk with his last bullet. He felt no grudge against Hassan. The man had been a good soldier, and had obeyed orders given him.

The sangar was a shambles. The men on their feet were less than those on-.the ground, and all were streaming blood. The white wolf standard had been torn from its staff and lay trampled under vengeful feet. Gordon bent, picked up a saber and looked about for Osman. He saw Mitkhal, running toward the horse-pen, and then he yelled a warning, for he saw Osman.

The man broke away from a group of struggling figures and ran for the pen. He tore away the ropes and the horses, frantic from the noise and smell of blood, stampeded into the sangar, knocking men down and trampling them. As they thundered past, Osman, with a magnificent display of agility, caught a handful of flying mane and leaped on the back of the racing steed.

Mitkhal ran toward him, yelling furiously, and snapping a pistol at him. The shaykh, in the confusion of the fighting, did not seem to be aware that the gun was empty, for he pulled the trigger again and again as he stood in the path of the oncoming rider. Only at the last moment did he realize his peril and leap back. Even so, he would have sprung clear had not his sandal heel caught in a dead man's abba.

Mitkhal stumbled, avoided the lashing hoofs, but not the down-flailing saber in Osman's hand. A wild cry went up from the Rualla as Mitkhal fell, his turban suddenly crimson. The next instant Osman was out of the gate and riding like the wind-straight up the hillside to where he saw the slim figure of the girl to whom he now attributed his overthrow.

Olga had come out from behind the rocks and was standing in stunned horror watching the fight below. Now she awoke suddenly to her own peril at the sight of the madman charging up the slope. She drew the pistol Gordon had taken from him and opened fire. She was not a very good shot. Three bullets missed, the fourth killed the horse, and then the gun jammed. Gordon was running up the slope as the Apaches of his native Southwest run, and behind him streamed a swarm of Rualla. There was not a loaded gun in the whole horde.

Osman took a shocking fall when his horse turned a somersault under him, but rose, bruised and bloody, with Gordon still some distance away. But the Turk had to play hide-and-seek for a few moments among the rocks with his prey before he was able to grasp her hair and twist her screaming to her knees and then he paused an instant to enjoy her despair and terror. That pause was his undoing.

As he lifted his saber to strike off her head, steel clanged loud on steel. A numbing shock ran through his arm and his blade was knocked from his hand. His weapon rang on the hot flints. He whirled to face the blazing slits that were El Borak's eyes. The muscles stood out in cords and ridges on Gordon's sunburnt forearm in the intensity of his passion.

"Pick it up, you filthy dog," he said between his teeth.

Osman hesitated, stooped, caught up the saber and slashed at Gordon's legs without straightening. Gordon leaped back, then sprang in again the instant his toes touched the earth. His return was as paralyzingly quick as -the death-leap of a wolf. It caught Osman off balance, his sword extended. Gordon's blade hissed as it cut the air, slicing through flesh, gritting through bone.

The Turk's head toppled from the severed neck and fell at Gordon's feet, the headless body collapsing in a heap. With an excess spasm of hate, Gordon kicked the head savagely down the slope.

"Oh!" Olga turned away and hid her face. But the girl knew that Osman deserved any fate that could have overtaken him. Presently she was aware of Gordon's hand resting lightly on her shoulder and she looked up, ashamed of her weakness. The sun was just dipping below the western ridges. Musa came limping up the slope, blood-stained but radiant.

"The dogs are all dead, effendi!" he cried, industriously shaking a plundered watch, in an effort to make it run. "Such of our warriors as still live are faint from strife, and many sorely wounded. There is none to command now but thou."

"Sometimes problems settle themselves," mused Gordon. "But at a ghastly price. If the Rualla hadn't made that rush, which was the death of Hassan and Mitkhal-oh, well, such things are in the hands of Allah, as the Arabs say. A hundred better men than I have died today, but by the decree of some blind Fate, I live."

Gordon looked down on the wounded men. He turned to Musa.

"We must load the wounded on camels," he said, "and take them to the camp at the Walls where there's water and shade. Come."

As they started down the slope he said to Olga, "I'll have to stay with them till they're settled at the Walls, then I must start for the coast. Some of the Rualla will be able to ride, though, and you need have no fear of them. They'll escort you to the nearest Turkish outpost."

She looked at him in surprise.

"Then I'm not your prisoner?"

He laughed.

"I think you can help Feisal more by carrying out your original instructions of supplying misleading information to the Turks! I don't blame you for not confiding even in me. You have my deepest admiration, for you're playing the most dangerous game a woman can."

"Oh!" She felt a sudden warm flood of relief and gladness that he should know she was not really an enemy. Musa was well out of ear-shot. "I might have known you were high enough in Feisal's councils to know that I really am-"

"Gloria Willoughby, the cleverest, most daring secret agent the British government employs," he murmured. The girl impulsively placed her slender fingers in his, and hand in hand they went down the slope together.

THE END

www.ingramcontent.com/pod-product-compliance
Lightning Source LLC
Chambersburg PA
CBHW031026030726
47497CB00004B/1017